The Roaming

The Roaming

The Toll

W.J. Hegarty

Valkyriur Song poem excerpt
by Felicia Dorothea Browne Hemans,
1793-1835
https://en.wikipedia.org/wiki/Felicia_Hemans

Cover art by Edward Moran
https://www.deviantart.com/edwardjmoran

Printed in the United States of America

First Printing, 2019

ISBN-13: 9781697005356

For updates on The Roaming, social media links and exclusive content
visit wjhegarty.com

CHAPTER ONE

Contact

Canvasback's Landing, South Carolina, was a small coastal town a few hours' drive north from Hilton Head; it lay deserted and largely in ruins. The city was left mostly untouched by the epidemic that swept the nation, though Mother Nature's fury wouldn't be so kind. It was a modest city. Even before the crisis, Canvasback wasn't the type of place anyone would mistake for a tourist trap. The city was composed of locals, mostly. A tight-knit community with ties to the sea. It was a quiet fishing town; most of its citizens were born and raised right here, mere steps from the ocean. The city was abandoned, and with it, so too was local infrastructure maintenance. Its drainage system had been irreparably clogged with debris that washed in from large storms.

Vast stretches of the city streets were flooded with ankle-deep standing water. Storm damage was extensive. With no one around to shore up buildings, the weather had its way with them. Awnings were ripped from their moorings, sent careening into other buildings, and left where they lay. Corrugated aluminum, bent and twisted, littered the streets. Shattered fencing, torn shingles, and entire sections of buildings were left strewn about the town. In some locations, sand had blown in from eroded beaches and piled so high against homes and businesses you would need tools to dig your way in or out.

Most of Canvasback's citizens fled inland to get out of the way of the season's first major hurricane. With the crisis having engulfed the region, rescue would be nigh impossible, should the need arise. The few people that remained rode out the storm—and the storms that followed. The ones that fled never returned. Whether they succumbed to roaming bands of carriers or violent drifters was a question their neighbors were left to ponder. In time, for one reason or another, and usually in small groups, the residents that remained left Canvasback's Landing for good. Now the city was nothing more than a ghost town.

A block from the ocean, a fully armed group of seven wearing black leather gear patrolled the city streets. If they weren't military or otherwise professionally trained, they at least appeared to be. This unit marched two by two with a single sentry bringing up the rear. Appearance-wise, they were an eclectic group composed of two women and five men. If anyone still lived in Canvasback to hear them speak, it would have been clear that all but one of them most likely hailed from foreign soil. This team moved with precision, with purpose. Each of them was well-armed, carrying an automatic rifle, a sidearm, and a close-quarters combat weapon. These implements were mostly long and bladed, no doubt to keep any attackers outside of arm's reach. One had a pair of nightsticks strapped to his back. Another carried what looked to be a comically large war hammer you might see in a fantasy movie. Not at all practical.

The black-clad team entered select buildings and ignored others. To the casual observer, it would have appeared that they had no rhyme or reason for which buildings they searched and which ones they passed up. Out in front marched the smallest of the group; the pair of them seemed to be signaling which buildings were of interest. One of them was a small blonde with yellow highlights on her suit. She sounded like she hailed from Eastern Europe. The other, a young black man, was the only American in the group. The woman pointed out a nearby two-story building. Its bottom floor was a drinking establishment named the Ruddy Duck Inn, and its second level looked to be lodging. The building itself appeared to be in relatively decent shape considering the state of its surroundings. Their leader, the one with the nightsticks and who brought up the rear, directed the group in. He was Hispanic and the only member of this group without markings on his pristine black leather uniform.

The interior of the building was dark except for what little light shone through hastily boarded-up windows. Garbage was strewn about, dried to the sides of the carpet and partway up the wall. The surface of the wall itself was stained up to a foot off the floor in spots. It was apparent that the place had sustained massive water damage, likely due to a storm surge. The two smaller members of the group hurried to the exterior of most rooms and yanked the boards from the windows, letting in much-needed sun. With this increase in light, a host of rats scurried back into large holes in the wall. The leader of the group wrinkled his nose as he entered. The stink of dried animal urine hung in the air. There were obviously many more rats living in the walls, or something much bigger had taken up residence in man's absence to produce such a stench. The African American rushed to the back room, where he opened a window. The airflow sucked in the ocean breeze, clearing away most of the foul odor.

Among the group were two giant men, each nearly seven feet tall and built of pure muscle. One was Scandinavian, the other Haitian. Both of them had white handprints slapped all over their armor. One wouldn't be wrong in assuming that these men decorated each other's gear just this morning with paint they found in a local hardware store. The Haitian's bald head was adorned with a cracked white handprint. The other had a hand decorating his face, with excess paint splattered into his long blond locks. Dried white stains around the cuffs of their uniforms told the tale. They had adorned each other as a form of war paint. Their leader directed them to guard the exits—one in the front of the inn, the other at the back.

The two smallest of the group took point again. They led the remains of the team farther into the building and up a flight of stairs. On the second floor, they spread out, each point man guiding another teammate to a particular room. Not a single movement was wasted. The smaller, quicker team members had obviously been here before. The leader paced the hallway as his team set upon its objective. He kept his rifle at attention, his head on a swivel.

The male point man led his group into a room at the end of the hall. He entered and paused for a moment before pulling out his sidearm. "Don't move."

A disheveled-looking pale young man was rummaging through a carefully organized pile of supplies near the center of the room. When he noticed the trio of armed soldiers towering above and saw the gun drawn on him, he scurried to the nearest corner. "Please don't shoot! Please don't shoot!"

A redheaded member of the team darted forward. His hair was shoulder-length, and he sported a matching beard. This one's leather was adorned with thick red lines that looked to have been applied with a large paintbrush or a small roller. He demanded answers behind a pronounced Australian accent. "Does this stuff belong to you?"

"No."

"You're goddamn right it doesn't. This shit's ours. We got here first. Hands off." The Australian snatched a can of peas from the frightened young man.

Another member of the team spoke up in the young man's defense. Like the others, she was dressed head to toe in black leather. Hers was carefully highlighted with blue paint at the seams. She was a light-skinned black woman with long, light-brown curls pulled back into a thick ponytail. She spoke in a soothing French cadence. "Take it easy. He's scared."

"He's stealing our shit," the redhead argued.

"Maybe this shit was *his* first."

"Look, you guys, I was just passing through. I don't even live here. I'm just hungry as shit, man."

The redhead studied the young man for a moment before relenting. "No harm, no foul, friend." He helped him to his feet. "I get a little worked up out on the road. Never know what you're going to run into out here. Know what I mean?"

"Yeah, I suppose I do."

"What's *your* story?" the Frenchwoman asked.

"Not much to tell. I'm homeless. I was homeless then, and I'm homeless now. When the crisis hit, I was in Fort Lauderdale. I was trying to get a job during spring break, but no one wants to hire the homeless guy. Anyway, I got out of there quick. I could see what was coming. On the streets, you could feel it. The people were already losing their minds, like a rage was boiling over. You ever been in a riot? Let me tell you, it fucking sucks, especially when you don't have a real home to go back to when it's all over. Afterward, everybody looks at you funny, like you somehow started it. Anyway, this was different, so I started walking, and thank God I did. It sounds like the cities turned into war zones. In the earliest days of this shit, when transportation was still kind of a thing, I snuck aboard a freight train, hopped off somewhere south of Charleston. Been following the coast north ever since. Can't say I've gotten very far. This is only the second town I've come across."

The team leader joined the conversation. "What's your name, kid?"

"Tate."

"Tate, I'm Cortez, and if you think you can pull your weight, we might be able to find a place for you with us."

"I'll take it."

"Not even a single question?" the Australian asked with a puzzled look.

"Are you kidding me? Life on the road sucks. You need help carrying anything?"

The Frenchwoman gave Tate a pat on the back. "Welcome aboard."

One of the large men yelled from downstairs. "Cortez, we've got contact!"

The alley behind the Ruddy Duck was slowly but steadily filling with the undead. Many of them had bloated skin that was sloughing off their bones like they were submerged for quite some time and had been washed ashore from some distant tragedy, perhaps even a far-off shipwreck. Their origin was unimportant. What was of the utmost importance was their destination. They were converging on the small building, and their numbers were swelling. It was as if the carriers' mere presence attracted more who were otherwise content to stumble around the area, oblivious to Cortez and his team.

The two giants took turns heading into the fray, the blond with a medieval battle-ax and the bald one with his hammer. When you saw him swing the bludgeon, any notion of its impracticality quickly vanished. They were careful to stay away from each other's wide arcs as they kept the back entrance secure. Any beast within reach was cleaved or crushed. From above, Cortez and the rest of his team took positions on balconies and fire escapes, offering covering fire from the high ground. Nearly every depression of the trigger was a headshot. Rarely was a bullet wasted.

"Cease fire! Cease fire!" Cortez yelled while waving his hand for the benefit of those who might not have heard his command. "Let's wrap this up. All that noise is bound to attract attention we don't need. We have what we came for. It's time to bug out."

Cortez and his people packed as much of the spoils as they could fit into their duffels. Tate helped as best as he was able with a thick contractor bag he packed as full as he could and still carry. Within minutes, Cortez, his team, and Tate were on the road.

W.J. Hegarty

CHAPTER TWO

Aftermath

Dawn's cleansing light blanketed Miller's caravan as it finally reached the highway. Blinding rays bounced off windshields and peeked through dried blood, casting foreboding shadows, an ominous reminder for the weary occupants of a disaster mere hours past. Tommy finally settled down. Little more than twenty minutes ago, and for the first time since before they escaped Pepperbush, silence filled the car. Tobias stole a glance around the interior, his youngest fast asleep in his sister's arms. Isabelle stared blankly out the window, emotionless, a state more common of late. He longed to comfort her but didn't know how; he had no voice for it. What would he say? That everything was going to be alright? *That* would be a lie or at the very least false hope. Everything was *not* going to be alright. Tobias knew that much. Their lives would never be the same again. He gripped the steering wheel tight and pressed on into the sunrise.

The remains of a downed 707 lay strewn across the highway. Miles of debris stretched as far as he could see. Was the pilot trying to land? What would cause him to attempt such a thing on a congested highway. Surely there were more people in these destroyed vehicles than his plane could carry. *It's feasible the pilot wasn't even trying to land*, Tobias thought. It didn't really matter anyway. Just another unanswered question for him to ponder at night. Negotiating the wreckage was a chore but manageable; it was as if someone had already attempted to clear a path. With any luck, this helpful stranger didn't stop halfway through the mess. Turning around in here would be nigh impossible.

Following the fall of Pepperbush, Miller was thrust into a leadership role he never wanted. Colonel Takashi was swallowed up in a sea of undead. There was nothing Miller could have done for him. His commanding officer and surrogate father figure of sorts was gone, another in a countless list of victims claimed by the undead crisis. "Put your back to the sea" was Takashi's final command. Miller would see it done; he would see these people to safety if it killed him. But first an inventory was needed; taking stock was paramount. How many members of his unit made it out of Pepperbush, and how many civilians did they have with them?

Five vehicles in total made up the caravan. Since their retreat from Pepperbush, some drivers stayed in contact with each other via the soldiers' short-range radios. Discussion ran the gamut of where they were going to who made it out. No real answers were forthcoming; "save your batteries" was the usual response.

The debris field was quickly narrowing. Miller called ahead to the lead car. "Soraya, tell Marisol to make a path. We're not stopping."

"Yes, sir," she responded.

"We should stop, Miller. There's shit all over the place. We could probably use some of it," Radzinski added from his end.

"Negative. Too many blind spots. If those things are mixed in with the wreckage, we could find ourselves surrounded, boxed in. We're not stopping until we find a clear stretch of road," Miller insisted.

"Yeah, but—" Radzinski started.

"Negative. We are not stopping! Miller out." Miller threw the radio onto the dash, displeasure with Radzinski written all over his face.

"This guy's fucking incredible." Radzinski's final transmission echoed through Tobias's truck.

"Maybe he's right, Miller," Tobias offered.

"I'm sure he is," Miller replied. "There are probably tons of useful supplies out there, but the risk isn't worth the reward. Are you willing to chance your family for a couple cans of soda and some shoes?"

"Of course I'm not, but—" Tobias tried to reply, but the soldier would have none of it.

"Then keep driving. We'll find somewhere safer to stop eventually."

"And if we don't?" Isabelle asked.

Miller didn't answer, though he caught the woman's glare in the rearview mirror, her contempt-filled eyes burning into his reflection. He knew that no matter what he said, she wouldn't be satisfied. *Best to avoid further conflict*, he thought.

Marisol's truck sped along out in front. She was careful not to get too far ahead of the caravan. For the most part, those with her remained relatively quiet since fleeing Pepperbush. The weight of what they'd witnessed, combined with Mayor Lancaster's cruelty, filled the truck with a thick, tense atmosphere. All morning, since the situation calmed, she'd been chain-smoking, adding to a particular occupant's discomfort.

"I certainly enjoy a good smoke as much as the next, but really, would you mind cutting back on the cigarettes? It has become absolutely stuffy in here," Mayor Lancaster suggested.

Marisol took a big drag, bigger than usual, and turned to face Lancaster behind the passenger's seat. "Feel free to get out anytime you like. If you want to walk the rest of the way, I won't stop you," she replied, exhaling the smoke into his face.

"My word, was that completely necessary, woman?" Mayor Lancaster gagged.

"Climb in the back, all the way back! I don't want to have to look at you."

"But—" he protested.

"Now!" she demanded.

"Let's go, old-timer. Over the seat." Seth helped Lancaster into the back of the truck, sufficiently far away from Marisol.

Up front and comfortable, she and Soraya shared a grin at the man's expense.

"Do you mind?" Soraya motioned for a cigarette.

"Please." Marisol flicked open the pack of smokes.

Mayor Lancaster slumped as close to the floor as he could manage, unable to escape the smoke. He pulled his filthy white suit jacket up over his face.

Bernie clipped a lone carrier with his truck, sending the ghoul careening through the air. It tumbled out of sight and into the overgrown brush that framed the road. With no one around to tend to such things, the vegetation on the sides of the highway had grown waist-high and up to the pavement's edge. In man's absence, the flora was quickly reclaiming the land. Almost fifteen minutes had passed since the debris field faded from view. Clear roads stretched ahead, seemingly to the horizon.

Miller returned to his radio. "Soraya, get them ready to slow down and pull over. We need to gather our bearings sooner rather than later."

"Yes, sir," Soraya replied. "Slowing down now."

Through gore-caked windows, Miller surveyed the coming road for a safe place to stop. The ragtag caravan of survivors had been moving at a steady pace since their exodus from Pepperbush roughly four hours prior. The five vehicles that managed to escape the assault were filled with most of what remained of the small town. For the most part, everyone was silent. Shock had set in over the loss of hundreds of their fellow townsfolk. Friends, family, and a lifetime of memories had been left behind, swallowed up by a tidal wave of infected.

"This is Miller in the rear vehicle plus five survivors. We're preparing to slow down and stop. If your radio's on, sound off. Identify yourselves and how many survivors are with you. Over."

"Radzinski, plus four. Two cars from the lead. Over."

"Soraya in front, plus four. Over."

"Markus, plus five."

"Jeremiah with four, sir. Over."

"All vehicles accounted for," Miller said. "I imagine it's safe to stop and assess now. We're going to be pulling over in thirty seconds. When we stop, I want a full perimeter sweep, twenty-meter spread. Miller out. Alright, Soraya, let's do this. Tell Marisol to put on her hazards and slow down. Don't bother pulling over. Just have her stay in the middle of the road and keep the truck running."

Tentatively at first and not without a few minor collisions, the caravan finally slowed. The soldiers were ready to hit the ground running, treating this no differently than putting boots down in a hot zone. Most of the civilians were obviously on edge but calm. Others, though, were on the verge of panic.

Samantha darted her view from left to right, searching the surrounding fields for movement. "Oh my God. What are they doing? Are we really slowing down?"

"We've been driving for hours. We need a break," Markus offered.

"They can't. No, don't stop. Let's just keep going," Ryan suggested.

"Relax, guys, it'll be okay," Markus continued. "Those things are way behind us now. It's pointless to keep driving until we can figure out a plan.

Besides, it's going to get real bad in here if we start using the back seat as a toilet."

Following Soraya and Marisol's lead, the caravan slowly came to a stop in the middle of the highway.

"Keep everyone in the car until I give the all-clear, Tobias, and be ready to bug out if necessary," Miller said.

"I'm ready." Tobias turned to his family. "Make sure your doors are locked and keep your eyes open. There could be anything out there."

As the caravan came to a stop Miller and the other soldiers rushed from their vehicles. In a circular formation, they slowly spread out, weapons drawn. Miller's unit inched its way farther from the transports, off the pavement, and into the deep grass. The fields stretched on for miles in all directions. Tiny gatherings of trees dotted the landscape far enough away that anything lurking in their shadows wasn't a threat. A few hundred feet farther down the road, a van and a smaller mid-sized car sat neatly to the side of the road, their occupants nowhere to be found. A jack, lug nuts, and spare tire lay strewn on the pavement.

Soraya yanked open the van's sliding door. Empty. The car was the same. "All clear over here, sir. No signs of struggle. Whoever was here is just gone."

"Ditto on this end," Miller responded. "Circle back around to the caravan. Give Marisol the all-clear to start unloading the civilians."

"Copy that."

• • •

The initial shock from the night's ordeal was finally wearing off, and suppressed emotions at last boiled to the surface.

"Oh God. Oh my God. All those people." Samantha crumbled to the pavement, slipping from Markus's helping hand.

"Easy now. Just breathe." He tried his best to comfort her. Truth be told, if he wasn't preoccupied with her emotional state, he would likely have needed consoling of his own.

A resident clamped onto Aiko's shoulder. "Thank you. Oh lord, thank you. God bless you, ma'am. If it wasn't for you…"

"Stay calm, ma'am. Are you injured?" Aiko asked.

"I… No, I don't think so," the woman replied.

"Okay, then stand over there for now. Let's clear the way for people who *do* need help." Aiko directed the woman to a growing crowd of survivors out in the middle of the road.

"Excuse me, son. Could you—" Mayor Lancaster was cut short as Isaac stormed past him.

"Don't you dare say a word to me," Isaac replied.

"Now wait just a minute, young man, I—" Mayor Lancaster began as Soraya slapped his face.

Soraya cursed him in Hebrew. "You say nothing." She pointed to a garbage-strewn ditch nearby. "Sit over there."

Wide-eyed, the mayor looked to Marisol.

"Fucking coward, stay out of my way, or I swear to God I'll kill you myself." She shoved past him, temporarily unbalancing the man.

Mayor Lancaster righted himself against an abandoned car. Shamed, he lowered his head and walked toward the growing crowd of survivors in hopes of disappearing into anonymity.

"I saw at least five other cars make it out. Three were headed north," said Seth. "The others, I have no idea which way they went or who was in them."

"I hate to sound this cold, but we can't worry about them right now, Seth," Tobias put bluntly.

"Agreed. Look, I'm going to check around. Make sure everyone has water and get an idea of what kind of injuries we're dealing with here." Seth turned to leave but stopped short, returned to Tobias, and placed a hand on his shoulder. "Hey, it's good to see you, man."

"I know," was all Tobias managed. He feared a breakdown in front of so many who only two days ago put their faith in him and his idea of safe passage to the sea.

Isabelle surveyed the aftermath. Many people, predominantly strangers, gathered about in the middle of a mostly deserted stretch of highway. Most looked unfamiliar; she feared the worst over the fate of her friends. For a mere second, a breach opened in the crowd, closed, and opened again. In the gap, a gorgeous woman stood alone, eyes closed, taking in the warm morning sun, its rays glistening off her perfect brown skin. Like everyone else's, her clothes were tattered, a little bloodied, but she appeared otherwise unharmed. Somehow, someway, Isabelle's oldest friend in the world was alive, standing right there, only twenty feet away.

"Oh my God, Nisha!" Isabelle ran across the pavement to greet her friend.

"Izzy?" Nisha dropped her water bottle, her eyes as wide as saucers as she pushed through the crowd to meet Isabelle.

"I thought I'd never see you again," Isabelle said, hugging Nisha tight.

"Me too." Nisha teared up a little. She rubbed Isabelle's back for a moment before holding her at arm's length. "Let me look at you. Are you okay?"

"I'm fine. Look at you, though. You're so dirty. Oh my God, what happened to you?" Isabelle wiped some dirt from Nisha's shirt and pants and brushed the woman's messed-up hair out of her face.

"I don't even know. One minute I'm wandering down—God, I don't even know what street it was—the next thing I know, Sam's shoving me in his beat-up old truck," Nisha responded, bewildered.

"I know what you mean. It all happened so fast it's like a blur. Have you seen anyone else?"

"No, you're the first I've seen." Nisha scanned the crowd for familiar faces. "Is Carla or John here? Who else got out in time?"

"I don't know. It looks like there's lots of people here, though." Isabelle also scanned the crowd.

Most of the survivors were gathering their bearings. Some were crying. A man across from the pair threw up all over someone else's shoes.

"Bonnie was in the car behind us. They didn't make it. The Petersons, too. It was awful." Isabelle closed her eyes. The thought of the Petersons' demise, especially their daughter flying through the air, was too much to contemplate.

"When it got real bad, cars were driving in every direction. I saw..." Nisha covered her mouth. "I don't even want to say. But Seth saw a few cars heading that way." Nisha pointed south, down the highway a few ramps back.

"Jesus, they're heading straight for Philadelphia." Isabelle gasped.

"I know. They probably won't realize it until it's too late."

"You have that headcount for me, Soraya?" Miller asked.

"Twenty-seven, sir."

"Casualties?"

"Mostly minor. Jeremiah and Aiko are tending to them, although one woman is very bad. I believe she has been bitten."

"Verify that, Soraya. If anyone else has been bitten, isolate them and have one of the police officers keep an eye on them."

Radzinski jogged up to Miller's location. "Northern side of the road is clear for at least a hundred yards, Captain."

"Good. Radzinski, I want you to take two of the civilians and police up the weapons and ammunition. We need to know exactly what we're working with before we go any farther."

"Goddamn bullshit! This is exactly what I was talking about," Radzinski snapped.

"Excuse me, Marine?" Miller stepped toward Radzinski.

Radzinski laid his rifle on the hood of a nearby car and got in Miller's face. "These fucking hillbillies couldn't hold the line. We were better off without them. Instead, we wound up burning through most of our ammo and still had to retreat anyway, like we should have done in the first place. I told you we should have left."

"That wasn't your call to make."

"You're goddamn right it wasn't, and we lost three of our own because of it." Radzinski pointed back in the direction of Pepperbush.

"You finished?"

Radzinski waved his hands in the air and began to leave. He took two steps, turned back around, and caught Miller in the jaw with a right hook. "This is all your fault, motherfucker! *You* could have talked Takashi into leaving. Now him and the others are all dead, and we're fucked. Fucked!"

Miller spat a mouthful of blood onto the pavement as he walked forward to meet his attacker face to face. He massaged his mouth with his tongue, checking for cracked or loose teeth as he addressed the man. "Are you finished?" Miller asked again, this time with finality, testing Radzinski's resolve.

Radzinski looked around at the gathering crowd, then back to Miller, and finally to the ground in front of his feet. "Yeah, yeah, I'm done."

"Then you have a job to do, Marine. I suggest you get it done."

Radzinski slung his rifle and set off for a group of civilians who were gathered around Bernie's truck, but not before shooting a defiant glance back at his commanding officer.

Miller knew his confrontations with Radzinski would continue to escalate, but he couldn't be bothered with that right now. For the time being, getting these people to safety was of paramount concern.

A few feet away from the conflict, Soraya stood at arm's reach, her hand wrapped tightly around her kukri's handle. Miller acknowledged her and sent her an appreciative nod.

Jeremiah and Aiko had set up a temporary triage area in the back of Bernie's truck. It wasn't much, but it was better than nothing. At the very least, it kept the wounded off the ground while he and Aiko worked on them. The amount of blood drying in the truck's bed gave the wrong impression. Most of the wounds inflicted during the exodus from Pepperbush were surprisingly superficial. Minor scrapes and cuts that under normal circumstances could go ignored had to be treated with the utmost urgency now. Because they were unsure of exactly how easily this infection spread, no unnecessary chances were taken. Jeremiah was finishing up with a young man's lacerated cheek and a bruised leg as Radzinski approached.

Aiko taped off the end of Isaac's bandaged ankle before helping him to his feet. "It's not even a bad sprain. Your leg isn't broken. Trust me, you'd know it if it was. Just twisted it. That's all. At any rate, I'd stay off of it as best as you can for a few days, if possible."

"Thanks, Doc," he said as he hobbled away.

Leg injuries seemed to be common as a result of the mad dash to escape Pepperbush. Jeremiah was seeing to one as well. "Keep off that ankle for a day, two if you can manage, Elliot. You'll be back up to speed in no time."

"Thank you, sir. I'll try," Elliot said, limping away.

Radzinski leaned against the side of the blood-soaked truck. "Hey, Jerry, how goes the clean-up?"

"Better than anticipated surprisingly. Except for the woman who was bitten, it's minor injuries all around. A few more sprained ankles than I'd like, considering, but manageable," Jeremiah replied as he wiped his hands clean with a cap full of whiskey.

"Glad to hear it. The last thing we need is these people being any more of a burden," Radzinski said, eying a patient that Aiko was sewing up.

"It could have been far worse, Radzinski. It probably should have been," Jeremiah replied. "We were fortunate to have survived at all."

"Yeah." Radzinski stared back at Miller. "Some of us were."

Tobias was touring the makeshift staging area, taking mental note of who was who and how best each survivor could contribute. "Ayn and Peter, is it? Why don't the two of you take inventory? See what we have in the way of food, water, or anything that looks useful, but don't wander too far. Stay in eyesight. Oh, and medical supplies, anything like that you see, bring it straight to Aiko or Jeremiah," he suggested.

"Yeah, okay, anything to get my mind off of what just happened. Can you give me a hand?" Ayn yanked on Peter's shirt sleeve. He was lost in thought, transfixed on something far off in the distance. She grabbed him by both arms and shook him gently. "Earth to Peter, you with us?" she asked in a soft tone.

"Sure, sure. Yeah, I hear you. Yeah," Peter mumbled.

"What are you staring at?" Ayn struggled against the bright spring sky for a glimpse at whatever it was that held Peter's gaze.

Open fields surrounded them, and overgrown grasses stretched to the tree line miles off.

"I'm not looking at anything, Ayn," Peter finally offered. "Just thinking, is all. Come on, let's see about those supplies."

Vanessa's hands and wrists were wrapped like a boxer's. A myriad of cuts made the danger of infection far too great to leave untreated for long. Her ribs were taped up similarly; at least a few were broken, no doubt due to Jim's handiwork. Her tumble into the dumpster didn't exactly help matters. Aiko made sure the wraps were good and tight and also applied a handful of butterfly bandages to the knuckles showing the most severe damage.

"How's that feel?" asked Aiko with a hint of remorse shown on her face as she finished applying the bandages.

"It hurts like shit, but I'll live, right?" Vanessa answered rhetorically.

"And that's all that really matters," Aiko replied. "Make sure to keep those hands bandaged and clean, at least for a few days until those cuts have a chance to close up."

Vanessa nodded in agreement. Ever the optimist, she wouldn't dare let Jim have this victory. She would have taped up her own hands had the medics not made it out alive. Either way, she would persevere.

Markus approached as Aiko was disinfecting her hands in preparation for her next patient. Vanessa fumbled with an old country band T-shirt

The Roaming: The Toll

Bernie had crumpled up in his truck. The shirt wasn't exactly her style, and it reeked of stale beer and ashtrays, but all things considered...

"Everything okay here?" Markus asked, happy to see his friend up and moving around after the state he found her in only a few hours ago.

"Superficial wounds mostly. A few deeper than others. Otherwise, she's fine. She's all yours."

"Cool, thanks, Doc." Markus noticed Vanessa struggling with the ragged shirt and froze, not sure if he should walk the other way or help.

"You mind giving me a hand here?" she asked, much to his relief.

"Sure, sure no problem," he said, hurrying to help cover her damaged body.

"Thanks, ribs hurt like a bitch," said Vanessa. "And thanks for stopping for me." She paused and looked to the crowd of survivors, wondering how many—if *any*—would have done what he did. She couldn't pick out one of these people that might have stopped for her, save for Sam and Lillian, of course.

Sensing a tinge of resentment in Vanessa's eyes, Markus offered a gift in hopes of curbing the emotion. "Here, I thought you might like to keep this. You know, for the memories." He handed her a dusty old photo of her and her husband, taken back when they first bought Mother Leeds. Clint was proudly showing off a dollar from their first sale. The memory brought a brief smile to Vanessa's face.

"Thank you, Markus." Vanessa broke her gaze with the picture, folded it neatly, and placed it in her pocket.

"What happened back there, Van?"

"Not now, Markus, please. I don't want to talk about it. I just want to be alone for a minute."

"Fair enough, but remember, I'm here whenever you're ready to talk."

"Thank you, again," she said before walking off behind a couple of abandoned cars.

Casandra pushed past the thinning crowd of injured gathering around the makeshift triage on her way to Aiko. She was waddling mostly; her stomach led the way. Casandra was on her way to the hospital for a routine checkup when her car gave out on her, stranding her on the interstate. The father of her baby was a deadbeat she met in the produce aisle of her local supermarket. They were inseparable for the first few months, until Casandra learned she was pregnant. Six and a half months later, she could count on one hand the number of times he came by for a visit. A local family stopped for the pregnant woman and convinced her to forgo the hospital visit; it could wait in light of what they were seeing on the news. Casandra agreed and would become one of Pepperbush's first refugees.

"I haven't felt my baby kick all day. She's dead, isn't she? Oh God, I know I crushed her when I fell down last night." Casandra was near a panic as she waited for her turn with the medics. She paced toward the side of the caravan before leaning against a car to steady herself while attempting to sit. As she made her way slowly to the ground her sundress bunched up behind her. Faster than she could react, the pile of cloth slipped, sending her fast to the pavement. Her ass slapped against the wet road, and her head bounced off the body of the car. "Oh God." She said, defeated. She slumped forward, her head hiding in her hands, knees framing her huge belly. The fall pushed her dress up, collecting the pile of fabric just below her shoulder blades.

Aiko offered an understanding smile. "Come on. Let's get you straightened up." She pulled Casandra's dress back down where it belonged.

The soon-to-be new mother didn't offer much in the way of help, other than muttering "my baby" a few times between sobs. Aiko was still able to get a good portion of Casandra's dress back under the girl, slight barrier that it was between her skin and the grimy pavement.

"What's your name again, sweetheart?" Aiko asked.

"Casandra," the pregnant girl squeaked.

"Nice to meet you, Casandra. I'm Corpsman Aiko Taniguchi, United States Navy. I'm here to help you."

"Hello," Casandra managed.

"You didn't crush your baby, Casandra. She's going to be just fine, but you need to calm down. The stress isn't good for either of you. Here, feel this." She guided Casandra's hand up under her dress and onto the girl's bare stomach. "See, can you feel that?"

"Is that…?" Casandra's eyes went wide, and she allowed herself a smile. "Is that my baby?"

"It sure is, kiddo. A minor fall or two is nothing to get yourself too worked up over. These little suckers are tough, though I'd stay away from stairs if I were you."

Casandra bit her lip, trying to keep quiet, her excitement palpable.

"You want to know a secret?" Aiko asked.

Casandra nodded, careful not to draw any more attention to the pair than she already had. Aiko guided the girl's hand to her own stomach. Even through the medic's combat shirt, her own slight belly bump was unmistakable. Aiko raised a finger to her lips and offered only a quiet "shh." Once more, Casandra nodded in a quick, silent agreement.

Bernie had laid Dana out in the bed of his pickup, a pillow behind her head and an old blanket pulled up to her neck. She was one of the survivors he picked up on his way out of Pepperbush. Once everyone started stretching out and moving away from the vehicles to converse, he thought it best to give the sick woman some fresh air.

She can't be past her late thirties. Pretty little thing, he thought as he wiped sweat from her forehead.

She was burning up one minute and freezing cold the next. The cool rag he fetched from his ice chest seemed to soothe her, at least until her chills returned. Bernie's truck was always packed and ready for a road trip. Clean rags were only a part of it. He kept plenty of supplies on hand: food and water and even ice. Bernie was always prepared. Even in the midst of a ragtag caravan, the man had ice water.

Dana coughed hard this time. If Bernie didn't know any better, he would have sworn she tore something loose in the back of her throat. She tried to get her trembling hand up to her mouth to catch any spittle but didn't make it. Tiny dots of fresh blood sprayed her chin and even came down on her cheeks and forehead. Unbeknownst to her, a large dribble of blood poured from the side of her mouth when she turned to talk with Bernie.

"I think I'm sick," she said, trying to hold back a laugh.

As she smiled, the red bordered every one of her perfectly white teeth. A constant stream of bodily fluids made their way into her mouth, causing little bubbles to form and pop as she spoke.

"Oh, you're fine," he said. "This ain't nothing a few Band-Aids and a shot or two won't clear up," Bernie offered.

"Are you sure?"

"I'm positive, darling. Just you wait and see. This time next week, I'll have you up and dancing."

"You're going to take me dancing?" she asked, her milky eyes widening.

"I promise." Bernie held her hand tight as he continued wiping sweat from her brow.

"You promise?" she said as she drifted off to sleep, a blood-drenched smile etched upon her face.

"Hi, Sam." Vanessa stood just off to the side of the caravan.

Sam turned and dropped his rifle to the ground. At the sight of her, his knees buckled, almost sending the man to the pavement beside his gun. "Vanessa!" he shouted. "Oh, thank God."

Vanessa rushed over to him. He did his best to meet her halfway. She leaped into his arms, nearly knocking the older man down.

"Goddamn, it's good to see you, girl!" he said.

"I know, I know," she replied, tears flowing.

"What happened to you? When I heard about the church, I thought I'd lost you."

"Never made it. I was on my way there, almost done boarding up my house, when Jim..." She paused. Her lip quivered for a moment before she righted herself. "I won't cry over that piece of shit."

"It's okay, darling. You don't have to say another word." Sam pulled her in for another hug.

Her battered body and bloody, torn-up hands told him all he needed to know.

CHAPTER THREE

Acceptance

As the afternoon wore on, relief morphed into frustration for some. For others, it was a time to contemplate in silence, to reflect. Radzinski, on the other hand, had questions.

"Anyone mind telling me just what the fuck happened back there? How the hell did we get surrounded like that?" he asked no one in particular.

"I've been contemplating that all day myself, John," Jeremiah said. "As it turns out, the explanation is rather simple—the cause of our predicament, that is."

"Well, by all means, let's have it," Radzinski asked, wide-eyed and flush.

"As I was saying, the timing and placement of the separate attacks suggest the initial group that followed us out of Philadelphia must have split into two separate entities in the time they were pursuing us."

"And how exactly does that profound statement answer my question, Doc?" Radzinski's eyes nearly rolled into the back of his head.

"Simple," Jeremiah continued. "The time difference explains everything. Roughly two hours passed from the time you first encountered infected by the southern defenses to when I first saw them in the north, my particular pack obviously coming from the west. During the roughly thirty-two hours it took for them to catch up with us, the two subsequent factions picked up stragglers along the way, thus increasing their numbers exponentially. By the time the two groups inevitably merged back into one solid mass, inside the town's perimeter no less, the battle was lost."

"I thought you said your group of carriers came from the north." Radzinski's face contorted in frustration.

"Yes, north of your position. Still west from mine."

"Whatever you say, man. You lost me at 'entities.' Sorry I even asked."

"The logistics of the attack are so simple a child could grasp the concept. Last night's defeat was simply the result of poor planning," said Jeremiah. "We should have anticipated this."

"You know what, Jerry? Anyone ever tell you you're a fucking weirdo?"

"Belittle me all you like, John. Our current circumstance is a testament to my conclusions." Jeremiah continued sorting medical supplies with barely an eye offered for the frustrated Marine.

"Give it a rest, Jerry. We get it. Radzinski does, too. He's just fried. We all are," Miller interjected. "I need you people to stay sharp. We've got wounded and scared civilians here that need our attention."

"You keep saying that, Miller, but these people are a liability. They're not even prepared for whatever the fuck's going on, much less combat-ready." Radzinski shook his head.

"That may be the case, but they're our responsibility now. We're all they've got."

"Yeah, tell that to Takashi and the others. If you ask me, losing three of ours for these civilians ain't worth it. Never will be." Radzinski spat in the direction of a huddled group of survivors ten or so meters away.

"I didn't ask, and haven't we been over this once today already? I get that you're pissed. Duly noted. Now go siphon the fuel from that van over there. We don't need this many vehicles, and I don't need your bullshit."

"On it."

Dana was wrapped in a blanket and locked in the back of an abandoned van, safely away from the group. Over the course of the day, while everyone else was licking their wounds or taking inventory, she had grown pale and was shivering violently. Her lips had gone blue, ears and fingertips blackening in what looked like frostbite. Occasionally, she would vomit, spewing bile and blood on her face and blanket. It had been hours since she was even responsive, longer since Miller made the call to quarantine her in the stuffy van. Every so often, Dana would manage to moan. Some—the naïve ones—would claim she was trying to speak and could even make out words.

Samantha's growing concern over Dana's failing health caught the attention of members of the group who weren't otherwise preoccupied.

"We can't just shoot her," Samantha pleaded.

"Put the gun away, man." Markus stepped between Damon and Samantha. He knew Damon was probably right, but as usual, his friend's methods left much to be desired.

"It's either put her down or leave her on the side of the road. Which would you prefer?" Damon motioned to a roadside ditch. His gun emphasized moving the girl from the van to the dirt.

"Put her down, huh, like an animal?" Samantha turned from Damon, focusing on Markus. "What do you think we should do with her?"

Markus lowered his head; he had no intention of being responsible for this decision. "I don't know."

"Thanks for the support," she added before storming off.

"Samantha, wait. It's not that simple." Markus begrudgingly chased after her.

Damon burst out laughing at his friend's expense. "You gotta be fucking kidding me," he snickered.

"I'm with that guy. I say we leave her." Radzinski pointed to an eager Damon.

Damon slapped his palm down on the roof of a nearby car. "That's what I'm talking about," he shouted, pointing back at Radzinski, who offered a grin in return.

"Of course you are, you inconsiderate prick." Rachel leered at the pair of them.

"Yeah, my heart bleeds for her. Maybe you forgot, but we left a whole fucking town behind this morning. One more makes absolutely no difference," Radzinski said.

"Last night we had no choice," said Rachel.

"And suddenly now we do, right? Please." Radzinski turned and waved her off. "Whatever."

The crack from a single gunshot echoed down the deserted highway. The sound brought the soldiers to attention, thrusting them from their differences to draw their weapons down on an assumed threat.

Conversations paused. Others around the caravan sprang into readiness, half-expecting another wave of infected to have appeared along the tree line in the distance. Mayor Lancaster locked himself inside Marisol's SUV, ignoring the pleas of some of the others to let them in.

Rachel was the first to make her way to the gunshot's source at the far end of the caravan. Off to the side of the road, away from prying eyes, Isabelle stood above Dana, a pistol at her side. At her feet, Dana lay unmoving.

23

"While all of you argue, she was suffering. If that ever happens to me, I hope one of you has the balls to put me out of my misery," Isabelle said as she tucked the gun safely away inside a nearby duffel.

Blood pooled on the cool asphalt beneath Dana's head. A small hole below her right eye leaked more of the same. Isabelle folded Dana's arms across her chest and tucked a makeshift bouquet in one of the dead woman's hands. She had picked them from the side of the road. Weeds, mostly. Isabelle pulled Dana's blanket up to hide her face. The covering was small. No more than a large bath towel, really. The sheet wouldn't cover the woman completely, even if Isabelle had bothered to try. Dana's feet peeked out from beneath the small sheet. She was missing a shoe. Her other foot wore a filthy white sock. Dana most likely lost her other shoe in the mad scramble to escape Pepperbush.

"Poor thing," said Rachel, eyes heavy.

Wearing a smirk as if his point had been made for him by one of the very citizens he repeatedly derided, Radzinski slung his rifle across his back. Satisfied with Isabelle's actions, he no longer felt the need to argue. "Well that's that."

"You son of a bitch," Rachel snapped while walking in the opposite direction, toward Isabelle.

Mercy killing or not, Isabelle was a civilian. She shouldn't have had to shoulder that burden on her own, especially not with a group of trained military and police only steps away.

Bernie stood motionless, just out of sight. He slapped his hat against his leg as he turned to head back for his truck. "Ah shit, goddammit."

Miller was at a loss. In his hesitation to do what everyone knew needed to be done, a civilian, a mother of two from a town that barely registered on the map, did what he couldn't. She made the hard decision for everyone. *Perhaps Radzinski was right*, he thought. *There really are no set rules anymore. All that matters is survival, and keeping Dana alive was a burden no one needed to bear, not to mention the danger she represented.*

"Soraya, get her out of sight. These people are shaken enough as it is. They don't need to see one of their own like this," Miller said. "Marisol, Aiko, calm these people down. Let them know everything is alright. We don't need them doing anything stupid like taking off with half of our supplies."

"Yes, sir." Soraya holstered her weapon and put on a pair of gloves.

Miller stopped her as she approached Dana's corpse. "Hey, wait a second."

The young Israeli's eyes went wide at her commander's change in tone.

"I haven't had a chance to ask yet, but are *you* okay?" He placed his hand on her shoulder.

"Sir?" she responded timidly.

"It was a mess back there. When I lost communication with you and the others, I thought... Well, I'm just happy you made it out in one piece."

"I am happy you made it as well, Miller. Now please, I must dispose of body." She smiled as best as she could in light of their situation and continued on with her task.

"Smooth, ace," Radzinski added as he came around the van.

"Been standing there long?"

"Long enough. What's the move here, Captain?"

"I see no reason to deviate from Tobias's plan. Not too far, anyway. Only difference is we head south toward the Outer Banks."

Radzinski gestured to the five still functional civilian-class vehicles lined up behind them. "This could be a problem. We just bugged the fuck out. We've got squat for supplies, and you can hardly call these pieces of shit reliable transport."

"No argument there. Our first priority is going to have to be a gas station or convenience store of some sort."

"You honestly think those places won't be picked clean by now?"

"Probably, but there's always going to be something useful overlooked by your average terrified scavenger. Not to mention, most of these people only brought the clothes on their backs. That girl doesn't even have shoes." Miller singled out Vanessa.

Radzinski's sudden attempt at camaraderie took Miller by surprise, though he wouldn't show it. He needed the Marine, and if a little gentle ribbing was all it took to get Radzinski on board, then so be it.

Hidden from sight, away from the group and behind the abandoned van, Seth propped up Dana's body as Soraya wrapped her with a sheet. Neither said a word as they prepared the woman's corpse. The wrap was tightly wound around the woman's body. The upper half of the wrap was soaked in crimson. Her bare feet poked out from beneath the sheet. Some thought it wise to keep her one shoe and socks just in case. Had Dana not soiled herself during her death throws they would have claimed her pants as well. The task complete, the two carried her off the road and down into a ditch.

"This should be far enough. I can't even see the tops of the trucks anymore." Seth cupped a hand over his forehead. The midday sun blurred his vision.

"Thank you for helping, Seth. I am sorry for your friend," Soraya offered.

"Appreciate the sentiment, Soraya, but I didn't know her. I don't think anyone did, really. She came in with a group of refugees a few weeks ago. I'd seen her around town here and there, but that's about it."

"This is a sad thing." Soraya knelt beside the wrapped body, touching its forehead through the sheet. "I think of her family waiting for her to come home."

"It is. The whole situation is sad. Fucked up, really. Do you have any idea how many people died last night?" Seth asked, more rhetorically than anything else.

"Many. Let's not speak of this. Come." Soraya led the way back out of the ditch. Dew from the waist-high grass soaked their clothes. Dried blood and grime from the previous night's encounter became liquefied and sticky once more.

"I've never had this much blood on my hands before." Seth wiped his soiled hands on his pants.

"Careful, do not get on your face," Soraya warned.

"That's all it takes, huh?"

"No one knows. I am sorry. We must be very careful now." Soraya looked at her own hands.

"Do you mind if I ask you something, Soraya?" Seth said with some trepidation.

"Please," Soraya answered eagerly.

"Is it like this back home? The infected, I mean, in Israel."

"I do not know this, Seth. I pray it is not, but I fear for my family."

"When you were in Philadelphia, before it got bad, had any of you or your unit had a chance to talk with your families? Any idea how they're coping?"

"No. We were not allowed to speak with anyone. Not even the civilians we were tasked with helping. Everything we did and saw was classified. Top secret."

"It would be nice to know, you know?"

"Yes. Now I fear I will never see them again."

"I'm sorry, Soraya. I shouldn't have brought it up."

"It is okay, Seth. What about you? Was your family in Pepperbush?"

"No, thank God. My parents retired to Florida years ago, and my sister... Well, my sister is in prison. Vehicular manslaughter. It crushed my folks. My father's had this look in his eye ever since, like a part of him died with that family. I can hardly face him anymore, and now... Now I'll most likely never see them again. Any of them." His lip curled with the thought.

"Then you and I are not so different after all, my friend," Soraya suggested, patting him on the back.

"No, I guess we're not."

"Isabelle can we talk?" Rachel asked.

"Rachel, right?"

"That's me," Rachel said. "I've seen you around today and a little back in town, but we've never been properly introduced."

"Well now we have. Look, I know what you're going to say, and I'm fine. I meant what I said back there, and no offense to you or anyone else, but that needed to happen."

"You'll get no arguments here or from any of my people. It's just that, well, you're a civilian. You shouldn't have had to do that at all. It's our responsibility to take care of that sort of thing."

"It's your responsibility to keep us alive. How we live is up to us."

"Fair enough, but if you ever—" Rachel began, but Isabelle would have no more of it.

"I think I've said all I plan to on this. Keep it from Tobias, would you? As long as you can, at least. He worries too much as it is," Isabelle asked with a nonchalance that would have betrayed her apathetic stance on the matter if it wasn't already apparent. The woman truly did not care what her husband thought.

"I'll do what I can, but this is a small group. Word's going to travel fast," Rachel warned.

Isabelle shrugged and walked off. Rachel watched her go, standing at the side of the road and rubbing down the raised hairs on her forearms.

• • •

Dusk had neared by the time it was decided that a slight deviation in the plan was in order. Miller had studied their planned route all afternoon. Something wasn't sitting right with him regarding their destination.

"We're not going to Cape May," Miller stated bluntly.

Tobias was understandably confused. He assumed Miller was on board with the plan all along. "What? But I thought we agreed to make a run for the ocean?"

"Take a look at your map. Tell me what you see."

Tobias unfolded his map atop the hood of his truck, staring at their intended destination. Confusion washed over his face. "Uh, pretty much a straight line from here to Cape May. Without traffic we'll be there in under two hours."

"Without traffic, sure, but we can't be certain the roads are clear. Not that far off the beaten path, anyway. There could be miles of abandoned vehicles when we near Atlantic City, and roadblocks equal death traps."

"We're so close. I say it's worth the risk."

"Normally I'd be inclined to agree, but Cape May's different. Look again." Miller was persistent.

This time both men looked at the map. A few moments later, an air of realization took Tobias.

"I get it," he said.

Miller nodded. "Cape May's located on a peninsula, surrounded on three sides by water. If—and I'll admit it's a big one—but if we get there and we can't find a working boat, we'll be forced to re-cover all that distance just to wind up right back in this exact spot." Miller tapped right above their position on the map.

"And if we ran into a bunch of infected on the way there, we'd have to fight our way back through them coming out," Tobias added with an understanding nod.

"Precisely."

"I take it you have an alternative then?"

"As a matter of fact I do. Have a look at this." Miller unfolded another map. This one covered the majority of the Eastern Seaboard. "We should still head south, obviously staying as far away from DC, Baltimore, and any other of the larger cities on our way. Southern Virginia and into the Carolinas should be our best bet." Miller pointed out various locations on the new map.

"You're right. The coast is littered with waterways." Tobias leaped at the prospect.

"And hundreds of marinas," Miller added. "But most importantly, if we can't find what we're looking for, we just keep going. No backtracking necessary."

Tobias returned to his truck. It had been a few hours since he last checked on his family. He was surprised to see Isabelle nowhere around, but he was eager to spend time with his children, who he found sitting on the road in front of the family vehicle.

"Lillian, you should eat something, honey." Tobias handed his daughter a small candy bar. "Here, I know it's not much, but it'll be something in your belly."

"Thanks, Dad." She took her time with the sweet morsel.

"How are you doing, sweetheart?" he asked, taking a seat beside her, careful to stay clear of the truck's grime-encrusted grill.

"I'm fine, Dad. Really. What's happening, though? Are the soldiers going to take us somewhere safe, to their base or something?"

"You bet they are, but no, there's no base to go to. Too dangerous to try. It may not seem like it now, but we're in good hands. Miller and his friends know what they're doing."

"You know you don't have to talk to me like I'm a child, Dad. I'm twenty-two years old," Lillian insisted.

"I know. It's just... Come here." Tobias hugged Lillian tight, the concerned father nearly cutting off the girl's circulation as he tried desperately to hold back tears. "I love you so much, baby. I'll never let anything happen to you. You know that, don't you?"

"I know, Dad. I know. I love you, too. Now, please, you're crushing me here."

Tobias released his grip and returned to his place beside her as Tommy came dashing from beside the truck. The boy jumped on his dad's lap and scooted in next to his sister.

"Hey! There you are, little man. Where have you been?" Tobias asked, elated to see his boy.

"Playing with Dusty," the boy replied.

"Is Dusty behaving tonight?"

"Mm-hmm."

"Here you go, squirt." Lillian handed the boy all but a small piece of her candy bar.

"Thanks, Lil."

Content, Tobias watched his children eat what might as well have been the last candy bar in the world. He let them be and simply smiled.

The group of survivors gathered at the center of the caravan. For most, the initial shock of last night's massacre had worn off; it was time for answers. This group of soldiers had pulled them from the brink, and they were grateful, but if Miller didn't have a solution, then all was for naught. Where they would go and how they would survive on the road were the two most frequent questions bandied about. Miller thought it best to keep everyone in the loop and make them feel like an equal part of the decision-making process, as he needed these people to function as a cohesive unit if he was to have any chance at leading them to safety.

The comfort of familiarity was not lost on Miller, hence the decision to include Marisol and Sam in the decision-making responsibilities for the group. Marisol had a no-nonsense attitude and a heightened bullshit detector. Plus, she was well-liked among the people of Pepperbush long before their worlds were turned upside down. Choosing her to act as an intermediary between the soldiers and civilians would be invaluable in assuaging any trust issues fostered by the group.

Marisol stood in the bed of Bernie's truck, talking with the survivors. She answered what questions she could and as best as she knew how. Mostly she let the group vent and voice their frustrations to get a feel for the group's needs and concerns.

"As mayor, I suggest that we put our options to a vote," Mayor Lancaster suggested, speaking above the crowd, as he was accustomed to doing.

"Mayor of what? Pepperbush is gone, in case you haven't noticed," Tobias was quick to point out.

"Hell, even if Pepperbush *was* still standing, we're at least a hundred miles away," Seth added. "You don't call shit, old man."

Marisol sized up the once-powerful official. Without his cronies, Lancaster looked small. Frail, even. "You're the mayor of nothing, Lancaster. Your days of calling the shots are over. From where I'm standing, it doesn't appear any of your thugs made it out alive."

Vanessa clenched her fists. The mention of Lancaster's thugs sent chills up her spine. The thought of Jim, in particular, was nearly rage-inducing.

"As far as I'm concerned, we're in their hands now," Tobias said with assurance as he gestured to Miller and Marisol. "The military and the police are trained to handle emergencies. I say we let them decide the best course of action here."

"Have it your way, then." Lancaster stood off to the side. He positioned himself halfway between the townsfolk he so despised and the new authority he held no sway over.

"Sheriff, do you mind?" Miller approached the platform.

"Please." Marisol gestured for the captain to address the crowd.

Miller hopped up into the bed of Bernie's truck. Marisol took a seat atop a cooler behind him.

"I understand you all have questions, and I'll get to those in a moment. I promise. I have a few things I'd like to say first." Miller jumped right into his semi-prepared speech. Addressing a crowd like this was not a position he was comfortable with, but Takashi's death thrust him into it, nonetheless. "You've all been through a lot in the last twenty-four hours, and for that, you have my sympathy. So I won't stand here and lie to you by saying the worst is behind us, because I honestly do not know. What I can tell you is that we are heading south in hopes of finding a boat. Getting off the road as soon as possible is the priority here."

Most of the crowd appeared relieved, others distressed. The idea of spending days on the road and looking for something that might not even exist was terrifying for some.

Miller continued.

"What you experienced last night was no fluke by any means. This is your reality now, people. This is what is happening around the entire country. The more populated an area, the worse it is. What we faced last night was only a fraction of the danger we'll find ourselves in if we get too close to a major city. That being said, the idea is to stick to back roads as much as possible for the duration of our journey. A few days ago, Tobias informed my commanding officer of a plan he had to head east in search of a boat. Colonel Takashi agreed the plan was sound. However, it was decided the original destination was not ideal. As I'm sure you are well aware, the southern tip of New Jersey is located on a peninsula. Great for finding water and possibly a boat, but bad for an alternative escape route," he said to a few moans and nervous chatter. "If we were to run into trouble on the way to Cape May or we are unable to locate a boat when we get there, we would have no choice but to turn back, returning through possibly unsafe territory. In a worst-case scenario, we would be trapped. Takashi devised an alternative route. He suggested we head south, to the Outer Banks, bypassing the larger cities along the way, of course, and stopping for supplies when the opportunity arises. Barring any unforeseen complications, we should arrive in a few days. This way, if we run into any issues, we simply keep going. In the event of a problem, there will be no need to backtrack. We simply go around."

"Should we pack up and get ready to go now then?" Bernie asked.

"That was going to be my next point, Bernie. Thank you," said Miller. "We've been here most of the day and it'll be dark soon, so it doesn't make sense to leave now. We will only travel at night if we have no other choice."

"Why can't we travel after dark? I don't think those things care one way or another," Markus asked.

Jeremiah answered for Miller. "It's simple. We need to see where we're going."

"He's right," Miller said. "Those things probably can't see us very well at night, but we certainly can't see them. There are other reasons, though, not the least of which are supplies. We are drastically low on food and water. We can't risk passing by a potential food source we didn't see in the darkness. Which brings me to the primary reason I wanted to speak with you as a group. It is vital that we ration our supplies."

"Now he's going to tell us when we can eat," Lancaster retorted, a little louder than was necessary.

"Not at all, sir. Just the opposite, actually. I'm leaving it up to each one of you to ration supplies. Use only what you need, and use *that* sparingly. Keep in mind that we may not come across anything else for days," Miller warned.

Radzinski stepped forward. "In other words, if you see your neighbor getting by on a can of beans a day, don't expect him to share when you've wasted all yours."

"That's not exactly what I meant, but Radzinski *actually* has a point." Miller's emphasis brought a snort from Radzinski. Was that a jab? Was Miller even capable of making one?

"Don't waste anything. Don't hoard anything. If we work together, we *will* make it through this. It's been a very long day and I'm sure no one wants to hear it, but we're sleeping in our cars tonight. Crack the windows if you need to, but keep your doors locked. I suggest making yourselves comfortable as best as you can and try to get some sleep. We leave at first light."

CHAPTER FOUR

Respite

Tobias and his family slept while Miller drove the SUV, leading the caravan through ever more rural streets. Old bedsheets hung around the interior of the vehicle, covering the rear windows. Another separated the passenger section of the truck, offering the illusion of privacy as a benefit for those resting. Rachel joined Miller for this leg of the journey, acting as his navigator while Tobias got some much-needed rest. Her primary goal was suggesting alternate routes to get around clogs in the road, but more importantly, she was marking clear roadways on the map in the event they needed to turn around. Detours weren' t always successful, and more than a few U-turns were necessary due to the badly dated map.

"This thing's damn near useless. Was it printed in the seventies?" she asked, opting for the binoculars instead.

"See anything?"

"No, sir. It's quiet. Clear. I'm going to take that as the first break we've had in a week."

"Enjoy it. We've got a long haul ahead of us."

"Five hundred miles? That's not so bad," Rachel added with an eye roll.

"Under ideal conditions, sure, but we have no idea what we're heading into. The roads could be flooded with those things or worse. Not to mention I've never escorted this many civilians before."

"Don't do that. Don't second-guess yourself. Takashi left you in charge for a reason. He believed in you. We all do."

"Takashi didn't leave me in charge. I was next in line. It's as simple as that."

"That's bullshit and you know it. The colonel was grooming you from day one. He saw something in you whether you want to recognize it or not."

"Try telling that to Radzinski."

"Fuck that guy. He's a piece of shit, and Takashi knew it. Why do you think the colonel insisted on that battlefield promotion? It was a safeguard. In case something happened to him, there would be no dispute over who would take command of the unit."

"I suppose you're right," he conceded.

"I am. You're just being modest, fucking boy scout. Besides, heading to the Outer Banks is just as good a plan as heading anywhere else. Think about it. Tobias is right. I'd much rather have the ocean at my back than hundreds of miles of blacktop."

"Tobias's plan *is* sound."

"It is. The guy's alright. I'll give him that much." Rachel peeked around the drawn sheet. The Burkes were out cold. Tobias was asleep with his kids in the middle seats. Isabelle slept alone all the way in the back.

"Yeah, he's a good man with a good head on his shoulders. A good father, too, and that's what scares me the most. If I make the wrong call, they all die."

"Enough with the Debbie Downer routine, will ya?" Rachel sighed.

"You're right, you're right, as usual. Shit, if it was up to Radzinski, we'd be headed to Tijuana in search of the last of the infamous donkey shows." He changed the subject rather than engage in another conversation over his worth.

"Well, in that case, Captain, I suggest we change course." She fumbled with the map again.

"You're disgusting." He managed a chuckle.

"What? I just want to see for myself. What's the harm in looking?"

"Where do I even begin?"

"Hey, you brought it up." Rachel returned to her scanning of the horizon, places to stop or threats in the distance never far from her mind.

Evening approached, and once again, Miller picked a large clearing off to the side of the road. The spot was far enough from the beaten path that any passersby might just miss them in the darkness but still close enough that returning to the pavement in a hurry would be as simple as loading the civilians and going. The vehicles encircled the makeshift camp with enough space left in between so as not to hinder a hasty retreat. For those who dared sleep under the stars, bedding was fashioned from cut tall grasses wrapped in sheets, though more than half opted for the safety of a vehicle. A modest firepit was dug and surrounded by a wall of stone; the barrier kept the light nearly invisible in the distance.

Tobias and Miller walked the outer perimeter of the encampment, as had become a ritual in the nights since fleeing Pepperbush.

"They're my life, Miller. If anything happened to them, I don't know what I would do." Tobias grew increasingly anxious the farther from home they traveled, as if some invisible force still tethered him to the small town.

"Don't think like that, Tobias. If we stick together, your family will be just fine. We all will." Miller tried his best to assure the man, though a mind so focused was not easily swayed.

"That's easy for you to say. You're trained to deal with this sort of thing. Two months ago, I barely knew the first thing about weapons." Tobias held his gun aloft as if to say, *Here, take it. I don't know what to do with it.*

Miller chuckled to himself at the display. Tobias was just fine with a rifle; he'd seen it firsthand. The man simply needed to relax.

"Trained, sure. For this sort of thing? Absolutely not. No one is," Miller said as assuredly as he knew how.

Sensing an air of frustration, Tobias attempted a change of subject. After all, how many nights in a row would he prattle on about the same misgivings to the young captain?

"Do you have any pictures of your family?" Tobias asked.

"No, no. Takashi frowned upon us bringing photos into the battlefield. Back at base, sure, but no, I don't have a thing on me."

Had the moon been a touch brighter, the twitch in Miller's lip would not have been missed.

"That seems kind of cruel. He could have at least let you have a taste of home."

"Like I said, reminders of home at base are fine, but out here, in the shit, it can be a distraction. If your mind is back home with your family, then your head's not in the game. That'll get you killed a lot quicker than any enemy," he insisted.

"I think I see your point, Miller, but my family's right here, not half a world away, and the enemy is at our doorstep, as it were." Tobias tossed a stone into the darkness, half-expecting to wake a sleeping carrier.

"My point is, Tobias, don't lose sight of the big picture while focusing on the details. My unit's sole purpose now is to keep these people safe. Trust me, your family is in good hands." Miller offered all he could to ease the man's concern, but the guy would either come around on his own or he wouldn't.

Lillian sat in the grass, leaning on someone's truck, her back against an oversized tire. Vanessa brought over a couple pieces of bread and a bowl of stew Bernie had slapped together. It wasn't much, but she appreciated it nonetheless.

"What are you doing sitting all the way over here? The fire's cozy and they don't bite, you know." Vanessa pointed to Bernie and a few of the others gathered around the campfire.

"I'm fine right here. I'm really not in the mood to listen to them go on again tonight."

"Fair enough. So how are you holding up?"

"Good enough, I guess. Just trying not to think about it too much, you know," Lillian said, a little flustered.

"Okay, we don't have to talk about what happened. How was school this semester? Anyone I should know about?" Vanessa playfully asked.

"No, nothing serious. A few dates here and there or hooking up after a party was about it. Living off campus makes it kind of hard, you know, not to mention my parents wouldn't let me move out until I graduate, so I figured, why even bother?"

"Ugh, I know the feeling. When I finally moved out on my own, my parents were up my ass every damn day, it felt like."

"I bet. None of that stuff matters now anyway, you know."

"Oh, I wouldn't be so sure about that. I bet some scientist in some top-secret lab has this whole thing figured out already. Things will be back to normal in no time. You'll see. Besides, everything matters. I think those little things matter now more than ever."

"Maybe, and thanks. I know you're just trying to cheer me up."

"Did it work?" Vanessa asked with a smile.

"You really want the truth?" Lillian finally made eye contact.

"Not really."

"Then it did, a little." Lillian grinned. "Thanks."

Around the fire, Bernie and a handful of the others were probably a little louder than they should have been, all things considered. Each night on the road afforded them a little more acceptance of their situation. With that acceptance came a degree of comfort, allowing them to push to the back of their minds what was happening just out of sight.

"I'll tell ya, Seth, Macaby's hole is right around the corner from here. Can't be more than twenty miles down the road. Catfish as big as your arm, I tell ya." Bernie held his hands high, measuring his imaginary catch.

"Man, that sounds great, Bernie. I can practically smell it frying up already." Seth closed his eyes, the imaginary aroma nearly intoxicating.

Sam joined the men by the small fire. "Don't forget the greens and potatoes, boys. Man, what I wouldn't give for a proper meal like that right about now."

"You think Miller and the others would agree to a slight detour, Sam?" Bernie asked.

"Doubtful, and I'd be inclined to agree with them. We need to be off the road and someplace safe yesterday. Besides, did you pack any fishing gear? I sure didn't."

"Now that you mention it, no, I did not, Sam. To be perfectly honest, I didn't think we'd have to leave town in such a hurry, so all I brought was my rucksack I keep packed for hunting trips."

"And what do you keep in there, man?" Seth asked.

"Not much, a couple of pairs of fresh socks and underwear, a pair of pants, and a shirt or two. Ah hell, fellas, I didn't know it was gonna be like this or I would have brought my gear." Bernie kicked the dirt.

"I wouldn't let it bother you, son. Most of us weren't prepared for this. Hell, in a few days, those underwear and socks will be worth their weight in gold," Sam said.

"Amen, brother." Seth adjusted his crotch. He lifted a leg to better arrange himself. "If we don't find a place to clean up soon, I'm going to smell worse than those things out there."

The three men chuckled over the thought, but Sam was distracted. Something else weighed on his mind—far from the luxuries of fishing gear and clean clothes. *What if this is it?* he thought. What if this was the last time they could sit around a campfire and laugh? He had no idea what the road held for them. The uncertainty of it all unnerved him greatly.

Sam and Seth stared at the flames. The momentary respite caught them off guard, but soon the men dwelled, their thoughts wandering to what-ifs and whys. The change in atmosphere went unnoticed to Bernie as he busied himself with rummaging through his things.

"Well, fellas, I do try to keep this handy." Bernie revealed a handful of small boxes tucked away at the bottom of his bag.

"Is that what I think it is?" Sam asked, excitement creeping over him.

"Whoa, Bernie, you've been holding onto these all this time?" Seth asked.

"Like I said, I keep the bag in my truck. Don't really think about it much, but yeah, there's a few hundred rounds in there at least. Shotgun shells, too." Bernie tossed the bag to Seth for a closer inspection.

"Well goddamn, Bernie, you're about to become real popular around here," Seth said with a childlike grin.

Isabelle sat near the flames with Tommy in her lap. The little boy used a stick to bat orange coals around. His mother held him tight, her arms wrapped around his tiny frame, her chin resting atop his head.

Tobias and Nisha stood out of earshot, watching them. Nisha and Isabelle had been friends since longer than either could remember. Was it fifth grade when they met or around the seventh? Neither could be sure anymore, but Isabelle would swear the two of them used to flick peas at the mean girls during lunch break. It went back that far.

Part of Nisha was jealous of Isabelle's family, though never spitefully. Two kids, white picket fence, and a loving husband—on the surface, her friend had it all. Though it wasn't the ideal family that Nisha yearned for, she was tired of sleeping alone. It was as simple as that. *How ironic*, she thought. Now, every night she slept beside twenty-odd people and all she could think about was a return to her lonely bed.

She pulled Tobias aside for a one on one regarding the group's next move. It wasn't that she didn't trust Miller and his unit. Any news, whether good or ill, felt more genuine coming from a friend.

"First thing in the morning, we head south. As long as we stay clear of the big cities, we should make it there just fine in a few days."

"They've been saying that for *a few days*. Tobias, I'm afraid. Scared shitless, if I'm being completely honest. We don't have much food, and well, goddammit, half of those soldiers didn't even make it out of Pepperbush. What chance do the rest of us have?" Nisha folded her arms. A sudden chill crept up her spine.

"Don't talk like that, Nisha. Honestly, I think the worst is behind us. Once we get to a boat, we'll be safe. You'll see."

"It's not me I'm worried about. It's Isabelle and the kids. They seem so apathetic, like they don't realize what's going on or, worse, don't care, especially Izzy," said Nisha.

"Do any of us really know what's going on? They're in shock. All of them. With any luck, the kids will be able to put this whole mess behind them faster than the rest of us," said Tobias before changing his tone to a whisper. "Isabelle worries me lately. It seems ever since this thing started, she's grown more detached, and everything I try to do isn't good enough. She despises me for spending so much time with Sam and the berm patrol or just trying to help out around town. I'm afraid I might have lost her, Nisha, and I have no clue how to bring her back."

"Hey, it's not that bad, Toby. Believe me, she loves you. She's just having a hard time with this, like the rest of us. She'll come around. You'll see," Nisha replied, though she didn't really believe what she was saying.

Something changed inside of Isabelle, and Nisha noticed right away. Unfortunately for Tobias, he didn't recognize it until she began lashing out. By then, Isabelle was weeks into her psychosis. A part of Nisha was resigned to the fact that Tobias lost his chance to ease his wife's troubled mind. At this point, she wasn't even sure if *she* was capable of helping Isabelle come around.

W.J. Hegarty

CHAPTER FIVE

Roadside Sanctuary

Camp was broken at first light. The caravan drove through the morning before spotting what looked to be a decent area to rest and hopefully rummage for supplies.

Nearly a week after fleeing Pepperbush, Miller was growing accustomed to leading the disparate group. Each day on the road, he and his navigator, Rachel, would ride in a different vehicle. Aiko suggested the idea of switching up car assignments on a daily basis as a way for the group to better acclimate themselves. If these people could move beyond the fact that they began as a bunch of strangers thrown together, it would make life on the road slightly more tolerable, not to mention that trust in Miller and his unit would naturally flourish as well.

Rachel took to the radio to inform the caravan a stop was finally coming up. "It looks like there's a strip mall up ahead in fairly decent shape. Probably picked clean, but we're going to stop, anyway."

"Copy that," Radzinski replied from the rear of the caravan.

To help alleviate the strain on batteries, it was decided days ago that only two radios at a time would be left on. The lead and rear vehicles would have them. Everyone else in the middle of the caravan would need to keep aware of any notable change in bearings. The first few abrupt stops were a little tricky, and the caravan had the dents to show for it. Hand signals and dedicated navigators promptly cleared up any confusion.

The caravan pulled up in front of a small strip mall. A line of stores stretched the better part of a standard city block. The mall was laid-out in an L-shape partially framing an expansive parking lot. The opposite end of the lot featured a simple gas station and convenience store flanked by a bank and a restaurant, both of which were burnt-out shells. A boutique and a printing press were all that remained of the strip mall's easternmost stores. A supermarket and a furniture store still stood on the north side of the L. The remaining shops in the mall had been burned out. Reinforced fire walls between each unit no doubt kept the few stores still standing unburnt.

The weary travelers exited their vehicles. Disappointment reigned at the realization that most of the shops were office buildings or ruined.

Marisol slammed her SUV's door shut behind her. "Looks like an office park mainly. Printing place, comic-book store, travel agency. Shit, almost every one of them is useless or burnt out." As she pointed out each shop, her voice grew more morose with every passing name. "Dammit!" she said, slamming a rifle down on the hood of her truck. Her skin glistened with tiny droplets of sweat; it beaded up and dripped from her forehead and nose. She waved her half-unbuttoned shirt desperately to air out her chest. "At the very least, we need to get out of this sun. Dehydration will kill us a lot faster than those things if we run out of water."

"Great, a bunch of office buildings. Lots of good that will do us," Ryan said, wiping his brow. "Oh, fuck this," he added as he yanked off his shirt and tied it around his head.

"Don't be so hasty. There could be something of value in one of them," Rachel suggested with a quick peek at Ryan's sweaty abs.

"Wait a minute. Is that a Travelers Mart?" Ryan asked, hopeful.

"See, what did I tell you?" Rachel playfully nudged him in the ribs.

"That's what I'm talking about!" Ryan shouted.

"Oh, the destroyed building with all the windows busted out? No thank you. I'm not even going to waste my time with that one," Elliot added.

"I don't get it. How is it a waste of time? What else do you have to do today? You have somewhere to be?" Ryan commented, perplexed.

"You can count me out."

"Whatever, dude. Their pizza is the shit. Sure, it's one step up from cardboard with sauce on it, but, man, I don't even give a shit. I love it!"

Radzinski leaned in with a grin. "You know, even if they still have some in the freezer, that crap melted a long time ago. You're shit out of luck, kid."

Ryan looked defeated. "Couldn't help yourself, could you? You just had to take that from me."

Radzinski quietly chuckled.

"What is Travelers Mart?" Soraya asked, a bit confused over Ryan's excitement.

"I don't have the slightest idea, but if the insides look like half of these other places, that kid's in for a disappointment," Aiko replied.

Samantha pointed to the ruined building. "Oh, I get it. It's the gas station. Look."

Across the way, a massive overhang formerly shielding the gas pumps from the elements was mostly knocked to the ground. All outward appearances suggested a large truck of some sort and obviously too tall to pass beneath slammed into the structure, collapsing it to the ground and smashing most of the pumps in the process. Two somehow survived the damage. At one end of the debris, remains of a large sign protruded from the pile. The first three letters, T-R-A, were exposed along with the partial remains of its logo, a caricature of a happy motorist with his thumb in the air and winking at passersby.

"I've seen that stupid thumb a million times driving," Samantha said. "He's right. It is a Travelers Mart, but I doubt there's anything in there. Just look at the place."

Miller interrupted. "There will be time to explore later. For now, I need you all to stay with the vehicles until we've better assessed the situation. We need to be sure there're no surprises waiting for us in any of these buildings before anyone gets too comfortable."

Miller's unit quickly assembled in front of him.

"Alright, everyone, listen up. We're going to do this quick and dirty. The supermarket and convenience store are the priority. We'll be spending most of the day there. Afterward, offices get a quick once-over, in and out," Miller said to a responsive unit before turning his focus on Marisol. "Once we've secured the area, I'll radio back. The rest of you can help look for supplies then. Marisol, you and your officers keep a lookout here. You see anything out of the ordinary, pack these people up and radio us ASAP. Clear?"

"Affirmative. But make it quick. I want these people out of the heat and in the shade as soon as possible."

"Copy that."

Miller and his unit swept the area for lingering carriers; the strip mall was devoid of movement. He soon gave the all-clear for the civilians to begin rummaging. The survivors of Pepperbush grouped off and spread

43

out, most simply enjoying the freedom to walk more than a few yards without an armed escort.

Miller's unit and Marisol's police traded shifts patrolling the parking lot. They were sure to keep watchful eyes on the civilians meandering about the place and rushing from one burnt-out store to the next, seeking supplies that simply were not there. Whether fruitful or not, the searches and the patrols gave everyone something to do. At the very least, it helped ease the growing tension from so many days spent on the road, forced to ride atop one another in too few vehicles.

Vanessa, Lillian, and Casandra took the time to scout out the boutique. The store was left largely intact, its contents obviously deemed worthless by previous looters. Rack after rack of black T-shirts stood untouched. Skateboard decks and posters still adorned the walls. Unbroken glass cases yet housed the rings and jewelry for a thousand piercings. A soda machine in the corner had been forced open and emptied of its contents. Otherwise, the place was mostly spared past vandalism.

It had been eight days since they fled Pepperbush, and Vanessa was still barefoot and wearing a filthy shirt she found among some wreckage miles back. The shirt smelled slightly better than the one Bernie gave her, but the woman was in desperate need of new attire.

"Hey, this is cute." Lillian handed Vanessa a small tank top.

Vanessa squeezed into the extremely small shirt, its tight fabric hugging every curve and line of her torso. She looked herself up and down in a cracked full-length mirror, hands pressed against her exposed flat stomach, the shirt ending a few inches above her belly button. "I like it. Thanks, Lily, but it's not very practical, is it? It'll do for now, though. God, this other thing smelled horrible when I found it. Good riddance." Vanessa balled up the grimy shirt and threw it behind a darkened display case.

"No, it's not very practical, but I'll keep looking. A light jacket might not be too bad. You could wear it over that and take it off when we're not running for our lives. Whoever got here first sure didn't leave much," Lillian replied.

"I can't fit into any of this, guys." Casandra held up a tiny tee to her huge belly.

"Just bring it with us, Cas. After you pop out the little one, we'll all be sharing clothes. You'll see," Vanessa suggested.

"Tropical beaches, bikinis, and martinis, huh?" Lillian held up a skimpy yellow bikini.

"Yeah right, more like this," Casandra said as she lifted a corner of a tarp duct-taped to a cracked window.

"Oh, stop it. You're not even that big." Lillian disregarded Casandra's attempt at self-loathing.

"As a matter of fact, try this on. Here, come with me." Vanessa pulled Casandra by the arm and led her to the changing rooms.

"Why did I even follow you guys in here?" Casandra said with a sigh.

"Hush." Vanessa slammed the curtain shut.

Lillian changed out of her bloodied clothes into something a bit more practical for travel: a tight long-sleeve yellow shirt over jeans and boots. The less loose fabric, the better, she imagined. She wouldn't give the infected anything to grab onto. She just wished her mother would do the same and change out of that damn dress.

Casandra inched from the dressing room with Vanessa close behind, lest the pregnant woman try to turn and flee.

"I can't believe I let you talk me into this."

"Quiet, you. Keep walking," Vanessa instructed.

"Whoa, you look amazing, Cas." Lillian's eyes went wide. She clapped and bounced in place as Casandra walked an imaginary runway.

Casandra's ear-to-ear smile was unmistakable, even after she raised her hands to her face, eyes welling with tears of joy. She returned to the storefront, bathed in light, a yellow string bikini accentuating her pregnant frame. She cradled her stomach lovingly, smiling at Vanessa's handiwork. "Thank you," she managed through the tears.

"Come here," Vanessa said.

The three women stood there, huddled together in the center of a clothing shop in a strip mall far off the beaten path. None of them knew what town they were even in, and it didn't matter in the slightest. Right then, trying on clothes with friends in a ruined store, Casandra was overcome with joy. Lillian held up another suit for the expectant mother. Casandra posed, her hips out to the side as she held the new bikini against the one she wore. Vanessa topped her off with a large, brimmed, straw sunhat. The three women's banter boosted each other's spirits, a much-needed rise from the despair brought on by the road.

"You got it, girl," said Lillian.

"I never lost it," Casandra replied.

"That's what I want to hear, ladies." Vanessa joined the other two in picking out future outfits for Casandra.

Outside the boutique, Radzinski peered through the window. "Goddamn, are you seeing this, man?" he asked a passing Jeremiah.

"I've got other things on my mind. If you prefer to keep yours in the gutter, then by all means, carry on."

"You're such a buzzkill, Jerry. For Christ's sake, would you live a little? This is the hottest thing I've seen in months."

"Like I said, enjoy yourself, and when you're finished, zip it up. Miller's been looking for you."

"Holy shit, I think that was a joke. It was, wasn't it? Dammit Jerry, I knew you had it in you." Radzinski waved off the thought of meeting Miller and returned to his show.

Jeremiah wasn't impressed with the man's immaturity. Disregarding a request from Miller was to be expected, though letting his guard down for a peep show gave the medic pause.

Markus chucked an empty soda can down the trash-strewn parking lot. "The pumps are all dry, man. Same with the store. Not even a fucking candy bar left. Someone beat us to it. You were right, Tobias. We should have put Pepperbush in our rearview weeks ago."

"That's what I'm hearing from everyone. The places that aren't burnt out have been thoroughly looted. We're not going to find anything here, but none of that matters now, Markus. This is where we're at and we have to make the best of it," Tobias suggested.

"Yeah, I guess you're right. Still sucks, though."

"It does, but you need to keep your mind off of it. Why don't you grab Bernie and check out those cars over there? See if we can at least siphon some gas from them. Grab the batteries, too, and anything else you think might come in handy."

While most of the civilians kept themselves busy by rummaging through ransacked stores, Miller was busy discussing options with some of the others. "Anything we find close to the highway like this is going to be similarly looted already," he said. "I think we're looking at two options here. We can stay on the highway all the way to the Outer Banks and get there quicker or take the back roads and maybe find supplies."

"If we don't find anything on those back roads, the extra miles could leave us out of gas and stranded in the middle of nowhere," Marisol suggested.

"That's a possibility I'm inclined to take my chances on. Middle of nowhere means less infected."

"Keeping that glass half full, I see," Rachel added.

"We have to," Miller replied. "That being said, it's going to be dark soon, maybe an hour of light left, so I want input. Now we can huddle up in and around the cars as usual or make use of that furniture store over there."

"The upside is there're beds for everyone and then some. Problem is, if we have to bug out, we're that much farther away from the caravan," Rachel added.

"Be nice to sleep in a proper bed," said Sam.

"I see no reason why we can't stay here, at least for a few nights," Marisol replied.

"Then we're agreed?" Miller asked.

"Yeah, I think this will be good for all of us," said Tobias.

"No arguments here," Seth responded.

"Good, then inform your people and start picking spots." Miller abandoned the group as it continued marveling over beds to rejoin Soraya out by the caravan.

"We stay, yes?" Soraya asked.

"Yes, we stay." Miller touched her shoulder. "Why don't you and Aiko take first watch. Then get some sleep. I'll see to setting us up with a few bunks."

• • •

Miller and Jeremiah patrolled the parking lot on midnight watch with Tobias in tow. Most of the others had already turned in for the night, exhausted from so many days of travel.

"I don't like this at all, Miller." Jeremiah's head was on a swivel. "Staying overnight in a place like this, out in the open in a strip mall no less, is far too dangerous. Any number of things could go wrong, not the least of which is the infected surrounding us with our guard down. This place is an open invitation for disaster."

"I don't like it, either, but it's really our only option. It was stay here or travel at night, and I will *not* do that. Not with so many civilians."

"Wait a minute," Tobias interrupted. "You're not suggesting those things are following us, are you? All the way from Pepperbush? I would have voted against staying here if I thought there was a chance of the infected catching up with us."

"Not at all, no," said Jeremiah. "We've covered far too much ground with the vehicles for them to catch up with us at this point. That particular group is the least of my worries."

"Oh, okay. Good. That's a relief. Then what's the problem? We have a clear view of anything approaching, and we even have doors we can lock at night."

"Jeremiah's concerned about roving gangs of looters," Miller admitted reluctantly. "We saw quite a bit of that in Philadelphia. It got real bad, fast."

"I'll never understand the mentality of people stealing TVs and game consoles during an emergency. Doesn't make any sense." Tobias scanned the nearby throughway, half-expecting to see a mob of looters descending upon them.

"It wasn't like that at all," Jeremiah said. "It was almost as if on some primal level the people knew this was something different. Like they sensed it, felt it. It wasn't luxuries they were after. It was the shoes on your feet, the gear or medicine in your pack. They wanted everything you had, and they'd kill you for it to avoid the conflict."

"My God, is it really that bad out there? Don't they realize we should all work together to figure this thing out?" Tobias was confused. The notion of killing an innocent was alien to him. He couldn't wrap his mind around it, no matter how hard he tried.

"Jeremiah's right. If—" Miller corrected himself. "*When* we run into a group of survivors out here on the road, and we will, let us do the negotiating, but be ready to act."

"Human nature dictates that desperate people are capable of nearly anything to ensure their survival," Jeremiah added.

"Well, that's comforting," Tobias replied.

Tobias returned to his family's corner of the furniture store. Two beds were pushed side by side, one for him and Isabelle and the other for Tommy, who was fast asleep. Lillian was sleeping somewhere else in the building with Vanessa and Casandra. The Burkes' area had a modicum of privacy. Tobias and Seth had pushed a wall of dressers around the beds and a couple of nightstands. The structure gave the illusion of a walled room. Little Tommy was in awe. He was convinced his dad had just built him a fort. Tobias crept in to find Isabelle still awake, sitting in a rocking chair near the center of the makeshift bedroom.

"You're up late. You want me to see if I can scrounge up something to eat? I think Bernie still has a whole bag full of jerky," he offered.

"No." She snorted, almost outright bursting into laughter.

"Oh, okay. What's got you so worked up tonight?" Tobias asked while attempting to rub his wife's shoulders. She immediately pulled away.

"What *is* there to say, Tobias? Don't cozy up to me now that we're forced to spend time together. Go play with Sam or your new friends," Isabelle said with a disdainful wave of her arm at Miller and Jeremiah, who were passing by in front of the building through a break in the stacked dressers.

"Isabelle, please, can we just talk?" Tobias laid his hand on her shoulder. She pulled away hard this time and shoved him back.

Tobias was momentarily off-balance. He tripped over an end-table display and fell to the floor. A lamp shattered on the ground beside him, alerting everyone inside to the commotion.

Isaac ran up, nearly ready to draw down on a perceived threat. "Is everyone alright over here?" he said but backed off before either of them could answer. It was clear what was transpiring. "I'll leave you be, then," was all he said.

Nisha heard the commotion, too, but wasn't about to back away over a case of embarrassment—theirs *or* hers. "I don't know what's gotten into you two, but now is not the time for this," she scolded. "Come on, you're sleeping with me tonight." She escorted Isabelle to another section of the store.

Tobias sat alone on the floor, stunned. He watched as his wife was led away, comforted in the arms of another woman. Nisha looked back and gave an apologetic shrug. The gesture helped, if only slightly, knowing Isabelle had someone to talk to, even if it wasn't him.

Seth offered a hand and helped Tobias to his feet.

"Don't even bother explaining, pal," said Seth. "Come on outside, man. I've got something for you. I found some cold ones. Well, they're warm ones now, but it's still beer, right?"

• • •

Dawn crept into the abandoned shopping center as the Pepperbush survivors slowly began to stir. Lancaster sat amidst the ash-laden ruins of a burnt-out liquor store two units down from the furniture shop. A blackened minivan was lodged into the front of a walk-in refrigerator at the far end; it appeared to have exploded on impact or was otherwise set ablaze. Most of the inventory that survived the ensuing fire was long ago looted, although if you dug deep enough through the remains, you could stumble across a gem or two. Lancaster found a half-empty bottle of the worst rotgut imaginable, dragged himself into a corner, and indulged. A far cry from his beloved Brandy, but the end result would be the same.

"You won't find it at the bottom of a bottle," said Sam, emerging from the shadows.

"Oh, the ever-so-wise Sam graces me with his divine wisdom. Spare me your false platitudes. A few weeks ago, your opinion meant less than dirt to me. Why should that change now?" Lancaster sneered.

"When everyone else was heading for the hills and looting places like this dry, we hid, cowering behind the berm, laughing all the while at the idiots on TV. Who's the fool now, begging for the scraps they left behind?"

"You and I could have accomplished greatness, Sam. Why were you always so against me?"

"You're either drunk or delusional if you can sit there straight-faced and tell me what you did in Pepperbush even resembled greatness," replied Sam, ire growing.

"Bah." Lancaster rose and steadied himself against a partially burnt wall. "What do you know about it, anyway?"

"I know those people were terrified of you, and for good reason."

"Is there a point to all of this, or are you here merely to gloat?"

"Honestly? I came in here with every intention of putting you down once and for all, maybe give Tobias, Vanessa, and Marisol some peace of mind," said Sam with a sudden air of serenity. "But seeing you like *this,* lying in the dirt, filthy, drinking bottom-shelf booze in the corner of a burnt-out liquor store, friendless and scared, I won't give you that release. You are *right* where you belong." He leaned on the doorframe, peering out upon a bright new morning. In days gone by, he would never have been so careless as to turn his back on Lancaster in any situation. By this point, the former mayor was nearly as low as a man could get. He wouldn't dare make a move against Sam or anyone else. Not anymore.

Tobias thought it best to let Isabelle cool off for the night. They could work it out in the morning before he joined Miller on patrol. After a few beers with Seth, he slept beside Tommy until well past dawn. He awoke to Isabelle gathering what little things she still possessed and quietly stuffing them into a trash bag.

"I didn't want to wake you, but I sent Tommy out with Bernie to look around the grocery store," Isabelle said while continuing to pack.

"Oh, okay. That's fine. Bernie's always been good with him," Tobias said through a yawn. "Why are you packing up already? We're not leaving until tomorrow."

"Tommy and I are going to start riding with Nisha and Sam. I'm putting our stuff with theirs," she said with no air of uncertainty.

"Just like that? No discussion? Can't we talk about this, Isabelle?" he asked, flustered.

Tobias tried to turn her around to at least look him in the eye before leaving.

"No, I don't want to talk about it, Tobias. Fuck." Isabelle pulled away. "Get off of me."

"Izzy, please," Tobias begged.

"For Christ's sake, would you stop calling me that?" she yelled.

"What? Izzy? I've been calling you that for years. I thought—" Tobias began.

"Well I fucking hate it! Sounds like you're patronizing me, like I'm a fucking child. My name is Isabelle, and you are my husband, not my father." Isabelle momentarily raged but calmed as quickly as she began.

"Okay, okay, Iz—Isabelle. I'm sorry. I didn't know," Tobias stammered.

"Talk *with* me, not *at* me, once in a while, and you'd know these sorts of things," she replied with a calmness. "Go find your son. He's not Bernie's responsibility and I shouldn't have to watch him every hour of every day."

Miller paced the length of an aisle. His position atop the empty shelves afforded a 360-degree view of the grocery store. He obviously couldn't see the goings-on of each and every aisle; that was what Marisol, Soraya, Seth, and Isaac were patrolling for. Miller had a clear line of sight to each exit; they wouldn't be caught off guard, not here.

A few pairs of survivors filed up and down each dusty, ransacked aisle. Not very dissimilar to better times when shoppers would be compelled to walk each and every aisle, rarely noticing their carts filling with items they didn't need. A good portion of which would be discarded weeks or months later with no recollection of where, when, or why they even bought the things in the first place. Now their eyes were wide. They didn't dare *not* scan every inch of every aisle for even the most mundane of items. A packet of ketchup would have been a godsend at this point.

"Oh my God, wipes." Lillian snatched up a plastic container of baby wipes that had been kicked underneath a shelf. "Do you have any idea how disgusting I feel right now?" she said rhetorically.

"Of course I do. I slept next to you last night," Vanessa replied jokingly.

Lillian grabbed Vanessa in a bear hug, trying to force the woman's face closer to her own filthy shirt. "I stink, huh? Well, what do you think about this?"

"Oh God, anything but that. Somebody, get me out of here." Vanessa laughed and slumped to the floor, sliding out of Lillian's grasp.

"Much better down here." Vanessa sighed, lying beside the moldy remnants of a can of beef stew.

"You love it," Lillian said as she stepped over her friend to continue her trek down the aisle.

Vanessa rose to her feet and brushed herself off as Rachel and Ryan pulled up beside her, brandishing a mostly empty shopping cart of their own.

"Sounds like someone's having some fun over here," commented Ryan.

"Trying to," Vanessa said before kicking the empty can.

The container rolled down the aisle and bounced off of Lillian's foot. The girl didn't bother to stop. She simply extended her arm and gave the trio the finger.

"That little bitch." Vanessa chuckled.

"That's right, sister. Every day doesn't need to be doom and gloom," Rachel stated adamantly.

"I guess you guys are having as much luck as us, huh?" Ryan asked.

"It's looking that way." Vanessa shrugged. "Luckily, we have enough to go around for now, but this place is a bust."

"Not entirely. I'd kill for a couple of those wipes. Just name your target," Rachel said, making the shape of a gun with her hand.

"Hmm, I'll have to get back to you on that," Vanessa replied.

"I've got an idea," Ryan said. "I'll jump in this cart. Tell Lily to get in yours. We'll race down to the frozen food section. If we win, you give us ten wipes. If you win, we'll do your guys' laundry for a week. Sound fair?"

"You've got yourself a deal, sir." Vanessa reached across the cart and extended her hand for a shake.

"Let's do this," Ryan replied, returning the gesture.

The race started simply enough, and Vanessa was off to an early lead. Although physically stronger than Vanessa, Rachel struggled to get the much heavier Ryan up to speed, but once she finally gained the advantage, Ryan's weight and her momentum easily carried them through the finish line first.

Nearing the end of the course and unable to slow fast enough, Vanessa lost control as Lillian's weight shifted, sending the two of them and their empty cart tumbling into a row of barren shelves. Plastic containers, boxes of sandwich wrap, scattered cutlery, and the like littered the surrounding floor. Vanessa slowly rose to a seated position, rubbing her shoulder.

"You okay, Lily?" She turned to find Lillian face-down, unmoving.

"Oh my God, Lillian! I'm coming. Don't move." Vanessa rushed to her side and gently turned her over. Still nothing.

She lowered her ear to the girl's chest when Lillian jumped.

"Gotcha," Lillian whispered.

"You asshole." Vanessa slapped her in the arm before collapsing onto her back. The pair burst into laughter.

Lillian crawled over to the relieved woman and rested on her elbows near Vanessa's face. They lay there panting, staring at each other expectantly.

Lillian brushed aside a few strands of hair from Vanessa's eyes. "You were worried," she panted.

"I knew you were fucking with me. Didn't want to ruin your joke. That's all." She lowered her eyes.

"Yeah right." Lillian laid her head on the cool floor beside Vanessa, who in turn proceeded to brush Lillian's hair with her fingers.

At the other side of the store, Bernie and Casandra were doing some shopping of their own. Tommy was half an aisle ahead, traversing the store by hopping from one shelf to the next. The floor was lava. Dusty would occasionally squeeze onto a shelf beside him.

"I don't think we've been properly introduced. My name's Bernie, ma'am." He leaned forward, took her hand in his, and kissed it.

"Oh, a gentleman? Well I do declare, sir," Casandra replied in a faux Southern accent, using her other hand like a fan to cool her blushing face.

She curtsied and Bernie held her hand high before taking her arm in his.

"Right this way, ma'am," he said. "It would be my pleasure to give you a first-class tour of the facilities."

Bernie guided Casandra down the empty aisle. They walked slowly as he described the treasures that used to adorn the shelves. She played along and enjoyed the momentary respite as the day's worries seemed to melt away. If that was Bernie's intention all along, he was doing a fabulous job of it.

Radzinski barged into the grocery store, scanned the surroundings, and made a beeline for Miller's position atop the shelf. "What the fuck's going on around here? Maintain discipline, huh? Oh, that's rich."

"What seems to be the problem today, Marine?" Miller asked through a half-smile.

"Oh, it is without a doubt *my* problem. I get it now. Your girl Rachel gets to jerk off with the locals. Anyone else steps out of line, though, it's get-in-your-face-time, right?"

"You need a push, Radzinski?" Miller kicked a box of detergent down from his perch and into a shopping cart beside the frustrated Marine.

"Funny. Oh, yeah. That's real nice."

"Relax, we're back on the road tomorrow, anyway."

"This is a joke, Miller. Look at these people running around all over the place. Is that a football they're tossing over there?" Radzinski motioned to Peter, Markus, Samantha, and Ayn tossing a ball around the remnants of the bakery department. "What are we supposed to do with them all?"

"They're letting off steam, Radzinski. What else would you have them do?"

"I don't know. Siphon gas? Loot the stores?" he responded, pointing back to the parking lot.

"That was all done yesterday and this morning. Listen, John, these are civilians. They just watched what was left of their town burn to the ground and get overrun with carriers. If staying here an extra day and letting them toss a ball around or race shopping carts boosts morale, then I'm all for it. Now, if that's all, be on your way—Marine," he added with a smirk.

"You got it," Radzinski grumbled. "Sir."

• • •

Across the lot, inside the gas station, Peter laid his shotgun on an empty chip rack and fumbled for his zipper while using his back to open the door to the lavatory. A carrier lunged from the darkened room, latching its putrid teeth deep into Peter's exposed neck. In his haste to escape the tormented creature's grasp, Peter lost his footing on the slick floor. He fell headfirst into a nearby countertop, and the impact knocked him unconscious.

The carrier was quick to pounce on the helpless man. Seemingly attracted to the warm, fresh blood, it licked at the wound at first, then quickly began tearing and chewing at the gash, widening the damage and digging deeper into Peter's scalp. The carrier promptly encountered hard skull but continued along the hairline, pulling and chewing flesh from bone until it reached Peter's soft eyes. The change in texture almost seemed to confuse the creature before it slowed its assault to concentrate on Peter's face.

Elliot and Ayn were doing some last-minute scavenging; the caravan was set to depart in thirty minutes. The pair of them were natives of Pepperbush and by chance were both attending university in New England. They carpooled to and from school a handful of times a year, but other than that, you wouldn't really mistake them as being friends. Elliot was in his final semester at MIT, and Ayn happened to be his roommate's girlfriend; the two of them were studying law. They were a part of a group of six coeds down from Boston, setting up job interviews in Philadelphia and hoping to land an internship. The rest of their group never made it out of the city; they lost track of each other when a riot broke out over bottled water distribution. Hitchhiking for rides eventually landed them safely home in Pepperbush.

Elliot held the door for Ayn and they exited the half-burnt-out building, prepared to rejoin the group and get back on the road.

"Hey, I'll catch up. Let me hit the bathroom before we head out," Elliot said, reentering the store.

"Fine, but make it quick. You know we're not supposed to be wandering around alone out here."

"Yeah, yeah, I know. *You* try shitting in a bag in a moving vehicle because no one wants to pull over. Fucking sucks," he said. "Don't worry. I'll be fine."

"Alright, alright. Don't fall in." Ayn laughed and continued back to the caravan while feasting on a small packet of crackers she stole from a rat.

Elliot waited a few moments for Ayn to be far enough away. Convinced it was all clear, he crept down, out of sight, and crawled his way around to the clerk's area behind the main counter. He stayed crouched as he reached up to yank the cash register down to the floor beside him. A few well-placed hits with the butt of his gun and the old register popped open.

"Ha, ha, jackpot," he said aloud.

The register was full of crisp, clean bills, easily five hundred dollars, he imagined.

"Somebody wasn't making their deposits," he said, shaking his head, satisfied over someone else's blunder.

A childlike grin stretched from ear to ear as he greedily stuffed his pockets with the money. Content with his findings, he stood up and brushed himself off. On his way to the door, he picked up a handful of rags to better keep up appearances that he was actually searching for supplies for the group.

"Now what possible use do you think that's going to have?" a voice called out from the back of the store.

"Christ, you scared the shit out of me, man. What are you doing in here?" Elliot's stomach dropped at the sight of Radzinski approaching from the bathroom, his excuse for being alone no longer an option.

"What you were supposed to be doing." Radzinski wiped his damp hands on the man's shirt. "Using the facilities, not stealing useless paper."

"Well, it's none of your business what I take." Elliot covered his pocket as if to prevent Radzinski from taking his score.

"It *is* my business, especially when it's my ass on the line when you refuse to do what you're told." Radzinski was resting his palm on his knife's handle, slowly moving it back and forth in its sheath. "You think you can use that money to buy your next meal? Or maybe you want to use it to pay me and my unit for keeping your sorry ass alive?"

"Now wait just a minute, Radzinski. I wasn't—" Elliot wasn't allowed to finish.

"Shut your mouth. When you break protocol, you put all of our lives in danger. I won't lose another man for you or your people, you hear me?" Radzinski pinned the smaller man against the wall, his forearm to the man's throat, cutting off his air supply. He finally unsheathed his blade and placed the tip just beneath Elliot's eye. "The next time you pull some shit like this, I'll do you myself and leave your ass here for the infected." Radzinski threw him to the floor, then stepped over the trembling man on his way to the exit. "Get your ass up. We're leaving," he said as he flung open the door.

"Headcount, Soraya." Miller gestured to the group of survivors gathered around the caravan.

The Israeli would be furious if she knew Miller assigned her to such menial tasks as policing up supplies and keeping track of the civilians in an attempt to keep her out of harm's way. In reality, Soraya was probably better qualified to take care of herself than anyone else here, him included. She was certainly not new to danger. After all, only the best of the best were handpicked to enter into the troop exchange program. The same could be said for her American counterparts back in her home country.

Miller's feelings for the young Israeli were growing harder to hide from the group, and this kind of favoritism would not go over well if indeed it got out. For now, though, he couldn't be worried about hypothetical scenarios. This new enemy was unpredictable and damn near unstoppable. He would do his best to keep everyone safe, but for now, Soraya stayed within his line of sight, period.

"We are missing one, sir. His name is Peter. They say he was last seen near the gas station," Soraya reported.

Miller shook his head slowly. Eyes closed, he pointed to Aiko and Seth and waved them toward the gas station. "Go get him." He sighed.

"Goddammit, another one?" Radzinski chimed in as he pushed Elliot into the crowd. "I found this one across the street by himself, looting a fucking cash register," he said accusingly.

"Take it easy, man. Not all of us are used to this sort of thing," said Elliot.

"And who the fuck is?" Radzinski asked rhetorically, nearly begging the man for a response. He grabbed a handful of Elliot's cash and held it up to the man's face in his fist. "The only thing this is good for is wiping your ass or starting a fire." He threw the wad into Elliot's chest.

Elliot snatched the money back as best as he could, "Whatever, man. Maybe that's why I took it."

"Oh really?" Radzinski turned back around to face the man, skin flush, eyes wide. "You're a funny little bitch, aren't you?"

"That's enough, John. Leave him alone." Rachel squeezed between the two men, gently pushing Radzinski back a few feet with her left hand. With her right, she pointed directly at Elliot's face. "You, disappear."

"Hey, wait just a minute. This isn't—"

"Go, now!" Rachel shouted.

"Okay, okay, I'm going, shit." Elliot backed down, cursing under his breath until he disappeared between vehicles.

Radzinski batted Rachel's hand away while turning to face the majority of the crowd. "Maybe you people don't understand that we follow protocol for a reason. If you can't follow a simple request, then we can't effectively keep you alive. How is that so hard to grasp?" He shook his head in disgust. "You know what? Fuck it. I don't even give a shit. Do whatever the fuck you want. I'm through babysitting you people." He walked from the group's sight, cursing to himself. "Fucking civilians."

Miller took point. "What Radzinski is trying to say is that most of us have escorted civilians through hostile territory before. So at least that aspect of our current situation is familiar."

"Ever the optimist, huh?" Radzinski added.

"That's enough." Jeremiah grabbed Radzinski by the arm and quickly pulled him away from the view of the civilians. "Listen to me. If you continue undermining Miller like that, this group will splinter. Are you prepared to deal with them if they begin questioning orders?"

Radzinski yanked his arm free from Jeremiah's hold. "Get your goddamn hands off of me, medic. If Miller loses control of these people, I couldn't care less. You all know where I stand. I say we cut them loose and double-time it to the nearest base. We could be of better use elsewhere," Radzinski suggested with a glare at the civilians.

"Well, thankfully for them then, you don't make the decisions. Miller has a destination in mind, and no, it doesn't include abandoning these people on the side of the road."

"Whatever, Jerry. Oh, by the way, you can call Aiko. Tell her she can stop looking for that missing civilian."

"Excuse me?"

"Yeah, what's-his-name, he's back at the gas station, face-down in his own filth." Radzinski shrugged. "One of those things was chewing on his neck last time I saw him. That was right before I found Elliot in the next building over. Should have shown him the mess, I suppose."

"Nice." Vanessa and Lillian were passing with boxes of blankets from the furniture store in time to catch the tail end of their conversation.

"And you left him there? Unbelievable." Jeremiah turned his back on the Marine. "I can't even bear the sight of you right now."

"Not my fault, Jerry. It was in the ceiling. Some dumb fuck civilian probably got bit and crawled up there to hide. You can figure out the rest. Besides, we've told these people over and over again not to go anywhere alone. Now maybe the rest will listen."

Jeremiah was disgusted with Radzinski's lack of compassion, and he needed space. For the time being, he would occupy his time by helping these people cope.

Vanessa, on the other hand, wasn't prepared to let the matter rest. "Look around you, you inconsiderate prick. People are terrified. We're not used to this kind of shit." She singled out Samantha, who was barely keeping it together. She cried into Markus's chest as he looked on, anger building.

"None of us are used to this, sweetheart. It's a cold world out there now and you gotta get hard if you want a chance at living in it," Radzinski responded, devoid of empathy.

Vanessa didn't bother answering. Instead, she ushered Lillian away from the confrontation.

Radzinski opened a beer and shrugged off the woman's comments. After all, what did she know? A few days ago, she was a bartender in a rural, backward-ass town in the middle of nowhere. She and her people were lucky to have stayed out of harm's way as long as they did. As far as Radzinski was concerned, every breath she took was by the grace of him and the other soldiers. If none of them spoke to him for the remainder of their journey, all the better.

As Radzinski sat in the sun, enjoying his warm beer in relative silence, Lancaster saw an opportunity to bond with a fellow outcast.

"They don't seem to like you very much, do they, son?" Lancaster's statement went ignored, although that didn't stop the man from edging closer to the Marine. "Would you mind terribly if I joined you? We seem to have much in common, you and I." Lancaster attempted to lean on the truck next to Radzinski but was denied.

"We have nothing in common, old man, so yeah, I would mind. Terribly, even." Radzinski tossed his empty bottle into the street. It shattered upon impact as a thousand tiny shards of glass skidded their way down the road. "And as far as being liked goes, they don't have to like me. They just need to stay out of my fucking way," Radzinski stated matter-of-factly. "That goes for you, too."

CHAPTER SIX

Ruin

Onward they pushed, farther south. Reading a map was one thing, but anticipating blockages in their path was another entirely. Avoiding the larger cities and congestion-filled popular routes led them farther off the beaten path. Rural one-lane roads seemed to be their curse. The caravan was careful to keep as much distance as possible as it crept past an abandoned campsite just off the side of the road. Remains of a makeshift shelter were strewn about. The only sign of life remaining was light from a battery-operated lantern still shining inside of a ransacked tent. A handful of carriers' silhouettes were illuminated on the walls of the shelter, their shapes clearly visible. They were feasting on the remains of a family apparently too slow to escape what was likely a surprise attack. The shadow of a severed arm was unmistakably being raised to a ravenous mouth. Spattered blood painted the tent's interior, casting an ominous glow for the weary onlookers. Slurping and crunching cut through the otherwise quiet afternoon. Content with their prize, these few infected took no notice of the trespassers' slow passage. The caravan continued on, careful to avoid the attention of the infected. Some in the group closed their windows as they passed, avoiding the scene altogether; others were captivated by the slaughter.

Rubberneckers, Marisol thought with a bit of disdain.

She'd been in law enforcement long enough to know it was human nature to be curious about the macabre, especially when it was at someone else's expense. She slowed down just a bit to allow her passengers an all-too-brief reminder of what these things were capable of. At the very least, maybe some of them would come away from the scene more cautious as a result, especially in light of Peter's mishap only a few days prior.

The caravan continued on, snaking its way through debris-strewn streets. Abandoned and wrecked vehicles made the travel slow going. A moving truck had flipped over and split in two, spilling its contents across the road. Large boxes and broken furniture hindered the group's movement. The SUVs would have most likely been fine navigating the remains, but the smaller cars could have been hung up on the wreckage. None would dare attempt to drive through the soft, rain-soaked earth beyond the road—the only alternative—but they couldn't risk losing a vehicle; conditions were cramped enough as it was. Miller had Tobias stop in front of the ruined rig. This was their second hold-up in as many hours. If these delays continued, they might never reach their destination.

Miller and his unit stood guard at the perimeter while the survivors of Pepperbush got busy with the task of clearing a path for the caravan. Rural back roads or not, the route Tobias and Miller agreed upon seemed fairly heavily traveled, at least traversed enough that every chance at resupply was a lesson in picking through someone else's scraps. For the most part, the group was beginning to find a rhythm as far as the delegation of tasks was concerned. Not everyone saw eye to eye on the subject.

"You starting to feel like we do all the work around here?" Damon asked, glaring at Jeremiah.

"You're getting that, too, huh?" replied Ayn.

"Look at them over there." He pointed out Radzinski leaning against a painter's van, smoking a cigarette, rifle slung. "It's the same thing every time we stop. They stand around looking busy while we do all the heavy lifting."

"No argument here, but what are we supposed to do about it?"

"I have no idea yet. I'll let you know when I do."

"Most of this stuff has been picked through already. Just junk mostly." Tobias tossed a box of comic books over the side of the road.

"Not surprising. There's no telling how long this mess has been here," Marisol replied.

"Story of our fucking lives, man. Give me a hand with this," Seth said.

He and Marisol heaved a smashed TV away from the road. Tobias continued on down the pavement, kicking or throwing larger items out of the way. His son followed behind, doing the same.

"It's fun breaking stuff," Tommy giggled.

"I know," said Tobias. "Watch this." He picked up a large lamp and tossed it like he was going for three points in a basketball game.

Unnecessary to be sure, but the joy on Tommy's face as the fragile lamp exploded into a million pieces was the desired result.

"My turn!" Tommy yelled, throwing plates and saucers as far as his little arms would allow. The boy's dog, Dusty barked with every shattered dish.

Rachel was in the middle of the road, dragging a long sleep sofa out of the way. One step at a time, she slid the cumbersome furniture backward, out of the path of the caravan.

"Let me help you with that." Ryan dropped his gun near an abandoned car's front tire and rushed to Rachel's side.

"Oh, I'm fine. I've got it," Rachel said with nary a grunt or sigh.

"No, really, I insist." Ryan lifted his end of the sofa and strained under its surprising weight. Embarrassment flushed his face. "Damn, this thing is heavy! You're stronger than you look, huh?"

Rachel smiled. She appreciated his help and found the gesture cute but unnecessary. "Gotta be. You'd be surprised how fast you build muscle mass lugging around eighty-pound packs every day. You ready? One, two, three," she said before they heaved the sofa away. The large piece of furniture rolled down a steep embankment, crashing into piles of various junk scattered about from the accident.

"Well, that takes care of that," Ryan said as he wiped his hands together, as if to be over the strain.

"Almost. For future reference, don't ever do that with your weapon. Never set it down in a place like this—ever," she advised.

"Shit." Ryan looked around to all the debris, and for the first time, he noticed the plethora of blind spots, any number of which gave the carriers a perfect opportunity for an ambush. He jogged back to where he left his rifle and slung the weapon over his shoulder before turning back to thank Rachel, who had crept up behind him. Mere inches from his back, she gave him a soft chop on his neck.

"You're dead." For once, Rachel's light-hearted nature wasn't showing through. Her warm, inviting smile gave way to a cold, unfeeling stare, eyes determined, fists clenched. "Remember, it's that fast these days. Sometimes you won't get a warning."

His face went warm. He cursed himself for being so absentminded. Ryan didn't need a mirror to tell that his face was as red as Rachel's hair, probably more so. The last time he felt this humiliated was at his brother's thirty-fourth birthday party. A buddy of his convinced him this girl he was talking to was into him. Within minutes, she shot him down within earshot of more than a few people. The feeling now was similar. In an instant, a harsh lesson was learned at the expense of some dignity, only this time he didn't have hours of drinking under his belt to lessen the sting.

Aiko lay prone against a tractor trailer's roof, scanning the horizon with the group's sole pair of binoculars. Untended to fields hosting waist-high overgrown weeds spread as far as the binoculars would allow her to see. A quarter-mile away, the scorched fuselage of a private jet lay wedged between a group of trees at the edge of a forest. The surrounding area was just as burnt. Shapes littered the crash site. Whether it was parts of the plane, luggage, or bodies was impossible to make out from this distance, as everything was so blackened.

Miller crept up beside her, lying down as well. "Contact?"

"I count three. They're far out there, sir. I don't think they've noticed us yet. Looks like they're preoccupied with a carcass. Big dog or baby deer, maybe. Could be a body from the plane crash for all I can tell."

"Keep an eye on them just the same. We're Oscar Mike in twenty, but if they come any closer, we'll bug out."

The largest portion of the broken trailer remained to be cleared before they could continue their journey. It blocked enough of their passage that squeezing by on the slightly elevated road risked their vehicles tumbling into the field. The rig itself was in fine working order and would be their only shot at clearing a path. It was assumed the truck's driver released the trailer before whatever accident split the container in two. Where he got off to and why was another matter entirely.

"That's it. A little more," Sam coached Radzinski. "You got it! Push that son of a bitch! Go, go, go!"

The trailer's weight wouldn't budge at first. Radzinski's tires screeched against the pavement. Smoked billowed from overworked rubber until at last the stubborn trailer gave up an inch. The smallest in was all he needed.

Radzinski floored it. This time, slowly the rig pushed the crippled trailer from their path, off into the grass.

"That did it." Sam waved for Radzinski to ease up.

Bernie let fly a triumphant string of hoots and hollers. A few of the others clapped, but most busied themselves with looting and foraging in the moments before being herded back into their vehicles. For some, the authority was welcome, as long as it afforded them another night among the living. Others, though, weren't so sure that the illusion of safety at the expense of any real say in their destiny was worth it. Some of them couldn't help but wonder if they'd be better off on their own. Tobias didn't share that particular set of misgivings. He didn't see it like that at all. He welcomed the help, as he'd been planning to flee Pepperbush for more than a week by the time Miller arrived. Having this large of a group together out on the road was more than he could have hoped when he posed the idea of flight to Sam, seemingly ages ago. If it meant keeping his family safe, sure he would defer the major decisions to Miller and his unit.

The low sun licked at the treetops. Already, shadows began to stretch along the pavement.

"Way to go, guys. You woke them up," Aiko informed from her perch.

In the distance, by the downed plane, a small group of carriers shambled toward the lonely patch of road, no doubt stirred by the commotion of Radzinski's moving effort.

"I reckon we should hit the road as soon as possible, anyway," Sam suggested. "Cover as much blacktop as we can while we still have the light."

"Agreed." Miller waved the group back to their vehicles.

• • •

More than an hour passed as they meandered country roads. Burning precious daylight, they turned from the blacktop onto an even more remote route paved with gravel. This continued for a few miles before rock gave way to dirt. The caravan stopped at the bottom of an incline snaking up into the hills. A shadowy structure stood halfway up the summit, barely visible in the dwindling light.

"It looks like a cabin, sir. I think it's abandoned, but it's impossible to know for sure from here." Rachel was struggling with the conditions, trying to best make use of the binoculars before handing them off to Miller.

"I think you're right. I can't make out any vehicles, no movement. A roof over our heads would be nice, and I don't like the looks of those clouds. We need to be off the road now. Screw it. We'll make camp there tonight."

Headlights cut through dense fog. A small cabin loomed on the horizon. The gravel road forked off in opposite directions before giving way to its smaller, less traveled dirt counterpart. Lining up side by side, the caravan's headlights flooded the small building with a cleansing light that drove away the darkness, a stark contrast to the blackness of the surrounding forest. Exaggerated shadows danced among the foliage as if in defiance of the light's penetrating glimmer of hope, its secrets remaining its own.

Weapons drawn, the soldiers approached the small cabin, their shapes blacked out by the intense light. Miller pointed to the dark perimeter of the structure. Soraya and Rachel headed off, engulfed by the darkness. Another gesture to the front door and Radzinski kicked it in, disappearing into the unfamiliar building and followed closely by Jeremiah. Miller remained outside of the cabin with Aiko; the pair kept a watchful eye on their surroundings.

Behind the caravan, Marisol and Seth trained their weapons on the darkness. Isaac, Tobias, Bernie, and Marcus watched the caravan's flanks, anxiety palpable in the day's newest unfamiliar locale. The mass of civilians, huddled safely away in their respective vehicles, awaited the all-clear.

"I get it now," Tobias said, careful not to take his mind off the task at hand.

"And what's that?" Seth asked.

"Why Miller insists on only traveling during the day. I've never seen it this dark. I can't make out anything out there at all."

"Yeah, if it wasn't so cloudy, it wouldn't be so bad, and all these headlights are doing is messing with our night vision. This is bad."

"You suppose there's anyone in there?" Tobias tried to focus on the blacked-out cabin, but the blinding headlights made it impossible to gauge any real detail.

"It's hard to say, man. No gunfire yet, so that's always good, right?" Seth wasn't exactly confident with his assessment of the situation.

"Let's hope so." Tobias inched a little closer to the nearest vehicle. If he couldn't adjust to the darkness, then he would at least position himself where his vehicle could act as a bit of protection from possible threats lurking just out of sight.

Isabelle agreed to ride this leg of the journey with Tobias, but only for their son's sake and with the stipulation that her husband not try to speak with her.

"Is Daddy safe, Mom? Are those monsters out there?" Tommy asked Isabelle. Tears welled up in the child's eyes.

"Your father is just fine, sweetheart. Him and his friends are just making sure it's safe for us to get out of the car. That's all," Isabelle reassured the child. Her confidence was all he needed. Whether she believed her own words or not became irrelevant in the face of her distressed son.

"Someone got hurt, Mommy," Tommy said.

"What do you mean, honey?" Isabelle asked and for once was grateful for the darkness, as the light would have betrayed the confusion written all over her face. "Why do you say that, Tommy?"

"I heard Mr. Bernie say lots of bad words and a soldier said Peter is gone. Where did he go?"

"He went away honey, like Uncle Danny."

Isabelle's attempt at consoling the boy did not go unnoticed by the others in the car. Lillian lowered her head and covered her mouth with a hand. She knew if she let her emotions show it would only serve to frighten her brother even more.

Vanessa took Lillian's other hand as she pulled the girl close. "Shh," she whispered in Lillian's ear. "He needs you strong."

Tommy continued. "You mean they're dead, like everybody at home," he said, this time with conviction as if the world's secrets had finally revealed themselves to the boy.

Isabelle hesitated as she stared longingly into the boy's eyes. He was so young, but at his age, he had witnessed more horrors in just the past few weeks than most people would in an entire lifetime. She owed him some honesty. "Yes, Tommy, they're dead. But they're with Grandma now, in heaven."

"I don't want to go to heaven. I want to stay with you and Dad."

"Why would you say that, honey?"

"Because the monsters have to bite you first. I don't want them to bite me."

"Those things will never bite you, Tommy. I promise," Isabelle replied.

Vanessa leaned into the back of Tommy's seat, her lips close to his ear. "You want to know a secret, little man?"

"Uh-huh."

"I'm scared, too, and I'm a big girl. I wish I was as brave as you, Tommy."

"You do?"

"I do, and Lily told me all about how brave you are. Didn't you, Lily?" Vanessa turned to Lillian for some much-needed support. A little sisterly advice was called for.

Lillian had taken the time to compose herself, quickly wiping away a few tears of her own. She joined the others in consoling her little brother. "That's right, Tommy. You're the bravest. You *and* Dusty," Lillian said while she pulled the dog up closer to Tommy.

"See, honey, there's nothing to worry about," Isabelle added.

Isabelle bit her lip and drove a thumbnail deep into her palm, drawing blood in both places. Pain helped drive away fear. More importantly, it allowed her to focus on remaining strong for her son.

Tommy smiled for the first time in days, it seemed. He wrapped his little arms around Dusty's neck, hugging him tight. The dog panted in recognition, though its eyes remained fixed on a far-away spot in the darkness.

Isabelle twisted the nail deeper into her hand. Her eyes rolled back as waves of pain *and* pleasure surged through her body. With her son content, she could focus her attention on the small cabin and what secrets it held inside.

Soraya and Rachel emerged from the shadows.

"No sign of anything, sir. No footprints or tracks of any kind. If I had to guess, I'd say the infected have never been here," Rachel said.

Behind them, Jeremiah exited the small cabin.

"All clear, sir. The cabin is empty. It appears no one's been here for quite some time."

"Food, supplies, anything?" Miller asked.

"A moldy loaf of bread and a small pile of rusted canned goods. Aside from a urine-stained mattress in the back corner, the place is empty."

"Radzinski?" Miller asked.

"He's still inside, getting a fire started."

"Okay, Soraya, set up a defensive perimeter. I want two on patrol at all times. You and Rachel are up first. And watch your six. No letting our guard down, even out here. Aiko, spread the word to start unloading the civilians. It's been a long night. Let's get some rest."

Tobias pointed at Damon and back to his position at the caravan's perimeter. Reluctantly, Damon got out of his vehicle and took Tobias's spot on watch. With a quick wave and a smile to his family, Tobias left the relative safety of the caravan for the cabin.

"It's quiet out here, Miller. Not so much as a cricket. So how does it look inside? You think we should stay the night?"

"The cabin is empty, Tobias. No signs of struggle or that infected have ever even been here. There's an unmade bed and a few canned goods in the back. If anyone lived here, they're long gone by now. I'd say this place is just about as safe as any to camp for the night. We'll reassess in the morning."

"That's a relief. After the campsite we drove past, I'm not sure anyone feels safe sleeping outside, at least not tonight anyway."

"Agreed. I've set up a perimeter watch and Radzinski's lighting a fire. We'll be safe—for the time being, anyway."

"Good, I'll let everyone know we'll be staying here the rest of the night then." Tobias returned to the caravan as he holstered his sidearm, the trace of a smile on his face, the first in days.

From their vantage point inside of the vehicles, the remaining citizens of Pepperbush took the sight as a small sign of relief. Fears temporarily quelled, the frightened people began to make their way to the cabin.

"One lonesome cabin out in the middle of nowhere? I like it. I bet the view is spectacular in the light," Lillian mentioned.

"I'm sure it is," said Vanessa. "Tomorrow I think I'll head down one of the other roads, see if they head higher into the hill. Maybe get a better view of our surroundings."

"Wonder why the rocks stop where they do. You'd think they could have given this guy a new driveway while they were at it." Lillian kicked a few stones around the dirt.

"The gravel road probably means new construction. That's what I'm hoping, anyway. If so, the cabin's most likely a holdout. The guy didn't want to sell so they'll just build around him."

"That's kind of messed up."

"Who are you telling? Same thing happened to my parents a decade ago. Developers don't give a shit. By the time ground's broken here, they're already planning the next site. They'll move on and not think twice about some old house or land that's been in someone's family for six generations."

"Depressing. What happened to your parents? I mean, after they had to sell."

"They moved in with us for a while. I think the whole ordeal broke them a little, losing the house. Dad passed away six years ago last winter. Mom followed him almost a year later to the day."

"Jesus, Vanessa. I'm so sorry. I had no idea."

"Don't be, really. They loved life and were proud to see me so happy. Besides, I wouldn't want them to have to live through this." Vanessa motioned around to the beat-up cars and worn-out filthy group of survivors. Bernie was engrossed in scraping the last remnants from the bottom of a bent can of food, Samantha still jumping at shadows. All around them, nervous survivors with guns patrolled the area. "As fast as we had to move and as bad as this is, I absolutely would not have left them behind. So the three of us would be standing right here now with you, or we'd all still be in Pepperbush, watching it burn."

Damon wouldn't take his eyes off Samantha. He watched as she daintily explored her surroundings, slowly leaving the safety of the vehicles and inching her way toward the cabin. Every rustle of a bush or peep from the forest's inhabitants sent the girl halfway back to the car.

"Stop jumping at every goddamn thing. You're pissing me off," Damon said, frustrated with her every breath.

"Excuse me if I'm not comfortable in the middle of the woods."

"You think I like it out here? I'm from Baltimore. I barely know what a tree looks like, you redheaded bitch."

Markus intervened. "What the fuck man? Chill."

"Enough, all of you!" Marisol demanded, just above a whisper but forceful, nonetheless. She put an end to all of it. "Keep it down. Start unpacking your shit."

Marisol barely gave the trio a second glance as she nudged by, closer than necessary. Her proximity only proved to heighten Damon's ire, though he kept it bottled up. Markus was merely thankful for the impromptu intervention, as even he was growing weary of Damon's outbursts of late. Marisol moved past them on her way to the back of the caravan, where Sam stood vigilant, one eye to the road behind them and the other on the darkened forest. She approached from behind and placed a firm hand on the man's shoulder to let him know she was there as she handed him a much-needed bottle of water. "Take a load off, Sam. I can take watch for a while."

"Appreciate it, darling, but I won't be able to sleep, anyway."

Marisol took up a seat beside Sam on the trunk of a car. She laid her rifle beside her and lay back against the rear window. "If you don't mind the company, I'd love to just lie here and look at the sky for a while."

"By all means," Sam said as he joined her on the trunk, though he wouldn't lie down.

Isabelle glared at her husband scurrying around with his new friends. He would point in one direction and someone like Bernie or Isaac would rush to the spot. She imagined the others merely humoring him, as he had no real authority. If it came down to it, they'd put him in his place in a heartbeat. She prayed for it.

Idiot, she thought.

"You should talk to him," suggested Nisha, who had crept up beside her. Isabelle was too deep in thought to notice.

"What is there to say that I haven't been repeating for weeks? I'm half-tempted to wait for everyone to go to bed and take Tommy to one of the shelters. Washington's suburbs didn't look so bad. You should come with," Isabelle suggested.

"Isabelle, no. I absolutely do not want to leave the group," replied Nisha sternly. "Talk to your husband, Isabelle. If you're up for it, first thing in the morning I'll sit down with the two of you and mediate."

"If I cared enough to speak with him, sure. Maybe some other time. I'm just over it. All of it." Isabelle scanned the group marching back and forth from the parked caravan to the cabin like so many ants. *Pointless, all of it.* She left Nisha standing alone to check up on her son. Obviously his father couldn't be bothered.

Tobias and Miller discussed a map unfolded on the hood of a car. Their destination was circled. Their current location, or at least where they thought they were, was marked with an X.

"I don't think a few days here would mean the end of the world," Tobias suggested. "After that, barring any unforeseen bullshit, we could feasibly be in marina country in, what, five days, give or take?"

"I'm inclined to agree. This place is secluded enough, and I think if we pile up some brush across the driveway down the hill a little, anyone driving by wouldn't be the wiser."

"I think a few nights in the woods will be good for morale, like a camping trip." Tobias slapped Miller on the back.

"Yeah." Miller grinned. "A camping trip from hell."

Aiko jogged up, sporting a wide smile and a dripping-wet bottle of water in hand.

"We found a hand pump for a well, sir, and believe it or not, the thing works!" she said excitedly. "We've got them filling containers now. They're piling up pretty quick over there, too."

"It's about time something went our way. In the morning, take a few of the civilians with Marisol or Seth and head back to the store we passed. Collect every container you can carry. By the time we leave here, water shouldn't be an issue, at least for a while, anyway."

"I would still recommend boiling it first. We have no way of knowing if the well has been contaminated," Aiko suggested. "One of those things rotting into the water table could feasibly infect all of us."

Markus approached, lugging two overflowing containers of water. "You want these inside the cabin? Is there anywhere in there that's out of the way to store them?"

"There's a small wine cellar under the cabin, or it could have been storage for food. Maybe the previous occupants were canners. I don't know. Doesn't matter. It's empty and cold as shit," Aiko said. "Steps down are right next to the kitchen. You can't miss it."

"Sounds perfect," Markus replied, turning for the cabin.

"Put the water in Bernie's truck, Markus." Miller shot an uneasy glance to the darkened forest beyond.

"Sir?" Markus dropped the water again.

"Just as a precaution, if we need to leave in a hurry, I'd hate to lose all this water."

Markus did as he was directed.

"You okay, Miller?" Aiko touched his shoulder. "You should probably try to relax, get a good night's sleep while you can."

"I'm not sure. Something doesn't feel right about this place. It seems too perfect, you know? I'm half-tempted to pack up camp and get back on the road now, dark or not."

"We *can* do that, sir. I'll have these people Oscar Mike in ten. Just say the word."

"No, not now, Aiko. It's probably nothing. Just paranoid is all. Keep your eyes open all the same, though."

Bernie lit a fire beneath a large cauldron held aloft by a spit, another amenity the cabin offered. Nisha and Elliot took turns stirring its contents.

Filthy road-worn clothes cooked in the stew, boiling away accumulated grime from nearly two weeks on the road. Save for the occasional sanitized wipe or damp cloth, the Pepperbush survivors experienced nothing resembling a bath since fleeing their homes. Hot steaming rags with a dash of soap never felt so good. A portion of the bathers scurried off to the side, keeping their modesty bathed in shadow. Others harbored no such qualms, cleansing themselves by the flickering firelight.

Hours passed inside the cabin. Most were settling in for the night or already sleeping. A calm swept the group, not a word of their trials spoken. A few remained active. Some poked around the cabin's interior, checking and rechecking empty cabinets. Maybe they had missed that vital item on their first pass.

Thump. The lid of an oversized ice chest slammed shut.

"You're an idiot if you thought there'd be food in there," Radzinski said.

"No shit. Had to check, though." Rachel shrugged. "You know, I half-expected this thing to be full of dead bodies."

Radzinski lifted the lid for a peek inside. "Three or four could fit, easy."

Rachel hopped in and lay flat on the bottom. Neither her head nor feet touching the cooler's sides, she raised an arm enough to just barely finger the box's lip. "What, are you blind? Eight, all day."

Those who wanted to bathed. Damp clothes were strewn about the cabin on makeshift lines or draped across the hoods and trunks of the vehicles out front, their owners wrapped in sheets or towels. For most, the flight from Pepperbush didn't afford them time to gather supplies on their way out, including fresh changes of clothing.

Part of the group opted to head straight for bed, forgoing a soak of their clothes or even a quick rinse of their bodies. The ex-mayor was one of those, as he would rather remain dirty than undress and debase himself in front of his inferiors. There would be time down the road in private to address such matters.

"If you still smell that bad when we leave here, you're riding with someone else," Marisol said, securing her towel firmly in place before lying down for the night.

"The lot of you may have left your modesty back in Pepperbush, but I for one—" Lancaster started.

"Save it," Marisol said, eyes closed. "No one cares."

"Dusty can sleep in the basement, Tommy," Tobias instructed adamantly.

"But, Dad..." the boy pleaded.

"I'm sorry, son, but we can't risk his barking attracting those things," Tobias insisted. "He's been acting up all day. He'll be fine."

"That's not fair!" Tommy shouted.

"I said he stays downstairs. Now that's enough. I don't want to hear any more about this! Put him in the basement and get ready for bed. We have a long day tomorrow."

"We always have a long day tomorrow." Tommy took his dog and stormed off into the basement, slamming the door behind him.

"That was a little harsh, don't you think?" asked Lillian.

"I know. I'll talk to him in the morning. I'm just tired. On edge, I guess."

"We all are, Dad. Come on, let's get some sleep. Tomorrow's a new day."

Tommy returned and promptly tucked himself in without a word for his father. Tobias wrapped himself up in a blanket opposite Vanessa; his children between them. He lay there, longing for his wife, who was across the room, asleep beside Nisha, Bernie, and the pregnant one.

What was her name again? he thought. Tobias still didn't know everyone in the group by name, another issue requiring his full attention. A good night's rest was what they *all* needed. Everything else could wait until morning.

• • •

Radzinski and Seth were on watch. Occasionally they talked out by the vehicles. Dawn was only an hour off. During their shift, they circled the cabin in opposite directions, crossing paths out by the driveway. Every ten or so passes when they met, they would chat for a few moments before continuing on. The cabin was silent and black. Even Miller and his unit were fast asleep in the relative comfort of the temporary abode. Soraya had nestled in beside Miller. Half-asleep, he pulled her close. She took his hand in hers, interwove their fingers, and pulled his arm tightly around her.

A rear window near the cellar door shattered the silence. A Molotov cocktail broke on the floor, showering the room with fire. Within seconds, curtains, furniture, and half of the cabin's interior were engulfed in flames. A second bottle smashed against the back door. Then a third fiery projectile barreled its way through a side window.

Soraya slept with one eye open. She had since she joined up with Miller's unit back in Philadelphia. She was on her feet in a flash, dragging Miller up with her. "Fire, fire! Everyone out!" Her warning roused the few survivors not already on their feet or out of the building.

The group made a mad dash for the front door. In their haste, they left behind mostly everything but the clothes on their backs, if they were wearing any at all. Most inside had taken advantage of a good wash, their clothes strewn about camp, hanging to dry. Out in the driveway, a few stood, dumbstruck, down by the vehicles or were left wandering around still half-asleep. Only Radzinski and Seth were at full attention as protection from unseen attackers.

Marisol burst from the cabin, weapon drawn and pulling a chain of survivors locked hand in hand behind her. She pushed them out into the clean air. Samantha was followed by Lillian, Vanessa, and Markus.

"Did anyone see anything?" Marisol yelled, all the while guiding more people from the smoke.

Sam emerged from the darkness, helping along Nisha, who twisted her ankle in the confusion. "Here, take this!" Sam offered his rifle to Marisol so he could better assist Nisha down the stairs and away from the cabin.

Marisol aimed the rifle's scope into the darkness and scanned up and down the perimeter. Nothing.

A cacophony of coughing and gasps for air threatened to drown out the crackle of the growing blaze. The group spread out in the dirt-covered lot, leaning against vehicles or bent over hands on knees for support.

Ryan lay on his back on the cool ground, gasping for air. Rachel paused for a second as she knelt beside him. He was fine, took in too much smoke. "Twelve, thirteen," she whispered. It was nearly impossible to get a proper headcount in all the confusion. Rachel stood back up, already on the move. She whistled for Radzinski's attention and pointed to the back of the cabin.

"What the fuck's going on?" Damon asked.

"Most likely a careless cigarette smoker, I'd imagine," Lancaster suggested.

"Oh, don't start your shit. You don't know that," Marisol replied. She stood at arm's length from Lancaster, barefoot and mostly naked save for a brown tank top and a towel haphazardly wrapped around her waist. Instinct took over when she awoke to the chaos. Getting as many as possible to safety took precedence over modesty. She wasn't the only one at a disadvantage clothing-wise, as others scrambled for still-damp clothes drying in the cool night air.

Bernie stood as naked as the day he was born, save for a pair of cowboy boots and a rifle draped over his shoulder, his trucker's cap firmly in place. "It was a bottle of gas," he said.

"Bullshit," Damon replied.

"Like hell. It flew through the window right above me. I was awake the whole damn time," Bernie insisted.

"Who would do something like that?" Samantha asked.

"We don't know what's going on yet," Ayn said.

"No, I saw it, too!" Casandra was panicked. "It came through one of the back windows and blew up on the floor. Lit the place up like the Fourth of July!"

"See, I know what I saw," Bernie insisted.

"Where the fuck are your pants, man?" Damon shook his head.

"In there." Bernie spat toward the flaming cabin. "And that's my favorite pair of jeans, by the way. Why? You wanna go get 'em for me?"

Damon ignored the comment, preoccupied with the situation at hand. "Goddammit, half of our shit's in there. Food, clothes. Fuck."

"Not now, man. We've got more important shit to worry about," Markus suggested.

"Like what?" Damon asked, irate.

"Like making sure everyone's okay, for one," Samantha added.

"How could I forget? Screw our stuff. Samantha needs to save the world first," Damon replied.

"Aiko, give me a headcount," Miller ordered. "Make sure everyone made it out. Soraya, Radzinski, Rachel, you're with me on perimeter search. Marisol, Seth, Isaac, secure the vehicles. The last thing we need is for whoever is responsible for this taking off with what little supplies we have left."

"Seth and I just got back, man... sir. There's nothing out there. Not a footprint. Nothing," Radzinski said.

"Whoever did this never left the tree line," Rachel added, out of breath. "We're not going to find them in the dark like this."

"Sir, someone really should keep an eye on the civilians," Aiko suggested. "We don't need anyone going off half-cocked and there could be injuries, so..."

"Go!" Miller pointed to the huddled masses. "At first light, we find this fucker," he said through clenched teeth. "In the meantime, I want eyes on every corner of this property until we're Oscar Mike. Is that clear?"

"Yes, sir," his unit replied enthusiastically.

"Utilize the police and stay in eye contact. No one goes anywhere alone. We don't know how many of them are out there or what their intentions are."

"I think it's pretty clear they want us gone," Radzinski added.

"They're more than welcome to try," Miller replied.

Over at the vehicles, the group was slowly acclimating to its latest misfortune. Tobias scurried his family off to the side, away from prying eyes.

"Are you okay, baby?" Tobias brushed mussed-up hair from Lillian's face.

She coughed an affirmative. "Yeah, Dad. Too much smoke. I'm fine," she replied, coughing again.

"Jesus, Tobias. Tommy was just sleeping in there. You said this place was safe." Isabelle was a black silhouette against the blaze.

"Everyone made it out safely, sweetheart. No one got hurt," Tobias replied. "We'll sleep in the car for the rest of the night."

Tobias caressed Isabelle's cheek, then pulled her in. He held her close, kissing her on the top of the head. Even under the circumstances, it was nice to have her back in his arms. She would give him this moment, if only for Tommy's sake. The sooner she was away from him, the better.

The cabin was more than two-thirds engulfed when a wind gust enveloped the couple in smoke. It stung, and Tobias averted his sight from the blaze and looked back to the darkened road whence they came. The thought they'd be back on the road first thing in the morning was demoralizing. Just a few nights indoors was all he really hoped for. Now that was gone, too, along with the bulk of their supplies.

Without warning, Tommy darted toward the burning cabin. "Daddy, we left Dusty locked in the basement!" Tommy yelled as he pushed through the smoke and disappeared into the burning building.

"Oh my God. Tommy, stop!" Tobias screamed. "No, no, no, no, no," he shouted, sprinting after his boy and into the smoke-filled home.

"Tobias, wait. It's too—" Miller rushed to the cabin. He wasn't quick enough to prevent the desperate father from running into the fiery building. A wall of flame shot up, separating the men. Miller was trapped outside, shouting over the crackling fire. "Tobias, can you hear me? Get out of there goddammit!" he yelled, though the hissing blaze and screaming civilians drowned out his pleas.

The flames intensified as another gust of wind whipped the fire up into a wall of waves that now splashed around the wooden structure, preventing Miller from pursuing.

Isabelle quickly followed but was tackled to the ground by a watchful Soraya.

"No, Isabelle," Soraya insisted.

"Let me go goddammit! Tommy!" Isabelle screamed. She struggled but to no avail. Soraya was strong for her stature, and she held on tight, pinning Isabelle to the ground. The soldier wouldn't budge. No one else was entering the inferno.

Radzinski ran up from behind the burning cabin. "Back door's fubar, man. We're not getting in that way."

"Goddammit." Miller shook his head in disbelief. "Alright, get everyone back. Christ, Tobias."

Vanessa escorted an unresponsive, nearly in shock Lillian down to the vehicles and away from the chaotic scene. "Come on, Lillian. Let's go back to the cars."

Miller pointed at Rachel and Aiko, then back to the fleeing girls. "Stay with them!" he shouted over the roaring flames.

"I'll go, too," Markus volunteered.

Isabelle continued screaming even after her voice gave out. By that point the sounds coming from her throat were nothing more than dry gasps and unintelligible ramblings. The fiery, crumbling cabin reflected in her eyes as she lay pinned in the dirt, helpless. Beneath the tears and sorrow, a rage was burning.

Miller knelt beside Soraya and laid a hand on her shoulder, tears welling. Her free hand found his. With urgency, she reciprocated and held tightly. The remainder of the survivors gathered around, ogling the spectacle, unable to process the scene. Flames licked the treetops and poured from every window and door. Their brilliant fiery orange glow illuminated the tortured spectators' faces.

CHAPTER SEVEN
Retribution

Before dawn, a thunderstorm rolled through the area, extinguishing the fire. Piles of ash turned to mud, and black water snaked its way from the remains of the cabin, down the drive and past the cars. Most of the survivors took care to stay from its path, convinced the water bore the lifeblood of Tobias and Tommy. Not much was left standing of the abandoned old cabin save for pieces of a blackened frame and a towering chimney that rose into the singed treetops. Those who were too distraught to help in the recovery effort stood around the burnt-out shell, reflecting on the senselessness of the night's events.

At first light, Marisol, Nisha, Sam, and Vanessa escorted Isabelle and Lillian to a nearby convenience store the caravan had passed in the night. Jeremiah suggested getting the mother and daughter away from the house until Tobias's and Tommy's bodies were recovered and properly dealt with. As an added measure of security, Miller sent Aiko, Markus, and Isaac in a separate car to follow. Safety in numbers, as it were.

Jeremiah stood near the center of what remained of the cabin, filthy from soot and mud digging through the burnt-out husk. Behind him, Radzinski and Soraya were knee-deep in debris. She would gently remove still-smoldering boards from her area whereas Radzinski was all too eager to throw each piece of debris aside with no rhyme or reason. Each of them had a different rationale for wanting to put this task to bed.

Soraya stopped digging. A quiet prayer from the young Israeli was signal enough. Jeremiah knew she found what they were searching for. He wiped his hands clean as best as he could before going for his radio. "Aiko, come in," he said, making his way from atop the rubble.

"You see anything yet?" Aiko asked.

"We found them."

"Status?"

"I'll let you know when it's safe to bring them back."

"Understood. Aiko out."

Sam looked on anxiously as Aiko put away her radio and sat down heavily in an old wooden chair. He didn't have to ask; her face betrayed the grim news from back at the cabin. Sam leaned into the rail on the store's front porch, gripping its surface hard. "Goddammit," he said under his breath, squinting his eyes against the bright morning sun.

Nearly three miles from the cabin, a lone convenience store stood at the side of the road. Its windows were mostly smashed, and its screen door, hanging on by a rusty hinge, blew in the breeze. Trash littered the small parking lot at its flanks and the road in front. A few busted-up cars were parked in the vicinity: two in the lot and one across the street directly in front of the shop. All looked to be stripped of anything useful, the lot and the vehicles slowly being overtaken by nature and the surrounding forest.

The store was previously ransacked. That was obvious enough. A given, really, but Marisol knew ahead of time that that was a distinct possibility before offering to get Isabelle and Lillian away from the smoldering cabin. She kept a watchful eye on the Burkes, though she wasn't sure what exactly she could do to help if the occasion arose.

Markus and Isaac stood in a corner near the front of the store, trying to remain invisible, though Markus never let Lillian out of sight. He had no words to comfort the girl but would be at her side in a moment if need be. Isaac tried not to be seen and fiddled with a few bobbles strewn about a small dusty shelf. He twirled an empty saltshaker between his fingers, trying to look busy, and for a brief moment, he found himself wondering how much salt he would put on a steak. The idea filled him with guilt, but he was entitled to his own form of escape as much as the next person.

Nisha shadowed Isabelle through the store, always two steps behind her lifelong friend. It seemed odd to her that Isabelle appeared to be staying remarkably calm despite the circumstances. Nisha would be in hysterics, had the roles been reversed.

"Isabelle, honey, I... I'm so sorry," Nisha finally offered.

"There's nothing to be sorry about, Nisha. Miller and the others will find Tommy. I'm sure he was hiding somewhere safe. You'll see." Isabelle showed no emotion as she rifled through a shelf of discarded items, things other scavengers before them had left behind. Useless things.

"Hey, sweetheart, can I get anything for you?" Vanessa approached cautiously. To an extent, she knew what Lillian was going through, but the loss of her husband was a slow build. By the time he finally passed, she was long prepared for it. Lillian's father and brother, on the other hand, were violently ripped from the girl mere hours prior. The suddenness of it all was shocking for Vanessa. How Lillian was coping was incomprehensible.

"I've seen so much death these past few weeks I've honestly grown numb to it." Lillian rifled through a ransacked shelf, stopping on a half-spilled bottle of iodine. "This should work. While we're here we might as well pick up as much supplies as possible, right?"

Vanessa clasped her hand to her mouth. She couldn't let the girl see her cry. Just as fast, she steadied herself. "Honey, it's okay. You can talk to me," she managed through trembling lips.

Lillian held up a badly dented can of sardines. "These things are horrible, you know, but it's food, right?" She tucked them away into her bag and continued down the aisle.

Vanessa approached a little closer but froze, her hand inches from the girl's shoulder. *Let it out*, she thought. *Let it all out. I'm here for you.* No, she wouldn't be the catalyst for Lillian's breakdown. Why push? If the girl has strength enough to get through this, who was Vanessa to jeopardize crumbling her walls.

Lillian turned. The suddenness made Vanessa's heart skip a beat. "I'm not ready to talk about this yet, Vanessa," she said softly. "But when I am, I'll let you know. I promise."

Vanessa nodded in agreement, hand still clasped tightly against her mouth as she followed Lillian deeper into the store in silence.

Isabelle was preoccupied with rummaging through a bag of toys. Nisha watched and imagined a family on the run, desperately trying to survive, a child's playthings disregarded in the confusion. Isabelle focused on a few small action figures strewn about the floor. She placed their tiny weapons in their even smaller hands, gathered up a handful of little accessories, and stuffed them into a bag of her own, her movements methodical, deliberate, like she'd done it a thousand times before.

Isabelle looked up at Nisha expectantly and held out one of the toys. "I'm pretty sure he has this yellow one," she said. "But I know he needs these two. Help me find the rest of their things." She dove back in, engrossed in the pile of plastic.

Nisha turned her head, avoiding Isabelle's gaze at all costs. She had no words for her friend, no comforting reminder that everything was going to be alright, because it wasn't. It couldn't be. Isabelle's husband and only son were dead. The reality of their situation hadn't truly set in for Nisha until that very moment. Isabelle's refusal to acknowledge the loss of half of her family finally made it all too clear for Nisha: life would never, *could never*, go back to the way it was.

Markus and Sam kept their distance but took in Isabelle's apparent breakdown in silence.

Markus had witnessed enough of the spectacle and turned his gaze back to the parking lot and Sam's truck. "I've lost friends before, you know? Back home, it was almost expected, though, where I lived. But this, this is bad, Sam. That little boy was burned alive. How are we supposed to get past something like that? How can *they*?" He waved his arm as if to shoo away the issue. He shook his head in disbelief as his eyes welled up. "I need some air, man."

"Alright, son, but you stay close. You see something, anything, you get back in here fast." He gave Markus that stern look of his, head tilted forward, eyes up. The stare conveyed the importance of his request far more efficiently than a few harsh words ever could.

Markus didn't reply as he left the store. He passed Aiko on her way in and disappeared out of sight.

"He doesn't look so good," Aiko commented, more of an icebreaker than anything else.

"He's not. I don't think any of us are after last night."

"Time, Sam. It takes time."

"I know."

"I saw this more often overseas than I care to admit."

"Ma'am?" Sam sensed the young soldier needed to get something off her chest. He wouldn't push, though. She would either talk to him or she wouldn't. Sam had more than enough history with the military to know just how difficult opening up to strangers could be.

Aiko looked back to Isabelle on the floor as she collected toys for a son she would never see again. Her lip quivered a bit and again she rubbed her belly. "A parent losing a child." Aiko straightened up fast. "You can see it in their eyes. Something dies inside of them." She turned from the scene; she'd witnessed it all before. "You know, there was a real, ever-present disconnect with the people when I first got in-country. After a while, though, you realize their grief is no different from your own." She pulled her hair out of her face and tied it up into a tight ponytail. Lately she'd been wearing her hair down. The look would have certainly had her reprimanded under normal circumstances. These last few weeks, trivialities like proper military regulations didn't seem to matter anymore or were slowly being overlooked in the face of a new paradigm. "A distraught father carrying the body of his maimed little girl through the streets resonates no matter the language barrier. When we got home, I thought for sure I'd never witness anything like that again. Things are worse now than ever."

Sam didn't say a word. It wasn't necessary. A few nods and some eye contact were all that was required. They both knew it. The release was what was important.

Markus burst through the door, quickly locked it behind him, and drew the shade. "Down, down, down. Everybody, down now. Get behind the counter!" he yelled.

"What is it?" Aiko asked, peering through a crack in the blinds, weapon ready.

"Just do it. Don't make a sound!" he snapped.

Deeper in the store, Vanessa threw herself and Lillian to the floor. The pair crawled on hands and knees toward cover behind an overturned soda machine.

"What is it?" Lillian asked, wide-eyed.

"I don't know. I couldn't hear what they were saying," Vanessa whispered with a finger to her lip. "Shh."

Nisha, with Isabelle in tow, made her way to the front of the store and toward Sam. She led the woman by the hand. Nisha stayed low, though when they stopped, Isabelle returned to her crossed-legged sitting position, still focused on her bag of toys.

Sam tipped an empty shelf over onto its side. Hopefully it was enough to block Isabelle from view. He grabbed Nisha by the arm. "Don't let her move!" he demanded.

It began as a low hum and quickly grew into a steady roar as windows rattled and dishes crashed from their shelves. Dozens of cars, trucks, and motorcycles were passing by directly in front of the building. A heavily reinforced school bus passed first, its windows shielded with aluminum siding and a plow attached to the front. The roof had a flat platform welded to it with chain-link fencing as a railing around its edges. Three men stood atop the platform, surveying their surroundings. Crates of what looked like Molotov cocktails clanked as they hit speed bumps in front of the store. The majority of the bus was caked in blood, not all of which was completely dry.

The men atop the bus were clad in makeshift armor. From Aiko's vantage point, it looked like chainmail, at least on two of the men's arms. Some sort of plating was attached to their thighs and shins. *Hockey pads, maybe*, she thought, though it could have just as easily been modified car parts. Their chests and backs were protected with fashioned sheet metal strapped in place with belts and rope. Trinkets and bones—trophies, it appeared—dangled from each man's neck and shoulder regions. Splatters of paint, she hoped. It could have just as easily been blood that adorned their armor from head to toe. One man had an ax strapped to his back. Others brandished long, pointed sticks. As they drove past, the men screamed and threw rocks at the building and any abandoned cars in the lot, Sam's truck included. Though its interior was dark, it was clear that those inside the bus were just as ferocious.

Marisol hoped the blood-drenched caravan merely drove through a pack of carriers wandering down the road. From her vantage point, she had a clear view of the gang as the passing convoy neared its end. A rough-looking bunch, the lot of them. Some of their motorcycles were adorned with skulls and various bones. Whether trophies or a warning was unclear. So were the bones' origins. Were they from the undead or fellow travelers unlucky enough to have stumbled across their path. It was impossible to tell. A few of the cars and trucks dragged corpses behind them from chains and rope. From her view, Marisol estimated that they were easily outnumbered by ten or twelve to one. She had no intention of finding out their true numbers or intent.

"I'll call the others, tell them we might need a little help down here," Isaac said, fumbling for his radio.

"You'll do no such thing. Put that radio down." Aiko snatched the device from his hand. "We have no idea what sort of resources those guys are working with." She made sure the radio was off and put it away in her bag. "If they're using radios, too, and happen to turn on the same channel, they'll hear everything we say. Just stay quiet. We'll wait them out. They don't appear to be stopping, anyway."

"I wouldn't count on that just yet." Marisol motioned for Aiko to make her way to her end of the counter, where she had a better view of the front of the store. Across the street in the other parking lot, three of the gang members were inspecting Sam's truck.

"Shit, I was afraid of this." Aiko grit her teeth.

A large burly man appeared from behind one of the bloody caravan's stopped trucks with a coiled hose in one hand and a long leash in the other. At the end of the leash, a young girl in barely-there rags crouched to the ground like an animal. Filthy matted hair stuck to her face, and grime hid most of her skin. She jumped up and down, pawing at the ground, tightening the leash as she lunged forward. He yanked her back forcefully, though she didn't lose her footing. This dance had been done many times before. The burly man threw the hose to the ground and yanked the leash again. This time she rushed to his feet, attentive. He patted her on the head not very gently and unclasped the leash from her collar. The girl scurried to the hose. Happy to be of use, she buried one end of the hose into Sam's gas tank, then furiously began sucking on the other. Moments passed before she finally spat a mouthful of fuel into a bucket and dunked the hose in as well. The scavengers laughed at the girl's expense and she smiled, hugging up against the burly man's leg, not much better than a wild beast seeking attention.

"Go on," he said calmly.

She jumped again, scurrying for Sam's truck, and spilled its contents out onto the pavement. The other scavengers wasted no time gathering up the group's hard-earned supplies.

"Keep an eye on her." The burly man pointed at the girl. He grabbed his crotch and aimed a thumb at the convenience store. His closest companion shrugged and got back to the business of removing Sam's battery, spark plugs, and any belts he could easily reach.

"Nobody move," Marisol whispered as the man approached the front door.

The burly man tried the handle a few times, but the door wouldn't open. He leaned in close to the glass. His hands up on the window and cupped against his face to shield his eyes from the sun, he kicked the door in apparent frustration.

Nisha jumped and squealed. Sam grabbed her and held her tight, covering her mouth with his free hand.

"Shh," he whispered. "He'll go away, darling. Just stay calm." Sam tried to reassure the terrified woman. Tears streamed down her cheek and collected against Sam's leathery hand.

The burly man kicked the door again. This time, Marisol slowly unsafetied her weapon. The others followed suit. She leaned into the crack for a better view, and a sigh of relief overcame her. She smiled wide as she motioned for Aiko to take another look. Aiko peered through the hole and shared Marisol's relief. Both women slumped to the floor, breathing again. The large burly man was leaning against the front door, pissing all over it. The yellow stream pooled at his feet, eventually seeping beneath the door and into the store. He leaned his head back, stretching his neck, and seemed lost in thought as he stared at the clear blue sky through a hole in the porch's overhang. A whistle from one of the other scavengers ended his brief downtime.

"Motherfuckers," he uttered as he quickly shook himself off and rejoined the dregs.

The three men and the young girl loaded themselves into their van and sped off in the direction of their caravan. Marisol holstered her weapon and breathed a sigh of relief. Once again it was quiet and they were alone.

Sam released his grip on Nisha. "You okay, girl?" he asked while brushing hair from her wet cheeks.

"No," she whispered, sobbing. "I'm not."

Sam put his arm around her, gently this time. Nisha hid her face in Sam's chest and cried. "It's okay, Nisha. They're gone. Just let it out, sweetheart."

• • •

Soraya found the scorched corpses of Tobias and Tommy just inside the cellarway door; it looked as though they were on their way out. She prayed that they succumbed to the smoke and not the intense heat. The dog was nestled beside the boy, hairless and black. Tobias's arms gripped his son's lifeless body, both victims charred, hair and clothing mostly burnt away. The blaze was so intense near the center of the fire that both bodies had large portions of exposed bone where the soft tissue had been completely incinerated. No skin remained on their extremities. Bone poked through their feet, heads, knees, elbows, and hands. The fire's heat fused the two corpses in an eternal embrace.

Jeremiah and Radzinski helped Soraya remove the bodies from the rubble. Seth and Bernie had just finished digging graves; they began the task soon after the surviving Burkes had been escorted away. Before Tobias and his son could be buried, one final decision fell on the group.

"We cannot bury them like this," Soraya insisted.

"I'm not wasting ammo on that. What's done is done." Radzinski was adamant. "Let's just put them in the ground and move the fuck on."

"Soraya's right," Seth added, barely keeping it together. "I don't want to think about them coming back like this."

"*If* they come back," Radzinski replied. "We're not even sure how any of this works yet."

"Sure we are," Seth bit back. "You die, you come back. What's so goddamn hard to figure out?"

"Whatever." Radzinski walked away. He was well and truly over the discussion.

"I will do it myself." For Soraya, the sight of half of a family burned alive, gone in an instant, resonated. The young Israeli didn't let on if her stance was in response to family of her own a thousand miles away or something else entirely. She was going to see to it that Tobias and his son had a proper burial, damn anyone else's thoughts on the matter.

Soraya jumped into the shallow grave before removing her dull-black kukri from its sheath on the back of her belt. She recited a short, solemn prayer in Hebrew before standing in silence and paying her final respects. Soraya's blade fell multiple times across the necks of Tobias's and his son's burnt corpses. She knew that wouldn't be enough to be sure that they stayed down, so one at a time, she sank her blade deep into their skulls. The crunching of burnt flesh could be heard as far away as the vehicles. Some of those who were within earshot vomited. Samantha covered her ears as best as she could and cried.

The deed done, Soraya placed the heads down by their feet. She gently moved Dusty over to the second grave, then made her way for the well pump to clean up. As she passed the largest portion of the group, she grabbed a blackened shovel and tossed it at Lancaster's feet. "You bury."

"Man, she hates that motherfucker," Radzinski commented. He tried to cover his grin as he stole a glance at Soraya changing her grime-encrusted shirt over by the water source.

"If you saw what he did while we were escaping Pepperbush, you would, too," Seth added. "It should be him in that fucking hole." He snatched the shovel away while shoving Lancaster, who tripped and fell to the ground. "Get away from him, you piece of shit. You didn't even like this man." Seth loomed over the former mayor while gripping the shovel tightly with both hands, its blade dangerously close to Lancaster's neck.

Lancaster scurried to his feet in silence and retreated to a large rock away from the rest of the group, frustration etched upon the man's face. Two weeks ago, no one would have dared treat him like this. "Fuck these people," he mumbled. The idea of stealing one of the trucks and setting off on his own dawned on him, though the thought of severe consequences should he fail to escape discouraged him from pursuing the scheme.

"Jeremiah, are you listening? Over," the radio blared. Any interruption was welcome.

"Aiko, this is Miller. I was just going to call. We need you back here on the double. What's your sitrep?"

"That's a negative, sir," she responded with a sigh. "We're going to need a pickup. We lost Sam's truck."

"Say again," Miller inquired.

"I'll explain later. Just send someone for us. We should stay off the radio."

Rachel was listening just beside Miller, her face contorted in a mixture of confusion and worry.

"Go get them," ordered Miller.

"On it," she replied, sprinting for Tobias's SUV.

"Rachel's en route. ETA seven minutes."

"Roger that."

Bernie and Elliot came into view from a trail on the north side of the burnt-out cabin. A scruffy old man in tattered rags walked ahead of them at gunpoint.

"Hey, Miller," Bernie yelled. "You're not going to believe this shit, but we found this old buzzard spying on you guys from the woods. Take a look at him. His hair, his clothes, they're all singed up. I think we got our firebug right here," he announced excitedly as he pushed the man toward the anxious group.

"He had a crate of these stuffed under a bush up the hill a way." Elliot handed Miller a Molotov cocktail.

"More than that, he's got all kinds of stuff up there. Axes, knives, baseball bats with nails in 'em." Bernie paused. "And they're all covered in blood, if you can believe that."

The sight of a possible culprit stirred up emotion in all of them; the gamut ran from sympathy to outright rage.

Radzinski grabbed the accused by the back of his shirt. "You burn this house down, old man?" he said up close to the man's ear as he shoved him along. "While I was in it?" he added.

The old man rambled behind a long gray beard, its ends curled and blackened. "Those things, those things are in my house. How do I get them out? There's only one way to get them out."

"What are you going on about?" Miller grabbed the man's chin and forced him to look the soldier in the eye. "Did you start this fire or not?" he demanded. "Answer me!"

The man continued. "Fire, they don't like fire. Fire keeps them away. If I burn down the house, they won't be in the house."

"Son of a bitch." Seth drew his sidearm and walked with purpose toward the old man, intent on shooting him on the spot.

Miller interceded. "Not yet. Radzinski, secure the prisoner. Tie him to a tree or something. Just get him away from the crowd. Jeremiah, radio the others. Find out where Rachel's at. I want them all back here on the double."

Seth holstered his weapon. He was shaking so badly he could barely secure it properly. Rage swelled. It took every ounce of his being not to tear this man apart. He walked away lest he take matters into his own hands, though he never took his gaze from the old man.

"You can't be serious. You were just going to kill him?" Samantha asked. "Just like that?"

"Fucking right I was!" Seth shouted. "Or were you too busy doing whatever it is you do to see Tobias and his boy all burnt up in a goddamn hole?" He grabbed her by her arms, demanding a response. "Answer me! Did you see him burned up?"

"That's not fair. Of course I did. It's just—" Samantha wasn't allowed to finish.

As Seth began to calm, he removed his hands from her body and lowered his head. "Tell that to Isabelle, how fair you think it is. If she doesn't do it, I'll shoot him myself."

Miller interceded. "No one is doing anything until the others get back here. That's Isabelle's family in shallow graves, not yours, not mine. Whatever decision she makes, we'll respect it. Am I clear?" He said with determination as he looked around at the gathering crowd. He tried his best to size them up, to gauge who could or couldn't be left alone with the prisoner.

"We'll see," Seth remarked.

"So that's it then. We're animals now? We get to choose who lives and who dies, just like that?" Samantha asked.

Damon made his opinion on the matter known. "Oh, get over yourself, you self-righteous bitch," He added. He never missed an opportunity to pile on. "These animals are the only reason you're alive. Maybe if you contributed once in a while, your opinion would matter."

"Coming from you? What the fuck do *you* do?" Samantha retorted.

"I don't get in the way and I don't ask stupid fucking questions. That's what I do," Damon replied.

"That doesn't even make sense, and who the hell do you think you are, anyway?" Samantha was boiling over with anger and confusion. She was normally inclined to take a back seat to the decision-making and exclude herself from arguments altogether, but there was something about Damon that stirred up mistrust in her. Whatever it was, she knew she didn't like the guy.

"That's enough, both of you." Miller wasn't about to let the group self-destruct. "If you need to work off some steam, help Seth bury the bodies. I want those graves presentable before Isabelle and Lillian get back."

• • •

Miller and Jeremiah watched from a distance as the old ragged man continued his incoherent ramblings. Bernie stood nearby. He had helped Radzinski bind the prisoner to a large oak. His legs and arms secure, his back to the tree, the old man was powerless to do anything save gaze upon his handiwork—the still-smoking remains of the cabin.

"He's probably been watching us since we arrived," Jeremiah suggested. "All he would have had to do was study our patterns, know when to move, and we'd never see him."

"Makes you wonder."

"What's that?"

"I don't think he's crazy at all. It's an act. As a matter of fact, I'm willing to bet he burned us out because there's so many of us. Imagine a small group. I mean like two or three people tops. What would he do with them?"

"Jesus, so the cabin's a trap?" Bernie asked.

Miller shrugged as Soraya appeared from behind the burnt-out husk. "You guys are going to want to see this. Over the ridge, just past the tree line, not half a klick away."

Miller, Soraya, Bernie, and Seth stood at the rim of a large hole in the ground with at least a foot of water in it. The hole had a cement bottom and cinder-block walls. This was obviously the basement of new construction, now a makeshift death pit where the hermit disposed of his victims. The cavity was filled with dozens of bodies of various ages and sizes. There was no discernible rhyme or reason as to how he chose his victims or why. Luggage, coolers, bags of what looked to be clothes, and maybe even some groceries all melted together in a grotesque soup. A few carriers that obviously fell in the pit were feasting away on the remains of unlucky souls foolish enough to stop at the cabin, themselves forever trapped as well.

"My God," Miller gasped. "There're dozens of them down there."

"Poor bastards," Bernie muttered. "Wonder what he does with their cars."

"There is another hole over there with cars in it." Soraya pointed out another plot of land a little farther down the hill.

"That cuts it, man. We can't let this guy go." Seth was enraged.

"Agreed," Miller replied through gritted teeth. "I've seen enough. Double-time back to the cabin. We're going to finish this and get the hell out of here."

When Miller arrived back at camp, the mass of survivors was gathered around the prisoner. The bound man and Isabelle were surrounded like this was a schoolyard fight. Insults and cheers erupted while she pounded on him. Her fists were bloodied as her delicate skin gave way to his coarse features. A pair of her knuckles split open on contact with his teeth. The teeth didn't fare as well, one chipping and the other breaking off completely. The crowd erupted as the man spat out a mouthful of blood and gurgled some nonsense no one understood.

Samantha came running up to Miller. Tears streaming fast becoming a trademark. "Do something, please. She's killing him!" she cried.

"Good," Seth answered, pushing past her and into the fray.

"You're just going to let this happen?" she pleaded.

"This *has* to happen," was Miller's only response.

Seth forced his way through the crowd and up to the scene, where he eased Isabelle aside. "Take a break," he said before getting in his turn. Seth sent a barrage of fists into the man's ribs, ending with a pronounced crack the entire crowd couldn't mistake for anything but a broken bone. He finished up his shot with a right cross that dislocated the man's jaw.

Isabelle returned for a final brutal volley, one that didn't end until long after the hermit's nose was broken and his right eye socket smashed. By this point, the man's jaw was so badly fractured that the right side of it flopped at a ninety-degree angle from the left. She leaned a forearm hard against the man's chest, her head slumped against her arm as she caught her breath.

Soraya approached. She gave Isabelle one of her knives and backed off. One final deep breath and Isabelle proceeded to stab him repeatedly in the chest, neck, and stomach. Blood exploded from the wounds, pouring down his front and covering both of them in red. The cutting only lasted for the briefest of time, as she was spent from her earlier rage. Isabelle collapsed at the old man's feet, panting. Seth reemerged with his sidearm drawn, prepared to shoot the old man in the head.

"No." Isabelle winced, holding a bloodied hand up before pulling herself to her feet. "Don't shoot him," she gasped, fighting for breath.

"He's right, Isabelle. If we leave him like this, he'll just become one more of those things to bite someone else down the line," Miller cautioned.

"He's not coming off that tree until he rots off of it." Isabelle smashed a fist-sized rock into the dead man's mouth, breaking most of his teeth in the process, and wedged it in deep, pushing it into the back of his throat. What remained of his jaw was forced open past the breaking point. She cut a sleeve off of the man's shirt and tied it around his head to secure the rock in place. "Now," she panted, blood dripping from her face and mouth, "he's not biting anyone."

For the most part, the group dispersed. Most remaining at the scene at least turned their heads. Samantha sat in the dirt with her head down, sobbing.

Radzinski eyed Isabelle from top to bottom as she passed. "Oh, I like this one."

• • •

After the group was given ample time to decompress, most of them lingered around the vehicles. It went unspoken, but it was time to go.

Miller joined Seth at Tobias's grave. Sam lingered nearby. Most of the others sat alone or in small groups and in quiet contemplation over the afternoon's events. The camp was solemn and quiet after Isabelle's display.

"What went down in Pepperbush. Shit, it all happened so fast it was almost like a dream. No real chance to take it all in, but now this?" Seth was pacing. "Man, it happened right in front of us. Everyone scrambling to escape, but it was just there, feet away, all around us, and there was nothing we could do to stop it." He was barely making sense, but Miller got the gist of it.

"You can't let yourself dwell on it, Seth. You have to pick yourself up and carry on. It's the only way."

"Harsh, man." Seth stopped his pacing, leered at the ruined old man across the property, then returned his gaze to Tobias's grave.

"Maybe, but it's the truth. Nothing is going to get you dead faster out here than being trapped in your head. If you need it, take a minute to gather yourself or pay your respects, but I need your help with these people and they need a familiar face, now more than ever," Miller replied.

Seth sauntered off to the shallow graves with plenty to think about. Maybe that wasn't Miller's intent, but it was the outcome nonetheless.

Miller watched as Seth knelt beside the grave, sobbing but doing his best to dry his tears with a filthy sleeve. What he told Seth was the truth: it made him feel like shit, but it was the harsh reality of it all. If the police started falling apart, where would that leave the rest of the civilians?

Sam turned to Miller and shook his head. "What the hell was that this afternoon, Captain?"

"I know what you're going to say, Sam, and normally I'd be right there beside you, but this was different." Miller could barely look Sam in the eye.

"Different? We murdered a man in cold blood today, Miller." Sam gestured to the killing tree. "These kinds of things change a person, rarely for the better."

"I can't do anything about that now, Sam. Half the camp was ready to erupt over what happened to Tobias. They needed justice."

"Well, they got it alright—in spades. At any rate, it's probably not safe to stay here tonight after all the commotion."

"There are a lot of reasons we shouldn't stay here tonight, Sam." Miller opened his hand to reveal a scorched locket. He brushed away some soot and flipped it open. Inside, a tiny portrait of Tobias and his family during happier times miraculously escaped the inferno.

Sam turned away from the memento and fixed his gaze upon the remains of the broken family. "Jesus Christ."

Miller tucked the trinket safely away in his breast pocket and nodded in agreement. "Gather everyone up, Sam. We're leaving."

CHAPTER EIGHT

Ben's Diner

Ben's Diner was situated at the inside of a sharp curve on an almost abandoned stretch of countryside. On the west end of the street stood a ransacked post office, windows smashed. Discarded mail and papers littered the road in front. The place looked to have blown up from the inside, but no scorch marks or the telltale signs of explosion existed. It was merely trashed, as if whoever did the deed wasn't simply scavenging for supplies. More likely they reveled in the destruction. The north side of the curve featured what remained of a small house. Maybe it belonged to the owner of the diner. It could have been Ben's house, if there ever was a Ben. A truck obviously took the curve way too fast. Black marks on the pavement went clear through the house and out into the backyard. What was left of the home collapsed in on itself some time ago.

The caravan pulled up alongside the diner. Some vehicles parked in the overly large lot; it was big for such a humble building. Most of the vehicles stayed in the road, just on the diner's side of the curve. Anyone approaching wouldn't know the caravan was there until they were on top of them.

The survivors had been on the road for hours without a stop since they fled the cabin. Still, Samantha refused to get out of the car. "She killed him. She stood there right in front of all of us and killed him, just like that, like it was nothing," Samantha cried in frustration.

"The guy murdered half her family, Samantha. Her son, her little boy," Markus replied sympathetically, though it was clear the previous night's events had unhinged the man.

"That doesn't make it right," Samantha answered without hesitation.

"I understand that, but what if we left him?"

"So what if we did?" she snapped. "We can't become animals. If we do, we might as well just give up because then we should be dead, too."

"Stop it. You don't mean that." Markus attempted consolation. "Besides, how many people did he kill before we found him? How many more if we left him? I'm sorry, Samantha, but Isabelle did the right thing."

"Why don't you go see if anyone needs help, Markus. I want to be alone."

Rachel, Seth and Sam stood sentry near the center of the curve, a decent vantage point down both ends of the road. Most of the group had spread out, looting supplies from wherever they could or just stretching after so many hours cramped in a vehicle.

"Keep an eye on that place." Sam referred to the collapsed house. "It's in bad shape, but I can still imagine something crawling out of the woodwork."

"If anything was in there, it's probably a pancake by now," said Rachel. "But yeah, I've got eyes on it."

"We never should have taken these goddamn back roads to begin with. If we just stayed on the highway, it would have only taken us a few hours tops to get there," Seth added.

"We can't be sure of that, son. If the highway was clogged with abandoned vehicles, we would have had to turn around, anyway," Sam suggested.

"Maybe. One thing's for sure, though: we wouldn't have come across that fucking cabin and Tobias and his boy would still be alive," replied Seth adamantly.

"What happened to Tobias was no one's fault. That old man was insane. There's no way any of that could have been predicted. You'll only drive yourself crazy dwelling on it, Seth."

"Yeah, I know. It's just I look at Izzy now and she's a shadow of her former self. She's broken, man. It's as clear as day. I've known her a long time, Sam, and I've never seen her like this, even when her folks passed, and they were close. Real close."

"It's too much. All of it," Rachel said. "The things we have to live with day in and day out. Now half her family's gone, just like that." She snapped her fingers. The sound startled Seth with a jump. "She'll come around eventually. It's going to be tough, but it'll pass."

"Let's hope so, 'cause she's all that girl's got now," Seth replied. "If it's alright with you guys, I'm going to head back over to the diner, see what's shaking."

Radzinski took stock of who was left lingering about the vehicles. Most had already gone looting. A few, though, could be put to use. "You, you, and you, with me," he ordered before making a beeline for the post office. "And for God's sake, keep your weapons aimed at the ground. I don't need the back of my head blown out by inexperienced yokels."

"You heard the man. Let's go," Damon added, much to Isaac's chagrin.

Isaac didn't mind taking orders from the soldiers. As a matter of fact, he welcomed it. Their experience in tough situations was just what this group needed. Damon, on the other hand, who was he to be barking orders at anyone? *Another time*, he thought. *Let's just get this done.*

Elliot was indifferent. He didn't care who was in charge. They could all bark orders as far as he was concerned. It kept any real focus off of him.

Radzinski kicked in the door. It was dark inside. Not a surprise. He motioned to the shade-covered windows. Elliot yanked them down, flooding the place with much-needed light. Two creatures at the far end of the room were torn from a meal by the change in illumination. As fast as they stood, they were just as quickly back on the ground, permanently. Radzinski waved the trio of volunteers in deeper behind him.

Upstairs was clear, the sole closet bare, save for a half dozen neatly pressed postal uniforms. Maybe the postmaster lived here. No matter, as no one was here now. That was just as well. More mouths to feed and all. Radzinski peered out onto the street below. The second story's northern corner room had an ideal vantage point over the front of the diner and a clear line of sight farther down the road past the sharp curve.

"Imma hit the head while we're here," Damon said. Halfway down the narrow hallway, he pulled open a door—the only one left that *could* have been a bathroom. He immediately slammed it shut. His back against the door, legs wedged into the wall. "Shit, there's two of them in there!" he yelled as he fumbled for his gun that lay by his feet; he had dropped it in the commotion. "Someone shoot these fuckers!"

"On it." Isaac lined up his rifle, waiting for Damon to release the door.

"Hold your fire. Stand down, Isaac," Radzinski ordered.

"But they're—" Elliot pointed at the crowded hallway.

97

"Yeah, man, what the fuck? I can't sit here all day!" Damon shouted.

"Leave 'em. We're not wasting rounds unless we have to." Radzinski kicked a sturdy nightstand toward the hall. "Wedge this in there. Those things are too stupid to unlock the door, and if they somehow manage, they can't push this furniture through that wall or break the door off its hinges. They're not going anywhere."

"You heard him. Bring that shit over here, damn," Damon insisted.

Ayn and Vanessa were rummaging through an abandoned pickup. Strangely for Ayn, she noticed it had two missing tires. Why only take two? *Whoever it was probably had to leave in a hurry*, she thought, squinting against the high noon sun for trouble. Ayn was as thin as a rail, and baggy clothes could only conceal so much. Her delicate blonde hair would blow from her face, exposing bony cheeks. She would act quickly, pulling the locks back down over her face, hopeful to avoid prying eyes.

Vanessa couldn't help but notice. Just one more sign that none of them were eating sufficiently, no matter what anyone said. "You getting enough to eat, Ayn?"

"I'm fine. I've always been skinny. Can't pick up weight to save my life. Never could."

"Okay, 'cause I might have something stashed away you're more than welcome to."

"Thanks, but really, I'm alright. Really."

"Suit yourself. But if you change your mind, let me know."

Ayn emptied the contents of the glove box onto the passenger seat. Nothing. She had already done the same for the trunk. She stood at the side of the car, tapping her palms against the roof and looking up and down the road.

"What is it?" Vanessa asked.

"I don't know. You find it strange this is the third car we've gone through and haven't found so much as a mint? Nothing useful at all."

"Eh, not everyone keeps a bunch of crap in their car."

"Maybe, I don't know. I don't like it. Something doesn't feel right about this place."

"Enough with that already!" Vanessa slammed her door shut. "Christ, every day you don't like this, or that doesn't feel right. Nothing feels right anymore, and you *shouldn't* like any of it. Just stop it, please."

"Sorry, I didn't realize I should be fine with living on the road or watching people killed ten feet in front of my eyes. Selfish me."

"I'm sorry. I've got a lot on my mind, too. I think we all do. It's just... I want Lillian to know everything is going to be alright, but I wouldn't know where to begin."

"Oh, I wouldn't be so sure about that." Ayn gestured to Vanessa's wedding ring. "You're just as qualified as any of us to console the girl. Probably more so."

Jeremiah and Markus were on fuel duty, the one task absolutely no one wanted but everyone save the pregnant Casandra was required to take part in. Bernie said he didn't mind siphoning the fuel. He did it all the time when he was a kid. So what if a little got in your mouth? The medics thought better of that idea and spread the task out among the group. Less of a risk of Bernie getting sick drinking gasoline every day.

"Damn, man, couldn't they have jumped out of a window or something?" Markus pondered.

"Excuse me?" Jeremiah asked.

"Tobias and his boy. How the hell did they get trapped in there, man? I mean, wouldn't you risk running out the way you came in?"

"Ah, I see," replied Jeremiah. "They would have become disoriented in the smoke and heat. Left becomes right. What looks like an exit is merely the next room deeper into the building. Situations play out similar to what transpired at the cabin more often than you know," he explained cold and logically, the only way he knew how. If you didn't know the man, he would certainly come across as unsympathetic.

"I'll take your word for it, but damn, what a fucking waste." Markus regretted even bringing it up. Talking about it out loud was far worse than he imagined. With no clear-cut idea of how to change the subject, he opted for walking away. "I'll just take these back to the cars." He picked up the fullest gas cans and began a light jog back to the caravan.

Nearly half of the group meandered about the diner, looting through what amounted to garbage for anything resembling supplies. Seth stood sentry near the entrance, one eye to the road. He wasn't about to add another set of hands to the project. Besides, he figured most of them knew there was nothing of value left to find; they were just looking for something to do. It wasn't long before the noise from the rummaging got to him. *Enough of this*, he thought while passing Marisol on his way out of the place. "They've got it covered in here. I'm just in the way. Hey, have you seen Isabelle?"

"I saw her about twenty minutes ago, over by the side of the building." Marisol pointed to the right of the diner, back toward the vehicles.

"How did she look?"

"The same. Poor thing."

"Well, I'm going to see if she's ready to talk about it. I can't stand to see her like this. Thanks, Marisol."

"Yep, let me know if you need anything."

Seth peeked around the corner of the diner. There she was, sitting in the dirt behind a row of shrubbery and playing with a decent-sized toad. She had her hands out on the ground, acting as miniature walls. The toad would hop to one side, she'd block him, and he'd hop the other way, just as trapped.

Seth slowly approached but was noisy enough to make himself known. The last thing he wanted was to startle her; she'd been through enough. "Hey, Izzy, what do you got there? A frog?" he asked, delicately.

No response. If she knew he was even there, she didn't show it.

"I know things have been rough and you're having a bad time of it. I just want you to know that I'm here for you. We all are. If you want, I can take you over and we can go talk to Lillian."

Isabelle miscalculated her wall placement, and the toad hopped away. She quickly leaped after it, landing on her belly in the dirt, where she continued to lay, covering the small animal with domed hands.

"Dammit, Isabelle, talk to me, please," Seth insisted.

Isabelle cupped the toad in her right hand as she rose to meet Seth. She placed her other hand on his cheek and lowered her gaze.

"That's it, Izzy. Let it out. Everything's going to be fine, girl. We both lost him," he said, cautiously advancing for a hug. He began slowly with one arm around her at first. When she didn't pull away, he hugged her properly with both arms and a gentle pat on her back. Isabelle lay her head on his shoulder, gazing upon his features. "Everything's going to be okay," he whispered.

Isabelle slid her arm up finally, stopping at his waist. Seth thought she was finally coming around. He continued with more words of encouragement as she began massaging his crotch. She hurriedly cupped his balls and slid her palm up and down the front of his pants, licking and sucking on his neck the whole time. Seth pushed her away, holding her at arm's distance by her shoulders.

"Isabelle, what the hell are you doing?" Seth demanded.

"From what I could tell, I was doing exactly what you came back here for."

"Oh, Izzy." Seth sighed.

"Besides, I know you always wanted me. Don't pretend you never saw me catch you checking me out, especially on those warm summer nights we'd have you over, in my barely-there shorts and shirt, leaning over and pouring you guys drinks. You loved every second of it."

"Izzy, sweetheart, I really don't know what you're talking about. Toby was my best friend. I would never betray him like that. You know this."

"You wanted to fuck me then. I know you want to fuck me still. Let's do it right here in the dirt. I couldn't care less who sees." Isabelle pushed against his grip, trying to get closer. When that didn't work, she reached out and grabbed his cock again.

This time Seth pushed her away, forcefully enough that she stumbled back a few feet. "That's enough!" he shouted. "I don't know what the fuck has gotten into you, but this ends now. You have a twenty-two-year-old daughter over there praying her mother comes back to her and you're pulling this shit? How fucking selfish are you?"

Isabelle stood silent, hands to her side, staring at Seth without the slightest hint of emotion.

"So that's it then? You're shutting me out again?" he asked. "Fine. Until you come to your senses, I don't want you near me anymore." Seth turned and left. He waved his hands over his head only to bring them back down hard against his thighs.

Isabelle watched him turn the corner and go back to the front of the diner, never looking back. Her arms remained at her sides, right hand clenched in a tight fist. Blood seeped from between red fingers. The toad's limbs twitched.

The small diner was devoid of even the most basic of supplies; looters had ransacked the place long ago. All that remained were plates of blackened, moldy food left behind by previous visitors.

Bernie kept coming back to an old plate of half-eaten meatloaf and potatoes. He poked the hardened baked potato with a fork but couldn't pierce its solid shell. He fiddled with it for a moment, batting it from side to side like a cat playing with its prey. He finally lifted the potato and quickly took a bite. The stale food made a loud crunch as he bit down, and he immediately spat the filth out. "Oh God. That's terrible," he shouted in disgust, trying desperately to spit out every last piece.

"Well what did you think it would taste like, Bernie? Just look at it. I wouldn't have tried that shit, and I'm eating for two," Casandra said with a smile.

Bernie smiled back as he let the remaining chunks of potato drip from his mouth like he was a child. With a flip of his wrist, he sent the plate sailing down the countertop. It reached the edge and teetered for a moment before crashing down onto the floor. Casandra laughed as she joined in sliding plates down the surface. The dishes knocked into each other and spread stale food all over the countertop and floor.

Bernie wiped a mound of dust and grime off a stool. "Have a seat," he offered. "I'll be with you in a moment," he said as he handed her a filthy menu.

"Don't mind if I do. So what's good around here?" she asked playfully.

"Oh gosh, best apple pie in town. That's for sure. Mable makes it from scratch. Her momma's recipe. She's off today, though." He looked around. "Huh, looks like everyone's off today." He shrugged. "I do have these potatoes, though."

"I hear they're great." She smiled.

"I'm sure they *were*," he said as he leaned on the bar. "I did find this for you, though." Bernie dropped a handful of sealed crackers and a couple packets of jelly onto the countertop.

"Thank you, Bernie," she gushed sincerely.

"So how far along are you?"

"Oh, seven months, I think. Give or take. Feels like he wants out now, though."

Bernie held his hand out. "Do you mind?"

"No, not at all. Please." Casandra placed his hand on her belly and guided it around, looking for the right spot. "You feel that? He's kicking. He likes you." She went wide-eyed over the idea.

"Or the little fella's saying, *Get off of my momma, ya son of a bitch*," he joked.

"Oh, stop. No, he's not."

"So you know it's a boy then?"

"Yeah, I figured since I was going to raise him on my own, I should get a head start on the planning."

"Smart thinking. My pop always said be prepared."

Casandra applied the smallest amount of jelly to each cracker, slowly savoring every bite. She leaned back in her stool to afford Bernie a better angle to feel for the little one. By this point, he had an ear to her belly. It was nice, she thought, someone showing her some attention. Especially

Bernie, seeing as if he were to drive off in his truck and head for the mountains alone, he'd probably fare much better than with the group. The imagined sacrifice was very appealing in her eyes.

For Miller, it was a relief to see at least some of them trying to enjoy themselves, despite the circumstances. It hadn't even been seventy-two hours since they lost Tobias. He knew the man well enough to know they were kindred spirits; duty and family were paramount to both men. The Pepperbush survivors looked to Tobias as a surrogate leader of sorts. Now he was gone. These people respected Sam and Marisol but kept them at arm's length, whereas Tobias was one of *them*. Sure, they deferred to Miller's leadership the moment Takashi was taken, but the kind of trust and camaraderie that Tobias instilled would take time—time that the young captain wasn't sure any of them had. Miller turned his attention to the front of the diner and the small pile of supplies they had gathered. It wasn't much. Mostly toiletries, enough for a week tops if they rationed. At least it was something. He looked out to the parking lot and squinted hard against the glare for a moment before diving to the floor. "Bernie, get her down, behind the counter. Now!" he whispered as loud as he could.

Dozens of motorcycles were pulling up and parking in the street in front of the diner. A majority of the riders appeared to be looking directly at Miller.

"Radzinski do you have eyes on this? Any idea how long they've been there?" Miller spoke into his radio.

"Copy that. I'm at your ten with Isaac and Damon. I've got eyes on the hostiles. Two dozen easy. Probably more. We've got the fuckers boxed in and they don't even know it. They go for their guns, we're lighting them up."

"Wait for my signal. If I can't talk these guys down, we can't afford to let any of them get away. If they're linked up with that crew Aiko saw the other day, then we're in trouble if they call for backup. We can't handle numbers like that."

"Roger that." Radzinski turned to the small group at his side. "Isaac, I want you downstairs. Anyone comes through that door, blow their fucking brains out. You two, either side of this window. The second I start shooting, put as many of those fuckers down as you can. None of them gets away. You understand me?"

"Oh yeah, I got this," Damon said, smiling for the first time in weeks.

"Well, you don't have to sound so excited about it," Elliot added.

"Whatever, bitch. It's us or them."

"Shut up, both of you. Damon's right. Those fuckers come out on top, none of us walk away from this. Am I clear?"

Miller emerged from the diner, unarmed with his hands in the air in front of him. "Hello there." Miller kept his tone light and welcoming as he inched forward, slowly positioning himself between a light pole and the bulk of the gang. "I assume we're both here for the same thing. Unfortunately, this place seems to have been picked clean. There's nothing left."

"Well, I could have told you that." A large gray-haired biker stepped forward, apparently their leader. "We cleaned this place out weeks ago. Bunch of heroes running their mouths then, too, huh, boys?" He leaned his head back in the direction of the gang.

Impressed by their leader's bravado, most of the gang laughed. Some simply lowered their heads in disbelief at Miller's approach. Others took a moment for a quick drink or to light a cigarette.

Miller took another step toward the pole but stayed just left of it. He didn't want to tip off the gang that he was inching toward cover. "We seem to have gotten off on the wrong foot, sir. Let me introduce myself. I'm Captain Miller, United States Army."

"I don't much care who you are, but it's about time you came out of that diner, boy. Was about to tell my men here to unload on your cars to wake your asses up." The head biker couldn't have been more unimpressed with Miller's credentials.

"That won't be necessary, sir," Miller replied.

"Those things aren't for you to decide." The head biker's demeanor changed in an instant. "Those are your vehicles parked over there, right? You know, the ones with all the people crouched down behind them?"

"I'll be honest with you, sir: we're just passing through. We don't want any trouble."

"You're a little thick, aren't you, boy? I'll make this real simple: your stuff, give it to us," the head biker demanded.

"We don't have anything. We're looking for supplies, just like you."

"Oh, I never said we didn't have anything. We just want more. It looks to me like you got some guns, and I'm sure you've got a bit of fuel in those vehicles. Not to mention I know I saw a few women over there. They're always useful, right, boys?" The head biker said, followed once more by laughter from his crew.

Behind the cover of the vehicles, the closest of the group could overhear the exchange.

"Oh God. They're going to take us. What are they going to do to us?" Samantha began to panic.

"Shut up. No one's taking you anywhere," Vanessa insisted while trying to force a pistol into the girl's hand. Samantha wouldn't take it.

Miller continued negotiations, though they were quickly deteriorating. "Sir, I understand now that this stretch of road is yours. We are obviously trespassing, and I apologize. If you'll allow us, we'll just turn around and go back the way we came. No harm, no foul, friend."

"Haha, *friend*. I don't think you understand, son. I call the shots around here. I tell you what to do, and you do it. We've got you outnumbered at least five to one from what I can tell. Maybe more. I want your guns, your gas, and your women. Now."

"Oh, fuck this guy. I'm taking his goddamn head off." Radzinski couldn't hear the conversation, but from his vantage point, the biker's body language spoke volumes. Damon and Elliot stood ready in the shadows.

"Wait just a second now. Perhaps a deal can be fostered here," Lancaster suggested from the relative safety provided by the vehicles. "If we just give him half of the guns and a few of the women, I'm sure he will let us leave peacefully."

"You're incredible." Marisol pushed him aside. "Shouldn't you be in a corner shitting your pants by now? Get the fuck down and keep still before I put you down." She turned to Soraya. "This isn't going to end well. Make sure everyone knows where this is headed and to be ready."

"I am on it." Soraya made her way down the line of cars, relaying Marisol's message along the way.

Miller continued negotiations. "We have no food and our vehicles are running on fumes. If you take our guns, we're as good as dead."

"Well, you got that part right. You are as good as dead, son. Look around you. There's no way out of this. I'll tell you what, seeing as I'm in a good mood today, I'll make a deal with you," the head biker said as once more laughter erupted from the crowd of anxious bikers. "Tell your people to throw their guns over the vehicles, put their hands on their heads, and stand up."

Lancaster attempted to stand but was yanked down hard by Marisol. "Keep the fuck down. I'm not telling you again."

The head biker continued his demands. "You and your men head back the way you came, on foot. Your women and supplies stay with us and everyone gets to live. That's the best offer I've got."

The laughing crowd of thugs went silent as the head biker fell flat on his back—a single gunshot wound to the forehead. A slight column of smoke escaped the breech of a sidearm Miller had concealed in the back of his pants. "Open fire!" he yelled as he felled a second biker, then a third before ducking behind the light pole. His fellow soldiers and the survivors of Pepperbush released a relentless flurry of bullets upon the unsuspecting gang.

The bikers scrambled for cover. They had done this many times before, but Miller knew by the way they carried themselves that they weren't accustomed to their victims putting up much of a fight. Most of the gang fired wildly. Some took cover while others tried to run away. Soraya carefully lined up her shots from behind the engine block of a truck. Each bullet claimed a raider. Marisol and Isaac likewise put down their share of would-be attackers. Lillian stayed behind cover while Vanessa stood above her, firing into the mass. The thought of what these men intended for her and the other women in the group enraged her. She thought of Jim and his attempt on her life as she indiscriminately unleashed on the gang with a hail of bullets. Radzinski's crossfire from his high vantage point sealed the gang's fate. The few remaining raiders who stood their ground panicked as those around them fell. Those still standing tried to run. Exposed and disoriented, they were all cut down in a merciless hail of gunfire.

Only a few weeks ago, most of these people, survivors of Pepperbush and gang members alike, had never even fired a gun. Now everyone involved, whether alive or dead, had a hand in the taking of another man's life.

The entirety of the gang was put down in mere minutes. Some tried to crawl away. Others lay in place in the hope of not being seen. A few disoriented and badly wounded scavengers crawled toward Miller's group in the confusion. They were put down permanently as Miller and the others pressed forward into the gang's ranks. Shoulder to shoulder, they marched, killing everything that moved. In the distance, a few gang members limped away, some helping their brothers in arms, others fending for themselves. All were cut down. Steady gunfire gave way to random pops. One here, two or three there. The untrained civilians were still randomly firing, unaware that the battle had ended.

"Cease fire, cease fire. Everyone, stop shooting!" Miller shouted, waving his hands in the air. "It's over. They're all down. Soraya, Rachel, fan out. I don't want any more surprises today. Marisol, Sam, go with them. If any of those assholes are still alive out there, put them down."

"Yes, sir," Rachel replied as she and the others made their way to the battlefield.

Shattered dishes and splintered furniture littered Ben's Diner. Those who managed to duck for cover were filthy with it. Casandra lay motionless behind the counter. A stray bullet had found its mark in her right shoulder. Another bullet grazed the side of Bernie's head as he heaved Casandra over the counter and threw himself on top of her just after the gunfire erupted. The hardwood floor beneath them was soaked in a puddle of blood.

Bernie was the first to rise. Dazed from the headshot, it took a moment to clear the ringing. Beneath him, Casandra lay unmoving, her wound gushing. Both of them were soaked in red. He flung off his shirt, balled it up, and applied pressure to the wound. "Somebody help me!" he screamed.

Aiko was the first on the scene. She was already en route to the diner for an impromptu checkup on the pregnant woman when the gang showed up. Her first obstacle was getting Bernie out of the way. He remained steadfast, pressing on Casandra's wound as if letting go meant her very life would pour from the hole.

"Okay, okay, ease off, Bernie. Let me in here," she said, guiding his hands away from her patient. No sterile blades in sight, Aiko ripped Casandra's top open at the bullet hole. "Help me lift her, Bernie. Let me see the other side." Aiko felt around while also listening for Casandra's heartbeat. A wave of relief washed over the medic's face. "You can lie her back down now, Bernie. Gently, gently."

"How bad is it, Doc?" he asked, balling his hat up in his hands.

"Bullet passed clean through. A couple of stitches, clean dressing, and some antibiotics," she began.

"You mean…" Bernie interrupted.

"Yes, she's going to be just fine, Bernie. Now, if you'll just have a seat over there, I'll be with you in a minute."

"Ma'am?" Bernie was at a loss.

Aiko tapped herself on the side of her head, followed with a nod at the man.

Bernie held his hand to the side of his face; it came back drenched in crimson. "Oh, yeah."

Seth lay in the street on his back, grasping his neck, his right shoe scraping against the pavement as his knee rose and fell. Jeremiah repeatedly pulled the man's hands away from the wound in an attempt to apply pressure to the drenched gauze. Blood gushed from the hole in his neck. He gurgled, spitting the red all over his face and the medic who was trying to help him. Seth allowed one blood-soaked hand free from his wound to grasp at the air, desperately pointing to a figure beyond Jeremiah. Isabelle emerged from the bushes a few feet from the scene. Her head tilted to the side when their eyes met. Both pairs of eyes went wide, his in terror, hers with wonder.

"You have to stop fighting me, Seth!" Jeremiah shouted. "Get over here and hold his arms down, woman! Yes, I am talking to you, Isabelle. There is no time to waste!"

Isabelle took her time getting there but eventually knelt as close as she could to Seth without interfering with Jeremiah. She kept his arms pinned to the ground, all of her weight leaning forward on his wrists. He wasn't going anywhere. She leaned in, appearing to apply more pressure, but she merely sought a better, a closer view of his face. She would not break eye contact. Neither would he, for that matter, as he choked on his own fluids. Jeremiah fought, desperate to pinch off the severed artery. Seth's spasms slowed. He blinked a few times, each breath taking a little longer than the previous until he stopped moving at all. The two of them never lost eye contact. Isabelle watched every last drop of life drain from Seth's face.

"You can get up now," Jeremiah said. "He was dead before he hit the ground. I don't like to let them die alone if I can help it," he said, searching for his next patient.

Isabelle said nothing. She released her grip, took a long look at her bloodied hands, and then wiped them off on her dress.

"I have other wounded, but if you need to talk, I can make the time," Jeremiah offered.

"Talk about what?" She looked confused.

"Your friend Seth. We did all we could for him. Take comfort knowing that he died helping us all."

"I don't know him," she replied coldly while walking away. Isabelle paused for a moment. She strained her neck, turning around to glare at

Jeremiah. Over and over she pressed her sticky hands together and slowly pulled them apart.

Jeremiah was in a hurry and already halfway across the street, his mind focused on the next patient.

Periodic shots could be heard in the distance as the group tended to its wounded and gathered supplies from the fallen gang. A few of the survivors jumped at every stray pop. Reflexively, Vanessa ducked for a moment, then continued policing up weapons and ammo. Lancaster grabbed his Stetson and ducked behind a car, nearly knocking her over in the process.

"Asshole," she muttered.

"This guy's got a pocket full of cash and not much else," Ayn said, throwing the useless paper aside.

"Same here. These guys weren't very bright for all the shit they were talking," Markus added. "Are any of you guys finding food? Anything to eat?"

"Nada," said Ayn.

"Not a drop. I know they said they had all kinds of stuff," Vanessa remarked.

"They *said*." Sam grinned.

Vanessa used all she had to heave a rather large man onto his back so she could better access his vest pockets. "These guys have to have a camp somewhere. It could be close. We should look for it," she suggested.

"Too dangerous, darling." Sam was against the idea of looking for trouble, regardless of the likely reward. "This might be all of them, but for all we know, they could have just as well been a small scouting party. No, I think the best course of action is to leave the area immediately."

• • •

Nisha was having a particularly bad time with Seth's death. A blood-soaked sheet covering his body would be her last image of the man. They never spoke much, but she saw him around town enough and Isabelle and Tobias were friends with him, so that made him interesting to her. As curious as she was, she never gathered up the nerve to ask Isabelle to introduce them. Now she never could. She often thought about it alone at night: the four of them getting together for drinks, her and Seth hitting it off, Isabelle taking notice and forcing Tobias upstairs early.

"We all must go sometime, my dear," said Lancaster with a smirk as he casually strolled by.

Nisha was trying to pull herself away. Her final goodbyes to the man nearly had her smiling again. Lancaster destroyed that. "Go fuck yourself," she sobbed.

"If it's any consolation, well, he wasn't a very pleasant man. I think you'll agree," Lancaster said as a quick aside, downplaying Seth's death.

Marisol thumped Lancaster in the stomach with the butt of her rifle, not once but twice, before throwing the weapon to the ground. He doubled over as she brought a knee up to his face, smashing his nose. The man stumbled backward before losing balance and falling onto his back, landing hard against the unforgiving pavement. She quickly straddled the man, pinning him to the ground before furiously landing blow after blow upon his face. "I'll fucking kill you, you piece of shit!" she yelled at the nearly unconscious man.

Lancaster's head rolled left and right, in sync with the former sheriff's continuous barrage of punches. Curious onlookers gathered around, not one interceding. If she killed the man, so be it. This had been a long time coming, which seemed to be the consensus.

Samantha burst forth from the crowd, crying, arms flailing. "Why isn't anyone stopping this?" she yelled, slapping her hands against her thighs. "Markus, do something!" she pleaded, but the man lowered his head before turning away from the scene altogether. "You're killing him!" Samantha pawed at Marisol's arms. She tried desperately to pull the madwoman off of Lancaster.

Marisol was off of the man in a flash. Hands at Samantha's throat, she had the girl pinned against a truck, fist raised and prepared to strike. Samantha went quiet. Tears streamed from ever-widening eyes.

"Hey!" Markus yelled from the crowd as he approached.

Marisol lowered her fist but did not break eye contact with the frightened girl.

"You were killing him," Samantha whimpered.

"Maybe, maybe not." Marisol let go of Samantha and continued. "That man will not disrespect Seth's memory in my presence." She pointed to the bloodied man who finally began to stir. "Seth was one of the few contributing to keeping this group alive. Lancaster, piece of shit that he is, does nothing to help. He's a drain on resources and a burden to morale." She yanked Lancaster to his feet and shoved him away. "Get out of here."

Marisol knelt beside Seth's corpse. His covering was bunched up and pushed aside during the fracas. She tucked the corners back under him again, wrapping the sheet tightly around his form. "Sam, you mind giving me a hand here?" she asked, wrapping her arms around Seth's lower legs.

"Where are we going, darling?" Sam replied. He got a good grip on Seth's torso, and they were upright.

"We don't have a shovel, thanks to the hasty retreat from the cabin, but we can *at least* get him off the road. Over there should be good, in the woods, just out of sight under that big fir," she suggested.

"That's the last of them, sir. Nothing's moving out there." Rachel took a seat in the bed of Bernie's truck. "If any of them got away, they're long gone by now."

"Well done. Rachel, I want you and the rest of the unit on the perimeter until we're Oscar Mike. I'm sure all this noise will attract carriers to our location. Stay sharp, people," Miller ordered as he eyed the weary group. "Make yourself useful, Lancaster. Every corpse you see without a hole in its head, you put one in it. Don't forget to collect weapons and ammo while you're out there, too," Miller told Lancaster as he shoved a pistol into the man's chest.

Lancaster stumbled away, wide-eyed and obviously frightened. "Well, I've never even fired a weapon before. Would you care terribly much to share some advice, young man?" Lancaster fumbled nervously with the gun.

"Learn fast. Here's the only advice you're going to get from me, old man. Stay away from Marisol and keep your goddamn mouth shut. Now get going," said Miller. "And one more thing. If I even think you're raising that weapon toward Marisol or anyone else in the group, you'll be dead before you finish the thought. Isaac, why don't you take a duffel out there and collect any weapons he finds. We wouldn't want the good mayor hurting himself, now would we?" Miller added with a smile.

"Yeah. Yeah, that's a good idea, sir." Isaac didn't have much to say. The shock of what just happened right before his eyes, the slaughter he took part in, weighed heavily on the man.

Radzinski tossed an empty bag to Isaac. "God forbid something happens to Lancaster. That would really be a tragedy, wouldn't it?"

"Why bother shooting all those assholes in the head? We're out of here, anyway," Damon asked. "Weren't you the one adamant that we shouldn't bother making sure Tobias and his kid didn't come back?"

"That was different. There're a lot of bodies out there, man." Radzinski kicked a dead biker. "This stretch of road will end up being a deathtrap for anyone else that comes by looking for a place to hole up."

"So. It won't be us."

"You're cold, kid. Can't say I totally disagree, but you're fucking cold."

Miller and Jeremiah were surveying the scene from the driveway of the ruined house. An abandoned vehicle blocked them from casual glances.

"Every move we make, something is jumping out at us." Miller was clearly frustrated. "We can't even take a goddamn break to let these people find their bearings and rest. Just a few hours is all I ask." Miller laid his rifle on the roof of the car with force. He kneed the driver's side door, leaving a considerable dent. He turned to face Jeremiah as he repeatedly stretched his fingers and balled them back into fists. "We can't keep going like this, Jerry. The road's going to take every one of them." Miller nodded toward the civilians gathering weapons from the dead. He watched as Nisha fumbled with an armful of rifles. She dropped one, then kicked it farther away as she bent to retrieve it.

We don't need seven more rifles, he thought. *Just the ammo.* How in the hell were the civilians supposed to know that unless otherwise told? They were trying. Shit, they were trying as best as they could, but he knew that unless he and the handful of soldiers and Marisol gave them constant pointers, the lot of them were in for a long, tough haul.

"More wounded, one more dead, and Isabelle has clearly checked out," Jeremiah added.

"She spoke to you?" Miller asked.

"No, she didn't say a word to me. Nothing of import, anyway. She was the only one around as I tried to help Seth, and I had to almost beg her to help me hold him down."

"That's a start. It's something, right?"

"It's not what you think. Isabelle didn't help me for Seth's sake. I believe she wanted to watch him bleed out."

"Are you sure?" Miller asked with a sigh.

"Not entirely. I suppose there's a chance I could be wrong, though I highly doubt it," Jeremiah replied. "Then there's Marisol. Sooner or later, she *is* going to kill Lancaster. The carriers are a constant menace, the hermit at the cabin, now a gang. This route grows more precarious every step of the way, Miller."

"I've noticed, and in light of that, not to mention our dwindling food situation, I've made a decision no one's going to like. We're driving straight through, no more stops. We can't be more than twelve hours tops from the Outer Banks, and there will be more marinas there than we'll know what to do with. We'll finally find a boat and get off this goddamned road."

CHAPTER NINE

The Emerald Star

Darkness slowly gave way to dawn. The sun's first rays burned away the night's dew, revealing previously hidden threats. Shadows danced between the trees more frequently. There was no doubt they had left the mostly rural portion of their trek behind. Carrier sightings increased the closer they came to civilization. Longleaf Bay lay before them, just across the bridge. The small ocean community lay in ruins, no doubt destroyed in the chaos and confusion of its inhabitants' hasty escape.

They arrived just before dawn. The caravan was parked at the northern side of the bridge leading into town and the marina. The expanse itself was barren except for a few newspapers and empty plastic bottles blowing in the wind. Feral dogs gnawed at a corpse lying in the street toward the other end of the bridge. Seventy-five yards from the stopped vehicles, a lone car sat in the dead center of the span. A handful of others dotted the structure. What was once a peaceful beach getaway had devolved into, at best, a ghost town. At worst, it was another death trap.

Longleaf Bay itself couldn't have taken up more than a quarter square mile. Even that modest acreage managed to house hundreds of buildings of all description. A wall of waterfront condos greedily obscured the best views of the bay and the Atlantic not far to the east. In its prime, the large marina was home to hundreds of docked boats. It also played host to frequent large gatherings. Just south of the bridge, now reduced to shambles, the marina hosted less than twenty boats. Most appeared to be in various states of disrepair. The boathouses, shops, and condos in the immediate vicinity didn't fare much better; they bore the stress of months of chaos and looting.

Burnt-out buildings were all that remained of the town proper. Hundreds of ruined, charred husks made up the city. Acres of trees in all directions were blackened, their foliage burned to the dirt. Everything in Longleaf Bay was burned black save for the marina. Somehow, it was spared. The road that adjoined the bridge, in conjunction with an intersecting highway just south, was all that separated the blackened trees from the town, the large stretch of pavement no doubt acting as a firebreak.

All that remained were the undead, many of them as black as the buildings. They scurried around the ruined town, their charred bodies afforded the beasts excellent camouflage. Hundreds of them meandered about in an endless search for food, their only prey fled long ago. Some merely stood in place, perhaps in wait for those unlucky or foolish enough to find themselves trapped in this ghost town. Others wandered about, aimlessly bumping into those with apparent purpose. A carrier would approach a locked door with what supposed experts could only assume was a sense of instinct. A sliver of memory perhaps would compel the beast to turn the handle in an attempt to gain entrance. They would continue like this for hours, sometimes days, before something else would grab their attention and urge them along their way.

The undead were kept at arm's length. A barricade of sorts had been erected on the city side of the bridge. Vans, moving trucks, and other large vehicles were lined up across its span, denying the ghouls access to the bridge and trapping them in town.

Jeremiah lay on the roof of an abandoned car at the center of the bridge. The vantage point wasn't ideal, but it was the highest location they had easy access to. Even still, it gave him a wide perspective of the downtown and marina areas. He was intrigued by the carriers' behavior. It fascinated him to watch their ranks swell around a perpetually locked door; within minutes, the original would be blocked from view by throngs of undead automatons. Down by the water's edge, others made their way to the docks, clumsily walking off the piers to disappear beneath the dark water. Like with the door, others would follow suit until none remained on that particular dock.

Each morning since they began their journey, Jeremiah spent the predawn hours studying his surroundings. This morning proved exceptionally fruitful. Studying these beasts was vital for the group's survival, even *if* no one else recognized it. Jeremiah mentioned he noticed during his morning research that a possible carrier was trapped in one of the cars near the summit of the bridge. Miller sent Soraya back up there with him to be sure before the group got any closer to town. The duo approached the car, its windows opaque with grime and blood. Jeremiah signaled that he would open the door. Soraya stood at the ready, her kukri trained on the filthy window. The door swung open, causing the soldiers to take a step back as they were engulfed in a cloud of wretched stench. A withered, nearly naked corpse slowly slid from the vehicle and desperately clawed at the soldiers' feet. They slowly backed off. Jeremiah kept his rifle aimed at the lone carrier's head. At a snail's pace, it pulled itself along the concrete on its belly. The carrier could only go so far, as its left foot was bent backward, trapped under the driver's seat. The thing was stuck; it could only move from side to side and just barely. The rough ground scraped the creature's flesh off down to the bone, where its elbows, knees, and hip bones met the unforgiving concrete. Jeremiah held up one finger for the benefit of those back at the caravan.

Miller returned an affirmative reply. Behind him, standing in a semicircle around the back of the caravan, Rachel, Marisol, Isaac, Aiko, and Sam watched the perimeter. Most of the remainder of the group hung out by the vehicles. Some wandered up near the bridge for a better view of the water.

"Grab that ax, would you?" Miller said to Radzinski. "Let's go."

"You got it, boss," Radzinski replied sarcastically.

"Mind if we tag along?" Vanessa approached. Lillian followed closely behind. "It doesn't look like there's much going on up there."

"I don't see why not," Miller replied, quickly scanning back and forth.

"God, I haven't seen the water in ages," Lillian commented.

"Just stay a few feet behind us, and if I say so, run your asses back to the cars as fast as you can," Miller added.

The girls followed Miller up the bridge and toward its apex. With ammunition low following an impromptu shootout, edged and blunt weapons were this task's weapon of choice.

"Giving tours now, are we?" Radzinski commented. He didn't wait for a response, nor did he want one. Miller wasn't about to risk losing his cool in front of the civilians, and Radzinski knew it. These little jabs simply amused him.

Lillian leaned in a little more closely to the trapped beast than anyone including her expected. She had never seen one up close like this before. Its shriveled skin was bunched up around its thighs and shoulder blades. It had sat for who knew how long in that car. The thing could barely raise its head. When it did, an arm shot out quicker than any of them anticipated, its bony, claw-like hand scraping less than a foot from Lillian's leg. The carrier's proximity to her and the others almost seemed to give the thing a boost of energy, apparent in the sudden lunge. Lillian stepped back, not about to test her luck any further.

"Fascinating," Jeremiah commented.

"Come again," Radzinski asked.

"For the last ten minutes, it lay there, barely moving or making a sound. The girl steps closer than the rest of us, and suddenly it has the strength for an attack."

"Yeah, we've seen it before. You get close, they fuck you up. No need to overthink this, Doc."

"Merely an observation. If we study them and learn to predict their movements, the results could save lives."

"Just one, alone out here?" Lillian asked.

"Look, she has claw marks all over her back!" Vanessa commented excitedly. "She must have got away from one of these things and locked herself in the car. Poor thing probably took days to die in that oven." She wiped her brow as if witnessing this thing's fate reminded her of her own rising temperature.

"You think that's what killed her? Those scratches, I mean?" Lillian asked.

"I would posit that the woman died of dehydration while attempting to wait them out," Jeremiah said. "The temperature in that car must have reached one hundred fifty degrees during the day. Windows aren't even cracked. No air circulation would have made it difficult to breathe. When she finally stopped moving after a few days or so with no water, the carriers likely lost interest and moved on. Sometime after that, she turned. Speculation, of course. Horrible way to go nonetheless."

"This thing is pathetic. It can barely even move." Radzinski teased the creature with his boot, nudging it in the ribs.

"Radzinski!" Miller shouted.

"Alright, alright. Jesus." Radzinski raised the ax and swung mightily, splitting the creature's head in two. Syrupy blood and brains oozed from the pie-shaped gash. The creature, or whoever it used to be, was finally at peace.

Upon further inspection, every alleyway in Longleaf Bay that Miller could reach with the binoculars was clogged, stacked at least ten feet high with junked cars, dumpsters, or anything that could act as a heavy blockade. For all intents and purposes, the town was sealed off. Barring some fool plowing headlong through one of the blockades, those things were trapped inside and couldn't get to anyone out of city limits. A shame the previous residents didn't leave signs making it as apparent.

"Jerry, I want you and Soraya to check out the eastern marina. This is a big area and we need to know what kind of numbers we're dealing with before we commit to a search. Get Sam to give you a lift and take Isaac or Marisol with you," said Miller.

"Yes, sir."

"Rachel, take Radzinski and Markus. I want you to circle around the highway. Come up behind the southern marina. Surveillance only. Keep your distance. Don't engage unless absolutely necessary."

"Roger that. Be back in thirty minutes tops."

Casandra lay in the back seat of one of the larger SUVs. Aiko recommended that she stay off her feet and remain as still and calm as possible for at least a few days. Casandra would be fine. As it turned out, the gunshot wound wasn't as bad as it looked, but the added stress on top of the blood loss and malnutrition could turn into an issue for the baby. Bernie cracked the windows. What little air circulated helped immensely, but it wasn't enough. Eventually, she won him over, and reluctantly Bernie opened a door, but only the one at her feet, directly across from where someone stood watch. Beads of sweat formed on her chest, forehead, and upper lip. Anywhere exposed skin remained undisturbed by clothes or touch beaded up. Her white blouse was drenched with it. Bernie removed her shoes to let her feet breathe. He dabbed her forehead with a damp cloth he'd dipped into the bay. With his pampering and the open door, she hadn't felt this good since before she was shot.

"Can you wiggle your fingers for me?" Bernie asked.

"Yeah, it hurts," she managed, dancing her digits along Bernie's forearm.

"I know it does, sweetheart." He kissed her on the forehead. "Don't you worry, Cas. I'll stay right here and change this bandage every day. You'll be as good as new before you know it," Bernie said as she drifted back to sleep. He stood watch outside the car. He'd let her rest for now, as they'd be running soon enough, he imagined. They always were.

• • •

Jeremiah and the others returned from their reconnaissance of the eastern marina. The situation appeared calm as their truck came to a slow halt.

"What's it look like over there, Jerry?" Miller asked.

"The eastern marina is gone, sir. Completely destroyed. I can only speculate what happened, but it appears a tanker ship crashed into the main mass of boats and exploded, igniting the marina and surrounding structures. There's nothing left at that location except for charred debris."

"Or it was blown up on purpose," Sam suggested. "It's possible those bikers might have stashed a few boats and destroyed the rest. We don't know if we got all of them. Hell, they could be watching us right now." He adjusted his hat as he peered off into the distance, searching for more raiders.

"Possibly," replied Miller. "Either way, that marina is of no use to us now and I don't plan on being here long enough to find out. Rachel, how are things looking down south?"

"The southern marina is stacked deep with those things, sir. I don't know what the hell they're doing down there, but I'd prefer not find out. No need to get any closer again and risk alerting them to our presence. You can see plenty from here. Take a look." Rachel handed off the binoculars.

Miller had looked at the closest marina a dozen times by now. He knew going in it was their only real option. The recon of the other two marinas was merely in the hope of establishing a backup plan. This close to their destination, he wasn't about to leave anything to chance. "There has to be close to a thousand infected down there. We'd never make it through, much less find a working boat before they swarmed us. The southern marina is out of the question." Miller turned and faced southeast again with the binoculars. "That leaves my least favorite of the bunch: the marina just past the bridge. It's obviously closest to us, but it's also closest to town and who knows how many carriers. I was really hoping to avoid it, but at this point, it's our only option."

Miller had a makeshift map scribbled down on an inside-out cereal box. The plan was simple enough. Three groups of three would hit the marina and spread out, clear any carriers wandering between the buildings, then meet up down by the docks.

"What do you see, Captain?" Sam asked.

"I make out about two dozen, maybe thirty or so infected wandering about. They shouldn't be a problem out in the open like that. What concerns me is the buildings. They could be full of useful supplies or a hundred of those things ready to jump on us, but we won't know until we're in the shit."

"Orders, sir?" Aiko asked.

"We're going to do this by the books, people. Hard and fast. Don't give those things a chance to group up. Radzinski, Soraya, and myself are on point. Jerry, Aiko, and Sam take the right flank. Rachel, Marisol, and Bernie cover us on the left. The rest of you, stay with the vehicles. If anyone approaches, detain them until we get back. If they refuse to cooperate, shoot them. If it comes to it, lethal force is up to your discretion, understood?" Miller looked around at the mostly receptive faces. The majority were checking over their weapons, sharing ammo, and discussing tactics should the gang reappear.

"Don't worry. We're not going to be taken by surprise again," said Markus.

"Good, one more thing," Miller added. "Single shots only unless you get boxed in. Ammo conservation and keeping these boats in one piece are priority. If everyone's ready, let's do this."

• • •

Dozens of bodies littered the marina. The aftermath of battle was apparent in the carnage left behind. Nine boats remained afloat in the once-thriving Longleaf Bay harbor. Scores more rested half-submerged in the relatively shallow water. Miller and his three groups cleared the area adjacent to the docks, between and behind every building, inside and under every broken-down vehicle, beneath upturned boats, and behind the smallest shed. If a door was open, they entered and did the same inside. Locked doors were passed by as time was of the essence.

Longleaf Bay proper was only just over a small ridge from the marina. Tops of burnt-out buildings were all that was visible of the town from its vantage point. The town remained full of infected, but Miller and his people had neither the time nor resources to clear the streets. Their only hope lay in finding a seaworthy vessel to leave this place behind, or else they would have to return to the uncertainty of the road.

"Every boat at the far end is either shot or halfway submerged," said Sam.

"Similar over here. We found one seaworthy, maybe, and that's a big maybe at that," Aiko replied.

Rachel came jogging up to the growing group at the dock. Markus, Isaac, and everyone else who wasn't otherwise preoccupied with boats were nearly finished transferring the supplies to the dock.

"No joy over here," Miller offered.

"Don't worry about it. I think we're good," said Rachel. "Bernie and Soraya are putting the finishing touches on one as we speak. They scavenged parts from these other heaps and now they're working their magic. He said it was a sword boat, whatever that means. The *Emerald Star* she's called. All I know is it's big and there's not a leak to be found."

"Outstanding," Miller replied. He turned to address everyone else who to his astonishment were already gathering up the supplies they had just dropped off. A few were already walking toward the boat.

"Well, would you look at that," said Sam.

"Impressive, boss man." Rachel patted Miller on the back on her way to give the others a hand with the supplies.

"Take a bow, Captain," said Sam. "You managed to get these people to come together, work as a team. Gotta admit, I never thought I'd see the day."

A puff of black smoke rose from the other end of the dock as the *Emerald Star* returned to life. Its engine purred. More than a few cheers erupted from the survivors.

"This one seems to be our best bet, Miller," Bernie said. "Three-quarter tank of gas and lots of fishing supplies. Looks like it's a sword boat. Plenty of room for everyone and then some."

"We are lucky. There was not much else to choose from," added Soraya. "The rest of the boats, they are all wrecked or too small for all of us. It seems we are not the only ones who had this idea."

"It'll have to do. This is just what we needed, you two," Miller replied. "Great work."

"Bernie did a hell of a job fixing her up, sir."

"Soraya's being modest, Miller. I couldn't have done this without your little lady here. She worked miracles in there with not much more than a roll of duct tape and spit."

The two mechanics exchanged a handshake. Bernie went back below deck for calibrations, leaving Miller and Soraya alone.

"I better get going. More work to be done," Soraya said. On her way below deck, she tossed Miller a smile and gently drew her hand down his arm, pausing momentarily when their hands met. He nodded and wondered how many days it had been since he saw her look happy. Any of them, for that matter.

• • •

The sun was at its highest and brightest by the time a small portion of the group had boarded the *Emerald Star*. Miller and Soraya were going over a few last-minute details while Sam and Marisol walked the deck, anxious to get going and put the road behind them.

"That is it. We have siphoned all the gas we could find from the other boats," Soraya said. "Extra batteries, parts, odds and ends, I think we have just about everything we need to get us to where we are going."

"Good, while we're here, I think we should give these marina buildings a once-over, then be on our way," Miller suggested.

"We should, yes."

A duffel bag flew over the side and landed on the deck by Miller's feet. Vanessa hoisted herself up behind it.

"Careful with that," said Soraya.

"Hey, guys. Sorry," Vanessa said, struggling with the slippery rail.

"Never let that happen again," Soraya teased with a smile as she helped Vanessa board the vessel.

"Thanks. That's the last of the stuff from the cars. I think we're just about ready to go, but we've got a problem."

"Now what?" Sam asked.

"Well, now that we're here and almost ready to go, it seems a few of the others have finally decided to speak their minds."

"Oh? And who has a problem now?" Miller asked.

"I'm sorry, Miller, but I promised I'd leave names out of it."

"Fair enough. What's their issue, though? Everyone seemed fine an hour ago."

"Cold feet mostly. I think a few of them thought we would never actually find a boat. That's my guess. And for the record, *I'm* ready to go. So are Lillian, Markus, and most of the others."

"Thanks, Vanessa. I figured you would be."

"Their main hang-up seems to be food and water and if it'll last. But I think the truth of the matter is that a couple of them, one in particular, is afraid of the ocean."

"That's understandable, but we can't start second-guessing ourselves now, and going back the way we came is not an option. We simply don't have the resources," Miller said.

"How much food and water do we have left?" Vanessa asked.

"If we tighten our belts, we've probably got about a two-day supply of food. Double that, maybe triple, for water," Sam said.

"Rations are one thing, but ammunition is going to be a problem soon," Marisol added. "We can't afford another shootout and we can be sure we'll see more gangs the closer we get to the larger cities. The boat really is the way to go. Doubt we'll run into many roving gangs on an island."

"Then that's it. We stick with Tobias's plan?" Vanessa asked.

"I don't see that we have any other choice." Miller peered through his binoculars, back toward the populated areas beyond the harbor. "Those things are still out there. They just haven't noticed us yet. My guess is, as soon as the wind changes direction, they'll be on us. We can't afford another encounter, not right now."

"They're all worn out. A good night's sleep is all they need," Sam suggested.

"And we're not going to get that on land. Not here, anyway," said Vanessa. "I say we take our chances out there, at sea. I mean, we've come all this way. Soraya and Bernie have got the boat working. What are we even talking about? I can tell the pessimists we're going with or without them. Maybe that will snap them out of it."

"I know what the problem is." Marisol singled out Lancaster, who was at the far end of the pier with a small group surrounding him. "He's a politician. He knows how to use people's fear to get what he wants. If they're busy doubting you and the plan, they won't notice as he slowly rebuilds his power base. Say the word and I'll tie him up in one of the boathouses. We can leave him here and be done with it."

"That won't be necessary." Miller almost smiled. "Gather everyone up at the pier. I'll brief them in five."

The ragtag group of survivors, filthy from weeks on the road, gathered around the end of the dock, awaiting Miller's briefing. Begrimed and torn clothes adorned their filthy skin. Weeks without properly bathing and the stench would be unbearable if not for the nearly coma-like daze most of the group had succumbed to. It wasn't dissimilar to their relentless pursuers.

Miller hated addressing crowds. He avoided it at all costs for as long as he could remember. Even with consideration of the bonds that were forming between him and some of these formerly complete strangers, he didn't want to do this. Rachel convinced him it was either a quick speech or take all day, pulling everyone aside individually. Miller pushed aside his misgivings and took his place at the center of the mass of nervous survivors. "Make no mistake, getting on this boat and heading for an unknown destination does not guarantee survival. I don't know what we'll run into out there. All I know is we can't stay here and we cannot continue on the road."

Some of the crowd nervously checked their surroundings for any sign of approaching infected. Others remained attentive to Miller's speech. Damon and former Mayor Lancaster had no qualms in showing disdain for anything their self-appointed leader had to offer.

Miller spoke up, ignoring the growing discontent. "We know now that there's more to worry about out there than carriers or infected or whatever we're calling those things today. For all we know, some of those bikers managed to escape and they could be tracking us. Hell, they could even be watching us right now. We have no way of knowing."

A few gasps emanated from the crowd. Some ducked from invisible attackers while most at least scanned the horizon. Every one of them felt for their closest weapon. Radzinski smirked in quiet pleasure at the civilians' fear. Unbeknownst to most of the audience, Radzinski, Soraya, and the rest of the soldiers were busy scanning the horizon for movement while Miller addressed the crowd. For the time being, at least, they were perfectly safe.

"Tobias had a plan. We make a run for the sea, find a boat, and head south for the islands. I had no reason to doubt the man then, and I see no reason to now. As a matter of fact, Tobias's plan could very well save all of our lives."

Lillian managed a smile at the mention of her father. Vanessa rubbed the girl's back in solidarity, a welcome attempt at comfort. Lillian returned the gesture with one of her own, her arm around Vanessa's waist, head resting on her shoulder.

Miller continued. "We desperately need supplies, but don't stray from the marina. Just because we don't see those things right now doesn't mean they're not out there."

"And what may I ask are we supposed to be looking for in the midst of all this wreckage, young man?" Lancaster asked.

"I know you are dead weight, but do you really need that question answered?" Soraya snapped.

"Vanessa and Markus are going to siphon as much fuel from the vehicles on the other side of the bridge as they can. The rest of you, pair up and look for supplies, anything that can be of use: life vests, rope, medical supplies, and food and water. Always be on the lookout for food and water. Oh, and you, Lancaster, *will* start pulling your weight or I'll leave you on this dock," Miller said confidently. "Do you understand me?"

"I was merely asking a question, son. There's no need for bravado."

"Punk ass soldier boy," Damon whispered for the old man's benefit.

Ayn was firmly with Damon and Lancaster. "I don't like this."

"Rendezvous back here in thirty minutes," Miller said. "I don't care what you've found or what you think you're going to find. Drop what you're doing and get back to the boat. We set sail at thirteen hundred hours. Hop to it."

The crowd dispersed, slowly at first, but an urgency overcame most of them and they flocked to the nearest buildings in a mad dash as if someone had told them everything they ever desired lay beyond the next door. The soldiers, Marisol, and Sam didn't participate in the looting; they patrolled the marina, weaving between buildings with a little less urgency than when they arrived earlier in the morning but with the same purpose, nonetheless.

Jeremiah poked his head into an ajar door. For a moment, he considered looking for something—anything. He reconsidered, though, as he knew it was futile. This whole place had been picked clean once too many. The sooner they launched, the better. He noticed Miller rounding a corner and took the opportunity to get a private word in. "I doubt we'll find much here in the way of supplies, sir," Jeremiah offered while pointing to the remains of heavily fortified buildings toward the town's center. "Whoever was holed up in that building dug in deep, from the looks of the nearby structures. They would have scavenged all they could."

"Hard to tell with everything burnt to a crisp. Where do you suppose they all went?" Miller asked.

"Your guess is as good as mine, sir. They could have had a similar plan as us and sailed away, or for all we know, we're looking at them now." Jeremiah gazed to the infected shambling about in the distance. "With all of these haphazard barriers strewn about, I would guess whoever lived here had lived here for a while. They were the ones who picked this place dry."

"Go on," said Miller.

"It took me a few hours to realize it, but the barriers and the complete lack of supplies, on top of a burnt-out town—the people who lived here did this. They believed by trapping the carriers and setting them ablaze, their problems would be over."

"But they didn't expect a constant flow of the things to continue pouring in from all directions afterward," Miller added.

"Precisely. They left the marina and surrounding buildings intact in hopes of relocating. But an unexpected surge of carriers forced them out to sea."

"Taking an entire town's worth of supplies with them."

Dozens of carriers shuffled just beyond the barriers across the road, their faces twisted in agony, eyes filled with rage and resentment. It was as if on some base level they knew that Miller and his people would be gone soon, just as the ones before, and with them any chance of satiating their appetite.

"Oh, fuck," Ryan shouted. He stumbled backward, dropping the flashlight as he fell to the ground. The cylinder rolled down the slight incline, casting large shadows upon the darkened boathouse. It came to rest against another carrier's foot. Not a second later, the thing fell backward, crashing to the floor and taking half of Ryan's well-stacked bottles with it.

Rachel stood just beyond the beast, checking the room for more threats. "Move!" she yelled.

Ryan scrambled to his feet. He grabbed what he could while Rachel continued laying down covering fire. She sent small three-round bursts into the darkness, hoping to keep any invisible threats at bay until Ryan made his way to safety. He was near the door when again he lost his footing. A strong arm yanked him off his feet. He was skidding on his back in front of the store when he saw Radzinski enter the darkness.

"Go!" Radzinski ordered.

Ryan wasted no time saying thank-you; that would come later. He picked up what little supplies were spread about the sand and bolted for the dock.

Just as quickly as Radzinski entered the store, he was backing out, rifle at the ready.

Rachel followed alongside him, pulling the door shut behind her. "Well, we're not going back in there again," she said, holstering her sidearm. "Thanks for the assist."

"Don't mention it. The boat's up and running and Miller's ready to go. I think we've picked this place clean of what little scraps it had to offer, anyway."

"Half a dozen buildings, little shacks, and this store and we didn't find shit, you?" she asked.

"Nothing. This place is a graveyard. I'm surprised we even manage to find a boat in working order."

"It makes sense, though. We weren't the first with this idea. We won't be the last, either. The next people who find this place will do the same thing," Rachel added. "Good luck to them."

"That's it, people. Gather up what you've found and make your way back to the boat!" Miller shouted at a row of nearby buildings as he approached. "We leave in five minutes!"

Ayn made her way through a darkened building to the doorway, carrying a cardboard box stuffed with various odds and ends. Nothing she was positive they needed. Mostly just stuff that caught her eye. She could better sort it later. The blinding transition from darkness to light was disorienting, and she missed the exit completely. After crashing into the wall, she dropped the box to steady herself against the doorframe.

"Everything alright there?" Miller asked, one eye to the scurrying group still inside.

"Yeah, I'm fine. I just got light-headed for a second there. Weird."

"Okay. Well, don't push yourself too hard. No sense in getting hurt now. We'll see you on the boat."

She gathered her things. After a little stutter-step, she was on her way as Soraya jogged up to the spot.

"Everyone else is aboard. The boat is running and ready to go." She eyed Ayn, who was down near the pier, making her way to the vessel. "What was that?"

"She's overworking herself. A lot of them are."

"Anything in this building?"

"Doesn't look like it. I'm seeing lots of stuff go by but not much in the way of food. We'll take a proper inventory once we're out at sea. I really just want to get out of here. That gang's got me spooked."

Below deck, Bernie and Aiko helped Casandra into a small bed they set up especially for her. The accommodations weren't exactly five-star, but they were comfortable and the tight quarters would prevent her from being thrown to the floor if they encountered rough seas. They lowered her into the bed, Bernie supporting her back and neck, Aiko guiding her arms and careful not to pull on her wound.

"Take it easy, take it easy. There you go, sweetheart," Bernie said as Casandra was finally flat on the bed.

"Thank you, Bernie." Casandra put her palm on his cheek. He kissed it and wiped the wispy blonde strands from her eyes.

"Well, I'll leave you two to get settled in then," Aiko said, feeling like the third wheel.

"Oh, Aiko, thank you so much for everything." Casandra smiled. "You don't know how much I appreciate this."

"Yeah, Doc. I don't know what we'd do without ya." Bernie tipped his hat.

"Just doing my job, you guys. Try to stay off your feet as much as possible, Casandra, and if you need anything at all, don't hesitate. Bernie can come find me." Aiko hurried back out into the light.

"Anyone seen Isabelle around? I know she's still not talking, but I don't want her getting accidentally left behind in the confusion," Isaac asked, straining against the horizon.

In unison, Ayn and Elliot pointed to the bow of the boat.

"She's been up there for a while now," Ayn mentioned. "I think she wants to go as much as the rest of us. She just won't say it."

"Well, that's a relief. Guess I'll leave her be then. You guys need a hand with anything?"

"I think that's about it for the supplies," Elliot said. "A few more stragglers and we're off, I think. I did have a few ideas about shift rotations I was hoping to bounce off you."

"Oh, sure. Glad to help," Isaac offered, relieved to be of assistance. Marisol cast a large shadow, and he was well aware that he would never be considered her equal. No one asked *him* for advice *or* to go out on recon. Some days he wondered why he even still wore the uniform at all. If Elliot wanted his input on putting together a list of shift rotations, whatever he meant by that, then Isaac was more than happy to help.

"Terrific, let's go down below deck, out of the sun, then. I think this will make a lot of sense if us civilians are going to carry our share of the weight," Elliot replied.

"Later, guys." Ayn watched them disappear below deck before grasping her stomach and holding onto the side of the boat for support. She took a few deep breaths before straightening herself, tears welling.

"Everything copacetic there, sailor?" Rachel came up from behind.

"Yeah, yeah, I'm fine, Rachel. Just need to find my sea legs. I haven't been on a boat in years."

"Tell me about it. Blah." Rachel stuck out her tongue and pretended to stick her finger down her throat as she continued on her way to the wheelhouse.

Sam took the helm. He'd never claim the title of captain, but seeing as he had the most experience at sea, which really didn't amount to much, he was the most logical choice. Black smoke poured from the exhaust. The engine, long-dormant, roared to life as they pulled away from the dock. The majority of the group stood watch on deck as Longleaf Bay, the final stop on the road from Pepperbush, grew smaller in the distance. The *Emerald Star* chugged along through the bay and out into open sea.

CHAPTER TEN

Adrift

Vanessa awoke to suffocating smoke filling the cabin. Lillian lay beside her, seemingly unfazed by the putrid cloud as some others scurried by in a mad dash for the exit. Fumes stung her eyes. The stench of burning plastic and chemicals filled her lungs. She could hear Miller from somewhere across the cabin near the exit, calling out for everyone to come toward the sound of his voice. Lillian began choking. The small fit forced her awake as Vanessa helped her to her feet. They stumbled toward Miller, the sun barely visible behind him, a dim beacon of hope. As they approached the exit, Miller grabbed Vanessa by the arm and yanked the pair to safety, flinging them out onto the sun-drenched deck and into Soraya's waiting arms. Soraya led them toward the front of the boat, away from the smoke and out of the way of those frantically searching for the fire's source.

"I can't breathe," Lillian choked out, panic-stricken.

"We're okay. Come on." Vanessa led the frightened girl away from the fumes and to the relatively clear deck of the boat. She caressed the girl's back. The rhythm of her hands gave the illusion of air circulating in Lillian's lungs. Vanessa's grandfather taught her that when she was a child. When she was only seven years old, she hit her head while jumping into a pool and swallowed what felt like half the water. For nearly thirty minutes afterward, her grandfather rubbed her back, magically pushing air back into the little girl's lungs. It was a simple lesson, but it was one Vanessa never forgot. Mind over matter. A psychological hoodwink, as it were. She

129

used the same technique on Lillian, and within a few minutes, the girl's hysteria had passed.

Ryan tumbled out of the darkness, in the process nearly bowling over Ayn, who leaned back, coughing hard into her clenched fist. Each fit doubled her over in pain.

"Just breathe. You're alright." Ryan helped steady the girl.

"Dammit, I was finally asleep, too." She coughed. "Been feeling like crap for days. Now this?"

"I know what you mean. I was finally alone in the bathroom, just me and my thoughts, when the place filled with smoke."

"Gross."

"That may be the case, but I got you to stop coughing, didn't I?"

Bernie emerged from the smoke-filled cabin. He wore a wet shirt around his head, a makeshift filter from the acrid fumes. He coughed and waved the cloud from his face. As he approached Miller, he threw the damp shirt to the deck to better take in the fresh air. "Fucking thick in there, boys," he said while clearing his throat. "Fire's out. Wasn't as bad as it looked to be honest."

"You sure about that?" Miller referenced the thick white smoke still pouring from the cabin. "It doesn't look like the fire's out from where I'm standing."

"Positive. The smoke's making it look worse than it really is." Bernie plopped down on the deck, spent. "It'll dissipate shortly. Lots of rubber and plastic down there putting off all that shit. Like I said, not as grim as it looks."

"Well, that doesn't sound so bad. Mostly cosmetic damage then?" Rachel asked.

"Ah, let's not get ahead of ourselves, red," Bernie cautioned. "We pushed the motor too hard too fast and burned up a belt. The thing exploded all over the place, igniting a pile of used oil rags. I reckon all the loose bullshit down there went up faster than hell. Good news is, the smoke should clear out soon enough, and luckily for us, the boat took no structural damage from what I could tell, so that's a plus. This could have been a lot worse—way worse."

"That's not all, is it?" Miller asked.

"No, unfortunately, without that belt, the motor is useless," Bernie said point-blank.

"There's no way to rig it up? A temporary Band-Aid till we can get back to shore?" Miller asked, careful not to let his creeping desperation show.

"Not unless you can direct me to a mechanic's shop within walking distance," said Bernie. "I'm sorry, fellas, but we are dead in the water."

Radzinski handed Bernie a bottle of water. "Well, that explains why no one else took this boat. The fucking motor's shot."

"We don't know that for sure. Don't jump to conclusions," Miller snapped. "Bernie, how about scavenging a belt from something not as vital?"

"Eh, it doesn't really work like that, Miller. When the smoke clears, I'll turn that place upside down for parts, believe me, but for now, all we can do is wait." After wiping sweat from his brow, Bernie adjusted his hat a little lower, closer to his eyes. "You're gonna want to keep these people out of the sun as much as possible."

"It's not that hot out here," Rachel pointed out.

"Not yet, sure. It's morning still. Give it a few hours." He pointed to the sky. "There's not a cloud in sight. Some people are gonna roast out here." Bernie nodded in Samantha's direction, her porcelain skin nearly glowing in the morning sun.

DAY ONE

"Oh, this is just great. Now what? We can't even see the fucking land." Damon strained his eyes against the horizon. As far as he could see in any direction, they were surrounded by open ocean.

"The soldiers will figure something out or maybe Bernie has a solution. He seems to know enough about boats," Samantha suggested, though she knew trying to have a conversation with Damon was usually futile. He didn't like her, and it showed, but for Markus's sake, she would continue to try.

"Yeah, you keep thinking that if it makes you feel better. Me, I live in the real world, and in the real world, we are stuck in the middle of the *fucking* ocean."

"Don't lose your head, man. We need to stay calm if we're going to figure a way out of this," Markus added.

"Keep calm? How the fuck is staying calm going to make our boat drift back to shore?" Damon asked, stupefied.

"It won't, but losing your shit every five minutes doesn't help us, either," said Markus.

"I'm glad the two of you are enjoying this." Damon waved the pair off.

"No one's enjoying this, but your constant bullshit doesn't help." Markus tried to grab Damon's shoulder before he could walk away.

"Fuck you. I'm going to get some water." Damon stormed off below deck.

For the most part, Miller remained a steadfast observer when it came to minor squabbles among those in his charge, only intervening when things steered toward a boiling point. Sam agreed with this stance of letting the group blow off steam when necessary. The pair kept a watchful eye, nonetheless. Insignificant as it seemed, Miller didn't ignore this conversation; there was no need to verbalize his thoughts.

"Aiko." Miller tossed a nod in Damon's direction.

"I'm on it." She hurried below deck.

"Oh what? Did I miss something?" Nisha asked as she approached Miller and Sam.

"Inventory, again." Sam shook his nearly empty water bottle.

"Already? You'd think we were cursed," Nisha replied.

"It sure feels that way, doesn't it, darling?" Sam offered the woman what little water he had left.

Atop the wheelhouse, away from the prying eyes of the group, Vanessa and Lillian sat, scanning the horizon for land. The view was only slightly better than down below, but the privacy the perch offered was what drew them to the spot. As it turned out, the boat felt nearly as cramped as the caravan, only instead of being stuck with four or five people in the confines of a vehicle, everywhere they turned, now someone new was there. At least in a crowded truck you knew what you were in for. The *Emerald Star* only offered the illusion of better living.

"They'll get the engine fixed and we'll be on our way in no time. You'll see." Vanessa tried to sound optimistic, though inside, she was just as concerned as Lillian.

"Are you sure? They don't sound very positive down there." Lillian couldn't hide her apprehension if she tried.

"Truthfully, I don't know. I just needed a break from all the bickering."

"I'm with *you* girls. All that fighting sucks," Rachel added, peeking her head over the edge of the wheelhouse roof from a spot on a ladder.

Lillian jumped, nearly falling over the side. Vanessa was quick to grab the girl's arm, and Rachel was ready to catch her as she anticipated startling at least one of them.

"Careful, girls. It's a long way down," Rachel said, peering over the edge to the unforgiving deck below.

"Dammit, Rachel." Lillian sighed as she returned to her spot.

"Sorry about that, Lily. I thought you heard me coming." Rachel chuckled.

"Well, I didn't. You better watch your ass. I'll remember this," Lillian said facetiously while pointing to her head.

"What's up, Rachel? Any luck with the motor?" Vanessa asked.

"Unfortunately no, and that's what I wanted to talk to you guys about." Rachel joined the girls on their perch, though she held onto a useless antenna for balance as opposed to sitting.

"I don't know the first thing about fixing motors. Do you?" Lillian asked Vanessa.

Vanessa shook her head no, closed her eyes, and waited for the bad news to come pouring in.

"Trust me, I don't, either," Rachel said. "Soraya and Bernie have been going at it all day. They don't want to admit it yet, but the thing's dead."

"Well, if you can't help with the motor, why don't you hang out with us for a while then?" Lillian suggested.

"I'd *love* to join you guys up here. Trust me. To just sit and relax, I almost can't even remember what it feels like, but no, I shouldn't. Maintaining discipline and all that," Rachel replied with a frown, disappointment obvious. "Anyway, back to why I'm here, you're going to want to cut down on your exposure time." Rachel flicked her wrist, pointing to the warm sun overhead. "There's no telling how long we'll be stuck out here, and heat stroke will become a real issue if we run out of water."

"How bad does it look? The water, I mean," Vanessa asked.

"Aiko and a couple of the others are going over that now. Early estimates are a day or two's worth of food. Three or four days after that, we'll be out of water," Rachel said as upbeat as possible, given the circumstances.

"Oh God." Lillian gasped.

"Look, I'm not trying to scare anyone. I just thought you should know."

"Thanks, Rachel," Vanessa said appreciatively. She sat up cross-legged, hands draped over her knees, looking to the horizon. "One day. All I want is one day without bad news or having to run for my life." She closed her eyes and tried to remember how welcome the sun felt on her skin only moments ago.

DAY TWO

Casandra lay sound asleep in her bunk in the stuffy confines of the ship's bowels. Perspiration beaded up and rolled from her forehead and onto the moist pillow. Bernie dabbed what he could from her warm skin, but his rag was long ago soaked. Now he was more pushing the stuff around than sopping it up. It was agreed upon to let her sleep as much as possible. Even so, Bernie still woke her up every few hours for her share of water *and* most of his.

"You're going to need to stop doing that, Bernie. You need fluids, too," Aiko insisted.

"I'll manage, Doc, but come on, ain't there something else you can do for her? She's hurting over here," Bernie pleaded.

"I'm sorry, Bernie. We have nothing else for the pain. Besides, anything more potent would jeopardize the baby. She's just going to have to make do. FYI, her wound is healing nicely and there's no sign of infection. Just keep her comfortable and hydrated for now. Eventually, though, we *are* going to have to make her eat something."

"Well, that's a relief, the first part anyway." Bernie stood. His legs buckled for a moment before he righted himself against the doorframe.

"Careful now." Aiko steadied him. "Water, get yourself some now," she insisted.

"Yes, ma'am," he relented. "But after that, I'm gonna mess with them nets, see if I can't do something about this food situation."

Below deck, Radzinski attempted to lecture Miller on command decisions. The two soldiers had been butting heads since their respective units were forced together during the Philadelphia siege. The subsequent week's trials only served to further divide the men.

Radzinski was nearly shouting. "This is why we don't leave the big decisions up to the civilians. You took logistical advice from a man you just met. Now look at us: adrift, God knows where. Fucking wonderful!"

"Don't come at me with this bullshit, Radzinski. I didn't hear you offering any suggestions. As usual you were, and remain, only concerned about your own well-being. When things are going good, you go with the flow, but when the situation goes fubar, you're always the first to toss around blame."

"We should have at least looked for Conrad's unit when we were near Alexandria."

"Well, we didn't. That was my call and I'll stick with it. We were beat up and on the run. There was no way I was going to lead this group into a potential massacre."

"Instead you led them to starvation. Much better." Radzinski held up the okay sign with his fingers, but Miller knew he was really calling him an asshole.

"We can have this out right now if you like." Miller got in Radzinski's face, nose to nose with him.

Before either man could escalate things further, Jeremiah interceded. "Enough, the both of you! Look around you. These people are frightened. They need to look up to us. They need to know that we have this situation well in hand. The two of you bickering betrays a lack of control." Jeremiah admonished both men equally.

Miller took the cue to peer at a small sample of the group just in earshot. Some were out on the deck, looking in. Others were down the corridor, farther away in the interior of the boat. Those who were paying attention looked on in wonder, perhaps asking themselves if they'd chosen the right leader following the deaths of Takashi and then Tobias. Miller couldn't help but wonder himself.

"Miller, I believe in you," Jeremiah stated calmly. "We all do, but don't get caught up in a pissing contest with him. He's only trying to unnerve you. No offense intended, John."

"None taken. Go fuck yourself, Jerry. I don't need this shit." Radzinski sauntered off topside.

Jeremiah spotted a few curious onlookers and pulled Miller aside, away from prying eyes, and leaned in for a whisper. "Keep in mind that society as we know it is finished. No matter how optimistic you may feel, it *is* over. We have no real authority over these people. If they become dissatisfied with our leadership, a revolt is not out of the question. They have the numbers, and scared people are capable of acting on impulse alone. We both know it. That is a situation we must avoid at all costs. We cannot risk the group's safety over the two of you measuring cocks." Jeremiah's sternness was not at all unusual, and Miller conceded to his wisdom.

"You're right, as usual. Thanks for that, Jerry. I don't know what it is with that guy, but he really knows how to push my buttons. He has since day one. When we're in the shit, I can count on him. Otherwise, he's becoming a liability." Miller turned his gaze back to the darkened motor room.

"John Radzinski is without a doubt a hard case. Unfortunately, in light of our current circumstance, that will have to remain a problem for another day," Jeremiah suggested.

Soraya rose early, as she always did. Instead of lamenting the group's newest problem, like so many others would on a daily basis, she instead focused on another route for a possible solution to their dilemma. She had the radio ripped apart down to exposed circuit boards. Every countertop in the room was littered with the stuff. The radio didn't work. It never did, or at least not as long as they had been on the boat. Back at Longleaf Bay, when she and Bernie brought the *Emerald Star* back to life, she didn't bother checking the radio. *Stupid*, she thought in hindsight, but at the time, getting off the road was paramount.

"Whatcha doing?" asked Samantha as she crept into the room, silently taking in what for her was an incomprehensible mess.

"Hello, Samantha. How are you this morning?" Soraya asked. There was always time for a proper greeting and manners, no matter the situation.

"The same, I guess. Scared shitless to be honest," she replied, arms crossed as if to fend off a chill.

"Stay positive. It helps. Believe me," Soraya offered, knowing it most likely wouldn't quell the woman's fears, but she'd try all the same.

"Thanks, I'll give it a shot. Markus has been a real help in that department."

"Good, it is important to have someone near to you." Soraya never took her eyes off her task.

"So what is all this stuff, anyway? Really, what *are* you doing? I have no idea what I'm looking at," Samantha asked while peeking over Soraya's shoulder, avoiding a small plume of smoke emanating from the soldering iron.

"This damned radio will not work no matter what I do," Soraya said. "I don't have the right parts, and the antenna is crap anyway, so..."

"Is there anything I can do to help, maybe?" Samantha asked, slowly pulling up a seat beside Soraya.

"You can keep me company, if that is alright," she offered with a smile.

"I'd love to," Samantha said while fingering a small blue capacitor. "So what does this do?"

DAY THREE

"Well, that's it. The rest of the food was eaten last night." Vanessa tossed an empty can onto the deck. It rolled a few feet before coming to rest against a growing pile of garbage.

"I saw some fish swimming around earlier. Maybe we can make a net with our shirts or something. What do you think?" Lillian suggested while nudging Ayn with an elbow.

"Go for it, guys. I'm going to go lie down for a while. I'm not feeling so well." Ayn slowly made her way across the deck.

"Is she alright?" Lillian asked.

"She's just hungry. We all are. Bernie's been trying to fish since before the engine broke. No joy." Rachel tossed an empty can into the water. She watched it float away, convinced the garbage would find land long before they would.

"Aaaargh," Damon screamed as he fired his sidearm into the ocean. While a cathartic release of sorts for the young man, the display was merely an annoyance for the others trapped alongside him.

"Relax, buddy. You're not going to catch any fish that way," Bernie suggested, upbeat as usual.

"Who knows? Maybe he'll get lucky and hit something," Isaac suggested as he passed with a box of garbage. "Lord knows we're due for some good fortune."

"Have at it then. Nothing else to do, right?" Bernie shrugged. "You want to give me a hand with this?"

"Sure, like you said, what else have I got to do?"

The men disappeared below deck as Radzinski leaned in for his own bit of advice. "We may need those bullets later, kid. Holster that thing. My advice, you got frustrations to let out, pick one of these sorry sacks and work them over. That's what I would do."

Damon nodded in agreement while scanning the crowd of frightened survivors and smiled. The thought of pounding on anyone of them appealed to him immensely. He already had a few in mind as he focused his gaze on Samantha over at the other end of the vessel. She too was scanning the horizon for land.

Damon and Radzinski's exchange and quiet laughter did not go unnoticed by Markus. If this situation didn't change soon, Damon and his new friend might become a problem.

DAY FOUR

Most of the group rambled about the deck. Gear and thick, impractical clothing days ago shed in an attempt to find relief from the heat and blistering sun. Even the soldiers stopped carrying their weapons, save for sidearms and sheathed knives. "What was the point?" became the consensus. Was a crazed civilian going to orchestrate a mutiny? Then what? Where would they even go? Four days adrift, and for the most part, arguments were a nonstarter. Again, what was the point? Most would agree. Not everyone saw it that way, though. Lancaster paced the deck. Fresh wounds still healing from the most recent beating he took less than a week ago stung in the salty breeze. No doubt adding to his own chagrin over current circumstances.

"You people and your plans. Making decisions for the lot of us has led this group to ruin," Lancaster announced.

"Now wait a second, Mr. Mayor, if it wasn't for the soldiers, we'd all be dead by now. We owe them our lives," said Elliot.

"You don't know that, son." Lancaster leered at a few of Miller's unit across the way. "For all we know, those creatures would never have set foot in Pepperbush if not for these so-called heroes leading them straight to our doorstep."

Soraya stood within striking distance. "Believe what you choose, old man. I know what I saw, for your part anyway."

"You saw nothing. You have no idea what you're even talking about. Delusional, the lot of you," Lancaster shouted.

"You left your family for dead. You are a coward. Marisol should have killed you." Soraya's clenched fists spoke volumes as she inched toward the man.

"Please," Lancaster grumbled. He waved her off as if the petite Israeli was no more than a bothersome fly. "I don't have to take this, especially not from some half-illiterate, Third World sand—" Lancaster stopped short of finishing his insult. He wasn't accustomed to losing his composure; the feeling was humbling.

Jeremiah stepped forward. "By all means, continue. Please don't stop on my account, Donald."

From Lancaster's vantage point, he had no idea the medic was observing from only a few steps behind him. "What I was trying to say was—" Lancaster stammered before being cut short.

Jeremiah continued. "Oh, believe me. We all know what you were trying to say, Donald. It's been written all over your face since the night we arrived in your precious little town. I'm sure you're not the first bigot Soraya has encountered. Unfortunately, even in these harsh times, you probably won't be the last."

Marisol quickly led the former mayor toward the darkened confines of the boat's interior. "Get your ass below deck, Lancaster. I've heard just about enough out of you today." She shoved him toward the stairs.

"It's far too bright out here, anyway," Lancaster retorted on his way below, implying that it was *his* destination in the first place.

"Everyone alright over here?" Marisol asked with a yawn. The commotion had stirred her from a nap.

"It would take a greater man than Donald Lancaster to unnerve me, but thank you all the same," Jeremiah answered.

"He is nothing. No problem. Maybe *I* beat him too next time, yes?" Soraya added, and the two women shared a much-needed laugh under the hot sun. Even Jeremiah allowed himself a smile, slight as it was.

Below deck in Casandra's makeshift quarters, she was finally awake and sitting upright. Her fever passed in the night, much to the relief of Bernie and also Aiko, who was running dangerously low on antibiotics. Bernie fashioned a sling out of an old sheet that, as it turned out, made for a horrible fishing net. Casandra kept her arm propped to her chest, keeping as much weight off the damaged limb as possible.

"I feel much better. It almost feels like I just passed the worst part of a cold. It's all smooth sailing from here, right?" She tried to chuckle, but her face contorted and her free arm shot to her wound immediately. "Okay, that sucked."

"Take it easy, girl," Bernie cautioned. "Keep that up and you'll be passed out again in a heartbeat."

"Yeah, I think you're right." Casandra carefully lay back down.

She looked up to Bernie, who already had a bit of water and a damp cloth at the ready. She held his hand in hers and smiled. "Thank you, Bernie. For everything."

"Think nothing of it, sweetheart. Now, why don't you get some rest?"

"Rest? I just woke up. What I need is a bath. I feel disgusting and I reek. If you even try to lie and say you can't smell it, I'll smack you." She waved her hand in front of her nose.

"Not gonna lie, girl, you are getting pretty ripe. Tell ya what, I'll head topside and fetch a bucket of seawater. See if we can't get you cleaned up. But only if you stay put. Deal? I don't need you falling down in here with those nonexistent sea legs of yours."

"Aye-aye, Captain." She coughed before pinching her nose closed. "Hurry back. I don't know how much more of this I can take."

DAY FIVE

"You really need to drink something, honey. Come on, help me a little here." Vanessa desperately tried to get Ayn to drink some water, but the girl was unresponsive. An occasional moan or a few incomprehensible words were the only indication she still lived.

Lillian stood nearby, arms crossed tightly against her chest, taking in the scene.

"Oh, man. She looks bad. Is there anything I can do to help?" Ryan asked.

"There's nothing *to* do," said Lillian.

"I'm fucking starving!" Damon shouted. "I told you getting on this boat was a stupid fucking idea."

"Oh, save it, man. Nobody wants to hear that shit today," Markus replied, already annoyed with the conversation.

"Just take it easy, Damon," Samantha calmly suggested. "Don't overexert yourself. The stress will only make it worse."

"Fuck you, bitch. Nobody asked you," Damon snapped.

"No. You know what? Fuck *you*, Damon." Samantha stood her ground this time. "This was a stupid idea? So what was *your* grand plan to save us all? Oh, that's right. You didn't have a plan. You never do. You've never had one single positive thing to say about anything anyone does to contribute. You're nothing but a waste of space and a drain on resources. You're an asshole, Damon. If we all die out here, I hope you go first. At least it'll spare the rest of us your mouth." Samantha turned her eyes from him, the bleak endless sea a far better sight.

"Guys, guys, calm down. All you're doing is wasting your energy," Elliot suggested as he sauntered by. "All of us just need to relax."

"Go fuck yourself, Elliot," Markus replied.

High above the deck in the wheelhouse Miller leaned into the window, resting his head against his forearm. The group's safety weighed heavily on him, always. The very real possibility of every one of them dying out here adrift, far from land, couldn't be ignored. The group was beginning to unravel. That was plain enough to see, though he would never admit it to the others, he wished Takashi was still alive. Takashi might not have had a solution to their current predicament, but at least the burden of leadership—a task he never asked for, much less wanted—would be off of Miller's shoulders. He observed the comings and goings-on the deck below from the relative privacy of the wheelhouse. The darkened room's contrast with the brightness on deck offered its occupants a certain advantage over those outside.

Circumstances had grown exponentially worse since the group fled Pepperbush. It seemed no more than a handful of days would pass between someone else dying on the road, and it all led to this: stranded on a boat with the slow death of dehydration looming on the horizon. For more than an hour, Miller watched as Bernie tried in vain to fish with a makeshift net; the only proper net they had drifted away days ago. Elliot and Ryan tried to use the thing unsupervised but with calamitous results.

Of the group, some took advantage of the calm and enjoyed the occasional breeze while others huddled in a corner, obviously terrified. At the front of the boat, Radzinski sat motionless, alone staring off into the horizon as if land would magically appear through sheer willpower. There was no love lost between the two, and Radzinski still had it out for him; that was clear. Miller was far beyond caring at this point. His only concern regarding Radzinski was the possibility of the man pointing out Miller's shortcomings as de facto leader. A splintering of the group would be devastating now.

Miller listened to the door open behind him but didn't care to look around and greet whoever it was. *Why bother?* he thought. Most likely they would just have more questions he didn't have answers to, anyway. Marisol entered, followed by Aiko, who gently closed the door behind her and joined Miller by the window. She rubbed her stomach as she leaned in for a closer look at the deck below.

Miller noticed her discomfort. His friend's seeming distress helped him regain focus. "You feeling okay, Aiko?"

"Who? Me? Oh, I'm fine, Miller. Just hungry is all." Aiko stopped fiddling with her stomach and moved to the wrinkles in her tank top, smoothing them out with the palm of her hand as if that was her intent all along.

"So how are we looking out there?"

"Well, half of them haven't even bothered to get up and walk around yet today. Obviously, that's not good."

"I don't blame them. Honestly, I'm feeling pretty weak myself."

"A few more days of this and things will start to get serious," Marisol suggested.

"Things already are serious." Aiko gestured below to Ayn. "The blonde still won't drink. She's almost unresponsive at this point," Aiko informed him. "They carried her out to the deck this morning, hoping the breeze or the sun would magically snap her out of it."

"She looks awful. Is there anything you can do for her?" Marisol seemed despondent.

"Unfortunately, no. Without fresh water and a minimal amount of protein, her condition will continue to deteriorate."

"And the others?" Miller asked.

"It's hard to say. It really depends on their individual health and mental fortitude. If they think they're going to die out here, chances are, they will. Obviously, age plays a role as well."

"Jesus, Ayn can't be a day older than twenty-five and she's obviously the worst of the bunch. What's that say for the rest of us?" Marisol took a step back from the window.

"Most likely she wasn't eating much these past few weeks, and just by looking at her, I'd say she wasn't keeping herself properly hydrated, either. Now it's caught up with the girl," said Aiko. "Expect to see more of this soon."

Marisol rubbed down the raised hairs on her arms. A sudden chill took hold of her when she heard Aiko's dire prediction. "Well, I'm going to go see if I can get these people up and moving, try to find something for them to do at least." Marisol left the wheelhouse. Alone in the stairwell, Marisol had a moment to compose herself. Her heart raced as she slowly got her breathing under control. *Was this what it was like to have a panic attack?* she thought. Whatever came over her was gone as fast as it reared its head. *Never, not me. I am stronger than this*, she told herself as she straightened her posture before exiting onto the blinding deck.

"Ayn's not going to make it, is she?" Miller asked.

"No, sir, she's not. Another day, two at most." Aiko had no inclination of softening the blow.

"One more."

"Sir?"

"One more dead civilian under my watch, Aiko."

"It's not your fault, Miller. None of this is. These people are alive right now because of you. Never forget that."

"I appreciate it, Aiko—your optimism, that is. Even if I don't share the sentiment." Miller turned his back to the window, resting against it for support.

"Keep your head up, sir. Things have a way of working themselves out. You'll see," she offered with a hand upon his shoulder.

"Do you really believe that?"

"I have to, but does it matter? If we are to die out here, do you want to spend your last days depressed and second-guessing yourself? You're still stuck on a boat in the middle of the ocean. Think about it." Aiko left as quietly as she entered but not before leaving Miller with a few things to consider.

In the corner, Soraya stirred, awoken by their conversation. She and Miller had been taking turns sleeping on a small cushioned platform that doubled as the lid over a small storage cabinet.

"I must have dozed off. What were you guys talking about?" Soraya stretched and let out a big yawn as she reached for her pants.

"Nothing worth repeating." Miller returned to his vigil over the deck.

DAY SIX

"Accept it. This is the lord's will. Everything will go much easier that way. Believe me," Isaac preached.

"No, I refuse to believe I'm going to die on this boat. It doesn't make any sense. We lived through hell only to die of starvation and thirst in the middle of the goddamn ocean?" Marisol replied.

"We can't begin to comprehend God's plan, ma'am."

"Oh, will you save it, Isaac? If you think he put us in this situation after we lived through Pepperbush, your sense of humor is more fucked than his."

"Have faith, ma'am. That's all he asks."

"I do have faith, Isaac, just not in him. What's gotten into you?" Marisol walked away, lest her temper get the better of her. After all, Isaac was a friend, and he was only trying to help, in his own way.

"Where did the sudden sermon come from?" asked Rachel.

"Isaac likes to dabble in the good book," She replied. "From time to time."

"We're really going to die out here, aren't we?" Lillian asked.

"I'd like to think not, but I just don't know anymore," Vanessa replied.

"I'm so tired."

"Me too, Lily. Try to stay awake, though. It's better if we sleep in shifts. Too many of the others are sleeping already as it is. Don't worry, Lily. I won't let anything happen to you." Vanessa pulled her close. "I promise."

Lillian lay in Vanessa's arms. She loved the feeling of Vanessa's fingers running through her hair, and for a fleeting moment, it reminded her of better times. She closed her eyes and listened to the waves lap against the side of the boat. She felt the warm sun against her skin, and for a time, she imagined all was well with the world and she could be at peace with whatever lay ahead. "I'm not afraid, you know. Of dying, I mean. If it's my time, I'm okay with it. I'm just glad I'm here with you, Vanessa." Lillian wrapped her arms tighter around Vanessa's waist. "I love you," she whispered.

"I know, sweetheart. I know." Vanessa leaned in and kissed Lillian on the top of her head. Tears welled in her eyes. It finally sunk in for her; they *were* in fact going to die out here. For the first time since her husband's death, Vanessa finally allowed herself to *feel* again. Here and now, on this boat to nowhere. It wasn't even a conscious decision at all, not something she pondered at night; it simply manifested without her even realizing it. These new emotions budding for someone who only a few weeks ago she considered nothing more than a friend and coworker were overwhelming. She was in love with Lillian, deeply, but she dare not speak it aloud under such hopeless circumstances. Instead, she sat in silence, tears streaming down her cheeks as she held Lillian under the warm sun.

Samantha lay in Markus's lap, knees curled up as far as they would go, her eyes raw from occasional bouts of tears. She kept a hand in close to her chest, the other clenching his baggy jeans tightly. Markus leaned back against the side of the boat, gazing off at wispy clouds, his lips dry and cracked, eyes regularly blinking against the light. He strained against the brightness to keep his eyes open. If he closed them for too long, they would never open again; he was sure of it.

"Look at them all just lying there, ready to die. Fuck that. Not me." Radzinski's contempt for his shipmates was etched all over his face. "They're pathetic. Every last one of them." He spat in the direction of a group lying on the deck. The wind took it and blew his mucus overboard before it could find a target.

"What do you expect? They all look up to that pussy, Miller," Damon added. "That shit's contagious, man. Look at my boy over there all hugged up on that redheaded bitch like he's checked out already. A few months ago, he would have been right here with us, plotting against these bitches. Man, fuck these people."

"You're going to have to let him go, kid. Your boy's weak like the rest of them. You gotta be hard to survive this shit. No time for making nice, not anymore."

"I hear you, man. It's just... We been through a lot of shit together, you know? And not just this whole end-of-the-world bullshit, either. I mean we put in time on the streets. We always had each other's backs. That's bond right there, man. That's blood." Damon insisted.

"He's not your blood. He's a lost cause. Sticking with him is only going to get you dead."

"I don't know, man. You might be right. I gotta look out for myself now." Damon could barely stand the sight of Markus anymore.

"I've seen it before, Damon. Shit gets too real and people want to curl up and die. Trust me, we'll get off this boat one way or another, and when we do, the first chance we get, we're out of here." Radzinski spat again, this time finding his mark on a sleeping Elliot.

Miller leaned on the glass overlooking the deck. He spent more time in this position than either him or those closest to him would admit. Soraya lay on the makeshift bed, fingers interlocked behind her head.

Begrudgingly, she took the spot as her own, as Miller insisted on sleeping on the floor. Neither had the strength to argue.

"Do you mind if I ask you something, Soraya?" Miller asked sheepishly.

"Of course not, Miller. You can ask me anything," Soraya replied as she sat up, a little flush.

"Back at the cabin with Tobias," he began.

"I know. He was a good man."

"Yes, he was," he started again. "When no one else stepped up to do what needed to be done, why did *you*? I mean, you were so adamant about them being treated with respect. We've seen so many die, yet there was something different about Tobias and Tommy."

"It was the boy," Soraya said after a pause. "I see families ripped apart every day back home. Innocent children killed or maimed for bullshit of others. I do not like this. Children should not suffer for our sins."

"Thank you."

"Miller?" she asked, perplexed, as she wasn't yet finished her thoughts.

"I couldn't have done that. What you did back there," he said. "Hauling their bodies out of the rubble and doing what was necessary. Especially the boy. I would have just left them there without even shooting them, so thank you. Thank you so much."

Miller collapsed to the floor, landing on his knees. A wall finally came down. Soraya rushed to his side. Miller reached around her waist, held on with all he had, and cried like he hadn't since he was a child.

"It is going to be okay, Miller. I am here." Soraya caressed his head and ran her fingers through his hair. She held him close but kept a watchful eye on the deck below. She would maintain his vigil for as long as necessary.

DAY SEVEN

"I just heard from Lily that Ayn died overnight. They've got her covered up out on deck." Samantha bit her lip until it bled. She didn't mean to. She didn't even mean to walk straight into Markus, but she kept moving forward, anyway. He caught her. Though his grip was loose enough for her to back away, she didn't. Samantha just stood there. So did Markus, the pair of them gazing at separate points in the dim living quarters of the boat. One of them stared hard at a broken clock, the other listlessly at the floor.

"Damn," Markus whispered. "She must have been way worse off than she was letting on, huh?" He gripped the banister tight. If he could yank it free and swing it around, he would. *Goddamit*, he thought. *What the fuck happened?*

Not a word was spoken as they found each other's hands. It became a game of who would silently beg the other for support first. He lost, as the cracks in his once hard exterior began to show.

"I don't remember seeing her eat anything. Maybe that's why," Samantha finally offered, in her own way pleading for affirmation.

Head down, she pulled on Markus's shirt. He had no relief to offer, and she knew it. He reciprocated as best he could, pulling her hand close to his chest. Finally, she relented. It was time to straighten up. With a blushed smile, she slowly and slightly pulled away from Markus. "I'm sorry," she began.

Markus wiped a tear from her cheek, returning a wide smile of his own. He brushed damp hair from her face and was about to offer a few words of encouragement as Damon piped up, seemingly never too far away at the most inopportune time.

"Oh yeah, you don't remember what she ate. What was the last thing I ate then?" Damon demanded.

"What's your problem? Who asked you anyway?" Samantha fully pulled away from Markus.

"You whine and you make shit up. That's my problem. You don't know what killed her, so don't act like you do."

"You know what? Go fuck yourself, Damon. I don't have to put up with your crap." Samantha stormed off.

"Samantha, wait." Markus tried to stop her, but she yanked her arm free. He watched her disappear into the sun-drenched deck before he returned his attention to Damon. "What is up with you, man? That shit was uncalled for. You fuck with her every chance you get."

"That country bitch is making you soft. That's why. Back home, you wouldn't give a fuck about that bitch or any of these other chumps."

"Country bitch?" Markus was incensed. "She's from Seattle, for Christ's sake. You know, that's the problem right there. We're *not* back home. We'll never *be* back home. The sooner you get your head around that, the sooner you can be of help to the rest of us and not such a dick all the time. Now excuse me, I think I need some fresh air. It stinks down here."

"She's playing you, son. No way that bitch likes your black ass. That cunt ain't shit." Damon insisted on having the final say on the matter.

Markus turned and landed a left hook on Damon's jaw. It would have incapacitated someone not accustomed to fighting. Instead, it sent Damon flying back into the corner, where he landed on his ass.

"Enough!" Markus shouted with finality before turning to leave the small confines of the cabin for the deck above.

Radzinski entered the room, obviously eavesdropping from the small corridor. "Your boy seems to have his priorities all fucked up, huh?" he commented as he helped Damon to his feet.

"Man, that bitch is fucking with his head. That's all," Damon replied, rubbing his jaw.

"Ignore it. This shit we're living in right now, right here, it brings out the best in people. Unfortunately for your friend, his best is being a pussy."

"That's what's up. You're probably right. He ain't been the same since we stumbled into that backward-ass town."

"Backward-ass town. Ha. You can say that again. These people have no idea how to take care of themselves. Shit, if it wasn't for me and my unit, none of them would have made it out of that shithole alive."

"You're right about that. All these motherfuckers do is whine and talk shit. Motherfucker, don't talk about it. Be about it."

"Words to live by, my man. I can see you've got drive. Same as me. People like us know the score, and if it comes down to it, I'll leave every one of these motherfuckers to die," Radzinski said with a shrug.

"I heard that." Damon nodded, offering up a fist bump.

"You're alright, kid." Radzinski returned the gesture. "I got your six. Stick with me. We'll make it through this shit just fine."

As the day wore on, the group slowly gathered out on the main deck. Something needed to be done about the lack of rations.

"We've been drifting for days, out of food almost as long, and unless by some miracle it rains, our water will all be gone by tonight." Nisha looked to the clear blue sky. Not a cloud in sight as she shielded her eyes from the blinding sun with the palm of her hand.

"I've been trying to fish. It ain't working, man," Bernie added, a tangle of discarded clothes at his feet, his makeshift net a complete failure.

"Of course you're not going to catch anything. We don't have any bait," Elliot added.

"Anything less than a shark and we're going to starve to death out here anyway. Look at all of us." Ryan pointed out the mass of people on deck.

"We need something substantial to eat," Jeremiah added. "Otherwise, when—*if*—we see the shore, we'll be too weak to swim to it, anyway."

"We'll have to swim?" Nisha asked nervously.

"Possibly," Jeremiah replied.

"There is another option," Radzinski began. "I know you've thought of it, too, Jerry. That analytical mind of yours is always ticking away at problems."

"What are you saying?" Vanessa asked.

"I'm not going to win any brownie points for this, and most of you don't like me anyway, so fuck it." Radzinski looked around at the curious faces. "We should eat the girl," he suggested.

"Who, Ayn? You can't be serious," Ryan said immediately.

"Absolutely not," Isaac said.

"What the fuck?" Elliot asked.

"I ain't eating no person." Bernie folded his arms tightly across his chest.

"How could you even say that about her?" Samantha began to well up.

"It *is* an option," Vanessa added.

"Vanessa, how could you? I can't believe you would agree with this," Samantha protested as the others grew silent.

"I'm not saying I want to or that I even would if it came down to it, just that it *is* an option. Look, we might all die out here, but if Ayn can help keep us alive a little longer, that might be all the time we need to get back to shore. I didn't know her that well, but I think she would want us to live, no matter what it takes," Vanessa explained as she gently pulled Ayn's hair out of her eyes, trying to make it look nice again.

Samantha began to cry. "I can't, I can't, I can't fucking do this. I won't!" Samantha broke down, beating her fist into her legs.

Markus put his arm around her and pulled her in. "Shh, it's okay. You don't have to do anything you don't want to. No one's going to make you do anything. I won't let them," he whispered.

Samantha buried her face in his chest. She pulled part of his shirt over her eyes. "I won't do it," she sobbed.

"I'll do it," Isabelle offered, emotionless.

"Mom, no," Lillian protested.

"This isn't happening." Ryan grabbed his head with both hands, and his pacing of the deck quickened.

"Wait a minute, Izzy. Let's talk about this." Nisha stepped toward Isabelle.

Before anyone could stop her, Isabelle sliced deep into Ayn's thigh, carving out a large chunk of muscle. She held the bloody flesh out at arm's length, presenting it up to the group. "Who wants the first piece?" Isabelle offered, waving the piece of meat around. With no one leaping at the chance to be first, Isabelle opened her mouth to take the first bite.

"Put it down now!" Aiko slapped the piece of meat from Isabelle's hand. The flank skidded off the side of the boat, disappearing into the dark water below.

"Now what did you do that for, Aiko? If you don't want to eat, don't eat. Should we all die 'cause this creeps you out?" Radzinski said, getting into the middle of it.

"You cannot eat that meat," Aiko insisted.

"I'll cut you a piece, too. There's plenty for everyone," Isabelle offered.

"What the fuck is wrong with you, Mom?" Lillian screamed in disbelief, tears finally bursting forth.

"Fuck it. Cut away, girl." Radzinski laughed.

Isabelle proceeded to slice off another piece, now from Ayn's calf. With this portion, she cut deeper, exposing white bone beneath. Pinpricks of blood dotted the wound, slowly forming minuscule droplets that splashed into a tiny pool at Isabelle's knees.

"Jesus fucking Christ!" Ryan vomited over the side of the boat. Yellow bile from an empty stomach stained his shirt. He turned back to the conversation and leaned his back hard against the side of the boat, sliding down to the deck and onto his ass.

"About time someone wised up around here. We are *going* to die if we don't do this, people," Radzinski said to the mostly horrified group.

"What are you doing to her? Stop it, please!" Samantha screamed.

"I cannot believe my eyes!" Lancaster shouted. "Is there no end to your people's madness?"

"It's not madness." Marisol put it as bluntly as she could, lest anyone not fathom the severity of their situation. "This is fast becoming a decision we're all going to have to live with if we want to survive."

"I don't know if I can do this." Nisha covered her mouth.

"I ain't doing it. No goddamn way," said Bernie.

"First time I'm up on deck walking around since we set sail, and *this* is what you guys are talking about? Wake me when it's over." Casandra ambled her way back through the crowd. Bernie rushed to her side to help guide her below deck.

"Enough! Stop! Stop it! Quiet, all of you!" The ordinarily composed Jeremiah yelled, nearly irate, bringing everyone to attention. "We cannot eat this," Jeremiah said with an ire unbecoming of the man.

"Oh, here we go again. Jerry, of all people, you *know* we have to do this." Radzinski was nearly pleading.

"See, I told you this is wrong," Samantha whimpered.

"Oh, shut up, crybaby." Damon shook his head.

"I said quiet! All of you!" Jeremiah raised his voice for the second time, eyes fixed on Damon, who quickly looked away.

"He's right, people. Let the man speak," Miller said, finally joining the discussion. Soraya stood at his side, fingering her kukri, her eyes transfixed on Radzinski.

"If you'll allow me to explain, please." Jeremiah sighed, exhausted from the outburst. "We know next to nothing about the incubation period of this disease. We all know that in a few hours Ayn will turn into one of those things. What we don't know is how exactly the infection works. If we eat of her flesh now, there's a strong possibility we could become infected as well."

"But she wasn't bitten," said Vanessa.

"I don't think that matters. Too little is known about this disease to make assumptions of that magnitude. Not with so many lives on the line," Jeremiah insisted.

"You don't know that for sure, Jerry," Radzinski said.

"That's exactly my point, John. I don't know that at all," Jeremiah replied, his voice rising again with each word.

"I say we tie her up then. If she hasn't changed by morning, she's not going to change," Radzinski suggested.

"In this heat, the meat would be rotten by then. Inedible," Jeremiah responded.

"So we're damned if we do and damned if we don't!" Radzinski shouted, hands in the air. "What do you suggest we do then? Just sit here and die?"

"For Christ's sake, just throw her overboard already," Ryan pleaded.

"How about I throw you overboard, runt? Shut up. Tell you what, Jerry, I'll watch her all night. Come morning, I'll get rid of her either way. At least we'll know," Radzinski offered.

"We'll know what?" Lillian asked.

"That the next one of you motherfuckers who dies out here is going to keep me alive," Radzinski replied, close enough to the girl she could feel his breath on her face.

Vanessa immediately stepped between the two and pushed Radzinski back a few paces.

"Get the fuck away from her!" she demanded, fists clenched.

The group continued to argue. Most of the survivors came down on one side or the other. The shouting voices abruptly went silent as a loud splash interrupted their argument. A bloody trail led to the edge of the deck.

"It's over. We ain't eating nobody. Not today." Markus wiped his bloodied hands on his pants as he reentered the group.

"Who the fuck are you to decide that for the rest of us?" Damon yelled.

"I made a call. Deal with it." Markus pushed past him.

"You made a call? You stupid motherfucker. You made a call?" Radzinski charged Markus.

"Come on. You want some, soldier boy?" Markus raised his fists, prepared for a fight.

Trained soldier or not, Markus had a few moves of his own and was about to show the enraged Radzinski just how they settled problems back home when three gunshots stopped everyone in their tracks.

"That's enough!" Miller shouted. "I've had it with all of you! Radzinski, stand the fuck down! Jeremiah said we can't eat it, and we *are* going to listen to him. What's done is done. This ends now. Everyone involved in this bullshit, fall out to separate parts of the boat, now!" he commanded, directly in Radzinski's face.

Slowly, the crowd dispersed, breaking off into familiar groups—as much as they could, anyway, on the not exactly spacious fishing boat.

Hours later, after the sun had long since gone down and anger brought about by slow starvation gave way to cooler heads, the survivors of Pepperbush again spread out. Each small faction claimed its own spot on the boat. Some remained below deck while others tried their best to remain calm out under the stars.

Exhausted from the day's drama, Samantha leaned her head in Markus's lap, hardly awake. "We forgot to shoot her."

"Come again?" Markus asked gently.

"We were all so tired and hungry and fighting, no one shot Ayn before we threw her in the water. She's at the bottom of the ocean, one of those things now," Samantha said calmly, not screaming, not crying, merely spent.

"Don't think about that. That's not going to do anybody any good. Besides, we don't even know if that's true. Just try to get some sleep, okay?" Markus peered off into the dark water. The moonlight cast eerie shadows along the boat's wake, and he couldn't help but wonder if what Samantha said was true.

Elsewhere on deck, Vanessa and Lillian sat alone, away from the prying eyes of so many desperate people.

"She hasn't said one fucking word to me since Dad and Tommy died, and the first thing she does is cut off Ayn's leg and try to give me a piece. What the hell is going on with her, Vanessa?" Lillian asked, racked with frustration.

"Your mother's having a rough time with what happened, Lily." Vanessa had no idea what to say. The truth of the matter was that she was just as shocked over Isabelle's actions as Lillian was.

"That was my family too, you know," Lillian responded.

"I know." Vanessa attempted to change the subject. "You want to know a secret?" she whispered.

"What's that?" Lillian asked suspiciously.

"You are *way* tougher than your mom. Seriously, you've got a better head on your shoulders than half of these people."

"Please don't be condescending, Nessa."

"I'm not. I swear. Look." Vanessa gestured for Lillian to look around at the various groups, some still debating the day's events, others already sleeping. Vanessa kissed Lillian on the cheek. "Let's get some sleep."

The two curled up under a blanket in their corner of the boat.

"Thank you," Lillian whispered, still unsure of what point Vanessa was trying to get across. She knew good intent was there, and that was enough.

Isabelle sat alone under the moonlight, peering off into the darkness. Her feet dangled over the edge of the boat. Following this afternoon's episode, no one seemed interested in speaking with her. Unaffected by her companions' lack of understanding, Isabelle stared blankly at the bright full moon. She fiddled with the inside of her dress for a moment before gently pulling a fist-sized piece of meat from one of the folds. Dried blood held it fast to the fabric as she tore it away. Tiny pieces of flesh ripped away from the larger chunk like a scab, leaving small pieces of meat behind on the material. Isabelle raised the flesh to her face, staring at it intently before biting down and chewing furiously into the hours' old drying meat. A large strip tore away from the flank, making it a more manageable piece, which was easily chewed and swallowed. She continued eating, savoring each mouthful. The center of the meat, still moist and almost warm, gently glided down her throat. It was much easier to swallow than the dry outer portion. Alone beneath the stars, Isabelle consumed all that remained of Ayn.

Day Eight

Throughout the day and long into the night, the *Emerald Star* rocked violently, listing from side to side and nearly capsizing with every wave. A relentless barrage of enormous walls of water assaulted the boat. What started as their first glimpse of hope in more than a week with lifesaving rains quickly escalated into a full-fledged hurricane. The group huddled below deck, holding onto anything that might help them withstand the storm. Yet another wave flooded the cabin, threatening to drown the nearly unconscious occupants. The tempest's fury battered the small boat relentlessly.

A wall of water smashed into the bow, up over the deck and into the living quarters of the boat, where the survivors were trying to weather the storm. Those nearest to the entrance were flung into the back of the boat. Unable to fight the strength of the waves, they were knocked into each other as they smashed into the walls of the cabin.

Another wave hit from the port side, sending the boat over on its edge. Everyone in the cabin was thrown violently into the ceiling. The entirety of the group, along with the contents of the cabin, washed back and forth from one wall to another as the boat listed from side to side. The survivors were helpless in the pitch-black darkness. Every few minutes, a flash of lightning would illuminate their surroundings just enough to prepare for incoming bodies and debris.

CHAPTER ELEVEN

CHAPTER ELEVEN

Marooned

Waves gently lapped at the side of the boat. A rhythmic, repeating thud followed by the strain of a water-logged rope moving with the ebb and flow of the tide revealed the unmistakable sound of floating debris still tied to the ship. Unable to drift away in the current, the detritus pulled away as far as it was able, only to be yanked back again to bang against the side of the vessel. Constant squawking among the seagulls helped stir Vanessa from her slumber. Hot sun beat down on her face as she began to stir. She licked her dry, cracked lips and squinted hard against the sun's rays as she awoke. Lillian lay on top of her in a tight embrace as if holding on for dear life. The girl was breathing. Somehow, they survived the night, even if by all appearances they had been washed out onto the deck, narrowly spared being carried overboard, it seemed. Vanessa managed to sit upright but was careful not to wake her companion. Though she was grateful to be alive, they still had the reality of no food and water to deal with. She slowly twisted from side to side until her back was straightened and more comfortable against the side of the boat. The sun was blinding; she blinked a few times, finally adjusting to the light before peering around, confused. She and Lillian, it appeared, were alone in the boat and with her wits quickly returning, it appeared the boat wasn't moving.

"Here, have some water." Rachel sprang up over the side of the vessel.

"Oh fuck, Rachel!" Vanessa jumped, rousing Lillian from slumber. "You scared the shit out of me." Vanessa snatched the water bottle from Rachel, who, oddly enough, seemed to be standing outside of the boat, resting her arms on its side at eye level with her.

"Careful, not so fast. You'll make yourself sick," Rachel suggested.

"Wait a minute. We're not moving. We're on land?" Vanessa asked, handing the bottle to Lillian, who proceeded to gulp the nourishing fluid just as fast as her friend.

"Where are we?" Lillian asked. Water dripped from her lips as she greedily took in the fluid.

"We, sleepyhead, are on a deserted island. Paradise, if you will." Rachel, arms extended, spun around as if to show off property to a potential buyer. "Okay, not really paradise, but we *are* on an island." She picked up a handful of sand and threw it in the air. The granules dispersed in the breeze, spraying the boat with a million tiny projectiles.

"Is it just us? Are we all that made it? Where?" Vanessa coughed. "Where is everybody else?"

Rachel smiled wide. "Amazingly, alive and all accounted for."

"How the hell?" Vanessa stood on the deck. Finally on her feet, she realized the boat was resting on quite an angle. She could walk easily enough, but a slick board and an ill-timed step would certainly put her on her ass.

"I don't have the faintest idea how we survived, if that's what you're asking," replied Rachel. "And honestly, I couldn't care less. I'll take it."

"So then where *is* everyone?" Lillian asked.

"Well, we found an abandoned campsite just up the beach that had some buckets spread out collecting rainwater. They're overflowing. Whoever set them up never came back. There's some food, too, a handful of canned goods, and some not-so-ripe fruit. It's not much, but it's something." Rachel couldn't hold back her childlike grin if she tried. "Most everyone is up there licking their wounds. A few are out scouting the island."

"Thank God. I never thought I'd be so excited for water. Rainwater at that," Vanessa commented.

"Oh, it gets better, ladies. They're cooking up a horse. An honest-to-goodness horse. We are going to eat *so* good today."

"A horse?" Vanessa was bewildered. "Where the hell did you guys find a horse?"

"The island is full of them. Bernie took it down. One shot, too. Very impressive." Rachel extended her arms as if she were holding an invisible rifle.

"Well, that *is* good news. What do you think about that, Lily?" she asked with a smile. Vanessa offered the girl a hand up. Lillian accepted but didn't rise. She remained on the deck, holding Vanessa's hand against her shoulder.

"That's awesome, guys," Lillian responded. "Where's my mom, Rachel? Have you seen her?"

"She's up near the tents with everyone else, sweetie." Rachel's demeanor faded.

"Is she still acting like a lunatic?" Lillian tried to force a smile.

"Well, honey, she's back to the thousand-yard stare. Sorry," Rachel said. "Hasn't said a word all morning."

"Thanks, Rachel. Just knowing she made it helps a little, I guess."

"Hey, it's something, right, kiddo? Look, everyone's still getting their bearings. That's why we let you sleep. So take your time. We're not going anywhere anytime soon. Come on up whenever you're ready." Rachel returned up the beach and headed toward the tents.

Lillian strained against the blinding light, trying to pick out the camp on the horizon. All she could make out were black shapes against a white background. Sparse trees and dune grasses dotted the landscape for miles, it seemed. If a camp was up there somewhere, she would just have to take Rachel's word for it. "She just left me here sleeping, Vanessa. What if it wasn't safe yet? If those things showed up while we were asleep, would she have left me *then*, too?" Lillian finally stood from her partially shadowed spot, stretching the whole way up. She shook her head back and forth and blinked her eyes furiously.

"Hey, don't think about things like that. You're safe with me. I won't let anything happen to you. I promise. Besides, look over there." Vanessa pointed out the top of a nearby sand dune. The silhouette of Sam's worn-out cowboy hat and a rifle was unmistakable, even beneath the blinding sun.

"You've got people here that care about you, Lillian, and not just me." Vanessa waved to Sam in the distance, who tipped his hat in response.

"Oh, I know, and I appreciate it. Really. I'm just pissed. What the hell is she thinking lately?" Lillian kicked a discarded life vest into the waves.

"When you're ready, if you want, I'll help you talk to her," Vanessa added as she wiped a tear from Lillian's eye. "Come on, let's go get something to eat. I'm starving."

Inland, about sixty yards from the shipwreck of the *Emerald Star*, the group gathered about an abandoned campground. Three tents remained mostly intact. Their owners had apparently left them behind in a hasty retreat from the small island. Two more tents lay farther up the beach, tangled and twisted into the bushes. The camp had been left in disarray. Old cooking utensils and a few pots and pans were scattered about. A few articles of clothing not blown away from the hurricane still hung on their lines. Whoever abandoned this camp did so in a hurry and most likely left with only the shirts on their backs. A small firepit centered the camp. Bernie wasted no time putting it to use in preparation for a long-awaited meal.

A massive horse leg roasted on a makeshift spit. Flames danced around the meat, and juices sizzled as they dripped into the fire. Weeks ago, eating a horse would have been considered taboo for most. Now, though, on this deserted island after days without food, the horse flank cooking was the most delicious aroma any of them could remember for quite some time. Bernie tended to the meat, carefully stoking the flames as not to burn their hard-earned catch. In the distance, a small herd of wild horses looked on this group of trespassers to their island home.

Away from the fire, at the other end of camp, Jeremiah and Aiko tended to the wounded in a makeshift triage center. Rough seas from the previous night's storm left most battered and bruised, though a few were worse off than others. Elliot was being treated for a dislocated shoulder while Aiko cleaned up a deep gash across Soraya's cheek. The medic had just finished applying more than a dozen stitches from just under Soraya's right eye, down to the center of her ear.

During the storm, Soraya was flung face-first into the corner of a table, splitting her face open and knocking her unconscious. Miller kept her head above water for the duration of the ordeal, though the constant struggle left no opportunity to address the wound. Nearly twelve hours later, Aiko tried her best to clean up and close the laceration.

"Almost finished, Soraya. One more stitch to go." Aiko tied off the final suture and held up a small shaving mirror someone had found half-buried at the campsite.

Soraya gently touched the skin around the wound. "This does not look so bad."

"I'll say. If you had hit that table any harder, you could have lost the eye."

"*Is* painful, though."

"The pain will recede with the swelling. Nothing is broken, thankfully. Give it a day or two. Besides, Miller will think it's cute. It'll give him more reason to look after you."

"What?" Soraya feigned ignorance.

"Please. I see the way the two of you look at each other. It's no secret. There's something there."

"Aiko, he's my commanding officer," Soraya stammered.

"Uh-huh." Aiko rolled her eyes. "And who's left to write either one of you up?"

Soraya remained silent.

"Back at the strip mall, when we had a bit of a breather, Rachel and I made a bet."

"Oh?" she replied with a grin.

"She says Miller will make the first move. I told her no way that boy scout goes against regulations. Sure, Rachel knows him way better than I ever will, but it's plain as day that Miller is still following orders. He thinks the brass is still out there waiting to chew him out for fraternizing. Anyway, I put my money on *you* making the first move. A month's worth of laundry is on the line here. Don't let me down, girl." Aiko grinned and shrugged. "We're finally off the road and safe on an island, just what we hoped for. What do you have to lose?"

Soraya smiled but quickly rose to her feet. "Thank you for sewing me up, Aiko. I should get going. There is a lot to be done." She hurried off down the beach. Her brisk pace quickly turned into a light jog until she disappeared over a dune.

"Hey, don't mention it." Aiko chuckled to herself as she wiped the woman's blood from her hands and glanced at a growing pile of soiled clothes. "Anytime."

Damon sat atop a small dune about a quarter of a mile from camp. Thick grasses obscured him from sight, but his vantage point offered a bird's-eye view of the goings-on in the group. He fared better than most through the maelstrom. Having locked himself in an empty storage closet, he was immune from the chaos of tumbling bodies and debris. More than once during the ordeal, a rap at the door and a jiggling handle signaled someone had the same idea as him. The closet was roomy enough for at least four comfortably, though he wouldn't have it. Damon remained silent. No one saw him go in there to begin with, and the hell with anyone who tried to prove otherwise. His policy during the storm applied to anyone who tried to get in, including a distraught Markus looking for safety for him and Samantha.

"Here, let me see that." Markus dabbed at a cut on Samantha's arm with a vodka-damped rag.

Samantha pulled back from the initial sting. After that, it was fine, and she let him continue tending to the wound. She cupped her forehead with her free hand. Squinting hard, she peered down the long-deserted stretch of beach. Calm seas lapped at the shore in stark contrast to the previous night's violence. As far as she could see, detritus from what she could only assume was their boat littered the beach. *That could easily have been bodies*, she thought. How they all survived the night was nothing short of a miracle in her eyes.

Her long red curls blew in the breeze, occasionally wrapping themselves around Markus's head. She did her best to hold them back with her free hand, but he didn't seem to mind.

"You know, I've never seen the water. Well, I've seen the Inner Harbor, and we went shooting out by Patapsco once, but the ocean... It's big. Bigger than I ever imagined," he said.

"I've never been much of a beach-goer myself. I mean, look at me." She held out her porcelain arm. "I burn just thinking about the sun."

"All done," he said. "Sure you don't want to have one of the medics take a look at it?"

"I'm fine. I'd rather not get in the way."

Markus leaned back in the sand beside her, resting on his elbows. "I'm never getting on another boat again. I'm done with the ocean. Once was enough for me."

"I don't blame you. Come on." She stood and held her hand out. "Let's go see if we can't find something useful in all this junk."

ISLAND: DAY THREE

Directly across from the narrow island, on the mainland, a small inlet disappeared behind a cluster of condos and waterfront cottages. Two-person paddleboats and kayaks littered the properties. All were as useless as the deflated banana boat that a storm wrapped around someone's dock. To their west, marshlands as far as the eye could see spread miles inland and around to a peninsula, affording the small sandbar of an island a natural barrier against the Atlantic Ocean's fury. The tip of the peninsula featured a lighthouse, no doubt as a warning for unfamiliar sailors to steer clear of certain doom upon the reef just beyond the island.

Eastward, the horizon offered a vast sprawling beach resort that disappeared into the distance. Hotels, restaurants, and amusements dotted the highway, which ran parallel to the miles of beach the resort had to offer. Now abandoned vehicles of all shapes and sizes littered the scenery. In the place of children playing and parents enjoying well-deserved vacations, packs of feral dogs teased countless undead for scraps of meat. Two dogs would pull and claw at a carrier's shredded clothes, each attacking from a different side. The frustrated creature would usually lunge at the animals, rarely making contact. Eventually, the brain-dead abomination would drop its meal and a third dog would pounce, absconding with the prize. The three dogs would then vanish down an alley and begin their own battle over the spoils.

Gone was the eye candy, all tanned a delicious bronze. The pretty girls in bikinis, one skimpier than the next, the guys chiseled from marble, vying for each other's attention. Countless corpses littered the streets and beaches. Garbage blew in the warm ocean breeze. A handful of buildings still smoldered from an unwitnessed disaster while others had their front windows blown in by out-of-control vehicles. A small plane, the kind that dragged long advertisements behind it, was embedded in the side of a high-rise, three-quarters of the way up the building, its streamer still blowing in the wind. The banner read—*Welcome to Poseidon's Rest! Home of Gianni's Pizza!*—for a city full of creatures with no taste for the stuff.

"I wonder if they're open," Radzinski asked.

"Probably not," Miller replied. "Do you see anything useful?"

"Yeah, a couple of dinged-up motorboats. Looks like they were dragged onto shore. The storm didn't do it. That's for sure."

"What do you think?"

"They look good from here, but we can't be certain until we're on top of them."

"Chances are they belong to our hosts," Rachel added.

"What if they come back?" Samantha, of course, was thinking of everyone.

"Doesn't matter. We'll leave the boats right where we found them once we're all across," Miller assured her.

"And no one will be the wiser," Rachel added.

"Let me see the binoculars," said Miller.

Radzinski gave up the device, and Miller focused them on the distant shoreline. "Yeah, I see them. Two small boats pulled up onto shore. Definitely put there with purpose."

"They might as well be on the moon," Isaac argued.

"Not necessarily. It looks to be about a mile of ocean between us and the mainland, and that's a doable swim, especially after spending the last few days gorging ourselves," Miller suggested. "We'll need both of those boats to get everyone and all of our supplies in one trip. We can't risk running out of gas and leaving people behind. It's on me, so I'm going, but I *am* going to need a volunteer to go with me. We don't have rope strong enough for a tow, and to be safe, I only want to go there and back once."

"This is suicide, Miller," Markus cautioned. "That's gotta be at least a mile of water, and if—*if*—you make it, you'll be alone over there, exhausted from the swim, and with no weapons or backup. If you get attacked, that's it, man. Game over. There's got to be another way." His apprehension had more to do with his newfound fear of water than anything else.

"We all die if we do nothing. I go, too," Soraya offered.

"Thank you, Soraya." Miller nodded. Soraya returned the gesture. "She's right, people. You better hope we make it, because if we don't, two more of you are going to have to try."

Miller and Soraya stripped down to their underwear before Jeremiah helped secure the gas can to Miller's back. Soraya strapped her kukri to her left thigh and a sidearm to the other. A good amount of duct tape ensured the weapons wouldn't be falling off during the swim.

"Are you sure about this, guys?" Markus's misgivings concerning the plan were clear.

"We don't have a choice, Markus. I'll see you soon." Miller gripped the man's shoulder on his way past to Rachel. "Keep your eyes on the shoreline, and if you see anything moving closer than a half a klick to those boats, fire three rounds."

"Yes, sir."

Miller and Soraya cut across the water, making excellent time, each deliberate stroke propelling them closer to the other shore. Miller had a love affair with the sea for as long as he could remember, though as time wore on, he found himself becoming less and less familiar with its touch. In another time, and certainly under vastly different circumstances, he would have found this place to be paradise.

For a moment, he imagined himself and Soraya swimming up to one of those abandoned cottages, closing the door behind them, and forgetting about the world. They could make a life together here, and why not? What was stopping them? She was lying in bed, cuddled up next to the spot he just rose from, and smiling in her sleep, content. Lost in thought, he barely noticed as his knee brushed the bottom. He stumbled for a second, then stood. They had hit land. He turned to help Soraya to her feet; she was already upright, helping him. The exhausted swimmers collapsed on the beach, faces skyward and panting like dogs.

"We did it, Miller." Soraya reached over and tapped Miller on the thigh a few times in congratulations.

He weaved his fingers between hers before raising both of their arms in triumph for the benefit of those watching from the island. The pair sat up wearily, leaning on each other for support that evolved into a long embrace.

"You okay?" he asked.

"Yes. You?"

"Perfect." He offered a smile that she was quick to return before adding, "We should get going." He helped her to her feet.

"Yes, you are right. It is not safe here." She started pawing sand off of her stomach and legs.

"Here, let me give you a hand." Miller swiped the grit from her back.

She attempted the same as a gunshot tore them from a moment's respite. The two were instantly at attention, scanning their surroundings for potential threats. As quickly as they took up defensive positions, Soraya had the pair of weapons freed from her legs and the two of them armed.

A mile away on the island, Radzinski laughed as he slung his rifle. "Oh, isn't that cute." He grinned.

"You asshole. There's nothing even over there." Rachel shook her head and returned to the binoculars.

"They can fuck around on their own time. Just get me the hell off this island." Radzinski peered down to his sand-covered boots.

"I agree completely, young man," Lancaster added. "This is hardly the time for foreplay."

"Shut up." Radzinski pushed past Lancaster, disregarding his comment. "They'll be back soon. Everybody, get your shit. We're out of here."

Miller's heart slowed its racing. There were no threats bearing down on them. He knew who was across the channel and why the shots were fired. He almost allowed himself a chuckle at the thought of Radzinski being right for once; they *should* hurry. "I don't see anything. We better get these boats in the water." Miller blushed slightly as he pulled his boat toward the shore.

"Yes," Soraya replied, biting her lip as she turned to the other boat in an attempt to hide her joy.

Miller allowed himself a smile as he poured half of the fuel into his boat's motor.

"Alright, everyone, look sharp. Here they come." Radzinski waved the tentative group forward along the shore. Miller and Soraya were moments away from their return, and he would prefer to be back on solid, paved land as soon as possible.

"I know it's only been a few days, but I really think I'm going to miss this place." Lillian turned to the still-new campsite.

In only a handful of days, they managed to turn what was essentially a pile of junk—abandoned leftovers, really—into the beginnings of a halfway decent miniature community. Once again, the uncertainty of the road lay ahead. Lillian pulled Vanessa aside, just a few steps away from the group.

"What is it?" Vanessa asked, scanning the crowd for Isabelle. Lately, Lillian's mother was about the only thing that could make the girl anxious.

"We don't have to go with them, you know." Lillian attempted to whisper, but she was in a hurry. The boats would be there any second now. With them, her chance to convince Vanessa to stay would be gone.

"Lily, we can't stay here. If something happens, it would only be the two of us," Vanessa said sympathetically.

"Since when are you afraid of *anything?*" Lillian replied.

"It's not that. It's that we're just better off in a group. Safety in numbers, you know?" Vanessa tried to appear as if she believed what she was saying.

"Dammit, Vanessa. Just think about this for a second. What's out there for us? More running? Who's going to die next? Don't you want to slow down, at least for a little while?" Lillian was nearly begging.

"Pardon me, ladies, but I tend to agree with Lillian." Sam couldn't help but overhear their conversation, as well as a few of the others who themselves were discussing the proposition.

Opinions one way or the other ran the gamut, from agreement to being vehemently against the idea. Most, though, seemed to be falling into the I'll-do-what-everyone-else-thinks-is-best category.

"You do? I mean, thank you, Sam," said Lillian.

"Don't mention it, darling. These old bones could use a good long rest. We should shoot this past Miller and the others, get an idea who wants to do what," he suggested.

"No need. Lillian's right, Sam. We're not leaving yet," Miller said while walking out of the surf. He nodded to Markus and a few of the others standing around him, then back to the boats. "Let's get these boats away from the water, up closer to camp."

"What do you mean? We're not leaving?" Radzinski was stupefied.

"We're staying here for now. We've got food and shelter, and we're surrounded by fast-moving deep water. Those things couldn't reach us out here even if they could swim." Miller gestured back to the resort on the horizon.

"For what it's worth, I second that idea, Miller," Sam offered. "Lord knows we can use the break."

"Thank God." Lillian let out a sigh.

"Not to mention that, without a set destination, we might as well be walking in circles. I mean, where are we going anyway?" Marisol commented. "I have no problem staying here a while."

"Agreed," Miller said before returning his attention to Radzinski, who was stewing. "It's been almost a month since these people got to slow down, Radzinski. They need to relax for a few nights without worrying about who or what's coming around the next corner," Miller insisted. "We all do."

ISLAND: NIGHT THREE

Most of the group took up spots in the sand around the crackling bonfire. Some wandered from the conversations and out on their own, down to the beach. For the first time in weeks, a few of them went unarmed. A pile of rifles within arm's reach of the fire stood as a testament to the growing sense of calm just a handful of days on the island had afforded the survivors.

"It's peaceful here. Quiet. It's a shame we can't stay longer," Isaac said as he stared off into the ocean.

"And who says we can't?" Elliot chucked a rock out into the water; it skipped a few times before sinking.

"Be nice wouldn't it, fellas? Living out under the stars and not a care in the whole damn world." Sam buried his feet in the sand. He hadn't felt the coarse but welcome grains between his toes since he was a child.

Marisol fiddled with a stack of discarded papers she'd found in the ruined campsite. "According to this map I found in one of the tents, I'd say we washed ashore in North Carolina. Deertongue Banks, to be exact." Marisol handed the map off to Sam.

"Well, that tells me exactly nothing," Radzinski chimed in.

"Ever with the positivity, Radzinski. Gotta love it." Marisol was unmoved by the brute's attitude but stole a glance at his shirtless physique nonetheless.

"Never heard of it," Damon added.

"Not surprising. You do know there used to be an entire world outside of Baltimore, right?" Marisol asked rhetorically.

"I've noticed. So far it's been great," Damon replied.

"Touché," said Marisol with a nod of her head.

"I know where we're at." Bernie perked up, nearly startling Casandra, who sat at his side. "I thought the landscape looked familiar. We're right on top of Mare's Point. My family used to travel here when I was a boy. That's Mare's Point lighthouse across the bay there. Well, goddamn, small world, huh? Even if it has gone to hell."

"Yeah, small world. Sure," Radzinski said. "Except for six billion carriers that all want a piece of your ass."

"You really think it's the whole world?" Nisha pulled her arms in close. The idea chilled her.

"It's *my* whole world, sweetheart," Radzinski asserted. "That's all that matters."

"Point taken." Marisol rolled her eyes as she lay down on her side in the sand.

Radzinski shrugged. He was already preoccupied with the view down Marisol's shirt.

Ryan attempted to change topics from talk of their usually grim reality. "I played NCAA ball for half a season. That's about the biggest thing I ever did," His nonchalance about his all-too-brief sporting career betrayed his true feelings on the subject.

Rachel picked up on it and decided it prudent to play along, lest someone else see it as a sore spot to exploit. "Why only one season? If you were good enough to get into a league school, they wouldn't have dropped you like that for no reason."

"Oh, there *is* a reason. I—" Ryan had no chance to finish before Rachel continued her ribbing.

"No, no, no, let me guess. Too much partying? No, that's lame. Everyone parties. Oh, you accidentally killed a rival team's mascot? No, that's not it. I got it. You knocked up a faculty member. That's it, stud. Tell me I'm wrong." Rachel stood up and pointed at him.

"I broke my ankle on a sprinkler head," Ryan admitted.

The campfire went silent for a moment until in unison everyone burst into laughter.

"Don't make me laugh like that, you guys. I'm still in a lot of pain over here." Casandra rubbed her shoulder, trying to hold back snorts of laughter. The sounds only made her laugh harder.

"I'm sorry, man. I didn't see that one coming at all," Elliot said trying in vain to cover his mouth.

"No need to apologize, bro," Ryan replied. "Oh, it's hilarious alright."

"Sprinkler, huh? Wow, I got nothing." Rachel sat down beside him, just a tad closer this time.

Nisha was smiling and laughing with the rest of them, though the here and now was never far from her mind. "There has to be more survivors out there," she said confidently, though the statement was more of a question she desperately needed someone to answer.

"Yeah, we saw them last week, and they killed one of us," Damon answered.

"Asshole," Marisol replied. "There's plenty of people out there and they're not *all* bad."

"You really believe that?" Radzinski asked, almost compassionately.

"Of course. How could I not?"

"The kid's got a point," said Sam. "Although I'm a little more optimistic than that. Given enough time, I'm hopeful we'll run into another group similar to our own."

"Yeah, strength in numbers. Then nobody can fuck with us." Damon punched his open palm.

"I think Sam was referring to security," Isaac commented. "But you *are* right. If we had larger numbers, that gang might have thought twice before confronting us." Isaac poked the fire with a stick. Small embers danced around in the smoke until disappearing into the sky.

"Do you think the government is still out there? I mean, trying to figure out how to fix this?" Marisol asked no one in particular.

"Who knows? At this point, who cares?" Radzinski answered. "We're on our own. Hell, for all we know, those assholes caused this shit in the first place." He picked himself up, sealed his bottle of whiskey, and disappeared down toward the water.

Off to the side, away from the smoke but within earshot of the group, Markus worked to ease Samantha's frayed nerves.

"Can't you hear that? Those things are still out there, aren't they? Everyone said this island was deserted." Samantha began to panic again, jumping at shadows and any stray noise the island offered out in the darkness and away from the fire. The neighing of distant horses particularly unnerved her. "We should head back to the boat, Markus."

"Trust me, this island is as deserted as it gets. There's nothing here but us and those horses. Otherwise, we are completely alone. Those things aren't out there. Believe me. At least not here on the island, anyway. Besides, sound carries on the water. I bet those bastards are miles away," said Markus, though his attempt at consolation wasn't going over well.

Jeremiah and Aiko sat alone in the darkness, away from the others. It wasn't that they were antisocial, far from it. They required a certain amount of time to themselves, especially Jeremiah. His brain basically needed time to recharge after being around a large group of people for an extended amount of time. He was an introvert, to be sure. The condition was usually manageable, but the past weeks pushed his senses beyond his limit, though he'd never let it show. In times like those, he would develop tunnel vision and dive headfirst into a task, only to come up for air when said task was complete. That was what he'd been doing for weeks now. It was finally time to decompress, alone on a beach with Aiko by his side, just far enough away from everyone else to relax.

"See that light in the distance? It's fire, a small city burning," Jeremiah pointed out.

"How can you tell?" Aiko said while adjusting herself to lie in his lap.

"It's unmistakable, the sight of a city on fire in complete darkness. Peaceful yet terrifying in its brilliance."

"Is that what it was like in Afghanistan?"

"Sometimes. Most nights were uneventful, though. Dark and quiet times, those were the worst, always. The anticipation was agonizing."

"I can imagine, but we're together now. That's what's important."

"You don't want to hear about fires or what I thought of the sandbox, Aiko. You never have. Be honest with me. There's something else on your mind, isn't there?"

"No fooling you, huh? Yes, there is something I want to tell you, but right now is not the time, Jeremiah. I really just want to enjoy this time alone together, where we can slow down and breathe."

"Given our current situation, we may not find a better time to speak with one another privately again."

"I know. I just need to do this on my own terms, okay?" Aiko insisted.

"If you feel it best," Jeremiah conceded.

"Thanks, but has anyone ever told you you're a fucking robot?" Aiko asked playfully.

"I may have heard it once or twice." Jeremiah managed a smile as he turned his focus back to the flaming town in the distance.

His smile, though fleeting, was what attracted her to him near two years prior. To see him content like this, at peace, made her heart swell. "Hey there," Aiko whispered. She took his hand in hers. "You're going to be a father, Jeremiah."

Eyes like saucers, he rose to his knees and reached for her belly. It was truly there, the smallest of baby bumps, but it was there. His child was growing inside of her. He had been so consumed these past weeks that he didn't notice. He leaned forward and held her tight, kissing her belly repeatedly. The typically stoic Jeremiah wept. "Thank you, thank you. I'm so sorry. Thank you, Lord. Thank you." He cried as Aiko looked on lovingly, caressing his head, tears of her own streaming. Even in a world gone to hell, the love they shared bore fruit. On an island he'd never heard of, under the stars with his young family, Jeremiah's faith was restored.

Miller and Soraya sat together, a little farther down the beach, away from the fire and the majority of the group. A bright full moon illuminated their spot just beyond the reach of the waves. When the wind blew a certain way, they could just barely make out the sounds from camp. Otherwise, it was peaceful. Twenty-four hours before he touched down in Philadelphia, Miller was at a local watering hole, relieving some civilians from the burden of heavy wallets over a few games of pool. He had been on the move ever since, nearly six weeks from the last time he was able to take a breath.

"I am glad you decided to stay, Miller. We needed this."

"Agreed. I'd been tossing it around in my head for a few days, weighing the pros and cons. Honestly, I wasn't sure what we should do."

"What made up your mind?"

"Sam did. When I overheard him and Lillian trying to convince Vanessa that it was a good idea to stay, that sealed it. They were right. We needed to be able to slow down, catch our breath, and find our bearings. I don't think anyone thinks we can stay here forever, though. Sooner or later, we *will* have to get back on the road."

"Enough of this road talk. Let's speak of something else. Tell me about your family."

"What's to tell? We're just your average suburban family: two brothers, two sisters, Mom, and Dad."

"There is always something to tell," she prodded.

The sound of the waves crashing and Soraya's voice brought him peace as he gazed up at the night sky. Tranquility allowed his mind to wander back to better times with his family, before his whole world went to shit. "I try not to imagine what they're going through with all of this. I mean, I have so many regrets, and it just kills me to think that they're out there, running for their lives right now, terrified, and there's not a damn thing I can do about it." Miller held his eyes shut for a moment. "I used to get so mad at them and for stupid shit, and all they ever wanted to do was spend time with me. I'd get an attitude if they asked me to do something. Being a stupid kid, I didn't realize they just wanted to spend time with their son. I miss them so much, Soraya. I would give anything to be back home right now, cooking on the grill with the old man and throwing back some cold ones."

"They know how you feel. You are a good man, Miller," Soraya said. "Do you know if they made it to safety?"

"God, I have no idea. I'd like to think they made it someplace safe, though. I have to, you know, think that way. It keeps me from losing my mind."

Soraya took his hand in hers. She wrapped his arm around her and held his hand in her stomach. "Someday, I will help you find them. I promise," she said while nestling in beside Miller for a long-deserved night's sleep.

Lancaster rummaged around inside the shipwreck of the *Emerald Star*, throwing seat cushions and life jackets about the wheelhouse as he searched. "I know you are in here somewhere, dammit," Lancaster said as he opened a compartment near the captain's chair. "There you are, my sweet. You are all the companionship I'll ever need, my dear, dear Brandy. To hell with that self-righteous garbage, the lot of them." Lancaster uncorked a liter of top-shelf Brandy, took a big swig, and sat back in the captain's chair, momentarily content.

Even farther still down the beach, within sight of the shipwreck, Vanessa and Lillian were enjoying some much-desired privacy.

"Do you still miss your husband?" Lillian asked.

"There will always be a place in my heart for Clint, but no, I don't miss him anymore. He wouldn't want me to," Vanessa replied. "It was hard at first, but he made me promise to let him go. I was angry with him for a long time for leaving me. Now when I think of him, I smile. I've learned to focus on the positive, so the negative usually bounces right off. Most times."

"If I think hard enough, will all of this go away?"

"Oh, Lily, I didn't mean to imply..." Vanessa sat up.

"I know. I'm kidding, mostly. Besides, I've seen so much crazy shit in the past few weeks I honestly think I'm becoming numb to it all."

"Tell me what you're thinking right now. The first thing that pops into your head," said Vanessa, quick to head off impending gloom.

"You know, and I feel awful saying it considering all we've been through, but I feel bad killing these horses like this. Look at them. They're beautiful. We've killed two so far, and the others still hang around like everything is okay." Lillian strained her neck to turn and watch part of a herd grazing beyond a nearby dune.

Radzinski interrupted, not content with merely eavesdropping. "If it makes you feel better, that little horsey is going to keep you and your girlfriend alive."

"Leave her alone. She doesn't have to like it," Vanessa snapped without hesitation.

"I'm just saying, some of you people complain an awful lot. I don't think you realize how good you have it here."

"No one's complaining. She simply said she feels bad about killing horses. Not a big deal, so why don't you move on?"

"Hey, don't listen to me. See for yourselves when we leave here, and believe me, we *will* leave here. When we're back in the shit with those things chasing us down again, you'll wish we were back on this island, killing your precious horses." Satisfied, Radzinski continued his trek down the beach.

"Thanks for that, but you don't have to stick up for me all the time. I'm a big girl, you know." Lillian was pushing and pulling on the blanket, trying to reset the divot they had made in the sand.

"Sorry, I just don't like people like that. The guy's a jerk. Here, let me help you with that." Vanessa took over straightening the blanket.

"I don't need your help to fix the fucking blanket!" Lillian yanked it back.

"Okay, sorry. Have at it." Vanessa backed away slightly, leaving Lillian to adjust the sheet.

"No, *I'm* sorry. It's just that you don't talk to me the same way you did back home. Then it was like we were on the same level playing field, like we were sisters or something else. Ever since we left Pepperbush behind, you've changed. It's like you think you're my mother now or something. I don't like it, and it's not fair." Lillian grabbed Vanessa's hand with purpose.

"There was always something more back at Mother Leeds, just beneath the surface. I saw it, and most of our regulars knew it, too. I don't need a second mother, Vanessa. I need *you*."

"I wasn't trying to act like your mom. I didn't realize I—" Vanessa began.

Lillian leaned in. Without giving Vanessa a chance to respond, she was on top of her former employer, gently kissing her lips while running fingers through her hair. They had kissed before, but it was always more of a playful thing, mainly for the benefit of their customers. This was different.

Vanessa reciprocated, slowly at first, but she was quick to catch up. A part of her couldn't believe this was really happening. She had only discovered her own feelings for Lillian days prior. There hadn't been ample time to process them before they were stranded on this island, and here was this girl, putting any doubt Vanessa might have harbored to bed.

Vanessa let Lillian pull away first. Truth be told, she didn't want the moment to end. "That was nice."

"It was."

"You want to just lie here for a bit before we head back?"

"Why? You holding out for someone else, Mom?" Lillian teased.

Vanessa threw the blanket over Lillian's head and laughed. "Shut up."

In the distance, the campfire seemed no more than a speck of orange against a sea of black. The light came into view and left again just as quickly while Isabelle bobbed up and down in the ocean. Easily thirty yards from shore, she gently swam in place, only moving enough to keep her nose above water. It had been at least an hour since she last felt sand beneath her toes. She floated, watching tiny shadows in the distance dance beneath the stars. Over time, the current would drag her away until the orange disappeared completely behind a dune. Eventually she would swim back to where she started and observe all over again.

CHAPTER TWELVE

Castaways

"I was wondering where you'd gotten off to." Miller stood watch halfway between the shipwreck of the *Emerald Star* and the inlet that separated their humble island from the mainland. He had shed most of his gear in the days prior. By day five on the island, boots, fatigues, and a simple white T-shirt were all that he bothered with. His rifle had gotten heavy. He kept armed, though: a combat knife and a sidearm. The rest of his unit had also adopted a more casual loadout in light of island living. Tank tops and T-shirts all around.

Rachel approached from atop a nearby dune, gliding over the sand barefoot. Her boots were tied together and draped over a shoulder, her rifle slung over the other. "Hiking. This island goes on for a few miles in both directions."

"Just us and the horses still, I hope?" Miller was more concerned about other potential inhabitants than he let on. The size of the island gave him pause. It was possible they missed something vital during their initial reconnaissance, like a land bridge, shattering the illusion of serenity that maybe this wasn't even an island at all.

"It's still just us. Over the past two days, I've hiked from one end of this bastard to the other. As far as I can tell, this whole island is one big campsite."

"You're serious?" he asked with a quick glance through his binoculars.

"Oh yeah. I found two more sets of tents out there, and there's probably more. Here's the kicker: I lost track of how many *pick up your trash* or *leave the horses alone* signs I came across. I'm fairly confident that this place is a national park."

"That would explain a few things."

"Yeah, really. Now, why don't you take a whiff of this?" Rachel leaned in, putting her hair up to Miller's nose.

He backed off for a second, unsure, but slowly inched forward for a smell. His brow furrowed and his neck tilted. "Is that what I think it is?"

"Two miles east is a fucking bathhouse with a working toilet and two honest-to-God hot and cold running showers. There's even a supply closet with travel-sized bars of soap and shampoo. Best I've felt in I don't even remember." Rachel pulled her short hair as close to her own nose as she could and breathed in deep. She held her eyes shut for a moment and smiled. "For the life of me, I couldn't figure out how the hell I wasn't running out of hot water *or* any water for that matter. I was about to start filling up all the trashcans I could find when it dawned on me: solar power. The well pump and the hot water heater are working off solar power; the roof of the place is covered with panels. Genius. No outlets or lighting fixtures, but big deal, right? I guess they were going for that *au naturel* roughing-it vibe."

"Well, this changes everything."

"Tell me about it. I let Casandra know already. The poor girl's got it worse than any of us. She and Bernie are over there now. They know to keep quiet and only tell a couple people at a time. No need to start a riot when everyone shows up at the shower at once."

"Good call. This'll be great for morale, pick these people's spirits up a little more. This place really is turning out to be paradise." Miller looked over to Rachel's bare feet, then down to his own boots. "I may never want to leave."

Steam poured out from the small stucco covered bathhouse; its only real ventilation was the crack beneath a thick wooden door. Inside, filthy clothes were strewn about the ceramic tile floor. No curtains adorned the shower stalls, and the facility's lone toilet sat adjacent the shower booths with only a waist-high cinder block wall affording minimal privacy. Bernie and Casandra didn't think twice about such inconsequential things as modesty. Both dove headfirst into the showers, barely ripping off their clothes before the first drops of water hit them. After weeks of travel, their attire was just as foul as their bodies, maybe even a little worse, though laundry could come later.

"Oh my God, Bernie. This is incredible!" Casandra shouted over the showers. "Why are you so good to me?" She giggled.

"Don't thank me. This is all Rachel."

"In that case, she deserves double rations tonight."

"Tonight? Hell, that girl's getting as much as she wants *every* night, from now on." Bernie cheered a series of hoots and hollers that would have had Casandra doubled over in laughter had her huge belly not been in the way. "What's so funny over there, girl?"

"Oh, I don't know. I'm just happy to have my very own cowboy in shining denim," she flirted.

"At your service, ma'am." He tipped an imaginary hat.

"Oh really?" she said boldly. "In that case, I have a spot over here I can't reach."

"Happy to oblige," said Bernie before shutting off his water and joining her in the next stall.

ISLAND: NIGHT EIGHT

"I feel safe here. First time in months, man," said Markus. "We lost a lot of good people getting to this island. It's a shame they couldn't be here with us to see it, too." He skipped a stone just over a breaking wave.

"People die. They weren't the first, and they won't be the last. No big deal, bro," Damon said, nearly laughing at his friend's compassion.

"Tobias died for nothing, Damon. Absolutely nothing. Some crazy old serial killer burned him up, and for what? A lonely cabin in the woods all by himself? That's no way to live, even in this fucked-up world. At least Seth went down fighting. What happened to Tobias just doesn't make any goddamn sense."

"Fuck that old man and fuck Tobias, too. Shit, fuck all of them. I'm alive and so are you, and that's all that matters. You should get your mind around that. And Seth? You're kidding me, right? We're calling cops our friends now, too? Is that it? Shit, fuck him the most." Damon was disgusted at the thought. He wore his disdain for those in authority on his sleeve. The soldiers were an issue for him as well. He could accept them, though, especially in light of he and Radzinski having so much in common, but the police? They were another story altogether.

"Jesus, Damon, where's your heart, man? They were good men trying their best to keep all of us safe. What good have you done lately? You barely even pull your own weight. Drop the bullshit and try acting like you're one of us for a change."

"One of us, huh? Is that how it's gonna be?" Damon looked Markus in the eye for the first time since their conversation began.

"No, that's how it *is*, Damon. If we don't come together, we're not going to make it. That's all there is to it. There are no more sides, man. We're all equals now, just trying to live. The quicker you see that, the better off you'll be."

"Make it? Make it where? We're in the middle of nowhere for fuck's sake, and as soon as you stop thinking you're one of them, the better off *you'll* be. As far as they're concerned, you're nothing but a thug. A city boy is all you'll ever be to them." Damon poked Markus in the chest in an attempt to drive the point home. Markus shrugged it off.

"It's not about us and them. It's just us now. It's been that way since the day Vanessa let us into her bar and gave us a place to stay. Why can't you see that? This little group that you despise so much? That's it, man. That's all there is. They might as well be the whole world, for all that matters now." Markus knew he wasn't getting through to him. The sooner this conversation was over, the better, he thought. It was getting so he could barely stand the sight of Damon anymore.

"Whatever, man. Fuck these people. And if Marisol or that cocksucker, Isaac even look at me sideways, I'll bury them out here. You feelin' that?" Damon pulled up his tank top. His 9mm was tucked safely in the front of his pants.

"You just don't get it, do you?" Markus watched his friend back away down the beach, still brandishing the firearm.

Damon made the sign of a gun with his hand and pointed it back toward camp. He slowly shook his head up and down and smiled as he pretended to fire off shots at his campmates. Markus ignored the bravado and continued his own trek down the beach in the opposite direction.

Nisha carried a portion of the night's meal out to the beach. For more than a week, Isabelle had remained alone. She normally stayed out by the surf, not speaking to anyone, and rarely ate. If Isabelle was eating more than she let on, it would have to have been stuff she caught with her own two hands.

Nisha knelt beside her friend and sat a portion of meat and a little fish between them. "Izzy, I haven't seen you in a couple days. Are you okay? Would you like something to eat, honey? Bernie put together quite a spread tonight." Nisha inched the dish closer.

Isabelle stared off into the blackness of the night sea. What little rags she wore—the remnants of the gray dress she had on during the night they fled Pepperbush—were hanging off her, blowing in the breeze. Nisha gently turned her head away. Her hand briefly covered her nose. Obviously, Isabelle gave up on any attempts at hygiene weeks ago.

"Tommy swam by earlier. He said he'd be back in a little while. You don't think it's too cold for my little boy to be swimming tonight, do you, Nisha?" Isabelle asked without so much as a peek in her friend's direction.

"Oh, honey." Nisha moved in close and put an arm around her friend. "Everything is going to be fine, Izzy. I'll wait here with you for a while. We'll wait for him together." Nisha attempted to pull the woman close, but Isabelle remained unresponsive. Unbeknownst to Nisha, Isabelle kept her right hand buried in the sand, fingering the length of a hidden blade for the duration of their conversation.

The waves crashing on the beach seemed to move in time with their delicate rhythm. Rachel wrapped her legs around him tight, forcing Ryan deep inside of her. They breathed heavily, in sync, mouths open. He could feel her warm breath against his face. It sent a rush of pure energy through to his core. Their lips brushed against each other's as her body rose and fell in time with his gentle thrusts. Their eyes locked onto one another's, neither daring to look away as they climaxed in near unison. They held their positions through each finishing spasm, continuing their embrace long after they'd both grown still. Lying on the beach beneath the stars, they held each other close as they continued to stare longingly into each other's eyes.

Rachel sat up. Still astride Ryan, she was silhouetted against the moonlight. Her toned body glistened as she gently caressed his sweaty chest and stomach. "I never noticed you had abs before."

"These aren't abs. This is what malnutrition looks like."

Rachel smiled. "So where do we go from here?"

"Oh, I don't know. Why don't we break off from the group, head over to the mainland?" he suggested. "We can set up shop in one of those high-rises, whichever one you want. Money's no option."

"So you're saying you want two-point-five kids and a white picket fence?"

"I mean, it doesn't have to be white. I've got the perfect spot all picked out." He arched his neck for an upside-down view of the darkened mainland in the distance. "What about that one? The condo next to the carnival with a view of the Ferris wheel. I'll show you when the sun comes up."

"You're adorable."

"Oh?"

"When everyone else is using the binoculars to search for supplies or signs of life, you're busy looking for carousels and Skee-Ball."

"Priorities, babe. It's the little things."

"Careful, Ryan." She rested her head on his shoulder. Her arm lay comfortably on his chest. "I may be falling for you."

Marisol and Samantha found themselves discussing the merits of one *ex*-Mayor Donald Lancaster and his place in the group. For most, it became commonplace to ignore the man or outright scold him, but for a few of the survivors, Samantha in particular, guilt had set in. From her vantage point, a near-elderly man was lambasted on an almost daily basis. Not a single person stood up for him or cared to ask why. Samantha had a history of volunteering her time, occasionally in shelters or community clean-up projects, but her passion was for abuse victims. This old man who she watched Marisol beat almost to death pulled on her heartstrings a little more than she was comfortable with.

Marisol, for her part, took it upon herself to keep Lancaster in his place, which as far as she was concerned was as low as humanly possible. Without a cell to throw him away in, she had no choice but to live with the man. And passing sentence, even now, was something she refused to consider as she became a police officer to uphold the law, not become an executioner. Lancaster's actions at Town Hall the night they fled Pepperbush was the crux of the argument, though the man's wife and her indifference toward the criminal ways of her husband was a bit of a sore spot for the now ex-sheriff.

"Not every woman has the wherewithal to separate herself from a bad situation, Marisol."

"You really think that was the case, do you?"

"I didn't know them, so maybe."

"No, it's not. That's a cop-out. Some women lust for money and power just as much as their male counterparts, but they choose not to get their hands dirty when someone else will happily do it for them. Catherine Lancaster and those like her couldn't care less what their husbands did to provide it for them. His wife and his cronies' wives were just as guilty as their husbands, maybe more so because they ignored it in exchange for a lifestyle. They were content with the big houses, new shoes, and jewelry. If Lancaster and his bought-and-paid-for officials got their hands dirty in the process, so be it," Marisol said accusingly.

"Then I don't understand. If he didn't help them and he basically let them die and you think they deserved it, why are you so angry with him?" Samantha asked. Marisol's reasoning was lost on the woman.

"He left an infant and two toddlers to die, not to mention his own son. I saw him backing out of Town Hall from across the courtyard. He was looking them right in the eyes as he locked the door behind him and tossed the keys in the bushes. He condemned those children to a horrible death. I couldn't care less about the wives. They got their comeuppance. Those children, though... They never did a damn thing to anyone." Marisol released a guttural sound, something akin to half a grunt, half a moan.

"My God, I had no idea." Samantha winced.

"Well, now you do, so next time I'm in his face or decide to smash his teeth in, I'd appreciate you not interceding on his behalf," Marisol snapped.

"Man, what a jerk. I see where you're coming from now, and for what it's worth, I'm sorry."

"You have no idea, girl."

Lillian suggested sleeping on the boat. Proximity to their campmates was beginning to take its toll. Comfort and safety in numbers had given way to frustration over the lack of privacy and constant commotion. The pair of them lay on the deck under a clear sky. This was the first either of them had set foot on the vessel since they washed ashore more than a week prior. The *Emerald Star*, though no longer seaworthy, still served as an excellent shelter. Had it not been for the abandoned campsite, the wreck would surely have not gone mostly ignored. The storm that brought them to the island pushed the boat far enough inland that there was no worry of a high tide sweeping them out to sea in their sleep. It would take another storm of equal or greater magnitude to even budge the thing.

The interior of the boat smelled of oil and machinery. Until someone bothered to clean it up, the deck would have to do as a small retreat from the island. A small emergency blanket and a pair of life vests were all they could scrounge up for comfort against the coarse wooden deck boards. The angle that the boat was resting was a little awkward, but they made it work. At least a modicum of privacy remained their primary concern.

Vanessa and Lillian were lying at the lowest point of the lopsided deck, the closest spot resembling an available flat surface. The angle of the deck availed them at least *some* privacy. Vanessa was on her back. Her hands were above her head, gripping the side of the boat tightly for leverage. Lillian had been down there for at least twenty minutes. Or was it an hour? Vanessa had no notion of time anymore.

Lillian slowly made her way back up Vanessa's body, gently teasing her stomach, breasts, and neck, then finally her lips. Their bodies pressed together, hands and legs pulling each other closer. Vanessa thought it was over ages ago, but Lillian kept going. If Vanessa possessed the will to ask, she would beg her lover to never stop. Vanessa knew that all things must end. She felt her partner slowing, though they kissed passionately for some time before Lillian eventually lay beside her. Both women spent, the pair of them breathed heavily under the moonlight. Beads of sweat glistened beneath its brilliance before they gently rolled down their curves and onto the sloped deck. The couple lay there, basking in each other's glow until long after their breath returned.

Lillian began to dress, lest Radzinski *accidentally* wander by. "How long do you think they'll let us stay here?"

"I'm not sure." Vanessa peered around the deck. "It would be kind of selfish on our part to claim the *Emerald Star* as our own private getaway."

Lillian smiled. "I don't mean the boat. I'm talking about the island. How long do you think they'll let us stay before we hit the road again?"

"Oh, man. I haven't really thought about it. This place, as nice as it is, probably isn't ideal for the long term. I'd hardly consider a small bathhouse, a few tents, and a shipwreck to be home. Then there's the weather to consider. A standard storm is bad enough, and hurricane season isn't even over yet. After that, we have winter to look forward to." Vanessa sat up, her smile fading. She gazed out into the blackened sea whence they came. Whatever momentary joy she felt from her brief time alone with Lillian was waning fast. "I've never been much of a survivor buff, but nothing about our island screams sustainable living to me."

"Sorry to be a buzzkill." Lillian felt the mood drop, that much was clear, and it was entirely her fault.

"Don't be. These are things we need to be thinking about." Vanessa snapped out of it nearly as fast as the depression reared its ugly head. Self-pity would do no one any good. "Come here." She pulled Lillian back down beside her.

They talked for hours, bathed in the moonlight while surrounded by the peaceful rhythm of crashing waves. A mare and her colt trotted along, pausing at the side of the boat to investigate their new island-mates. Lillian's eyes watered at the display. Vanessa wiped a tear from Lillian's cheek and looked on at her with a full heart. The island was overflowing with beauty, if only you took the time to look.

The new couple's conversation lasted long into the night. Snippets of their dialog and brief bursts of laughter could easily be heard farther down the beach, where Isabelle sat alone, waist-deep in the surf, staring out into the black water. She had sat down hours ago when the tide was out and the waves were only just nipping at her toes. Each time the women's laughter made it to her ears, she covered them with her palms in a vice-like grip. Isabelle eventually relented and lay flat on the sand underwater, watching as the waves passed overhead. Beneath the surface, only the crashing surf broke the silence, and she smiled.

ISLAND: DAY NINE

Miller strolled down the beach in a pair of cargo shorts he found in an abandoned tent. He wore nothing else. He didn't even carry a knife or sharp stick for protection. He leaned down for a rock and sent it skimming across the water and grinned when he counted one more skip than the last time. He had grown to love the island, especially at sunrise; it was fast becoming a home. From swimming laps and collecting driftwood during the day to spending his evenings talking with Soraya, then snuggling up next to her at night, it was the ideal of perfection in his mind.

Most mornings, he would meet Sam down by the shower house for coffee and conversation. His elder felt it wise that someone keep watch when those inside were left so vulnerable. Miller didn't think it was necessary, but if it made Sam feel a little better, then who was he to argue. He enjoyed these talks quite a bit. If asked, he would say he very much looked forward to them, as he valued the man's wisdom, but more than that, Sam reminded him of his own father and how much he missed him.

"Been meaning to ask. Why the change of heart, Captain?" Sam asked from behind a steamy coffee mug.

"Honestly, it was the swim," Miller said. "When Soraya and I finally reached land, we had a brief moment to relax and catch our breath. In that instant, I forgot about everything: the running, the fighting, those things, and what we've lost. And just like that, it was gone and we were back to back, weapons drawn, ready for anything. I wanted to slow down. I needed to slow down."

"Well, you made the right call, son. You've earned this break." Sam offered his hand.

"Thank you, sir." Miller returned the gesture.

The door to the bathhouse opened. Soraya and Rachel cut through the steam and strode into the cool morning air. The ladies would keep watch now.

"All yours, boys," Rachel said.

"Much obliged." Sam tipped his hat. He wasted no time entering the bathhouse.

Miller briefly paused as he exchanged smiles with Soraya. While they passed, the pair of them instinctively extended their arms, unconsciously reaching for one another. Their palms gently ran the length of the other's forearm as they each went their separate ways.

Inside, Miller wiped steam from the mirror above the facility's lone sink, and it dawned on him that he hadn't seen his own reflection since sometime before touching down in Philadelphia. His hair was at least an inch longer, and his beard was not much further behind. Miller let the warm water wash over him. He stood beneath the spray for a time, far longer than he had at any point since before enlisting. If felt good. Having nowhere to rush to was a godsend, but the quiet and the tranquility of it all instilled in him a sense of peace long since forgotten.

Truth be told, Miller was growing fond of the slight lack of responsibility. More importantly the closest carrier was a mile away. The people in his care could sleep at night. And if they could sleep, he could sleep. He found himself of late going hours at a time without thinking of the carriers or the true horror of what they represented.

Marisol was eager to beat the rush to the bathhouse; she dragged a still half-asleep Isaac with her. Soraya and Rachel were relieved of sentry duty. Soraya had to meet with Aiko anyway. She had promised the medic that she wouldn't try to remove her own stitches.

The medics had a humble makeshift facility set up just outside of camp. It wasn't even remotely sterile, but it served their needs so long as no one got themselves too banged up.

"One more to go," Aiko said enthusiastically. She gently tugged on Soraya's sole remaining stitch with her tweezers, lifting it just enough to get the scissors beneath, snipped, and pulled it free. "All done, and it's healing nicely, I'll add," she said as she wiped the area down with whiskey.

"Thank you, Aiko." Soraya pressed gently on the scar. To her surprise, there were very few raised spots. "It feels much better now. Should I still bandage?"

"I don't think that's necessary. Maybe when you sleep so you don't accidentally bang it up, but no, let it breathe. If it bleeds at all, come see me. Otherwise, I think you're good."

"I am glad to hear this, Aiko." Soraya rose and stretched as she looked out to the horizon.

"So what's on the docket for today?"

"I do not know. Rachel and I have discussed rowing over to the lighthouse. I have wanted to see the view from it since we arrived."

"Sounds like fun. If the place is secure, it could make for a good storm shelter at the very least."

"I have thought of this as well."

"Be safe out there."

"We will. Take care, Aiko."

Soraya and Rachel had two choices: drag one of the boats two miles across sand and rocks or swim the half-mile distance to the lighthouse. There was really no decision to be made. The span from their island to the lighthouse was only half the distance, maybe less, that she and Miller had swum a little over a week prior. Only a week ago, this impromptu jaunt would have been considered foolhardy and voted against, but now, when everyone had full bellies and their strength had returned, no one batted an eye at the idea. Soraya had to insist that Miller not join them, much to his dismay, but she was adamant. Rachel was offended at the implication that they needed a babysitter, so Miller backed down.

The swim was refreshing and surprisingly quick. Afterward, they pulled themselves safely ashore before marching to the far side of the lighthouse, but not before lying on the cool wet sand closer to the water to catch their breath, always with a wary eye on their new surroundings. The dry sand farther away from the beach was hotter than they expected; they laughed and raced to the shade offered by the towering structure.

The entrance to the lighthouse was not visible from the island. Otherwise, Soraya and Rachel would have realized that this was a wasted trip. The door was burned from its hinges. Inside the lighthouse was charred black. Ancient wooden steps leading to its peak had collapsed in the fire. The lighthouse was a bust. Amidst the rubble, a handful of skeletons poked through the debris. Odd limbs were raised like corn growing out of a burnt field. It was impossible to tell if they were the lighthouse keeper and his family or a small group of infected. It didn't matter who it was. The lighthouse would remain nothing more than a landmark.

"You think they're going to get up?" Rachel nudged one of the bony stalks.

"The skeletons? No. Their brains would boil in their heads in the fire. They are dead."

"Comforting. Gross. But comforting."

"We should go." Soraya pointed to several infected that were approaching the lighthouse property from the mainland. A small strip of land connected the lookout to the once-bustling city beyond.

"I'm sorry, Soraya. I know you've been looking forward to this."

"Is okay. We still have the island. Come, let us go home." Soraya could feel her eyes welling, her frustration mostly over what she imagined the lighthouse could have been. If Rachel had asked, she would have blamed it on the salt spray. Had the lighthouse worked out, she had every intention of surprising Miller with their own private retreat, a place where they could be alone and intimate. Instead, she had to return empty-handed to a crowded campsite.

Later that evening, as she and Miller sat beside the fire, listening to the group's tales of the way things used to be, Soraya lamented the loss of the lighthouse.

"I'm sorry the lighthouse didn't work out for you." Miller kissed her hand and offered sympathetic eyes.

"Thank you, Miller. Is no big deal. Something else will come along." She ran her fingers through his hair, mussed it a bit, and smiled. "Your hair is getting long."

He scratched his beard. "It is. I hadn't thought about it until today. I should check the *Emerald Star*. Maybe there's an old pair of scissors lying around."

"Keep it. I like it this way."

Miller kissed her on the top of her head.

Soraya snuggled in beside him. Firelight danced around them, and all was well with the world.

ISLAND: DAY TEN

For someone who was fast to denounce the idea of staying on the island, Radzinski was the first of Miller's unit to abandon his gear. He could often be seen wandering their new home in nothing more than black boxer-briefs. Occasionally he armed himself with his knife or pistol. Usually, though, he simply carried a piece of driftwood that he liked to swing around at imaginary foes. He and Marisol had been meeting randomly for nearly a week at various private locales around the island. The shipwreck was a favorite spot when it was available. Marisol couldn't stand the guy, and Radzinski, for his part, well, didn't care for much of anyone. They were kindred spirits in a sense, at least in that neither of them had zero fucks to give regarding what people thought of them. They each desired something the other possessed, and that was the extent of it.

"Oh shit, oh shit, oh shit," Radzinski panted.

Marisol was bent over the main console in the wheelhouse of the *Emerald Star*. He mounted her from behind, pounding harder during each thrust. Radzinski kept a firm grasp on her hips, he pulled her toward him in time with her rhythm, and with each of their movements, both of them worked faster and faster. Their naked skin slapped against each other's bodies repeatedly, echoing in the small chamber and out into the open air beyond the sun-drenched deck.

"Oh God!" Marisol reached back, desperately pulling Radzinski closer. She dug her fingernails into the back of the man's thigh, all the while forcing herself backward onto him. She was concentrating on a third orgasm and trying her hardest not to think about the brute behind her when Radzinski pulled out moments before release.

For a moment, the two stood there, panting, spent. Her elbows were digging into the console. His arms dangled at his side. Radzinski slapped her on the ass a few times, followed by a series of grunts she couldn't imagine turned anyone on. Marisol rolled her eyes and pulled herself up off the uncomfortable perch.

"If you're finished, you can get off of me now. I've got things to do today." Marisol pushed Radzinski's weight off of her, and he collapsed backward into the captain's chair, his sweaty naked ass slapping against its surface as he came down.

"Like what? We're doing all there is *to* do," he replied, followed by another series of grunts before he cleared his throat and spat a thick mucus ball across the room.

"Washing your stink off of me, for one. Now get out of the way," she said wearily. "God, you're disgusting."

"What's your problem?" Radzinski asked rhetorically as he squeegeed sweat from his chest and stomach with a finger before flicking it onto the floor.

"Keep fucking me like that and we won't have a problem," she quipped while wiping her body off with a crumpled-up shirt. She placed extra emphasis into cleaning her back.

"Now that's my kind of girl. No strings attached. Just the way I like it." He leaned back in the chair, interlocked his fingers behind his head, and grinned from ear to ear.

"And why in the hell would anyone want strings attached to you?" Marisol shot back while quickly dressing.

"Never liked strings myself, babe. But hey, I think I got a little more in me. Why don't you help me out over here? Put those lips to good use." He shook his cock in her direction, slapping it against his stomach.

"What makes you think I want any more of your dick today? You're pretty limber for a big guy. Blow yourself. Next time I need something, I'll let you know. In the meantime, stay out of my fucking way." Marisol slid on her tank top and headed for the exit.

Radzinski chuckled and followed that up with another nice wad of spit for the floor. He leaned over to retrieve his clothes. His smile quickly faded as he picked up his crumpled shirt, the same one Marisol had just discarded.

"You cleaned up with this?" he asked before he threw his soiled shirt at the door, barely missing Marisol on her way out. "You bitch." He laughed as he lit up another cigarette. Radzinski leaned back in the chair and exhaled a small cloud of smoke. "Fucking paradise."

ISLAND: DAY TWELVE

The shipwreck of the *Emerald Star* had become a popular getaway spot. For some, it was a reminder of how lucky they were to even be alive. For others, though, the ship offered privacy not afforded elsewhere on the island without having to first walk miles out of the way. Elliot rounded the corner on his way topside. He was quickly buttoning his pants. In his haste, he crashed into Marisol, sending her back a few steps. She nearly drew her sidearm.

"Oh, hey, Elliot. What's the rush? A couple weeks ago and I would have shot you dead," she joked.

"No rush. Just need some air is all. I forgot something back at camp. Need to check on something. Gotta go." Elliot hurried up the steps, snatched up his shoes, and hopped over the side of the boat.

"Okay. See ya later, I guess." She rolled her eyes at the man's strange behavior and continued below deck.

Marisol hung her sidearm on a hook on the wall before kicking her boots off and stretching her toes against the hard floor of the cabin. She peeled off her tank top, draped it across the top of a cabinet, then did the same with her jeans. Standing there, it occurred to her that she hadn't worn her sheriff's uniform or badge in weeks, it seemed, and come to think of it, she didn't miss them in the slightest. An early evening swim would do her good. It would help take her mind off being so bored, she hoped. Sure, they were safe for the first time in ages, but they were living on a giant sandbar. This wasn't exactly what sprang to mind whenever she thought of an island paradise.

A thump from a nearby closet caught her attention. She slowly backed toward the recess as she pretended to look herself over in a badly cracked mirror. When she was within reaching distance, she turned quickly and yanked the door open.

"Radzinski, how many times do I have to..." Marisol was rendered speechless at the sight of Isaac standing naked in the closet, covering his manhood with his hands.

"I can explain, ma'am. It's not what it looks like," he stammered.

"Isaac, what the fuck? Wait a minute. Were you...?" Marisol pointed topside. "And Elliot? Really?"

"Oh my God. Ma'am, please. Please don't say anything. Please," Isaac begged.

"Um, Isaac, I've known you were gay for years. What's the big deal?" Marisol said, slightly offended.

"Not for me, Sheriff. For him." Isaac nodded in the direction Elliot had run off in. "It's Elliot. He says he's not fitting in well with the others, and well, I can just tell it would devastate him if he thought anyone knew about this."

"What people get up to on their own time is none of my business." She shrugged. "His secret is safe with me."

"Thank you, but do you mind passing me my pants, ma'am? I'm feeling kind of exposed here." Isaac blushed. "They're right over there behind the console."

"Oh, sorry. Here you go." Marisol tossed Isaac's clothes in his direction, but they landed just out of reach, far enough for him that he had to lunge from his darkened closet and out into the light.

"You did that on purpose," he sneered as he quickly held the tangled pants in front of him.

"Modesty went out the window a long time ago, in case you haven't noticed." Marisol motioned to herself. A pair of black panties was all she wore. If Isaac had waited a moment longer to make a noise, she would have been completely naked herself.

"I know, ma'am. It's just..." Isaac stammered again.

Marisol wasn't about to make the man explain himself. It was no business of hers how he felt. Besides, *she* was the one who barged in on *them*, unwittingly or not. "Hey, to each their own, right? And how many times to I have to tell you about that 'ma'am' shit? Do you see a badge on me?" She pointed to the spot on her chest where a gold star had rested for years.

"Yeah, about that, I've been meaning to ask you what's been going on lately. Is everything alright? You loved that uniform," he asked with an air of slight concern before he bit his lip and pressed a little further. "And Radzinski, what the hell is that all about?"

Marisol shrugged. "I know *exactly* what I'm getting with him. Besides, he's hung like a fucking horse."

"Sheriff!" Isaac blushed.

"What? Like you've never gone after the wrong one because of what he's working with. There's nothing more to it. Believe me." She gestured to his state of undress. "You're not the only one around here with needs, Isaac. As far as the uniform goes, I don't need it. The clothes don't define me. I put on that uniform to help people, and I can still help without it. I loved what it stood for. If Pepperbush needed me, I was there, no questions asked. The badge, the uniform, it helped me keep people safe and, well..." Marisol curled her lip before stretching her arms against a wooden overhang, allowing the joints in her shoulder blades to crack. She stood there a moment, arms outstretched, tapping her fingertips against the wood. "I'll put it to you like this, Isaac," she said. "I am far from done helping these people or any others we may come across in any way that I can, but that uniform, the one *you're* still wearing, it represents Pepperbush, and Pepperbush is gone."

"You did all you could for them, ma'am. A lot of souls made it out of there that night thanks to you," Isaac offered.

"I refuse to beat myself up or even give a second thought to those we've lost. I did all I could, when I could. I have nothing to be ashamed of. No regrets here, but I choose to move forward. I have to leave the past where it belongs. Same as this conversation. Anyway, Isaac, I've got a swim to get to. Care to join me?" Marisol stripped off her panties and stood in the doorway, hand outstretched, her body a black silhouette against the fading sun outside.

Isaac paused for a moment. There she was, naked for the world to see and bathed in the day's fading light. Her cards were laid on the table, and she was unafraid. Marisol never looked back or backed down. She'd always been that way, he realized. Nothing to hide. Ever. It only took an awkward moment in a shipwreck at the end of the world to make him see. He dropped his pants to the floor and took her hand. The gesture was liberating. The simple act of standing nude in front of her stirred a sense of confidence never before felt in the man. "I'd love to join you, Marisol."

ISLAND: DAY SIXTEEN

On the deck of the *Emerald Star*, the dawn's first rays broke over the horizon, already warming Vanessa and Lillian from a cool but not at all cold night's sleep. The couple had been staying on the boat more often of late. Not a soul seemed to care. Lancaster, of course, grumbled, but no one paid him any mind.

Lillian rose first and slowly untangled herself from Vanessa's limbs before rising to her feet and stretching.

"Hey, you. Been up long?" Vanessa asked, lips slightly quivering as she reached for Lillian's hand.

"Only a minute. Sleep well?" she asked, tucking the blanket back around Vanessa.

"Mm-hmm," she answered while wrapping the blanket around herself. "Didn't wake up even once."

"Same here." Lillian leaned on the edge of the boat, letting the warm sun engulf her face. Its warmth brought a smile and a sense of contentment she never thought possible.

Vanessa opened the sheet and pulled Lillian back down to the deck. "I could stay here with you forever," she said as she wrapped Lillian up.

"Me too."

Sunrise on the island was always quiet, peaceful. Jeremiah usually took this time to walk the beach and contemplate their current situation without the distractions of his fellow island-dwellers. Instead, he and Aiko woke Miller and Sam early for an impromptu but much-needed discussion on present and future issues.

"I'm of the mind that we should be leaving this place soon," Jeremiah said without a hint of doubt. "We cannot stay here indefinitely, and people are becoming complacent. Just yesterday I witnessed two of them skinny dipping without a care in the world."

"Since when did you become a prude? What's wrong with that?" Miller's face contorted with confusion as he handed Jeremiah a cup of coffee.

"Thank you. On the surface, there's absolutely nothing wrong with the act. Do as you will. Enjoy yourselves while you can. I'm not here to judge. My point is that there wasn't a weapon in sight," he said accusingly. "At the very least they should have had someone standing guard."

"And complacency breeds outright laziness if left to its own devices," Aiko added. "I could name a half dozen of them right now who haven't lifted a finger to help since we settled in. When we inevitably get back on the road, that behavior will be a liability that jeopardizes us all. I'll defer to your judgment on this, of course, Miller, but you know where we stand."

"While we're at it, I *have* noticed some folks are beginning to splinter off into separate groups. We're gonna need to keep an eye on that," Sam commented.

"You're right about that. We can't afford to have anyone feeling like an outsider. Not now, not here," Miller replied.

"It's unreasonable to think we can stay here indefinitely. I'm beginning to wonder if some of these people consider this island the end of the line. I get the sense that the majority feel we can sustain ourselves on horse meat alone," Jeremiah said with an air of astonishment.

"Jeremiah's right. After all, this island *is* nothing more than a glorified sandbar. One good storm could wipe us out. There'd be no sign we were ever here," Sam added.

"True, but the end of hurricane season is right around the corner. We've already discussed that. What's the rush?" Miller asked. The sudden urgency to try to instill a sense of discipline onto a majority group of civilians seemed out of place in light of their new home, the first real home they'd ever known as a group.

"For one, the infected across the inlet have been growing in numbers daily. It was foolish to assume they would stay out of the water," Jeremiah stated. "I've been studying them since they arrived over the past few days, and they've been testing the surf. An individual carrier or a small group of them will walk in our direction until a wave knocks them over. By the time they right themselves, they've usually been washed back ashore, down current, and the process starts all over again. Sooner or later, they *will* figure out how to get past the waves," Jeremiah warned.

"Those are rough waters out there between us and the mainland. Even if they figure out the surf, there's no way they can make it past the current," said Sam. "I'm all for caution, son, but I honestly can't imagine those things ever making it over here."

"Maybe, maybe not. Are you willing to take that chance?" asked Jeremiah. "For the sake of argument, let's say they do cross. Then what? This isn't the road. We can't just run away. You and everyone else, myself included to an extent, may feel safe here, but the truth of the matter is that we're trapped." Jeremiah slowly spun, pointing out the endless Atlantic on the horizon and the growing number of infected, which had no doubt originated from the resort, gathering just across the inlet.

Miller straightened his posture, as if the conversation had awoken a dormant sense of duty. "If we're airing worries, then there's also the matter of the swim if we lose the boats for one reason or another. I'm up for it again. Are you? What about Sam and even Lancaster? Zero chance Casandra makes that swim. I can pick out half of the civilians off the top of my head who have no chance at making it, either. No offense, Sam."

"None taken. You'll get no arguments here. Hell, I'm not sure if I could have made that swim thirty years ago."

"So we need an exit strategy, but more importantly, we need to consider moving on," Miller said, trying not to reveal his disappointment. "Some of them are not going to like it, but I really don't see any other choice now that you've brought it up."

"Correct. There *is* one additional immediately pressing issue, though," Jeremiah added.

"Why do I get the feeling that what you're about to say is what brought this talk up in the first place? It's not like you to bite your tongue. What is it, Jerry?"

"I'm pregnant." Aiko stepped forward and spoke before Jeremiah finished processing exactly how to go about revealing the news. Aiko stayed quiet for most of the discussion for this very reason, weighing the pros and cons of even telling Miller in the first place. More than once she considered pulling Jeremiah away and backing out of the planned reveal entirely.

"We've been hiding it, but that will be impossible soon." Jeremiah put his arm around her, and it all clicked for Miller. The pair of them acting distant and setting up their own separate camp far away from the others should have been a clue that something was going on, but he completely missed it. In his contentment with the island, he had become blind to the details. What else had he missed?

"How far along are you, sweetheart?" Sam asked.

"Three months, give or take. I only found out a few days before we were deployed to Philadelphia."

"That long ago. Why didn't you say anything?" Miller asked.

"When was I supposed to do that? When we were running from infected or when we were being shot at? I'm telling you now."

"Point taken. How are you feeling otherwise?"

"Morning sickness and cramps are manageable, and I can still run, but give it another six weeks and, well... Let's just say I'd like to be in someplace a little more secure by then. Honestly, I'm fine. You wouldn't know I was pregnant if I didn't tell you. It's Casandra that I'm worried about. I don't want her giving birth on the road, and I'd really prefer not to have to do it here. We can leave now with an extremely pregnant Casandra *or* in a few weeks with a crying baby. I vote we head for the mainland, all of us. When we get there, we barricade the shit out of one of those hotels, soundproof an entire floor, and go from there."

"That's good enough for me. It's settled, then. Getting you and Casandra someplace secure and out of the elements is the priority," Miller said with a purpose not seen in weeks. "We're leaving in forty-eight hours."

ISLAND: DAY EIGHTEEN

Nisha awoke on the beach again. She had lost track of how many nights she'd spent out there, waiting and hoping Isabelle would come around. Warmth surrounded her body on all sides. She blinked, then covered her eyes. *Wow, that's bright*, she thought. She must have passed out last night. Early morning, more like it. Why did she even bother anymore? The group would be leaving tomorrow, first thing, and Isabelle was nowhere to be found. Nisha noticed that the meal she offered her last evening was partially eaten. That was a good sign, although it was just as likely crabs could have been nibbling on it.

Nisha noticed a head out in the surf, just above the waves. It was staring back at her. It startled her for a moment, a million thoughts passing through her brain in a matter of seconds. She was on her feet and ready to dash back for camp when she realized the face staring back at her wasn't one of the undead; it was Isabelle. Nisha gasped a sigh of relief as she approached the water. Smiling over her paranoia, she waved to her friend. "What are you doing out there, Izzy? Aren't you worried about sharks or the undertow?"

As had been typical of late, Isabelle didn't respond. Nisha assumed she wouldn't, but she had to try, anyway. Isabelle merely stared back at her, eyes cold and lifeless.

"Why don't you come on out of there, Isabelle? I'm worried about you. Let's go see if Lillian's awake yet. Would you like to talk to her today?" Nisha pleaded, trying not to sound demanding, but these little fits of Isabelle's were wearing her thin.

Isabelle slowly swam toward shore, snaking left and right, taking her time, and toying with Nisha's nerves.

"That-a-girl. Come on out of there. Let's get you warmed up." Nisha held up Isabelle's ragged dress; it would have to do as a makeshift towel.

Isabelle emerged from the surf naked and bloody, a shiny blade in her left hand. A long crescent moon–shaped gash beginning at her right clavicle continued down and over her left breast, ending just below her right hip bone. The wound seeped blood. Everywhere from her chest to her feet was red with it.

"My God, Isabelle. What did you do to yourself?" Nisha shouted.

Isabelle remained listless while Aiko sewed her up under the mid-afternoon sun. If she felt the pain of hundreds of stitches, it didn't show. She spent most of the operation picking grime from her fingernails. When that bored her, she would tug on fresh stitches, which of course incensed Aiko. Her little show, if that was what it even was, concerned those in attendance. Even the medics had never witnessed someone grow this detached and unstable so rapidly.

Lillian looked on in distress, eyes growing red, though she held back any tears due in large part to Vanessa's presence at her side. Isabelle hadn't bothered to say one word to her since their arrival on the island, and it hurt. The more Lillian dwelt on the issue, the more she realized that her mother hadn't spoken with her at all since her father and brother died. The realization turned grief to ire as she wanted to scream at the woman.

Look at me. I'm your fucking daughter, goddammit! She wished she could roar but couldn't. As furious as she grew, Isabelle was still her mother, and whether she deserved it or not, at this point, at the very least, she would have Lillian's respect.

Others in the group had gathered around, curious to catch a glimpse at Isabelle, considering most hadn't even seen her since their arrival.

"Do you think she was trying to kill herself?" Samantha asked.

"Suicide by shark? No fucking way. Who's ever heard of such a thing?" said Elliot.

"Who's ever heard of the dead returning to life?" Marisol added. "Yet here we are."

"Well, tell me then: why would anyone cut themselves and then go swimming in the ocean?" Nisha asked rhetorically, still visibly shaken.

"I don't know, but I think the woman has a death wish. That much is clear. If we let her, she *will* become a danger to us all," Marisol said sternly and without remorse.

"We could leave her a gun and supplies. When we find a safe place, maybe we send someone back for her," Elliot suggested.

"No, she'd be trapped on this island and most likely not make it through hurricane season," said Miller. "We've come this far together. We take her with us. This isn't even a discussion. I refuse to leave Tobias's widow alone on a deserted island, no matter how far gone she is."

"Studies suggest she's just as likely to suddenly snap out of it or progressively get worse. There really is no way of knowing," said Jeremiah.

Aiko finished up with Isabelle, who casually walked off afterward. "Isabelle really fucked herself up." Aiko was in disbelief. She shook her head back and forth slowly as she watched Isabelle disappear back out beyond the waves. "She started cutting somewhere just above her left collar bone, down over her left breast, across and down her stomach, then over her right hip bone and off the top of her right thigh. She took it slow, too. It was easily a twenty-six-inch-long gash, deep enough to need attention but far from life-threatening, even on a nearly deserted island—almost as if she knew what she was doing. And that's what worries me the most."

Rather than gawk at Isabelle, most of the others decided to get a jump on preparing the boats for the next day's journey. Halfway to the boats, Bernie sat down, his arms full of supplies, and silently stared off into the distance.

"What is it?" Casandra asked, wrapping her arm around Bernie's waist in the process.

"I sure would have liked to check out that lighthouse while we were here," Bernie said, adjusting his hat while staring at the landmark.

"Well, it's not like you were pressed for time." Casandra elbowed him in the ribs. "Besides, Soraya said the place was a wreck, anyway."

"I know. I just would like to have seen it myself, is all."

"Aww, there'll be other lighthouses. Just you wait," Casandra replied. "I *am* going to miss that shower, though."

Bernie smiled. Casandra hugged his arm, forcing him to drag her along to the boats and dropping half of his supplies in the process.

Camp was quiet that final evening. The mood had soured thanks to Isabelle. The group spent its last night on the island, sorting through their dwindling supplies. Everything they couldn't live without was in one pile. Everything else was in another. It would be left behind for anyone else who might find themselves in need. A never-ending supply of horse meat and whatever seafood they bothered to catch gave most of the group a false sense of security. Hot showers and miles of private beach only exacerbated the feeling. In the almost three weeks spent on the island, nearly all the Pepperbush survivors fell victim to apathy of one degree or another. Even most of the soldiers were not immune to the island's charms. In reality, they should have left a week ago, maybe more, and Miller knew it. It only took a conversation with a trusted friend to make him see. He had become just as complacent as those Jeremiah had warned about. Miller was sure that a large portion of the discussion that morning was Jeremiah's way of pointing out Miller's own shortcomings, and it worked. They would be leaving in the morning.

W.J. Hegarty

CHAPTER THIRTEEN

Migration

The streets of Poseidon's Rest were empty, save for trash and discarded items blowing in the ocean breeze. Up and down the main drag, buildings were boarded up and ransacked, or in more than a few cases, only burnt-out shells remained. Corpses in all stages of decay littered the pavement. Most had obviously been gnawed upon by human teeth. Others were dismembered and scattered. Wild dogs chewed on a corpse in an adjacent alley, rending flesh from bone. Many of those feral animals still adorned collars, a grim reminder that in the not-too-distant past, most of these man-eaters were someone's loving pets.

"Oh my God, that's horrible." Samantha shied away from the grisly sight. She turned to Markus, covering her eyes.

"This way. Come on. Don't look," he said as he put his arm around her, directing her away from the gore.

None of this went unnoticed to Damon as he walked a few meters behind them. He raised his hand into the shape of a mock gun. Pointing in Samantha's direction, he made sounds of false gunfire. Radzinski snickered at the display. Elliot pretended not to see it.

Jeremiah was indifferent to the carnage; he took little notice of the gore and destruction. This was life now, and in his eyes, the faster you adjusted, the better chance you had at survival. "It's in their nature. Every living creature will do what it must to subsist. Survival remains the basest instinct that drives us all, man and beast alike."

Radzinski leaned in to offer his two cents on the observation, whether welcomed or not. "They're just hungry dogs, Jerry," he whispered, perhaps trying to spare the one member of the group he respected embarrassment. "No need to get all deep on us."

Jeremiah ignored the comment but continued his observation of the ruined city just the same.

Lillian listened to the exchange and couldn't help but steal a peek in her mother's direction. Isabelle's attempted cannibalism only a few weeks ago would not soon be forgotten. Everyone was starving, and of course, they all wanted to live, but if Aiko and the others hadn't stopped her, Isabelle would have surely eaten Ayn's flesh. The love she once felt for her mother was slowly fading in the face of what the woman was apparently capable of now that half of her family had been killed. It was selfish of her to act like this. To cut herself off from the group was one thing, but to completely ignore her daughter was unforgivable. Lillian lost her family as well that night. That trauma shouldn't have been her mother's burden to bear alone.

Isabelle walked apart from the bulk of the group, close enough so as not to be constantly reminded to keep up but far enough away that it was clear she wanted to be left alone.

The sight of her mother still wearing that threadbare gray dress disgusted Lillian. "If you didn't know any better, you'd think she was one of them," she finally said.

Vanessa simply rubbed Lillian's back as they walked. What more needed to be said on the issue? Day by day, it was becoming increasingly clear that Lillian had lost her entire family that night at the cabin.

Vanessa periodically turned to look back at the horizon. The home she grew to love in only a few short weeks was nearly invisible in the distance.

"You keep looking back. The island's getting pretty small now, isn't it? What, did you forget something?" Ryan asked.

"No, no. I'm just wondering if maybe we should have stayed after all," Vanessa replied with a final glance back at the place.

"I was thinking the same thing." Ryan gave the island a final look himself. "If I asked, I know Rachel would have said yes."

"Then why didn't you? A few more people on board might have changed my mind, too."

"Because she worries about him." Ryan nodded toward Miller, who was up on point. He returned to form as soon as they put boots down in Poseidon's Rest. "She admires the guy," Ryan continued. "I can respect that, and she wouldn't be able to live with herself wondering every night if he made it or was dead in a ditch somewhere."

"We'll make it someplace where we can *all* settle down," Vanessa replied. "I really believe that." She kept her eyes forward this time. No more looking back.

"Let's hope so." Ryan tightened his bag's straps and picked up the pace.

• • •

The road-weary survivors roamed the city's abandoned streets for what seemed hours. Every building they passed was either completely destroyed or long ago looted of vital supplies. Coming upon the first halfway decent vehicle they had seen since leaving its boats behind, the group stopped in near unison. It had done this before with no luck. Elliot dropped his bag and leaped behind the wheel. He didn't know the first thing about a functioning vehicle, much less one left in disrepair.

"What does he think *he's* doing?" Casandra asked.

"Not a clue. This should be good," Bernie replied.

Elliot fiddled with exposed wires beneath the dash. Obviously someone else had tried this and failed. He would have loved help, but it was clear that no one else was interested in this heap; they just wanted to move on. Frustrated, he slammed his hands down on the dash, bringing the car's long-dormant alarm system to life. The warning was deafening. Its piercing whine echoed off the empty buildings and down alleyways for blocks in all directions.

"For Christ's sake, turn that thing off!" Miller yanked Elliot from the car. He dove into the driver's seat and fiddled beneath the dashboard, yanking out every loose wire and fuse he could reach. Nothing he did would stop the incessant sound. "What did you do to this thing?"

"I don't know. I just leaned against it, man. It's not my fault." Elliot paced outside the car, hands to his head in panicked desperation.

Bernie slammed both of his hands down hard on the car's hood. "Pop it, man. Pop it!"

Miller fiddled beneath the dash until he came across a set of levers. He pulled each one furiously until finally the hood unlatched. Bernie threw the cover open and began furiously rummaging. While Casandra held the hood aloft, Bernie dug deep behind the engine cavity. His face strained, his body twisted as he reached deeper into the maze of metal and wire.

"I think I got it," he said as he yanked a handful of wires from their housings. "Fuck." A second handful of wires came free, and the ear-splitting whine ceased.

Miller let out a sigh of relief. He closed his eyes as he let his head go forward to rest on the steering wheel. Raised voices from outside of the car jostled him from his all-too-brief moment of quiet. The upright hood of the car blocked his view of the commotion. Yet another issue requiring his attention—he was sure of it.

"You fucking asshole!" Damon yelled before punching Elliot in the face. Off-balance, the already embarrassed man fell backward over a downed motorcycle, landing back-first on the curb. Damon continued his assault. As Elliot lay on the ground, Damon began kicking him in the ribs and stomach, all the while cursing his clumsiness. Lancaster slunk behind a nearby van, lest anyone take the opportunity to let out their frustrations on him again.

"I'm sorry, man. I didn't do it on purpose," Elliot pleaded while shielding his face from Damon's unrelenting blitz. The pummeling continued long after Elliot felt a rib snap beneath Damon's heavy boots.

Radzinski laughed and turned his back on the beating as Miller passed en route to intervene. Miller knew Radzinski was an asshole, there was no denying it, but to let an innocent man take a beating like that was beyond even him, or so he thought.

"Goddammit, that's enough!" Miller grabbed Damon around the neck in a chokehold and pulled him backward, off of his victim, while Soraya dragged Elliot off the street and into a grassy patch near the sidewalk. By this point, the remainder of Miller's unit and the Pepperbush survivors joined the scene.

"Get the fuck off me!" Damon struggled against the soldier's hold. He swung wildly. His fists occasionally landed harmlessly against Miller, who squeezed tighter and leaned into the man's ear.

"Calm down, and I'll let you go," Miller whispered.

"Fuck you, man!" Damon yelled, struggling to free himself.

Miller said no more. He gently applied more pressure, quickly cutting off Damon's air supply. Within seconds, the man's flailing arms began to slow, and Damon's eyes rolled into the back of his head; he was unconscious.

"Let me take a look at you." Aiko bent down to examine the bloodied Elliot.

"I'm fine," Elliot said, shooing her away, more embarrassed than injured. "You people are fucking crazy. That guy's gonna kill someone!" he shouted, waving his hands in Damon's direction.

"Hey, man." Miller reached out in an attempt to calm Elliot.

The battered man pulled away from the attempted compassion. "I said I'm fine. Just leave me alone," he insisted as he limped into an adjacent building, one slightly less ruined than its neighbors.

Aiko attempted to go after him, but Miller stopped her short.

"Give him some space. He'll be fine," he said as they watched Elliot disappear into the structure.

Elliot's face was dotted with blood. It blurred his vision as he entered the burnt-out building. The contrast from light to darkness inside didn't help matters. A large portion of the ceiling had collapsed into the first-floor lobby, cutting off access to the nearest restroom. He made his way, stumbling through the debris, into the kitchen; it was in complete disarray, much like everything else they came across in this town. Enough light made its way into the wreckage for him to find a large washbasin still filled with dirty dishes and rotting food scraps. A hole in the ceiling allowed some light in, but in reality, all it accomplished was preventing Elliot's eyes from properly adjusting to the darkness.

He felt around the sink for a faucet and opened the valves. They were dry. *Of course they are*, he thought. Turning on the faucet released built-up pressure, causing a stirring in the pipes behind the wall. They moaned and creaked in the darkness, rattling some dishes loose from their perch above Elliot's head. The plates and saucers crashed down into the sink, clanging and shattering against unseen pots and pans.

"Motherfucker!" Elliot yelled.

He was incensed over the lack of even the most basic of needs. Much like the pipes releasing pressure, his built-up frustration over the afternoon's events boiled to the surface. He threw pans and plates in all directions, cursing his luck and circumstance as they bounced away into the darkened kitchen. Calming, he backed from the sink and tripped over a pile of rubble. The misstep put him flat on his back on the filthy floor. As he lay there motionless, his gaze caught a sliver of sunlight tearing through the roof. All the while he tried to distance himself from his predicament. The cold floor offered no comfort as tears of frustration streamed down his face. He kicked the sink. A cathartic release of sorts, it helped, if only slightly. He kicked it again and jarred more dishes loose. His outlet appeared to create a domino effect. Though he could barely see it, he could certainly hear *and* feel more dishes raining down into the sink and onto his legs. By this point, he couldn't help but laugh, and for a moment, he relaxed. It was almost peaceful, he thought, being alone in the darkness and lying atop unseen filth. Aside from the constant rattle in the wall, it was quiet, too.

He began to chuckle at the absurdity of it all. It seemed unreal even now, and a smile finally overcame him, if only for a fleeting moment as clawing hands from beneath a nearby counter scratched at his face. Those things were in here the whole time, he realized, watching him from the shadows. Two more leaped upon his chest, knocking the air from his lungs. Within seconds, more than a half dozen previously unseen infected were on him, clawing and biting at any piece of exposed flesh they could find. Elliot began to scream as another clamped its jaws down tightly over his mouth, nearly severing his lips and breaking a few of his teeth. Muffled moans were all that escaped the kitchen as Elliot was crushed under the weight of his attackers. To no avail, he swung wildly at the one attached to his face, his flailing arm a tempting lure for yet another ghoul, who immediately began rending the flesh from Elliot's fingers. The young man kicked wildly as all trace of him was covered by an ever-growing swarm of undead.

Radzinski's increased lack of discipline and outright contempt for Miller's command had become a problem that threatened to tear the group apart. Weeks on the road had only reinforced what Takashi warned Miller about nearly two months ago. Dissension in the ranks in the midst of a volatile situation like this must be dealt with swiftly and harshly. Doubt had the potential to spread like a cancer, infecting otherwise loyal subordinates or placing doubt in the minds of those you were protecting.

Miller handed his rifle and sidearm to Soraya and took off in a sprint after Radzinski. This had gone on long enough. The lingering stares from the civilians every time Radzinski piped up and questioned orders or flat-out refused them and the constant undermining of every little detail of Miller's leadership would end here and now. One way or the other, they would settle this.

"Miller, wait," Jeremiah protested. He was ever the voice of reason, but it was too late. Miller was on top of Radzinski before Jeremiah could finish his thought.

Miller lunged to shoulder the larger man in the small of his back. It knocked the wind from Radzinski, and he stumbled but stayed on his feet.

He turned and in one fluid motion elbowed Miller in the spine, sending him to the ground.

Radzinski threw down his weapons and stripped off his gear to square up against Miller. "You must have lost your fucking mind, boy." Radzinski snorted as he reached down and grabbed Miller by the back of his shirt. Radzinski's other hand firmly clenched Miller's belt. He used the momentum to slam Miller face-first into the side of the abandoned car.

Winded, Miller crawled to his knees as Radzinski pulled back his leg for a kick. Miller deflected the blow, throwing his attacker off-balance, and punched the man in the side of the knee. The ground went out from beneath Radzinski as he fell hard to the pavement. Miller didn't give him time to recover and was on top of him the second he hit the pavement, landing several blows to the man's face.

Sam stepped forward with every intention of putting a stop to the brawl. "We need to end this now!" he demanded, but Jeremiah held out his arm as a barricade.

"No," Jeremiah interceded. "This has been a long time coming. They have to sort this out now before we go any farther." Jeremiah stood by his assertion but watched the bout closely. If it got out of hand, he wouldn't hesitate to break it up.

Sam saw the logic in Jeremiah's opinion, although he wasn't comfortable letting them fight like this. He *would* remain a spectator as well.

Miller forced Radzinski's back against the car, prepared to continue the beating.

"Go ahead," the bigger man whispered.

Miller paused, his bloody fist held aloft while Radzinski spoke through red-rimmed teeth.

"Go ahead and beat me down. It won't change the fact that you're incompetent." Radzinski pushed Miller off of him and rose to his feet. "Look around you." He gestured to the ruined city and the ragtag group surrounding them. "None of this shit matters anymore. If Damon beats the shit out of Elliot or Marisol tries to kill Lancaster on a daily basis, so fucking what?" He spat a mouthful of blood onto the curb. "They're all dead anyway. All of us are, and there's nothing you can do to change that." Radzinski unsheathed his knife and pressed it hard against his throat. "All you gotta do is pull this fucker. Go ahead. Do me a favor. You want me gone so bad? Do it right here, right now."

The stubborn men stood eye to eye, each waiting for the other to make the next move. Miller turned his back on Radzinski.

"That's what I thought," Radzinski said as he put his knife away and began collecting his gear. "The road is going to kill every one of us eventually. You really think I give a shit if it's here and now at your hands instead of by one of those things when I finally slip up?"

Miller wiped blood from his busted lip. He rolled the fluid around his fingers with his thumb until it became sticky and began to dry. Radzinski wasn't completely off the mark, and once again, doubt crept in. Did he just make things worse within the group? If they had doubts, did this little scene help to dispel them or exacerbate them? "Save the self-righteous act, Radzinski. You're not fooling anyone." He turned to gather his own gear but paused mid-stride to confront Radzinski once more. "You *will* fall in line, and you *will* help me get these people to safety. Like it or not, we *are* still following command structure," Miller stated with finality. "If you don't like it, I'll leave your ass here. You want to die? Fine. I really don't care anymore, but you die alone. Otherwise, you *are* going to help me."

"You're gonna get us all killed," Radzinski added.

"You might be right. Things certainly don't look good for us, now do they?" Miller calmed. "We very well may all die out here long before we find somewhere safe, but until that happens, I'm not giving up on these people. They need us. So if you're done feeling sorry for yourself, get your shit together. We're Oscar Mike in five."

The crowd of onlookers was silent. If that was any indication of their stance on Miller's actions, he couldn't tell one way or the other. He would have to press on and hope for the best.

• • •

"Miller, you better take a look at this!" Rachel shouted from her perch atop a wrecked bus, urgency in her voice. She remained at her post as a lookout while the others busied themselves with drama. Her attention was fixed on something she was viewing through the binoculars. Rachel frantically waved her arms and pointed back in the direction they'd come from. "We've got movement," she said as Miller sprinted to the bus and joined her on its roof.

"Let me see those," said Miller as Rachel handed off the binoculars. "Shit, they must have heard us." Miller squinted against the midday sun. Though partially blinded from the glare, he could make out hundreds of infected closing in.

"Do you think they've been watching us?"

"Doubt it. I don't know if they even watch anything. I was afraid of this. Whatever they *were* doing, all this noise we're making has got their attention now." Miller jumped back to the ground. He pointed west, farther down the main stretch of the road opposite the encroaching mass.

Around him, the group frantically gathered up its belongings; some had already begun a fast-walk in the direction he'd signaled.

"That way. The big one in the distance." He singled out a tall hotel about thirty blocks away. It was easily the largest on this portion of the strip and towered over the horizon. "Let's go, people. Only take what you need. We are leaving!"

A pair of gunshots followed by three more rang out from the nearby building. Noise from crashing debris and steady footfalls grew closer to the street. Another short burst of gunfire preceded Soraya tumbling from the darkened building. She dove out of it and fell into a combat roll, then rose to her feet and ran toward the group, looking over her shoulder most of the way. "Elliot is gone," she said, out of breath. "Many inside. We must go."

Miller helped steady Soraya. He brushed some debris from off her back as the pair began running in the direction of the hotel. "We're gone, people. Move it!" he yelled. As he picked up the pace, the group followed suit and quickly left the little building behind.

In pursuit, undead poured from the structure, quickly filling the streets in the group's wake. They came from every darkened corner and burnt-out building. Two or three at a time quickly escalated into dozens, hundreds, and possibly thousands of undead shuffling down the main drag of Poseidon's Rest. Above all of it, the large hotel loomed in the distance.

Isabelle casually strolled down the center of the street as the gap between her and the rest of the group widened. Throngs of undead closed in, barely slower than the woman's nonchalant stride.

"What the hell are you doing, woman?" Miller picked off a carrier just behind Isabelle's left shoulder. Soraya took out another to her right as a third carrier's knee was blown out a second before its head exploded.

"Mom!" Lillian screamed.

Vanessa grabbed her by the belt and shirt, turning her in the direction the group was running. "Keep moving, goddammit!" Vanessa yelled, pushing her along. She fired off a few shots of her own, mostly for Lillian's benefit.

A carrier closing in on Isabelle took the brunt of Vanessa's impromptu attack, showering the woman with gore.

"Miller, we must go. We have no choice!" Soraya ceased her covering fire of Isabelle and yanked on Miller's arm. "It will be her or all of us. I am sorry. We must leave her!"

"Fuck." Miller turned his rifle to infected converging on him and Soraya. "Go!"

Isabelle wandered across the street and out onto the beach. She stood at its edge for a moment and wiggled her toes in the warm sand. She looked back at Lillian as the group became smaller in the distance. If her daughter could have seen her, she would have noticed that for the first time since Tobias and Tommy were killed, her mother looked happy. A creature lunged at her, but unsure footing in the sand hindered its progress. Another tried for the assumed easy target. Isabelle grabbed onto its shirt and used the beast's momentum to tumble over the sand, knocking down a few more of its grisly brethren. She was on her feet in a flash, slowly backing toward the sea. The beach in either direction was swarming with undead. Back on the road, her companions had grown to nothing more than indeterminate specks against the backdrop of a ruined city and hundreds of undead pursuers. She grinned before she turned and dove beneath the surf.

Isabelle slowly swam backward, out beyond the breaking waves, until the sandy bottom was far below her. She kept only her nose and eyes above water, not too dissimilar to how she observed her campmates from a distance back on Deertongue Banks. Waves crashed in front of her, disorienting or knocking down any infected that approached, then washing them away. Lillian and the rest of the group were barely more than silhouettes blending in with the detritus of the once happy resort. From their vantage point, Isabelle went completely unnoticed. As far as any of them could surmise, she had been swallowed up on the beach.

Isabelle let the current take her, only ever gently fighting its pull if she felt unseen hands grasping from the depths. She was in a riptide. Any infected that tried to claim her were powerless against its strength. The bottom was where the creatures dwelled; farther out was where she swam. Her dress was tangling, suffocating. She slid out of it in a single swift movement, and for a moment, the dress still held Isabelle's shape, high above her before the tide sucked it away. She was free to swim as she had countless hours before. When she finally surfaced, Isabelle was blocks away, her road-mates gone. She smiled before disappearing again beneath the ocean's cold inky surface.

For the most part, the strongest of the group picked up the slack for the weaker ones. After Isabelle wandered off, no one was left behind. Even so, they still managed to keep a steady pace. The hotel was quickly within reach. Its giant neon sign bore the remnants of a decadent era when gaudy was the rule of the day. It still hung proudly atop the building. The Blue Oasis would be their stronghold. The unfamiliar building would have to do, as their strength was fading. Even the strongest of the group was finally succumbing to fatigue. There was no choice; they had to rest.

The twenty-minute run to the hotel put a considerable distance between them and their pursuers, but if Pepperbush had taught them anything, it was that the undead would be here fast and in far greater numbers than when they last saw them. Eighteen blocks behind them, the legion of undead grew. The larger the mob became, the more bodies it attracted to its mass until not a square foot of asphalt could be seen beneath their crushing numbers. Countless undead resembled an army of ants descending upon a wounded animal. Soon it would encircle its prize and move in for the kill. Their sheer numbers easily rivaled the mob that attacked Pepperbush nearly two months prior.

Miller was the last one inside. As he dashed through the entrance to the lobby. He slammed a set of large double doors closed behind him. "Radzinski, Markus, bring that desk over here. Everyone else, find heavy furniture to barricade this door with!" Miller shouted on his way through a secondary entrance that left the lobby and opened into a sprawling three-story atrium capped with cathedral ceilings. Wraparound walkways overlooked the floor and stretched deep into the hotel's interior.

With the main entrance secure, Ryan was one of the last through the secondary doors. In his haste and more as a result of looking behind instead of ahead as he ran, he sent his leg crashing through a pane of glass. Blood immediately sprayed the broken window and the wall on his way to the floor. "Oh fuck!" Ryan's panicked scream echoed throughout the chamber.

"Grab him!" Markus yelled. He and Sam pulled Ryan back into the lobby by his pack and shirt and laid him onto a sofa in the waiting area.

Rachel immediately dove on the wound.

"Keep pressure on it, Rachel. I'll go find Aiko!" Vanessa sprinted off, farther into the hotel.

"I fucked up. Goddammit, I fucked up," Ryan cried.

"You're going to be okay. I've seen way worse. Trust me." Rachel tried to reassure him, but she knew the wound was bad. She pressed firmly against Ryan's thigh. Blood soaked through the thin cloth and collected in a pool on the sofa beneath him, soaking them both.

"It's bad, isn't it?" Ryan began to go pale.

"It's not good. Come on, let's get this thing elevated," Rachel suggested.

Ryan tried to lift his leg and screamed in agony before passing out. His dead weight yanked his leg from Rachel's grasp.

"Hey, stay with me, Ryan. I need you to stay awake. Can you hear me?" Rachel pleaded. "Lillian, hold his leg up. Try to keep it above his heart. Markus, grab as many cushions as you can find, on the double. We're going to get through this. You're going to be just fine." She began to sob.

It was tough for Lillian to watch. All throughout this ordeal, Rachel had been a bastion of strength and a role model. But more important than any of that, they had become friends. To witness Rachel on the edge of despair for the first time since meeting her was crushing.

Deeper in the hotel, at the atrium, a booming voice echoed throughout the chamber. "Nobody move."

Above Miller's group, spread around the second-story walkway, a group of seven armed fellow survivors drew down on them. Each of their faces was obscured behind a balaclava or a similar covering, and they were clad from head to toe in leather of various hues and tones. They brandished automatic rifles of their own.

"We have the high ground!" their leader shouted with a heavy Mexican accent. "Drop your weapons or we open fire."

They were surrounded. Miller knew it. Everyone in Miller's unit knew it, too. *How could I have been so careless?* he thought. *Clearing any unfamiliar space is always priority.* Maybe he *did* get soft on that island.

"We surrender." Miller slowly held his gun aloft, then lowered it to the floor. He turned to his companions. "Everyone, put your weapons down."

"Are you fucking kidding?" Radzinski was irate. He trained his weapon on one target, then back to another.

"He's right, John. Do as he says. They have the tactical advantage." Jeremiah lowered his weapon as well. "If they desired, we would have never seen them. All of us would be dead by now."

CHAPTER FOURTEEN

Farewell

Four of the armed group frisked Miller and the others, gathering all of their weapons into a shopping cart in the center of the room while the remaining three kept watch from the walkways above.

"Who are you and what is your business here?" their leader asked while checking for any hidden weapons on Miller's person.

"My name is Captain Miller of the United States Army," he began, arms still raised. "My unit and I have been on the road for weeks, trying to escort these civilians to safety. We shipwrecked on an island a few miles up the coast nearly three weeks ago, and due to unforeseen circumstances, we were forced to leave this morning. It wasn't much longer after that when we were overrun by a horde of those things out there. We lost two more of our own before we fled to this hotel. It looked secure enough from the outside. We didn't realize we were stepping on anyone's toes."

The black-clad leader remained motionless. He kept his gun trained on Miller, never breaking eye contact. Miller and his group were at their mercy.

"Nice to meet you, sir." The leader lowered his weapon before removing his cover. "It's good to see a friendly face on the road. That's a rare find these days. I'm Capitán Segundo Alejandro Cortez of the Mexican Army. You can call me Cortez." He slung his rifle over his shoulder and signaled for his group to do the same. "All clear, everyone. Lower your weapons.

These guys check out. You'll have to excuse the inhospitality, but you never know who you're going to run into out here," Cortez said before pointing to one of his men. "Simon, give these people their weapons back."

"On it, Cortez." Simon pulled the cart up next to the largest part of Miller's group. "No hard feelings, huh?" He grinned.

"Not sure yet," Radzinski said as he snatched up his weapons.

The remainder of Cortez's group filed in, removed their coverings, and began talking among themselves, most with pronounced accents from around the globe, all still sizing up Miller's group. They all had close-quarters combat weapons strapped to their backs, each more deadly than the next. Bludgeons and slicing weapons all around. Cortez's group had a cocksure swagger about it, was a testament to its effectiveness as a unit.

"This is quite the eclectic group you've got here, son," Sam mentioned.

A red-haired Australian with a thick beard and accent to match spoke up. "That's because we're from an international cruise ship, old-timer. Hence the flavor. Ever been on one?"

"Don't mind him, sir. He's got no couth, but he's harmless. We call him Ahole for a reason. I'm Simon, by the way." The short African American with large eyes and a warm smile offered his hand. Sam reciprocated.

"No offense intended, mate. Here, I think this was yours." Ahole handed Sam Markus's gun.

"Close enough, son, and none taken," Sam replied as he exchanged weapons with Markus.

"Nice leathers, Mad Max," Radzinski added. "I thought I saw the Interceptor parked out front. Was that yours?"

"That's funny." Ahole was wide-eyed but still smiling. "You know what's even more funny? Watching a hard-ass, smart mouth soldier get ripped to shreds cause his standard-issue fatigues aren't worth a shit."

"You still look ridiculous."

"Keep laughing, jarhead. I guarantee you those things bite and claw their way through your BDUs long before they get through this leather." Ahole gave his armor a good slap.

Ulrich chuckled. He was another of Cortez's unit, an enormous hulk of a man with long blond hair flowing halfway down his back and chest.

Ahole shook his head and gave the big man a fist bump. "Fucking amateurs."

Radzinski turned to Damon. "I think I'm going to like this guy."

The groups tentatively mingled while their leaders continued exchanging words.

Ahole, for his part, wouldn't or simply couldn't sit still. "We're not getting anywhere like this. Let me help break the ice around here. Jesus, you guys are stiff." He pranced around the room, stopping in front of each of his companions. "The big guys over there, that's Ulrich and Bull. Whatever we can't run past, they cut in two, baddest motherfuckers around." He slapped the pair of giants on their backs. Standing between them, the men towered over Ahole, who himself was nearly as tall as Radzinski. Ulrich stood proud, his hands resting upon the hilt of a giant double-bladed battle-ax. Beside him was Bull, his massive frame nearly bursting his leather armor at the seams. Like his comrades, the Haitian was fully armored below the neck. Only his bald head showed through. He carried a large war hammer that he draped over his shoulders when at rest. The both of them had their armors splashed in white war paint.

"If you don't want to lose that hand, little man, I suggest keeping it to yourself." Bull snorted.

"Aye." Ulrich nodded in agreement.

"Did I forget to mention that they're not exactly house-broken?" Ahole added, slipping between them and back to the group.

"Where the hell did you dig these two up? Impressive," Marisol asked, sizing them up.

A coffee-skinned beauty in black with blue trim strode toward Marisol. She had wild, full curls that bounced to just below her collarbone when she walked. She spoke with a soothing French accent that was known in her circles for putting people at ease. "Believe it or not, before all of this happened, they were kitchen staff aboard our ship."

"Interesting."

"Yeah, leave it to the apocalypse to bring out the beast in all of us, right?" Simon added. As he passed the ladies, he handed Marisol one of the weapons. He was over caring whose weapon belonged to whom.

Ahole continued introductions. "The blond with the flowing locks is Scandinavian. Swears he's a fucking Viking. Who am I to argue? And Bull, don't let him scare you. He's a pussycat. The guy's a family man from Haiti."

Bull spoke up. "I was working aboard Captain Kayembe's ship, saving money to buy my family passage to America when the crisis began. But that time has passed. They are gone now." Bull grimaced before smashing a nearby table with a mighty swing from his hammer.

"They *will* be avenged, brother." Ulrich consoled the man.

"What happened to his family?" Miller asked.

Cortez came in close, away from the distraught man's earshot.

"Port-au-Prince, where his family lived, was leveled in the earliest days of this bullshit. The assholes in charge thought if they bombed the shit out of the hardest-hit areas, they would have a chance to clean up the mess and retake the district. Obviously, it didn't work."

Ahole had a sudden solemnness about him. "Sorry about that, big guy. I get ahead of myself sometimes. Need to think before I speak."

"Don't apologize, Ahole. We're good." Bull slapped him on the back in a show of camaraderie. The gesture nearly bowled the Aussie over.

"Thanks, mate." Ahole regained his spirits. "Now, where was I? You lot obviously know Cortez over there is the big boss man, and Simon is returning your gear. You'll never forget me, so that leaves the lovely ladies of our illustrious troupe: Genevieve and Petrova." Ahole pointed out Petrova first, who was sporting a tight blonde ponytail without a single stray hair out of place. Curious, considering that she was wearing a brown balaclava only minutes ago. Her leathers were a deep brown with yellow highlights. "She happens to be the daughter of a prominent Russian diplomat. What the hell she's doing out here with us lot, I'll never know."

"I'm out here to be of use to the people of the ship. I am no better than the lowliest passenger," she said sternly. Her English was impeccable, though it was clear she hailed from Eastern Europe.

"Yeah, her father hangs with the uppity ups aboard our boat. The guy's got a stick so far up his ass, I swear—" Ahole began as Petrova punched him in the side, and not at all that gently.

"He *is* still my father, Ahole," she snapped.

"Who's the a-hole, me or him?"

Petrova raised her fist again.

"Okay, okay." Ahole backed off. "Yeah, yeah, I get it. Damn." He scurried away. "Fucking broad can throw a punch."

"And *I* am Genevieve." The Frenchwoman curtsied, her long curls bouncing against her leathers with the gesture. "Former French police on holiday. Now a glorified looter."

"I know the feeling," Marisol added as she approached her fellow law enforcement officer, followed closely by Isaac. The trio wasted no time discussing the difficult position that stealing just to stay alive had put the former police in. The consensus was that living in perpetual hypocrisy faded fast when your life and the lives of those you cared for were on the line.

"By the looks of things, this is a well-oiled group you have here, Cortez," Miller commented, visibly impressed.

"We get by," Cortez replied. "We keep our teams small and we travel light. We don't take unnecessary chances, and everyone on the team knows a bag of canned goods or a case of whiskey isn't worth your life, no matter what the Elite would have you believe."

"The Elite?" Miller asked.

"Yeah, the guys that run Haven. Petrova's father is one of them," said Cortez. "In light of our current situation, they've taken the whole 'haves versus the have-nots' thing to the nth degree. Their attitudes are sickening, but don't let me give you the wrong impression: life aboard our vessel is paradise compared to living out here on the road. I don't know how you did it with this many people in tow, and I certainly don't envy the idea."

"We started off with a hell of a lot more than this."

"We all did."

"Guess I'm getting rusty, but you guys had a serious jump on us back there. It could have been bad."

"We heard you coming from a few blocks off. There was a chance slight as it was that those things would have kept going had you not been so loud breaking in here. Doesn't always happen, but sometimes. You'd be surprised just how often a simple locked door keeps those things out. Of course, you guys kicked it in and led a ton of them straight to us, so now a change of plans is in order, and we *are* out of here ASAP."

"Are you guys holed up close by?"

"Yes and no. As you've heard, we *are* from an ocean liner. A cruise ship. Goes by the name Haven. We were looking for supplies, just like you guys. The only difference between our groups, as far as I can tell, is that we have a home to go back to. Roaming like this is only going to get you killed. Come with us, and I can promise you safety, security, food, and community. That's a hell of a lot more than anyone else is offering these days."

Miller pondered this a moment. A safe haven in every sense of the word. Finally, they could rest for real. No more running, no more surprises around every corner. Cortez's ship was just what they were looking for.

"Do you have room for a few more?" Miller asked hopefully.

Without hesitation, Cortez answered with a grin. "We always have room, amigo."

Miller was relieved. "What do you need us to do?"

"Well, first of all, you need to drag your own weight out of here. I won't have my people risk their lives for *anything*, and that includes potential survivors. We've gotten this down to a science over the last couple of months, and it's paid off in spades. I'm not just talking about finding good scavenge, either. Follow our lead, and we *can* get you out of here."

"He's referring to refugees. Dozens of people have come home with us," Genevieve added. "We've had no deaths on the road under Cortez's command and only a few injuries. Every one of those was when someone broke protocol."

"One caveat." Cortez's demeanor grew rigid, and his eyes went steely. "When we leave this hotel, if anyone falls behind, we *will* not stop for them. My people are the priority. Every one of them comes home alive. Every time."

"I see. So *do* you have a way out of here?"

"I do. The other exits are jammed up with God knows how many infected, but the west wing should be relatively clear. It empties into a parking lot, which is adjacent to a sand dune. The exit was barricaded when we arrived, so it's going to take some muscle to clear. The previous occupants must have fled. We found no one here. The place was deserted. The parking lot bellies right up to the dunes. We're going up and over. On the other side of that sand dune is a pier going right out into the Atlantic. That's where our pickup will be."

Aiko cut across the atrium in something just shy of a light jog, her torso and thighs soaked to dripping with blood. "Ryan's in a bad way over here, Miller. I've got him patched up but... Just follow me."

Miller and Cortez followed the medic back to the lobby, where Rachel and Lillian were looking over Ryan. Despair hung like a fog. The air in the lobby tasted of iron, and the floor and the sofa Ryan rested on were covered in blood. So were all of those who helped Aiko stabilize him. Samantha stood in a corner, nearly in shock. Markus and Vanessa worked diligently to keep her calm.

"How bad is it?" Miller asked.

"Any deeper and we wouldn't be having this conversation, so it goes without saying he missed the femoral artery, but only just."

"So what's our next move?" Rachel asked.

"He needs a transfusion. Obviously, that's not going to happen here."

"Fuck." Rachel paced the room. "He's come all this way only to die in a fucking hotel lobby?"

Cortez was obviously deep in thought, his face wrinkled and contorted as he mulled over options. "We *do* have a hospital aboard Haven," he finally said. "Our doctor is short-staffed, but we should have all the equipment you'll need to patch your friend up and see to *that* one when the time comes." Cortez motioned to Casandra, who was sitting on the sofa with Ryan. His head was in her lap. She ran her fingers through his hair as he drifted in and out of consciousness.

"If we can get him safely there, he may have a chance." Aiko put the diagnosis as gently as she knew how.

"Thank you," Rachel said, suppressing tears. "Both of you."

"Don't thank me just yet, chica," Cortez replied. "We still have to get past all of those things outside."

Radzinski and Damon watched from a far corner of the lobby. While the two groups took the time to mingle, they were busy sizing the lot of them up.

"I'm not getting fucked up over his crippled ass. If it comes down to me or Ryan, I'll leave him right here." Damon stared across the atrium to the lobby and the small group tending to their injured companion.

"You think *I* won't?" Radzinski replied. "I don't know what we can expect aboard this ship Cortez mentioned, but anything's better than this. I say we stick with these guys and get on the first boat out of here. Any stragglers can rot for all I care."

"Sounds like a plan," Damon responded with nary a stray thought toward Markus.

• • •

Preparations to leave were finalized over the following hour. A large portion of the group met in a second-story corner-room overlooking the westernmost parking lot and a long narrow alley to the north. The supplies Cortez's crew gathered were few. Even still, they were spread evenly throughout everyone's bags. Gear was strapped down tight and anything deemed not vital was discarded. Miller and his group's impromptu entrance had unfortunate consequences on an otherwise routine supply run and extraction. Large masses of infected were commonly encountered on these missions, but Cortez and his crew had become proficient in stealth, so they rarely found themselves with this many carriers aware of their presence. Regardless of the mass having thinned a little over the course of the afternoon, a deviation in the plan was deemed necessary.

"Why don't some of us go out to the end of the pier and dismantle a section from the middle? Halfway out and a six-foot gap would work just fine. It's not like those things can jump or climb," Miller suggested. "Then we can shuttle the rest of the group out there a few at a time."

"No can do, mate." Ahole shook his head. "Because of you lot making so much noise, we've had to cut this excursion short."

"What Ahole is trying to say is that we've barely even explored this part of town," Cortez explained. "We might want to come back when these things have forgotten about us and move on. For all we know, these hotels are loaded with useful supplies, so no, dismantling the pier is not an option."

"That will not work, anyway. There are too many of them out there for us to do the job." Soraya was peering out of a window and into an alleyway below that stretched east and west along the backside of the hotel.

"Right. So does anyone have any ideas how we can reach the pier without being spotted?" Miller asked.

"We need a diversion," Cortez suggested. "Someone needs to lead them away from here before we make for the pier."

"We can send one of *them* out." Ahole gestured to Miller's unit.

"Wait just a minute here. My people are exhausted. We've got wounded and two pregnant women. We barely made it this far to begin with."

"Hey, I don't like it, either, mate but someone's gotta go, and it ain't gonna be us."

"Is this how you treat all the survivors you come across? We just need a little help here," Vanessa said as calmly as she was able, not wanting to make matters worse.

"It's called brutal reality, babe. Nothing personal."

"That's enough, Ahole," Cortez interrupted. "Look, it *is* nothing personal. I feel for you guys—I really do—but I have a responsibility here that supersedes any feelings I may harbor toward refugees. All my people come home safe. Bottom line."

"Refugees, ha. Where have I heard that one before?" Markus commented.

"We're people, too, you know?" Samantha appealed. "You can't just treat us like livestock."

"Fuck these guys, Miller. They're outnumbered three to one." Radzinski fixed his rifle on Cortez.

Ahole pointed his weapon at Radzinski. Soraya unsheathed her kukri. In less than a second, a dozen guns were aimed at various heads in the room.

"Just give me the word, Miller." Radzinski fingered his trigger. "I'll grease this motherfucker right now."

"Try it, moron." Genevieve pressed her pistol to the back of Radzinski's neck. "You kill us, you're still stuck here with no place to go. Fucking macho idiot." She holstered her sidearm.

"Stand down, Radzinski. They're right. Everyone, lower your weapons. We brought this to your doorstep, and for that, I apologize, but we *can* fix this. I'll go. Just promise me you'll look after my people, Cortez."

"I'll take care of them like they're my own, Miller. You have my word."

"Outstanding! That is very magnanimous of you, young man." Lancaster had the audacity to offer Miller a handshake.

Soraya dropped the old man with a left hook. "No, I go. I am faster."

"That is completely out of the question. There's no way I'm letting you go out there alone."

"This is not for you to decide, Miller." Soraya placed her hand on Miller's chest. "The mission comes first." She looked around at the worried faces of the group and back to Miller, who had lowered his head and closed his eyes.

"No," he whispered, voice cracking, exhausted, as if the weight of the world simply refused to budge from his shoulders.

"I'm sorry," Cortez said. "But from what I can tell, this is the only way."

Jeremiah was full of remorse over what he was about to say, pain etched on his face. "She's right, Miller. I am so sorry to have to tell you this, but Soraya *is* the quickest among us. If anyone in this room has a chance of outmaneuvering those things, it *would* be her."

"Goddammit, don't you think I know that, Jerry?" Miller shouted. "Just hold on a minute. Let me think about this. There's got to be another way."

"Yeah, she looks fast to me." Damon shrugged.

Jeremiah darted across the room. He forced Damon into a wall with his forearm pressing firmly against Damon's neck. The drywall caved under the impact, leaving Damon partially embedded in it. "Never interject yourself into my conversation again. Am I speaking slow enough for that street-trash brain of yours to process?" Jeremiah pushed harder.

Damon's face went red as he choked. "Yeah, yeah, okay. Fuck, man, I can't breathe."

Jeremiah pushed forcefully again before letting go. Damon fell to the floor, gasping for air. Jeremiah watched him fall. He stood above the downed thug, daring him to get back up.

• • •

The room was illuminated in red by the day's waning light. Cortez and the others backed away to give Miller and Soraya privacy. Their conversation was so hushed that the others in the room struggled to hear. Miller's body language told the tale.

Soraya still had her hand on his chest. She used her other to raise Miller's head by his chin. His eyes were welling as they made contact with hers. "You know I am the fastest. Everything will be okay. I will make my way to the inlet, go back to the island. You can pick me up later, when everyone is safe," Soraya said with a serenity usually reserved for goodbyes.

"Soraya, it's three miles back to the boats. It'll be night soon and..."

"Then I better get going." Soraya held her palm to his cheek. "Sometimes we have to do what is best for everyone, not ourselves." She used her thumb to blot a tear for him. "We *will* meet again, Miller."

He held her gently by the waist. His fingers trembled as they danced along her belt. "I..." he tried, tears flowing freely.

Soraya gently pulled the fragile soldier's head down. She leaned up on the tips of her toes as far as she could manage to kiss him on his forehead. "I know."

The room was silent. Some looked on while others couldn't bear to watch the dying throes of yet another person they had come to call a friend.

Radzinski turned his back on the scene before quietly exiting the room. He found a spot out in the hallway where he leaned heavily against the wall.

Lillian hid her face in Vanessa's shoulder and began to sob. She clenched tightly onto Vanessa's shirt. "She's not coming back, is she?"

"Shh," Vanessa whispered softly as she gently rubbed Lillian's head. "I don't know." She wrapped her other arm tightly around Lillian. "I don't know."

Miller was frozen. The twisted reasoning of her sacrifice began to blur, and he imagined himself denying Cortez's offer and continuing the journey he and the others had started so long ago. Muffled sobs from across the room pierced his heart. He knew the survivors of Pepperbush were depending on him. He knew that continuing on like they had was futile. The road would be the death of them all. Cortez's ship was the only option left. "There's so much I want to say right now."

"I know." Soraya understood that they lived on borrowed time.

Cortez approached. The weight of their decision was not lost on the stranger. "For what it's worth, I'm sorry. Truly I am. But it's time."

The rope of bedsheets held strong. Miller, Cortez, Bull, and Ulrich slowly and carefully lowered Soraya to the alley below. Jeremiah, Genevieve, and Ahole were there to offer cover, if the need arose. She waved the all-clear when she finally reached solid footing, quickly cut herself loose of the sheets, and ducked behind a nearby dumpster. Alone in the darkening alley, she steadied herself, taking in deep breaths, preparing to sprint for an unknown location.

"You run. You run like you've never run before." Miller's voice echoed in Soraya's mind and she wondered if she would ever see him again. She looked up to the window a final time. She locked eyes with Miller and smiled for him. She gently nodded and mouthed the words "it's okay."

Miller yearned to leap down into the darkened alley with her. They could face that uncertain future together, just the two of them, instead of dying alone. He couldn't, though. Once again, the needs of the many trumped two people's desires. He had many lives that depended on him. He was their leader, and they needed him. Finally, at the end, he understood. Every decision made from the moment he saw Pepperbush's lights in the darkness was to get them to this place, right here, right now. If they had left the island a day before or a day after, where would they be? His group's best chance at survival lay with Cortez and his crew aboard this much-hyped Haven of theirs. All the sacrifice had better be worth it.

Soraya turned on the smoke detector that hung from her neck like a medallion. Its piercing wail shattered the silence. While Miller and Cortez had crafted a makeshift rope from bed linens, Soraya got to work bringing a busted smoke detector back to life. If Elliot's mishap with the car earlier in the day was any indication, the racket this thing made should lead the throngs of undead away from the hotel. There was no turning back now as she banged a steel pipe against the hollow dumpster. The commotion was working fast. At the east end of the alley, the first of a wave of undead stumbled into view. She jumped up and down, waving her arms in frantic desperation for their attention. Soraya banged on the dumpster a few more times, and the carriers finally took notice. Their pace seemed to quicken as they marched deeper into the alley.

Miller raised his rifle and quickly lined up a headshot on the infected nearest to Soraya. He was well aware that what he was about to do was wrong. His fingers trembled as he felt a stern but compassionate hand on his shoulder. Jeremiah said nothing. He simply looked his friend in the eye, his stoic facade briefly weakened at Miller's pain. To fire even one shot would risk everything. Giving away their position would render Soraya's sacrifice moot. Miller lowered his weapon and gazed south again in time to see Soraya disappear down a side street as hundreds of infected pursued her. The plan was working. As fast as the decision had been agreed upon to sacrifice one life in the best interest of the many, Soraya was gone.

Ulrich was no stranger to loss. He had a tale of his own that only Bull was privy to. He felt Miller's pain as deeply as any stranger could. Empathy was an old friend. Ulrich stepped forward, eyes lowered, sullen. He recited an old poem his father read to him as a child while the alleyway below filled to beyond capacity, overflowing with undead.

There are songs in Odin's Hall,
For the brave, ere night to fall!
Doth the great sun hide his ray?
He must bring a wrathful day!
Sleeps the falchion in its sheath?
Swords must do the work of death!
Regner!-sea-king!-thee we call!
There is joy in Odin's Hall.

At the feast and in the song,
Thou shalt be remember'd long!
By the green isles of the flood
Thou hast left thy track in blood!
On the earth and on the sea,
There are those will speak of thee!
'Tis enough-the war-gods call
There is mead in Odin's Hall!

Regner! tell thy fair-hair'd bride
She must slumber at thy side!
Tell the brother of thy breast
Ev'n for him thy grave hath rest!
Tell the raven-steed which bore thee,
When the wild wolf fled before thee,
He too with his lord must fall
There is room in Odin's Hall!

CHAPTER FIFTEEN

Turning Point

No one discussed Soraya's sacrifice; now was not the time for tears. They simply put their heads down and got the task of living done. Everyone in this newly merged group had seen death. They'd grown accustomed to it, but none of them had witnessed such a selfless act like hers before. Soraya gave them a chance to live. They owed it to her to do *their* part. Miller, Cortez, and Sam reviewed logistics. Radzinski and Jeremiah helped Bull and Ulrich remove the barricade from the west wing's exit. Vanessa and Lillian assisted Genevieve and Ahole with the proper packing of all of their gear and scavenged goods. Simon helped Aiko, Rachel, and Bernie prep Ryan and Casandra for transport. Markus, Samantha, and Petrova were at the far end of the hotel, making as much noise as possible to try to distract at least a portion of the horde away from the western side of the building. Lancaster and Damon stood off to the side, uninspired and uninterested.

Cortez issued a final briefing of what lay ahead. "The first team out of the door will clear a path through the parking lot to the base of the dune. They'll remain staggered along the route to pick off any stray carriers until everyone is out of the hotel. As soon as the way is clear, Petrova will escort the first group of you to the edge of the parking lot. Just keep your heads down and stay on her ass and you'll be fine. When she hits the summit, Simon and his group will be up next. By the time they get to the base, the first group will be up and over the dune. That's how it's going to work until we're all on the other side, heading for the pier. This is going to go down fast. If you have any questions, now is the time. There will be no second chance at this. Just follow my men and this will all be over in a few minutes. Fall behind and you get left." Cortez zipped up his bag and Genevieve secured it to his back. A hard slap let him know he was ready. "How are we looking, Simon?"

"It's about as clear as it's going to get out there, boss," Simon informed him as he gently peeled back the curtains for one final look.

"We'll just have to deal with it. We're overdue as it is and losing daylight fast. The extraction team won't wait. They'll assume something happened and leave."

"They would just abandon you? That doesn't make any sense." The logic was lost on Miller; it stopped him in his tracks.

Ahole was headed toward the rear and the second group. "We may not all be military, but we do follow protocol. Maybe you're familiar with the term?"

"The extraction boats departed Haven over thirty minutes ago," said Cortez. "They are out there idling as we speak, waiting for our signal. We have exactly one hour from when they left to contact them or they return to the ship."

"And that's it? They would just assume you were all dead and move on?" Miller asked.

"They would try for pickup again tomorrow at the same time. After that, yes, they would cut their losses and move on."

"It's the fuel, isn't it?" Sam suggested.

"You're exactly right, sir. Every minute we're late, they're burning fuel we don't have." Cortez held up his hands as if shushing an unruly classroom. "Listen, we'll have time to get into this later. Trust me. But right now, we have to go."

"Lead the way." Miller wouldn't question Cortez's leadership; it wasn't in his nature. Cortez had a point, and that was that. He would have to take a leap of faith and trust in Cortez's methods, stranger or not. His unit appeared to know what it was doing, and the man was right: there would be time for discussion later.

Casandra was standing in a puddle. "Guys, I think my water just broke."

"Are you sure you didn't piss yourself?" Damon chuckled.

"Fuck you!" Bernie took a step toward Damon before his good sense took over and he returned his attention to Casandra. "I've got you, sweetheart. Don't you worry about a thing."

"We don't have time for this," Petrova snapped.

"Can you make it to the pier?" Aiko asked with urgency. "I have to know now."

"I... I think so," she said. "Bernie, help." Casandra gripped him hard, trying not to fall. Her legs buckled worse by the minute.

"I'll carry you to the damn boat if I have too." Bernie was struggling.

Sam slung his rifle and stepped forward. "We'll do this together, son." He draped Casandra's free arm around his neck.

"Straighten up. We are leaving *now*," Petrova said.

"Knock it off. We're fine." Bernie's ire was growing.

"She's right. We've already wasted too much time." Cortez made his way to the exit.

• • •

Simon and Ahole stood at the ready, each holding a doorknob and awaiting the signal to swing the barrier open and let the first group depart, the official point of no return.

Cortez stood facing his crew, checking one last time for loose straps or open pockets, anything that could potentially slow them down. "Remember, no gunfire unless absolutely necessary. Melee weapons only. My team clears the path to the other side of the parking lot. When I give the signal, Petrova will follow. Only engage the carriers if one of them gets in the way. Otherwise, get your asses to the dune as fast as possible. We'll keep your way clear. This is it, people." Cortez nodded to his men at the exit.

Simon and Ahole yanked the doors open. Cortez, Miller, and Ulrich made their way through the parking lot, followed closely by Radzinski, Genevieve, and Bull. Most of the undead had been drawn to the other side of the building. A few stragglers remained in the parking lot, wandering aimlessly. They were put down without incident by the first group.

Miller and Radzinski were resigned to using broken table legs as bludgeons in light of the no-firing order. Close combat with such primitive weapons was alien to them; their technique was sloppy but effective nonetheless.

Genevieve's deadly precision with her naginata was a sight to behold. Its long reach allowed for ample distance between her and the carriers' disease-racked bodies. Her dance with the undead almost seemed choreographed in its beauty.

With each swing of his mighty war hammer, Bull dispatched any carrier within arm's reach. Skulls collapsed beneath every blow or simply exploded upon impact.

"Holy shit!" Radzinski shouted, taken aback by the spectacle.

"What can I say? They love their work," Cortez replied proudly as, one after another, he crushed the skulls of nearby infected with a pair of nightsticks.

Ulrich's battle-ax came down heavy, cleaving a ghoul's head in two though burying his weapon deep into her chest cavity in the process. A swift kick to the thing's breast released its grip, and he was on his way.

"Tis a glorious day for battle indeed," he sang while swinging his giant ax into another target, seemingly enjoying the carnage.

Petrova led her group past Ulrich and deeper into the parking lot until they reached the rendezvous point. Once there, they spread out amongst a line of abandoned vehicles and ducked down out of sight.

"That guy can't be serious?" Bernie was dumbstruck.

"Don't ask me. He's been like that for as long as I've known him." Petrova peered under the cars for hidden threats.

"Fucking guy really thinks he's a Viking."

"I don't care who he thinks he is, Bernie, as long as he keeps putting those fuckers down." Casandra did her best to stay low.

Safely at the edge of the parking lot, the only obstacle between a city overrun with undead and rescue was the towering two-story sand dune.

"We made it," said Samantha excitedly.

"This isn't over yet! Everyone, stay in the parking lot. Do not approach the dune yet." Cortez pulled a short-range radio from his bag. "Zodiac One, this is Cortez requesting immediate evac from Landing Zone Seven. Over." Cortez was silent as they waited for what seemed an eternity for a reply.

The small plastic box finally crackled to life. "Cortez, this is Zodiac One. Release flares for location confirmation. Over."

"Negative, Zodiac One. Repeat, negative on flares. Hostiles in pursuit. LZ compromised. Over."

"That's an affirmative, Cortez. Zodiac One en route to Landing Zone Seven. ETA six minutes. Over." The box went silent again.

"Copy that." Cortez put away the radio while addressing the survivors. "Okay, people, it's game time. Everyone, keep your heads down and stay in the parking lot until I give the all-clear. We climb the dune in ninety-second intervals. When you reach the end of the pier, your boat will be waiting. You'll have thirty seconds to board. That's a lot longer than it sounds. Stay calm, jump off the pier, and swim for the boat. They'll help you aboard."

"We have to jump?" Samantha asked nervously, wearing a hole in Markus's jeans.

"It's nothing to worry about, red. Just don't swallow too much water." Petrova attempted to assure her with a slap on the ass for good measure.

Lancaster began to rise from his position beside a van. "We are surrounded by those monstrosities. Surely you don't expect us to simply stand here, waiting?" He looked around expectantly.

"They're right, Lancaster. We have to stay put," Miller chided. "If those things notice us bunched up on the pier, there will be nowhere to go if they catch up to us." He attempted to reassure the frightened man.

"Listen to your friend, sir," Cortez said before addressing the lot of them. "People, we have done this before. Do not panic and we will all get through this in one piece."

"I am afraid not, young man." Lancaster rose from his crouched position. "I will not be staying in this godforsaken parking lot for one moment longer. I am going to that pier right now to await my liberators." Lancaster took a step toward the dune as Petrova pulled her knife, holding it inches from the stubborn man's ear. She looked to Cortez for authorization.

"One more step toward that beach and you die," Cortez calmly explained. "Return to cover immediately."

"Good Lord, Miller, are you seeing this? Do something, man!" Lancaster pleaded.

Marisol leaned in close to Cortez's ear. "Look at him," she whispered while casting an accusing stare at Lancaster. "This man is a self-centered, worthless piece of shit. We've lost good people in the time it took to get here. How he's still alive, I'll never understand. Here we are, moments from rescue, and still all he can think about is *himself*. He's about to walk out on us like he did to his own family back in Pepperbush. He left them to die. He will do the same here to all of us in a heartbeat. Stab him. Stab him in the fucking stomach and leave him here for those things as a distraction." Marisol fingered her knife as Cortez and Petrova exchanged questioning glances.

"He's right, Lancaster." Miller did all he could to keep himself from choking the man dead on the spot. "Get back into cover now, or I swear to God I'll let both of them cut you down where you stand." He turned his back on Lancaster. Cortez could decide his fate. Miller was well and truly done with the man.

A single tear streamed down Lancaster's leathery face as he did what he was told. Cortez approached as Petrova put away her knife, readying for the climb.

"Listen to me and listen carefully, old man. I don't know what you've done to make these people so angry with you, and frankly, I do not care. You and your people will have plenty of time to hash things out later. But for now, this is what matters." He turned to show off his pack. "These supplies are going to help keep hundreds of people alive, maybe more. I've lost count of how many souls we look after." Cortez looked around at Petrova's group kneeling for cover in a parking lot surrounded by infected and shook his head in disbelief at one man's selfishness. "Getting these supplies *and* my people back to Haven is all that matters to me. If I have to put you down to make that happen, then so be it. When it comes to the well-being of Haven and its crew, *you* are expendable. We won't have this conversation again." He turned his attention from the old man and back to the issue at hand.

Petrova nodded in agreement. As did Miller and Marisol. The remainder of the group were stunned by Lancaster and still processing his irrationality.

Cortez waved at the dune. "Petrova, now!"

• • •

Ahole couldn't have cared less for the drama unfolding at the other end of the parking lot, though he kept an eye on it anyway, in case things escalated. He spent the downtime jogging in place in the safety of the hotel, shadow-boxing an imaginary opponent. "Whew, get ready to run, kids. This is my favorite part," Ahole said enthusiastically. Sufficiently hyped, he sent one last uppercut into the air before cracking his knuckles and stretching his left knee up to his chest, followed by his right. "Yeah, you ready motherfucker?" He slapped both of his hands against Simon's chest, nearly knocking the smaller man over.

"Let's do this," Simon responded with a grin while bumping fists with Ahole.

"Are you ready for this?" Vanessa leaned into Lillian, who nodded in the affirmative.

"Stay close to me," Lillian whispered. "I'll see you on the boat." She released Vanessa's hand and prepared to run.

Ryan was propped up against the door. His group was next, going with Simon. It was decided that both he and Casandra, considering their conditions, shouldn't be in the same group. A pregnant woman took precedence, which he agreed with, so he would be in the second and final group, led by Simon. By this point, Ryan was able to limp around a little on his own, so long as he kept any real pressure off his leg. The problem was that any kind of exertion nearly knocked him unconscious due to blood loss.

"Jeremiah and I are going to carry you to the boat, Ryan. Do you understand?" Rachel asked.

"Uh-huh," he managed.

Aiko didn't like the idea of Jeremiah carrying someone all the way up a dune and back down the other side into God knows what, but what choice did they have? "Be careful out there, Jeremiah." Aiko gripped his wrist tight.

"I'll be right behind you. Don't stop for anything until you hit the end of that pier."

"Okay." Aiko nodded slowly. There was no use in arguing the matter. Her fiancé's mind was made up. He would see Ryan through. "Will you hold me until we leave?"

He felt no need to reply verbally as he wrapped her up in his large arms. She stood there, warm, comfortable, and safe. Jeremiah rested his chin atop her head, waiting for their turn to be called.

Step after breathtaking step, Petrova's group scaled the dune, reaching the top in just over the allotted ninety seconds. One at a time, they disappeared from sight, over the other side. Samantha shot a quick glance back to the hotel, hoping to catch a glimpse of the others, but Markus was moving too fast, leading her forward by the hand. The uppermost floors of the hotel were all that she could see.

At the bottom of the dune, Miller awaited the last group. "That went smooth."

"Like I said, Miller, we've done this before," Cortez replied, waving on Simon in the distance.

As Simon's group mounted the dune, Rachel, Ryan, and Jeremiah pulled off from the pack. Ryan leaned against a car, trying to catch his breath.

"Jeremiah, Go. We'll catch up," Rachel said.

"Don't be absurd."

"Your fiancé, your *pregnant* fiancé, is about to board a ship that we don't have the first bit of intel on. I'm not saying I don't trust these people, but you shouldn't take the chance on getting separated from her when we have no idea what we're heading into," Rachel insisted.

"Rachel, I..." Jeremiah was speechless.

"You know I'm right. Go," she said. "I was never going to let you fall behind with me, anyway."

Jeremiah cursed under his breath. Rachel knew exactly where to hit him. He kissed her on the forehead. Reluctantly, he pressed on up the steep dune.

Rachel watched Jeremiah climb for a moment. She knew it tore him up not to be able to lend a hand, and she hated doing that to him, but she meant what she said. She returned her attention to Ryan. "We have to go, sweetie. It's now or never," she said calmly but urgently.

Ryan's head bobbed side to side, eyes barely open.

"I can't feel my leg," he mumbled.

"That man over there should have gone with the first group." Miller pointed to Ryan who was still in the parking lot.

"Take a good look at him. That man over there isn't going to make it," Cortez fired back, waving Radzinski, Ulrich, and the other perimeter guards onto the dune. "You all saw it, but you can't admit it. That kind of baggage gets people killed."

"You can't expect me to just leave him here."

"Look, I respect your position and how far you've brought these people, and on next to nothing, no less. You feel responsible for them—I get that—but it's time to hand the ball off. They're in my hands now. The many outweigh the few, remember? It's a concept I know you're familiar with. How many did you lose along the way? Did you go back for any of them? Or did you carry on with the greater good in mind?"

"Let me try. Please."

"I don't want to leave you, but I won't risk my team for a dead man. If he makes it to the pier before the last boat leaves, he can come with us. In the meantime, we are done here." Cortez pushed past Miller as he joined the final group on its ascent.

"Miller?" Rachel choked. She didn't need to ask, nor would she ever have to. Her eyes were anxious with the idea of Ryan not making it to safety with the rest of them.

Miller and Rachel carried Ryan to the top of the dune, one slow step after the next until finally the summit was achieved. Before them, the vast beach opened up below, the pier and the final zodiac still waiting beyond. A minefield of infected dotted the landscape between them and salvation. The other group's dash to safety obviously piqued the carriers' attention.

Light-headed, Ryan tripped over his own feet, sending the trio to their knees. Thrown off-balance, Miller plummeted down the dune, landing hard on the beach two stories below. Dazed, the soldier slowly rose in time to flip an incoming carrier over and away from him as another lunged. Miller kicked its knee, snapping the bone backward and out of its socket. He sprang to his feet, spinning, his knife unsheathed. In one swift move, he buried the blade deep into another carrier's temple. Miller let the knife fall with the body as he equipped his sidearm. Three more fell in as many seconds. Just behind him, another infected dropped. Its body crumbled to the sand inches from his feet. He never heard that one coming. Three-round bursts sang out on Miller's left. He ducked instinctively and stole a glance as the bullets whizzed by his head. Cortez had returned. He was making his way back toward the dune base from the pier, all the while laying down suppressing fire. Short, controlled bursts kept the enemy at arm's length, buying Miller precious seconds to regain his composure.

"Go!" Cortez shouted.

Miller was seasoned enough to know that Cortez had bought him the time he needed. His main concern now was Rachel and if she could make it from so far away.

"He came back for us," Rachel gasped. "Stay with me, Ryan. We're almost there." She struggled under Ryan's weight as they made their way across the top of the dune to better line themselves up with the pier. Their feet became heavier with each footfall in the soft sand. Traces of red began to form on Ryan's bandages; the fall had reopened his wound.

A carrier lunged from the tall dune grasses, knocking the pair over. Rachel tumbled halfway down the hill before she managed to right herself. Her rifle, however, continued the journey down. She fought hard against the sand, dragging her heavy feet one step at a time back to the top of the dune. Ryan landed face-down, the creature atop him, the infected's weight pinning him in the soft, warm sand. Weak from blood loss, he could hardly struggle as the creature buried its face into his newly gushing wound. He managed the strength for a scream as more infected reached the hill's peak. Wrestling with a small female carrier, he was able to send it over the steep dune face. It narrowly missed Rachel on its way down. Blood drained from Ryan's fully reopened injury. His world began to spin.

"Hold on, Ryan!" Rachel yelled, trudging up the mountain of sand. Every step, it felt like she was carrying a lead weight attached to her feet.

Cortez pointed to the scene. Both he and Miller offered covering fire. Undead plummeted past Rachel as she ascended the dune for a second time. Another carrier approached Ryan. Rachel fired off four shots before she managed to drop this one, fatigue taking its toll. Her aim and balance were thrown off by the steep dune. Not willing to chance hitting Ryan, she holstered her sidearm to better climb.

Ryan's sight was blurring, but he could still make out Rachel climbing the dune, coming to his rescue. Even in his condition, to see her so close, returning for him, brought a smile to his face. He held out his hand. If she could just help him to his feet...

"Ryan, Ryan!" Rachel shouted. She shook him hard. His limp head rolled from side to side. There was nothing left to hold up its weight. She was too late; he was gone. Even in the summer heat, Ryan's hands had already grown cold. She held his head in her lap for a moment and whispered a silent prayer as dozens of infected tumbled down the surrounding dune. Most were falling victim to Miller and Cortez's continued assault, though many unstable-footed carriers tripped and fell of their own accord.

"What is she doing?" Miller shouted while backing toward the pier.

The undead's numbers continued to swell on the beach below, the trail from the dune to the pier quickly closing. A sharp pain pierced Rachel's stomach. In the moment she spent praying for him, lamenting his loss, Ryan turned. The newly birthed monster took advantage of her exposed belly. He bit hard and deep, removing a good portion of skin. No one would ever know if Ryan turned because of the hot sun, the severity of his wound, or its closeness to a major artery. The only thing that was certain was that he changed, and he changed fast. Even back in Philadelphia, she never witnessed a transformation occur so quickly. Her moment of grief might have just cost her life. She kicked Ryan's reanimated corpse away as a second carrier grabbed her by the hair, forcing her into the sand. As it fell on top of her, her mouth filled with the coarse granules. Ryan was quickly making his way back up to her belly. Cold, undead fingers clawed at warm living flesh, digging bloody trenches into her skin along the way. Rachel grabbed the unfamiliar one by the throat, barely keeping it away from her face. In her haste, she shot it in the head, sending the monster careening backward down the dune. Its putrid blood and brain matter sprayed her in the face.

"Miller, there's no more time!" Cortez pulled Miller onto the pier.

Dozens of undead converged on their location. Hundreds more approached from all corners of the beach. Miller watched helplessly as the silhouette of Rachel atop the dune fought for her life.

With enough wiggle room to move, Rachel kicked her reanimated lover in the teeth before starting a forced tumble of her own down the hill, quickly putting distance between her and an increasing number of infected. Dazed from the plummet, she pulled herself to her feet. Agony coursed through her body as the wound in her stomach leaked and pulsed. Her eyes and lips burned from the filth splashed on them. All around her, fallen undead regained their footing as still more plummeted down beside her. *They don't matter*, she thought. The pier was within sight. She willed herself forward, step by painful step. Behind her, more infected fell down the dune. A rather large carrier had a good head of steam as it came barreling straight for her. The impact knocked her back to the sand. Whether by instinct or a primitive form of intelligence, the gathering infected quickly took the opportunity to close the distance.

Undead littered the pier as Miller and Cortez sprinted its length side by side to the final boat. The end of the pier reached, neither man hesitated before jumping into the water far below. Blackness surrounded Miller. He was weightless for the briefest of moments before swimming to the surface. Cortez was already being helped aboard.

The boat's pilot chastised Cortez. "You stupid fuck, I almost left you. They're going to be pissed you broke protocol."

"I made a call. They're going to have to deal with it. Just get us out of here." Cortez reached out a hand for Miller.

An infected latched onto Rachel's calf, biting deep. A third of the muscle was removed before she could spin around and kick the ghoul in its face, shattering its nose and busting most of its teeth. Lying on its back, undaunted by its shattered mouth, the creature continued to chew on its meal. Pieces of Rachel's calf leaked from the thing's greedy maw and landed on the sand. The monster, momentarily contented, gave the wounded soldier a brief chance at escape. Rachel limped to her feet in a vain attempt to reach the pier. From her vantage point, she had no way of knowing if her boat, the last boat to safety, was gone.

Limping toward the pier, Rachel fired into the approaching horde. Two more fell as she used the last of her bullets. She threw her empty gun at another, missing completely. Desperate, she unsheathed her knife and jumped onto another carrier to bury the blade into its skull. The creature fell, and she rode him down to the pier's hard surface. Rachel tried to get up but collapsed. Her leg was ruined. It didn't work at all. The impact sent her knife skidding across the boards and into the water. Reduced to crawling on all fours, Rachel slowly made her way down the pier. She wasn't about to give up, not after coming this far. Miller would make the boat wait for her. She was sure of it. Nearly to the pier's edge, she saw it. The boat was gone. She watched it grow smaller in the distance. Delirious, she decided to lie at the end of the dock and wait for Miller to come back.

Barely conscious, Rachel hardly noticed as a group of five carriers ripped away her pack and most of her shirt, exposing soft, warm flesh. The first carrier bit into her stomach. Two more fought over the same leg, tearing fist-sized chunks of meat away from bone in the struggle. Three more joined in, ravaging her chest and neck. The pier was swarming with undead in a matter of moments. More than two dozen infected vied for a place of their own. As new carriers joined the fray, others were forced off the dock into the waters below. The mass clawed and scratched, ripped and tore, desperately trying not to lose their spot in line. A large portion of Rachel's entrails went over the side with a careless carrier's misplaced footing. Her intestines, still attached somewhere inside her torso, dangled from her body to the water. Her right arm came off at the elbow. It violently passed from hand to hand until it was cleaned of all flesh, then discarded. The bone was kicked back and forth around the pier until it fell beneath the water below.

A small, child-sized carrier gnawed ferociously on Rachel's remaining hand. Warm fluids still pumped out onto the already drenched pier. Her limb chewed to the bone, the greedy creature made its way up her arm. Rachel was semiconscious as yet another fiend pulled her bottom lip from her face. In her state of shock, the myriad wounds felt warm. Rachel imagined she was in a hot tub, soothing water flowing over her exhausted body. Ryan was sitting next to her in the pool and smiling. It was so relaxing she wanted to take a nap. Only for a moment, though. "I need to rest my eyes, Ryan. Just for a few minutes."

Miller watched helplessly as the expanse grew and throngs of infected ravaged and consumed Rachel. In minutes, she was buried by them, each one trying desperately for its share of their hard-earned spoils. Miller dared not blink, lest he miss her fade from sight. He would watch her for as long as he was able. He owed her that much. His thoughts drifted to Soraya and the image of her sharing a similar fate, hundreds of filthy hands clawing at her delicate tanned skin, rending her limb from limb.

Miller remained silent, watching Rachel's overwhelmed silhouette grow smaller. At this point, he couldn't help but wonder if Radzinski had been right all along: maybe they *should* have ignored Pepperbush in the first place. It began with Takashi and the others. Now Soraya and finally Rachel were gone, too. He wondered how long the needs of the many would outweigh his own feelings. For the first time since their journey began, an anger swelled inside him.

The shoreline of Poseidon's Rest grew small in the distance. He strained to locate the hotel they came from as a fog began blocking out the horizon. Barely visible, the Blue Oasis stood as a gravestone, a testament to this journey's steep toll. Miller lost track of how many days it had been since he touched down in Philadelphia. Too many. For the first time since he was tasked with the burden of leadership, the future for what remained of his unit and the survivors of Pepperbush was in someone else's hands.

The Roaming
Haven's Promise

Book III
Coming
Winter 2020

For updates on The Roaming, social media links and exclusive content
visit wjhegarty.com

Printed in Great Britain
by Amazon